WHAT MATTERS MOST

His heart was drumming in his chest. That light perfume in the freshness of the summer night blended with the nearby magnolia tree. Her hand nestled in his was soft, and he knew her body would be softer still.

Not altogether realizing he would, he rose and pulled her hard against the length of his body. He worked out most days and tried to keep in top shape, but his body was betraying him now, demanding something—somebody—that could only hurt him again.

He wasn't planning to let it happen, but he found himself locking her tightly in his arms, his hardness pressing into her wondrous softness. He might have stopped with only a nuzzle, but her lips came to his—her lush, open lips—and he was lost. His heart thundered against her like a racing stallion, like Black Steed racing on the hill that day.

"Derrick." She moaned softly as his tongue explored the honeyed moistness of her mouth. With deftly probing tongues, each relished the splendor of the moment. He kissed her thoroughly then, ending in the upper hollows of her collarbone within her off-the-shoulder dress. His heart hurt with her beauty in the moonlight. But something came more sharply alive in him than he had known in ages.

Other books by Francine Craft

DEVOTED
THE BLACK PEARL
"Misty's Mothers" in A MOTHER'S LOVE
LYRICS OF LOVE
STILL IN LOVE
"A LOVE MADE IN HEAVEN" in WEDDING BELLS
STAR CROSSED
BETRAYED BY LOVE
FOREVER LOVE

Published by BET/Arabesque Books

WHAT MATTERS MOST

Francine Craft

ARABESQUE

BET
BOOKS

BET Publications LLC
http://www.bet.com
http://www.arabesquebooks.com

ARABESQUE BOOKS are published by

BET Publications, LLC
c/o BET BOOKS
One BET Plaza
1900 W Place NE
Washington, DC 20018-1211

All Kensington Titles, Imprints, and Distributed Lines are available at special quantity discounts for bulk purchases for sales promotions, premiums, fund-raising, and educational or institutional use. Special book excerpts or customized printings can also be created to fit specific needs. For details, write or phone the office of the Kensington special sales manager: Kensington Publishing Corp., 850 Third Avenue, New York, NY 10022, attn: Special Sales Department, Phone: 1-800-221-2647.

BET Books is a trademark of Black Entertainment Television, Inc. ARABESQUE, the ARABESQUE logo and the BET BOOKS logo are trademarks and registered trademarks.

First Printing: March 2002
10 9 8 7 6 5 4 3 2 1

Printed in the United States of America

*Dedicated to Herschel and Marietta Lee—
lovers extraordinaire. Love you both.*

*Special dedication to Dr. James B. Finn—
with deep appreciation
for your patience and your help.*

ACKNOWLEDGEMENTS

As always, I wish to thank Charlie K. for his magnificent help, and June and Bruce Bennett for assistance way out of the ordinary.

One

Ashley Steele stood in the middle of her meadow and looked at the white rail fence separating her place from the Quinns' horse-breeding farm. Brushing her dark reddish brown hair back from her oval allspice-brown face, she breathed deeply, then put on the wide-brimmed straw hat she carried.

Black Steed, her jet-black stallion, neighed softly as if in greeting to a man who came down the hill on the Quinns' side of the fence.

It was the first Monday morning in July, and hot, as Ashley began walking toward the fence. She looked back to see her young daughter, Eleni, joyfully riding her tan and beige Shetland pony, Goober. "Take it easy," she called to Eleni.

"Sure, Mom. I'm just having fun."

The tall, rangy man reached the white-boarded fence before she did, put his foot on the bottom rail, and waited, his eyes narrowed. He saw when she drew near him how she had changed.

"Derrick!" she exclaimed. "It's good to see you again!"

"It's good to see *you*."

"How are you? It's been quite a while."

He nodded, seeing her in a totally new light. Had she always been this appealing? The last time he'd seen her she had been in the midst of a divorce and had looked drawn.

She was ten to fifteen pounds beyond slender, but on her it looked damned good, he thought. A fist seemed to grip his belly as he looked at her. He had come up with the Steele children. After he moved away to college, he had come to visit his brother for many years before Marty had died of a heart attack the past spring. He had always considered her good-looking.

Now he stood with eyes half-closed, enjoying what he saw. Those sparkling, diamond-bright dark brown eyes were something else. The full lips, the high cheekbones, the high forehead all drew him, but there were other matters that came first.

Ashley smiled a bit bashfully. He was gazing at her, his head lowered, and he hadn't answered her question.

He shrugged. "I've been okay, I guess. I've missed Maria. And speaking of my wife, I want to apologize for not acknowledging your telegram and your beautiful wreath when she died. Hell, I haven't known whether I was coming or going for a while. . . ."

"It's okay. I understand. I would have come, of course, if I hadn't been on tour in Germany." His brother, Marty, and the Steeles were longtime neighbors. While they weren't very close, they observed the niceties.

Derrick's face suddenly looked bleak. "Maria was away when her accident happened."

"Mama sent me the papers. Derrick, I'm so sorry."

His smile was brief, sad. "I know. You expressed your sympathy beautifully. As for how I've been, I'm getting there. Life goes on, and my son needs me."

"Did Corby come with you?"

Derrick laughed a bit. "You bet he did. He tries not to let me out of his sight. Poor kid. He and Maria were especially close."

"How's your farm?" Derrick Quinn owned a highly successful animal farm out from Norfolk in the Tidewater area.

"It's okay. Julian, my assistant, is managing while I try to give Delia some help. If I can find a really good manager for her, she won't be forced to sell."

"I wish you luck there."

"Thank you."

A chocolate-brown, tall, thin boy came down the hill swiftly, skidding to a stop beside Derrick.

"Hey, Dad!"

Derrick looked amused. "I'd swear we'd been separated more than a week, Corby, not just a few minutes."

The boy closed his eyes. "Ah, Dad. You know."

And Derrick thought he did know. The boy was going through torment, just as he still was.

Corby licked his lips and looked at Black Steed. "Hello, Ms. Ashley. I really missed Black Steed."

The horse raised his head and whinnied in the direction of the boy, whose face lit up with a grin.

Seeing Corby, Eleni came trotting up astride Goober.

"I'll let you ride if you want to, Corby," she said.

He grinned. "Thanks, kid. Maybe I will a little later, but I'm kind of too big for a pony." He turned to Ashley. "Maybe, Ms. Ashley, you'll let me ride Black Steed sometime."

Derrick shook his head vehemently. "No, absolutely not, Corby. I thought we'd settled that. You won't get on a horse. Not now, not for a long while."

"Gee, Dad. I'd be careful."

"You know very well it takes more than being careful. It's a closed subject, son. I'm sorry."

To soften his stance, he reached out and hugged the boy, but Corby drew away.

Ashley looked from the man to his son. Now Corby vaulted over the fence to their side, and Ashley marveled at the spurt of his growth. A year or so ago when she'd seen him, he'd seemed half the size he was now. His rangy build was the same as his father's, but the rich chocolate brown of his skin was like his mother's.

Eleni got down off her pony, walked over, and took her mother's hand. "Mom, I want to show Corby how Grampa refurbished my dollhouse."

Ashley smiled at the child's use of the word *refurbished,* borrowed from Ashley.

"Is Gramma home?" Ashley asked.

"Yeah. They're *all* there."

"Okay, but don't stay longer than a half hour or so."

Turning to Corby, Ashley said, "Unless you're too grown-up now to want to see a dollhouse. Are you?"

"Ah, I'll look," Corby said, "to please the twerp."

Eleni laughed. "You're still calling me *twerp.* I'm going to call you *boy twerp.*"

"No problem. I can take it."

The little girl and the rangy boy walked back toward Ashley's parents' house.

When the children were a short distance away, Derrick ran his tongue over his dry bottom lip. Ashley wore white duck shorts and a dark blue T-shirt that proclaimed LOVE IS EVERYWHERE. Her breasts under the cotton jersey were beautifully rounded. Her satiny brown skin was without makeup except for a hint of green eye shadow, accentuating her bright brown eyes, which were enhanced by ridiculously long black lashes. Her big, white teeth were perfect.

Ashley knew he studied her, yet she was calm beneath his gaze.

She smiled inwardly, doing some studying of her own. She thought his six-foot, sinewy body a great match for her five-eight. His rough coal-black hair was brushed straight back. Thick black eyebrows topped gray-blue eyes. *And that mouth,* she thought, *that wickedly, sensually curved mouth.* Small thrills ran the length of her body. His olive brown arms in his black T-shirt were well muscled, and his masculine chest seemed to threaten to break through the cotton jersey.

What in the world was wrong with her? she wondered.

She was twenty-eight, not a teenager any longer. She was the mother of a seven-year-old. Oh, well, it felt good to *feel* again. Lord knew she hadn't felt much since her bad days of the divorce from her ex-husband, Reese. And even before the divorce she had had to suppress her feelings. Helplessly she had watched as her husband had become a full-blown alcoholic, verbally if not physically abusive, and an accomplished skirt-chaser.

With a start, Ashley remembered the times lately that she had dreamed of and felt close to someone whose presence wasn't clear. But, oh, how wonderful his spirit was, and the feelings he evoked in her.

Derrick chuckled. "We're standing here like a couple of bashful juveniles—early juvenile at that. I'm so glad to see you, Ashley. You're looking extraordinarily well."

And there it was, she thought, the old Quinn charm.

Ashley couldn't stop the thrill that tingled from her scalp to her toes.

To change the subject, she said, "You're not letting Corby ride?"

"No. I'll keep him off for a while at least."

"He loves horses."

"So did his mother." His voice was sharp.

"I'm sure you'll do what's best for him."

Derrick pursed his lips. "I wish I could know what's best for him. I wish I knew what's best for *me.*"

Her heart went out to him. She wanted to pull his head down to her breasts and let him nestle there. Comfort him. Stroke him. She wanted to feel that wonderfully wicked-looking mouth on hers, and . . . *Oh, Ashley, stop it!* she commanded herself, but she owned a free mind and it kept dancing, beckoning. Derrick wasn't the only one who needed someone.

Smiling, he asked her, "Mind if I jump the fence and come to your side?"

"Be my guest."

He vaulted the fence as effortlessly as his young son had done. Standing beside her, his whole body was tense. It had been a very long time since he'd felt this kind of attraction.

He stroked Black Steed's forelock.

"Beautiful horse." *Beautiful woman,* he thought. Would she think him out of line if he said it? It wasn't as if they were strangers. He and his brother hadn't visited each other often, but he knew her. He and Maria hadn't traveled. They'd had each other and their son, and that had been all he had wanted.

Ashley touched his arm and an electric shock went through him.

"You seem bothered," she said gently.

"It's okay," he said grimly. "I'll get over it one day." Then he added, "If I'm lucky."

Ashley brushed the back of her hand across her forehead. "It's getting hotter. Come to the house and I'll fix you some lemonade, or I've got fresh root beer. A refrigerator full of stuff . . ."

"I think I'll take you up on that. I'm kind of dry."

"I even have beer."

"I don't dare drink these days."

"Count your blessings."

His big hand touched the side of her shoulder. "Ashley, I haven't asked you. How's the gospel music coming along? We have so many of your CDs. Your albums. Corby loves them, as I do. I forgot to ask. I've come to be a thoroughly selfish man, locked up in my grief."

"They're doing wonderfully well." Then her voice grew warm with sympathy. "One day you'll feel better."

"I'm sorry about your divorce."

"So am I, but life does go on. I've got Eleni."

They stood there lost in the moment, as if she hadn't invited him home with her, and as if he hadn't agreed to come.

Suddenly he grinned broadly. "Let's go."

Even with the heat bearing down on them, he could have stood there a long while, basking in her presence. He'd always thought she had a way about her.

"Just a minute," she said, slipping the halter from Black Steed's neck. She stepped back and slapped the horse's rump and he went flying, straight to the top of the hill a few hundred feet behind Ashley's house. The black stallion raced from one end of the hill to the other and back again. Ashley's breath never failed to catch when she saw him do that.

As they walked toward the house, Derrick put a hand under Ashley's elbow. "It's kind of rocky along here. I think you told me Alpha and Omega was Black Steed's sire."

"Yes. One of the racing greats. It would have cost us a fortune, but Dad and the man who owned Alpha and Omega grew up together. He refused to take payment. Not that we particularly cared about racing him. Dad wanted the bloodline."

"Why has he never raced?"

"Broken leg when he was younger. I'm not sorry. He's all mine now. Mine and Eleni's when she's older."

"You like having things and people to yourself?"

"Sometimes. I can share, but not indiscriminately."

Her hair and her body smelled like castile soap and very light perfume, and he wished the walk were longer.

In her white enamel and stainless-steel kitchen, she closed a window, then went to an alcove and turned the air conditioner up.

"Sit down. Make yourself comfortable."

He chose a chair near the windows. She uncovered a platter of saucer-sized cookies.

"They're still warm from the oven. Help yourself."

"Those had better be oatmeal, because my appetite is hurtling toward them."

"They *are* oatmeal, and loaded with plump, juicy raisins. I brag on them and my chocolate-chip lace cookies."

He took a cookie and bit into the chewy mass of it. *Superb!*

"I'm calling you the cookie wonder woman," he said, grinning. "I'm not sure I've ever tasted one like this. You ever think of going public with them?"

"Thank you, but no, I'm already public with more than I can handle wisely. Now, what are you drinking?"

"Root beer. I haven't had one in ages."

"Then I guess I'm joining you."

She got a pitcher of root beer from the refrigerator, filled two heavy glass mugs from the pitcher, and brought them back on a tray and sat down. She smiled at Derrick's root beer–foam mustache. Oh, but he made her heart dance! And never mind ascribing that to a lingering trace of the juvenile inside her. Full-grown women went gaga, too, over certain men. Men like Derrick.

Then common sense kicked in. One year and a half ago, she had sat at this same table crying her eyes out. Reese hadn't come home all night, and when he did come home early the next morning, he had stumbled in and fallen on the couch facedown, dead to the world.

"Penny for your thoughts," Derrick said gently.

"They're not worth it," she answered. "You don't want to know."

"I see you're still touring with your glorious gospel music."

"Oh, yes." She added bitterly, "It cost me my marriage, but I'm still touring. It's my life."

He felt a heavy twinge of regret. Maria had loved the spotlight. . . . Ashley was saying something and he'd missed it. "I'm sorry," he said.

"Your face got such a woebegone look. Were you thinking of Maria touring with her centered riding, her dressage?"

More harshly than he had intended, he told her, "You'd better believe I'm still remembering. Look, I guess I was wrong. Everybody has got to live his or her own life. I loved my wife, but I wanted—I *want*—*a woman who's there most of the time. Maybe I'm just an old-fashioned chauvinistic jerk.*"

Ashley placed a soft, slender hand over his. "You're not a chauvinistic jerk, Derrick; that's just what you want. There's someone for everybody. It's just that . . ."

He finished for her: "It's just that sometimes the one you want is not for you."

"That's what I was thinking."

The sunlight from the windows struck her hair and enlivened the red in it. Her face was suddenly full of pain.

"Did I hurt you with what I said?" he asked.

"No. I've been hurting a little less each day. How long have you been here?"

"A couple of days. I've had my hands full making plans for Delia to link up with someone who can do a really good job with the ranch. She's petrified, poor soul. I had planned to walk over this way later today."

The side door slammed and a merry voice rang out, "Burglar coming through, and Lord, how I hope there's a hunky man here for me to steal."

Ashley's sister, Annice, paused at the kitchen doorway, embarrassed and full of giggles. Her smooth almond face was alight. She held out her arms as she walked toward the table.

"Derrick!" she said, giggling more. She flung her arms around his neck. "Oh, I'm so glad to see you!"

Derrick hugged her and patted her back, saying, "Hi, Neesie." She had always flirted gently with him, and his wife hadn't minded; she liked Annice and Ashley.

"Simmer down," Ashley laughingly told her sister. "You're welcome to cookies and root beer, or whatever you want, but you'll have to serve yourself."

Annice frowned. "Nope, I don't want what you're having. How about some of that popcorn crayfish you got from

Popeye's last night and a nice, frothy light beer. No, better make that lager. Oh, Derrick, you're a sight for sore eyes."

Derrick grinned, pleased. "So are you. How's the head-shrinking business?"

"Fabulous. When I get rested from my studies and my psychology residency, I've had a job offer from a Pennsylvania university treatment center."

"Congratulations!"

"I knew you'd be happy. Derrick, you look so wonderful." Her face softened, her expression becoming more serious. "How are you holding up?"

"I'm surviving." Both women were aware of a shadow that passed over his face, a tautening of his body.

"Don't mind my being silly," Annice said. "It's just my way."

"Don't apologize. I know you're the salt of the earth. I like your sense of humor. It lifts me."

Annice sat there, delaying getting up to get her food because she enjoyed looking at Derrick Quinn. Derrick, his wife, and Annice had had so much fun together. Ashley had had her hands full with her music and her errant husband, Reese.

Annice's almond skin, dark brown hair, and natural beauty set her apart, but her homey manner brought her closer. She wore her hair cut short and back from her brow. Her medium height was well filled out, but lacked the lushness of Ashley's.

"How long will you be here?" Annice asked Derrick.

He repeated what he had told Ashley about getting things straightened out for Delia.

"We really must go riding," Annice said. "If my sister permits it, I'll take Black Steed. I love to ride that horse."

Derrick's breath nearly stopped. "I'm not riding these days, Annice," he said, and added nothing more.

Annice nodded. "Oh, yes, how stupid of me. Maria's accident. Derrick, I'm so sorry."

He patted her hand. "Don't feel bad about it. Some people take things better than others. This one threw me. We can go for a long walk. Talk. What if I took you both around to my brother's place, let you know what I'm planning for Delia? And yet another walk over part of your parents' spread. Are you two girls game?" He grinned.

Annice perked up. "Wonderful, but Derrick—*girls?* We're women, you know." But Annice laughed merrily.

"Remember," he said, "I told you both when we were way younger that we'd always stay girls and boys. We were having too much fun to grow up." He laughed ruefully. "Hell, there's no way I wouldn't know you two are women." His look at them was warmly appreciative.

The two women smiled. Very gently Ashley said, "Grown-ups have fun, Derrick. You know that. We've both just hit a rough stretch of road. I'm sure it will smooth out later."

"I wish I could be so certain," he said thoughtfully.

Two

The doorbell rang and Ashley answered to find a chilly Delia standing there.

"Is Derrick with you?"

"He is. Won't you come in?"

Delia stepped inside, her long, silky black hair framing her pale, haughty face. Fairly tall, she was reed-thin and graceful. Her stance said she knew she was beautiful, and she expected everyone to do obeisance.

Ashley led her back to the kitchen and asked her to be seated, offering food and drink.

"No, I don't think so." She excluded the two women as she spoke to the man. "Derrick, have you forgotten you were to take me over to Maryland to meet a man about the ranch?"

"No, as a matter of fact, I hadn't," Derrick said evenly. "I was thinking about putting it off until tomorrow, though."

"No. I have things to do tomorrow. Melissa and I begin canning tomorrow. We will go today." It was an order, not a request.

Derrick sat thinking. He was less than fond of bossy women, but he had long noted that Delia was bossy only where other women were concerned.

"Please, hon, let's get going. I have so much I need to do when we get back."

"Yes, ma'am," Derrick said drolly, but he was irritated.

"Sorry you can't stay," Ashley said. "These are first-rate cookies, and when did you last have homemade root beer?"

"I don't like root beer," Delia answered, "and I'm not especially fond of oatmeal cookies. Derrick, shall we go?"

Derrick got up without answering. He touched Ashley's face. "It's so good to see you again, Ash." He was slipping back to the times when he and Maria had visited his brother. "I'll be seeing you soon."

Delia linked her arm in his as Ashley saw them to the door. Delia chose to ignore his stiffened body.

When Ashley came back to the kitchen, she found Annice standing by the window watching Derrick and Delia cross the meadow. She came to Ashley and extended her arm upward, inviting a responsive high five. Ashley's palm met hers and Annice laughed.

"What's the occasion?" Ashley asked.

"I'm happy for my sister," Annice told her. "I saw the hot glances between you and Derrick."

"You've got a great imagination, sister, dear," Ashley scoffed.

"I don't think so. I'm trained to deal in reality, and I saw what I saw." Annice made a comical face, turned up her chin, and gave a wolf whistle. "He's a hunk, sis. Grab him!"

Ashley blushed. "You're in the right field, Neesie. I'll be glad when you go into training analysis."

"I'm going to go in later," Annice said, "not now."

"Isn't it going to bother you, getting your psyche probed?"

Annice shrugged. "You'd better believe it is. I've got so many skeletons, beginning with my adoption by your parents—and mine, of course."

"I couldn't love you more if we were blood."

"I know that, but I find myself more and more haunted as

I grow older. You might as well know, Ash, I've begun my search for my biological parents."

"I see. You know I wish you luck."

"Thank you. If I develop an illness later on, I'd like to know which forbears it came from."

"That would be helpful."

Annice's face brightened. "I forgot. Whit's coming in day after tomorrow morning. Our big brother—*another* hunk!"

Ashley smiled, thinking of her older brother.

"Mom's planned waffles with thin strips of bacon cooked in with the batter. Ham. You name it. She's got a morning feast laid out, and she wants you over about nine. He gets in early."

"I've missed him."

"And I've missed you both."

Annice's ratty gray T-shirt and navy shorts were in keeping with her less-than-formal style. She grinned again.

"Shall we talk some more about our own substitute for Denzel Washington—Derrick?"

Ashley laughed. "Let it go, will you? You're not going to be a matron of honor anytime soon, at least not for me."

"Well, we'll see, won't we? Listen, I've got to run. Mom's running me ragged preparing for her darling son."

"Okay. You're always a prize to have around. Send Eleni home, will you?"

"Sure. She and Corby were in the kitchen having lemonade when I left. That Corby has grown three feet since I last saw him."

"One and a half anyway."

At the phone's sudden jingling, Ashley picked up the receiver on the first ring.

"I'm taking Delia to Maryland," Derrick said. "Do me a favor? Please keep Corby until I come back."

"I'll be glad to. He's still at my parents' house. I gather they got through the dollhouse tour in a hurry."

He chuckled and she hung up.

Annice wasn't smiling now. Her loving face was concerned. "I want the best for you. I'd take over Derrick myself, but you got there first and we were never sharp competitors. I want you to be happy. Reese put you through hell. You deserve love, sis, a lot of love."

"I've got Eleni to love."

"Eleni isn't a man who can rock your world."

"Maybe Derrick isn't either. Maybe no one can ever rock my world again." She felt sad saying it.

"He's already doing it. I can see it from the outside. You're lit up in a way I've *never* seen you, and isn't this your first day seeing him since he's been visiting this time?"

"It is. That's why I know you're seeing fairy dust."

Annice shook her head. "I'm seeing attraction, plain and simple. Anybody will tell you human attraction is full of fairy dust, and my girl, does it ever lend a sparkle to the eyes. Ash, how about singing me a song before I go? I'm a little bluer than I'm letting on."

"I know. I can always tell."

"I'll sit on the floor while you turn on the stereo."

"What would you like me to sing?" Her voice was soft, concerned.

"My favorite of favorites: 'Talk about a Child that Do Love Jesus.' "

Ashley walked over and turned the stereo on, listening to the soft strains of the music for the song. Annice had crouched down and put her head on her knees. After a few minutes she lifted her head and recited the full title of the song she so loved: " 'Talk about a Child that Do Love Jesus, Here's One.' "

After a few minutes of letting the music sink into the core of her, Ashley set the disc back to the beginning. Her glorious voice rose in gorgeous waves of sound with the song she loved so much.

As she sang, she thought about her family, formerly well known as the Singing Steeles. Her parents, Caroline and Frank

Steele, sang with Ashley and Whitley, two of their children. They had traveled widely, had had record contracts, and were greatly beloved. But it was when Ashley and Whitley went out on their own as soloists that the glory began.

Ashley was a warm, entrancing mezzo-soprano, Whitley a stunning baritone. They were taking their music to the heights, whereas Frank and Caroline had been satisfied with their success at a lower level.

The song Ashley sang had long been in the public domain, so she had also written her own set of lyrics, which she often sang for family and friends.

> Talk about a child
> that's known a lot of trouble,
> it's me.

She substituted the words *it's me*, for *here's one* because she felt it more; it went deeper. The torment she had known with Reese drifted away as she sang. All the joy and love of the life she'd known with her close-knit family came into her voice.

> Love him with my heart and
> all my reason,
> Love him through the years
> and every season.

Annice looked up for a moment, her eyes brimming with tears. She hadn't been home long. She would talk sister-to-sister with Ashley soon. And she would talk with Frank and Caroline.

> Talk about a child was born
> to trouble, it's me
> I was set on high, yet
> scorned and hassled,

> I've lived in them all,
> the hut, the castle
>
> Talk about a child was born
> to trouble, it's me.

No, Ashley thought as she sang, she hadn't been born to trouble. Her early lot had been wonderful. Sublimely in love, she had married Reese at twenty. Her family had been supportive but had never liked him. It was only when her marriage to Reese had begun to splinter, leaving painful needles in her heart, that she had begun to substitute her own words for the better-known ones.

Ashley swept on, her mellifluous voice shimmering.

> Jesus came to me one night
> around midnight—
> yes, he did.

She repeated that set of lyrics and went on.

> Left alone to die, and
> made to suffer.
> Ev'ry hour it seemed
> the pain got rougher.
> Jesus came to me one night
> around midnight—
> yes, he did.

And as she listened, a hint of tears came to Annice's eyes, and her heart overflowed with love for her sister.

Three

Ashley sat in a cane-backed rocker on her screened back porch, fanning herself. A yellow jacket buzzed her face and she swatted it away. A peach tree at the corner of the house hung heavy with fruit; tomorrow she would harvest them. Oh, it was wonderful to be in the country in summertime. There was no place she loved more than Crystal Lake and its countryside.

The root beer and the oatmeal cookies had left a pleasant taste and a pleasant feeling. Derrick seemed to have really enjoyed the repast. She touched her face as he had touched it when he was leaving. It felt good to feel good about a man again, but it frightened her. She wasn't nearly ready to be involved again. But then, maybe he wasn't either.

She watched Eleni and Minnie, her mother's helper, cross the meadow. The woman held the child's hand as they moved along; they were fond of each other. Ashley waved as they neared her, and they waved back. Minnie was tiny, with dark brown skin and black Indian hair. Both the woman and the child wore big straw hats, which they pulled off as they reached the porch and came in.

"I came to help out however you want me to," Minnie said, her black eyes serene. "Your mom said to tell you she'll bring you some strawberry preserves tomorrow. The glasses were still hot when we left."

Eleni stood with her eyes half-closed, looking at her

mother. "You look happy, Mom," she said. "What're you up to?"

Ashley laughed. It was a question she often teasingly asked her daughter.

"Nothing I can talk about, sweetheart," Ashley told her daughter. "Aren't *you* happy?"

"Oh, yes. Corby played with me in the playhouse. I served him tea and strawberry jam on crackers."

"Oh, you made the tea? Sweetie, remember I told you I didn't want you actually cooking in your house unless I am or Gramma is there."

"Oh, Gramma gave me some of her nettle tea and fixed the jam and crackers for me. I just served it."

"And you had a good time playing hostess?"

"Uh-huh. He was showing me how to whittle. He said he's coming back. He's neat—for a boy."

Ashley shook her head. She took Eleni's little face in her hands. "I have to say I think you're too young to be whittling, love. . . ."

"Aw, Mom. We were having fun."

"No, Eleni, you're too young to be whittling. I'll have to talk with Corby."

Eleni whimpered for a moment. "He's going to think I ratted on him." Ashley raised her eyebrows. Already the child was picking up Corby's language.

Ashley patted Eleni's face. "No, he won't. Corby's a responsible kid. He'll understand."

"Can I keep playing with him?"

"May I keep playing with him, love. Sure, but he's six years older, and I don't want you to be a burden on him."

"Mom?" The child hesitated. "Am I a burden to you?"

Ashley pulled her to her bosom. "No, my darling, never. Where did you get that idea?"

"Oh, last time I was over at Daddy's house and I wanted to come home early, he said I could be a burden."

"I'm sure he didn't mean it."

"Yes, he did. He was frowning. Mom, you won't let him take me away from you, will you?"

"No. Never."

"He asks often if I want to stay with him all the time."

Ashley seethed a moment. It was so unfair of Reese to try to make the child choose sides. Annice had tried to talk with him about this and he had gotten angry.

"Wait'll you have children," he had barked. "Then you'll understand."

Now Ashley stroked the child's delicate back.

"Gee, Mom, that feels good."

"I'm glad. I'll never let you go, Eleni. Count on that."

"Okay." She pulled away then and went out into the yard to look for butterflies.

Minnie came out of the kitchen. "I helped myself to some cookies and the root beer," she said. "I'm going to shine the glassware in that top cupboard."

Ashley looked at the small woman who was fifty and looked thirty. She sparkled with energy.

"Minnie, be a love and sit down," Ashley said. "Talk to me. It's hot, too hot to be polishing glasses. They'll wait. You and Mom have put up preserves all morning. Rest, woman. Rest!"

Minnie had a delightful, deep laugh, so at odds with her small stature. "I love working for your folks," she said. "Twenty years and never a cross word. And you know I love working for you."

Minnie sat near the edge of another rocker, perched as if she would fly away any moment.

"Let's get something straight," Ashley said. "You work *with* us, not *for* us. I don't know what we'd do without you."

"Well, you won't get a chance to find out. I'll be here until they drag me off to the old folks' home."

"Thank heavens for that, and that's a long way off."

Minnie shrugged. "The boy, Corby, has grown a whole lot since I last saw him. He and Eleni had a good time playing.

I looked after them. He was real nice to her. Too bad about his mother."

"Yes." Thinking about Maria's death brought to her mind the sharp desolation and loss she had seen in Derrick's eyes.

Later, after she had put Eleni to bed, Ashley paced the house. There was no point in going to bed; she couldn't sleep. She glanced at her Movado watch. Nine o'clock. The sun had recently set, and she had watched the red-gold rays spread across the sky before they went completely below the horizon.

It bothered her the way Reese kept haranguing her about Eleni not spending enough time with him. Yet the child had said he spoke of her being a burden. How dare he? Well, Reese was Reese. No changing that.

She wanted something and she wasn't certain what it was. She, Minnie, and Eleni had fixed and eaten tuna salad spread onto Ritz crackers and carrot and celery sticks. Dessert had been more of the oatmeal cookies.

Now she felt lonely, a bit blue. She looked at her reflection in the mirrored panel in the living room. Her off-white and off-the-shoulder cotton crepe dress with its capelet and its deep-bottomed ruffle on the full skirt flattered her. She looked better than she had looked lately, but she felt haunted. When was she going to get the mess with Reese together? It had been an acrimonious divorce, with him even accusing her of having an affair with Max Holloway, her agent. God knew Reese had had many affairs. He argued constantly that men were not meant to be faithful; women were.

"I'm of the Old Testament persuasion," he'd often said when he was drinking. "I believe in stoning the hussies who cheat on their men."

She'd stopped letting him drive her pressure up and simply let it slide from her system.

She twisted the long coral necklace she wore and played with the coral bracelets on her wrists. What was bothering her so? Then she knew: she was lonely. She usually worked too hard to let herself get lonely.

The house was silent, with only the steady purr of the fifty-gallon aquarium filled with many goldfish, its bubble machine sending myriad bubbles through the water. Black, white, gold: goldfish got along. They didn't fight. The big and the small. All colors. Humans could take a lesson from them.

She got up and went back to her study. It was cooler here. A lighted painting on the wall never failed to lift her spirits: the great Mahalia Jackson, all-time queen of gospel singers. She had paid Dale Borders, a San Francisco artist, a lot of money to paint that portrait from a photograph. She had paid him twice what he usually charged because she had known the inspiration it would bring. And it had.

She stood before the painting, studying the deep brown skin, the powerful features of a woman who had seemed to be on excellent terms with God and the heavens.

"You were blessed. Your life was blessed," Ashley murmured. "You gave the world so much."

She felt warmth suffuse her body, then put her spread-out hand on her bosom and breathed deeply. "I feel grateful singing the same songs you sang, even if I could never do them the justice you did."

She'd go to bed. She had a busy day tomorrow. The doorbell buzzed suddenly, and she went to the door and glanced out, then opened the door quickly.

Derrick stood there. "I hope you'll forgive me," he said. "I didn't intend to walk this far, but I saw your light. I knew I wasn't going to sleep."

"I know the feeling. Come in."

"I wonder if I could ask you to come out. Have you noticed that full moon?"

"Not this time, but I usually do. I always find it beautiful."

"Would you walk in your meadow with me?"

Ashley glanced down at her coral strap sandals. She had been about to pull them off when he'd buzzed.

Where was he leading? But without hesitation she said she would, and left him standing there. She wrote a note telling Eleni where she was in case she woke up, then left it safety-pinned to her daughter's pajamas. She locked the door behind them and they set out.

Four

At first they were silent, walking in the part of the meadow closest to the house, then going farther back. Ashley couldn't think of a time when she'd felt more peaceful.

"I guess it was selfish of me, coming over like I did."

"No. There are times when we need somebody else."

"You understand. I thought you would."

"That moon is gorgeous, and it looks like the stars are tripping over each other. The heavens are one glorious spectacle."

"Yeah." His heart was thumping at her nearness.

Ashley glanced over at Delia's house. Only one or two lights shone.

"Let's cut across here," she said when they were halfway across the meadow. With her leading, they walked toward the fence that separated her property from her parents'.

"There's a big oak nearby, if you remember. We can sit and talk."

"Or keep walking. I'm restless."

"I know. I can sense your body thrumming."

He wanted to pull her close to him, stroke her, feel her heart beating against his. *Steady,* he told himself. *You've got a long way to go before you'll be comfortable taking a chance with a woman.* But Ashley wasn't just a woman.

She sensed him pulling away and was relieved. She

wasn't ready to handle even the beginning of a new relationship.

The lights along Crystal Lake were shining brightly when Ashley turned around and said, "Look at the lights on the lake. But then, you've got the Tidewater region. Do you like water?"

"Love it. I enjoy being in the Tidewater area, but it takes nothing away from Crystal Lake. It's beautiful, and since they put the new lights around it, it's spectacular."

Both felt more comfortable talking about land and surroundings.

"Tell me about your farm," she said. "Are you succeeding with it?"

"Beyond my wildest dreams. Julian Harkett is my right-hand man, and he's handling things while I try to haul Delia's chestnuts out of the fire. She should have called on me earlier. Things are pretty much a mess for her now."

"Does that mean you're going to have to stay awhile?" She felt happy thinking about that.

"Oh, I'll go back and forth. If we can get the man from Maryland, Ace Carter, to take over for Delia, I'll still need to be here to train him, but my stay here will be shorter."

He stopped a moment and looked at her closely. "Speaking of my success down in Tidewater, we've got tourists coming out our ears. Large numbers of schoolkids, older people. I'd like to take you down to see it."

"I'd love that."

"Now, what about your life? Your wonderful gospel singing?"

"It could hardly be better. I'm happy with it, and I'm glad you like it."

"Love would be a better word."

"Thank you."

As they stood there in the moonlight, the heady scent of her floral perfume wafted to him, and without meaning to he reached out and took her hand.

"The name of my game seems to be moving too fast with you," he said. "I hope you'll forgive me."

"Forgiven. Maybe I invite you to move too fast. If I do, I apologize. You said once before that it isn't as if we're strangers. I feel comfortable with you."

He chuckled mirthlessly. "I can't say the same. I'm full of thoughts about you, yet I've got to make it clear: I'm not a free man. My heart's been shredded, and I find myself wondering if it will ever heal. I'll never hurt you. I know your divorce hurt you. I've run into Annice and Whitley a couple of times. We talked about you."

"I'm sorry about Maria, sorrier than I could ever tell you. As for Reese, the less said, the better. Yes, he stripped me bare and poured acid on the wounds. The last year was truly dreadful. Then there was the court fight over Eleni."

"I read about it. Marty used to send the paper to us."

"If it gets better at the rate it's been getting better, then by the time I'm eighty, maybe I can chance loving someone else," she said bitterly.

"Ashley, believe me, it does get better."

"Are you judging based on yourself?"

Her answer brought him up short; he thought she knew damned well he was nearly as deeply in pain as he'd been when Maria had died over a year ago, but he wanted to comfort Ashley.

"We're both the walking wounded," he said slowly. "All we can do is try."

Ashley felt her breathing grow shallow. "I'm afraid to try," she said simply. "I hate pain."

"So do I. Being with you helps me feel better."

"I feel the same way about you."

They walked then, and she led them to the big, gnarled oak near the barn at the foot of the hill. Black Steed's high whinny came once from his stall in the barn.

"You lock him up at night?"

"Yes. And we've got security for him. There's been a lot of horse thieving going on around here."

"We've had trouble, too. I've got a lot of security. Delia needs more, but she's hardheaded. Doesn't see the point."

"She'd better. All those valuable horses. Do you think she'll want to keep on with the stables?"

"It's hard to tell. Delia isn't a woman who's easy to figure out. I'd like to see her sell. Get out. She isn't really interested."

"She likes you a lot."

"What makes you think so?"

Smiling a little, she thought, *How do I know the moon is lovely tonight? Because I see it clearly.* And any fool could see that Delia was smitten with her dead husband's brother. Ashley shrugged. Well, he was a free man, a widower. No, he had just said he wasn't free.

A ferret scurried across their path, and a hoot owl sat on a big branch of another oak tree. They sat close together on the wooden bench built around the oak. He was the only person she knew, she thought, who seemed in greater pain than she was.

Her mind had wandered when he jostled her hand. "You didn't answer my question. Why do you think Delia likes me so much?"

"Intuition. Possessing a woman's powers of divining things. You're a very likable man."

"Do *you* like me?"

"I do. I think you're good for me, but as you said, we're the walking wounded, so . . ."

When she was silent so long, he ventured, "So why can't we give each other what comfort we can?"

"I'll go along with that."

"Are you willing to listen to me talk a little longer, since I haven't talked about Maria's death nearly enough?"

"I'd love to listen."

It was a long time before he started. "I think it hurts so

badly because so much had begun to go bad between us. I keep feeling guilty. If I can't get over it any other way, I'll talk with my minister or a mental-health professional."

"That would be a wise move." Should she question him further? *No. Let him go at his own pace.*

"It's more than likely the two of us would be wise to stay friends only. We could be valuable to each other."

"Why do you say that?"

"You're tied up in your music the way Maria was in her riding." After a moment, he seemed to become lost in what he was saying, talking to himself as much as to her.

"Centered riding was her dream," he said. "Dressage." He pronounced it to rhyme with *massage*. "She was friends with the top people in the field, and she traveled all over, giving exhibitions. Training. She was planning on setting up a dressage training stable on our ranch. It's mostly a woman's field, but Corby loved it, the way he loved his mother."

She took his hand in hers and her other hand covered his.

"You're lucky it was a divorce you had to contend with," he said. "At least you have him around to be angry with. I didn't want Maria to be away from us so much. She loved the travel and said she'd continue to travel even after she set up her stable with us—"

He stopped and abruptly asked, "I know this sounds pushy, but do you plan to always travel?"

"For the foreseeable future, I'd guess."

"And you love it, don't you?"

"I love gospel music, love bringing it to people who would only have my CDs. Yes, I guess I do love it, even the travel."

When he said nothing, she continued, "One day I'll set up a music school here, hire other teachers. I think I'd make a superb teacher."

"I think you're a superb woman!"

She felt a golden arc go through her. "Thank you. I return the compliment."

"You're like Maria," he said. "You belong and she belonged to a world that isn't mine. I'm a homebody to the bone. Marty and I both were. He married a woman like him."

His saying it cut like a knife through her heart. *Hold on!* she silently admonished herself. *I'm seeing Derrick Quinn today for the first time in well over a year. I know him, but I don't know* him. *And he's telling me the two of us could never make it. Why is he telling me this?*

His heart was drumming in his chest. That light perfume in the freshness of the summer night blended with the nearby magnolia tree. Her hand nestled in his was soft, and he knew her body would be softer still.

Not altogether realizing he would, he rose and pulled her hard against the length of his body. He worked out most days and tried to keep in top shape, but his body was betraying him now, demanding something that could only hurt him again—somebody who could only hurt him again.

He wasn't planning to let it happen, but he found himself locking her tightly in his arms, his hardness pressing into her wondrous softness. He might have stopped with only a nuzzle, but her lips came to his—her lush, open lips—and he was lost. His heart thundered against hers like a racing stallion, like Black Steed racing on the hill that day.

"Derrick." She moaned softly as his tongue explored the honeyed moistness of her mouth. With deftly probing tongues, each relished the splendor of the moment. He kissed her thoroughly then, ending in the upper hollows of her collarbone in the off-the-shoulder dress. His heart hurt with her beauty in the moonlight. But something came more sharply alive in him than he had known in ages.

A sweet fire ran the length of her body, and she trembled with longing—for what, she wasn't certain.

Derrick crushed her to him, kissing the column of her throat, and ran his tongue along her collarbone. The lovely off-the-shoulder dress let him kiss that soft bareness, and he was grateful.

Half fainting, Ashley dug her fingertips into the flesh of his shoulders and back, which were covered by the shirt she wanted to tear away. It seemed that someone else was moaning softly, not her. *I cannot remember ever being out of control,* she thought with surprise. Well, she was out of control now.

For a moment she struggled to stop the flash fire that threatened to consume her, but his lips were ardent, relentless. His hands alternately held, caressed, stroked her. He was taking her on an emotional journey more brilliant than the stars.

"Derrick." She whimpered. "No!"

But he listened to her heart, not her voice, and the delicious onslaught continued. He didn't know what had come over him, only that he wanted and needed this woman, needed everything she had to give. And he would give her everything he had in return.

Finally he paused to say lazily, "Ashley, yes!"

By then she was speechless. Was she mad? Derrick Quinn wasn't a stranger, but he was a friend. She shuddered, afraid of where this wonder would lead. She had never been kissed like this, never been swept away like this.

Every cell of his loins ached with wanting her, and every part of his emotional and spiritual being longed to meld with her. He would not stroke below her waist—there was a little safety in avoiding that—but he rose mightily against her. She was so damned soft, so yielding. How much more could he take of having her in his arms and not possessing her?

Almost abruptly he let go of her, and she stumbled slightly.

"We've got to go back," he said gruffly.

She didn't answer, half-ashamed of feeling so strongly, but then not ashamed. She had free will, and it didn't have to happen again.

On the way to the house, he was silent again, but at her door he laid his fingers against her face and said huskily, "Thank you for a wonderful walk."

Five

Two mornings later, Ashley still felt happier than she had in a long time. On the way to her parents' house, she stopped in her meadow to stroke Black Steed, then paused to help a bluejay trapped in a pile of frayed rope.

"It's too beautiful a day to be on the ground when you can fly," she told the bird. She glanced over her shoulder at Delia Quinn's house, and a twinge of jealousy fluttered in her breast.

When she finally reached her destination, she was high with good spirits. She found Frank and Caroline, her parents, Whitley, her brother, and Annice seated around the big oak table in the kitchen. Rows of gleaming jars of freshly made strawberry preserves lined the counters.

"Come and have some of Whit's flapjacks," her mother said. Then, "My love, you look pleased about something."

Eleni had come over earlier. Ashley asked about her now. "Oh." Ashley's father laughed. "She's out in the backyard, playing with Corby. He came over to spend some time with us. His dad's taking Delia again to see a man out in Maryland, something about managing her farm."

Her brother started to get up, but Ashley came and stood behind him. "Don't you dare let your flapjacks get cold just to say howdy to me." She bent and hugged him. "I'm so glad you're here. It's been a long time. I followed you in the papers."

He grinned. "I'm glad you all were able to follow me in

the newspapers. This was a grueling trip. I hardly had time to breathe. But it *was* a success."

"Will you be here awhile?" Ashley asked.

"I'm not sure. I need the rest. I'm certain of that."

"Stay. I enjoy having you around. You and Annice aren't home nearly often enough for me."

Annice shook her head. "I like Crystal Lake all right, and I loved growing up here, but San Francisco and I have a love affair going on. Now, Ash, should I give away your secret of why you're so happy?"

Ashley's breath caught. "Don't you dare go spreading gossip," she said, laughing. "Mom said I look pleased. I am, about many things."

"Okay, I won't," Annice answered. "They'll find out soon enough."

"How are you, Ash?" her father asked, rubbing his short grizzled beard. His tan, leathery skin was unlined. "You look happy to me. Don't mean to be nosy, but I like finding out secrets, especially my kids' happy secrets."

"Let's change the subject," Ashley said, smiling. "Who's in your life lately, Whit? You were linked with an English lady in one of the gossip columns."

"Hazards of the trade." He shrugged. For a moment his eyes were as bleak as Derrick's had been. "There's no one special, Ash. Sometimes I wonder if there ever will be again."

Ashley looked at her brother, who had been studying her. The two sisters and their brother were close, but did not see each other often. It bothered Ashley and Whit that the adopted Annice was not as close to them as they were to each other.

At thirty, Whit was a steadily climbing gospel singer who toured the United States, Canada, and Europe. A handsome, sturdy man, he was just under six feet, broad-jawed, with pleasant rather than handsome features. Like so many men, he worked out and took care of himself. He wore smooth, long, dark brown dreadlocks that hung to his shoulders. The dreadlocks added to his male splendor.

"Sure you won't have some breakfast?" her father said.

"You keep asking, and you've made your point," Ashley said, going over and tweaking his chin. "I'll have one or two pancakes in a minute. I'm going to pour myself a couple and let them brown the way only I can make them to suit myself."

"Whit brought us lots of raspberry-chocolate coffee," Annice said. "You've got to try some."

"Okay. In a moment."

Ashley went to the window and looked out at Eleni in the gym swing, being pushed by Corby, her long, crinkled black hair tangling in the wind. Strange, the patience the thirteen-year-old had with the seven-year-old. At times Corby's face looked so sad. Strange, too, how this was only the boy and his father's third day here this visit, and she felt as if they'd been here all along.

"When's your next concert?" Whit asked. "And when are you touring again?"

Ashley pondered his question a moment. "My next concert is at Constitution Hall in D.C. in November," she said. "I'm still thinking before I do too much touring. The divorce hit Eleni hard, and she's still clinging to me. She's spending this weekend with Reese. Sometimes she comes back all torn up. He's trying to win her over to his side completely."

Whit shrugged. She was glad he didn't say they'd told her so. None of them had liked Reese. Frank, her father, who liked most people, had been noncommittal, telling her that only she could decide.

"That's bad news." Whit expelled a small stream of air. "Eleni's too precious to be messed up by a divorce. Is Reese still drinking?"

Ashley frowned. "He hasn't been as drunk when I've seen him lately. I hear he's seeing someone. Maybe she'll be better for him than I was."

"Don't you dare blame yourself for that jerk," Whit said with irritation. "You did all the right things. You can't compete with a tall bottle of good liquor. Your ex needs treatment. Think he's getting it?"

Ashley shook her head. "I asked him and he said no, that he could and would do it on his own. He said he'd always needed a good woman and I wasn't it. Let's see, how did he put it? Oh, yes, that he needed a woman of his own, and I belonged to the public."

"Loser." Whit looked angry.

"I'm here to tell you, love," Caroline said, "you were a good wife. Reese never did his part."

They all fell silent as Ashley poured and flipped her pancakes on the sizzling hot griddle and poured herself a cup of coffee. She took her plate and the coffee back to the table and sat in one of the empty chairs. She selected a sausage patty and two pieces of Canadian bacon from a platter on the table.

Minnie came in the back door with a big basket of strawberries she had picked in a nearby patch.

"These are for you," she told Ashley. "I'm going to your house when I'm finished here and making you some scrumptious preserves and syrup."

"Thank you." Ashley smiled at the small woman. "Have you had your breakfast and some of this great coffee?"

Minnie laughed, a deep, husky laugh that seemed to shake her small frame. "At least three cups. It's the best I've tasted."

"Sit down and have a bite," Caroline said to Minnie. "You've been going like a house afire all morning. You haven't eaten a thing."

Minnie chucked. "That shows how much you know. King came early to help me in the garden. I fixed up French toast and maple syrup and made coffee. We stuffed ourselves. You know how King can eat. Any more and I'd pop. Even after picking the strawberries, I didn't work it off."

"Where's King now?" Caroline asked.

"Over at Ashley's. He's cleaning out her stable. That man is always looking for something to do." She beamed with affection.

Ashley and Minnie always teased each other. Now Ashley said, "Hear ye! Hear ye! Mark the expression on Minnie's face. Now, that's happiness. Study it and maybe you won't be so quick to call my merely feeling pleasant *happiness*."

Whit's eyes narrowed. "Methinks thou dost protest too much, Sister Ash." He often prefaced each sister's name with the title. Less often they called him Brother Whit.

"You like the maple syrup?" Caroline asked.

"Very good. One of my favorites, after strawberry syrup."

"A fan in New Hampshire sent it. A long time ago he used to write to us. He stopped, but now he's coming down this way and wants to stop in."

"Take one tin back with you," Caroline said.

Minnie moved about the kitchen, so sprightly she seemed to be skipping. "You and Eleni have got to stay for dinner. We've got three wild rabbits your dad and King brought in from hunting. I'm frying them, then smothering them in wild scuppernong wine gravy. And I'm fixing macaroni with so much cheese you won't believe it. Even as full as I am, it makes my mouth water."

"Also blackberry cobbler." Frank smacked his lips. "One of my favorites. And we're all getting together on this. King shot two of the rabbits. We're all going to be a family this afternoon."

"How can I refuse?" Ashley smiled around the table.

The back door slammed and Eleni came in, then went to her mother and flung her arms around her neck.

"Sweetheart," Ashley said, hugging her. "Close doors more quietly."

"Sure, Mom. I'm sorry."

"It's okay."

"Can I go with Corby to ride Goober and just look at Black Steed? He really likes your horse."

Ashley nodded. "Wait a little while and then I guess it's okay, but don't go out of sight of the kitchen windows. Understand?"

"Sure, Mom. Can Corby and I have some strawberries? We want to pick them."

"Uh-huh," Ashley murmured, thinking that the strawberry patch could be seen from the kitchen windows. All summer Minnie and Caroline picked and made strawberry preserves and syrup as gifts for their many friends and for the community people who helped Caroline with her efforts with lower socioeconomic groups.

Around nine-thirty, Minnie put her hands on her slender hips and declared, "I'm ready to begin making dinner."

All three women said they'd help her, but Minnie shook her head. "No-o-o. Today I'm going to strut my stuff. Whit's back and I want a dinner fit for a king."

"What about me?" Annice said. "I got no such celebration."

Minnie laughed. "You're a woman. You can do your own. Besides, your cooking shows mine up sometimes."

A lumbering giant of a brown-skinned man came through the kitchen screen door.

"Howdy, folks," he rumbled, taking off his straw hat and wiping his brow.

"It's about time you showed up again," Minnie scolded.

"Now, Minnow," he teased Minnie. "No bigger'n a minnow."

Minnie rolled her eyes heavenward. "One of these days . . . You play too much, King Johnson."

A smile spread across the big man's face. "Tell you what. You marry me and I'll be a real serious soul. I'd never play the fool again. What do you say?"

Minnie's face grew hot with embarrassment. He was serious about marrying her. King Johnson was a healthy, virile forty; she was fifty. He had never been married; she'd been married twice, the last husband leaving her a widow. King frolicked and played much of the time; she was serious, even glum sometimes, although she did tease Ashley on occasion.

The people in the room had grown quiet, listening to the banter.

"I'd be happy to be a maid of honor," Annice chirped.

"Likely you'll need a maid of honor yourself long before I'll need to ask you to be one for me," Minnie shot back.

"Aw, Minnow," King pleaded. "Show me love."

"What I'm showing you is the door," Minnie retorted, leaning way back to look up at the big man. "You know how you like to eat, and you're invited to dinner. We're eating out on the back porch."

"Country style," Caroline cut in. "Between twelve and one o'clock. We're having the rabbits you and Frank brought back and a whole lot of other wonderful dishes."

"Since Minnie's putting us out, why don't I set up the Ping-Pong table out in the backyard? Who's game?" Whit asked.

With great merriment, they all agreed. They knew better than to take King's marriage proposal to Minnie any farther. Minnie had a temper and a thin skin where marriage talk was concerned.

Minnie frowned. "On second thought, King, I know it's a little late, but please go pick me some butter beans and cut some more okra. Plus anything else you think'll be good."

"Is Whit why you're doing all this? You always did favor him," King grumbled. Whit laughed but didn't comment.

Minnie shot King an exasperated glance. "Maybe I favor him because he's not always making me feel foolish."

"Ain't got a foolish bone in your body," King said staunchly. He got a basket and a pan from the cupboard and went out, telling Ashley, "I left Corby and Eleni over in your meadow. He looks after her real well. You know, he told me he's always wanted a little sister, and before his mama died she told him she was working on that."

Ashley looked out the window again and saw Corby shooting hoops with Eleni in Ashley's backyard. Reese had put up a regular basket for himself and a much lower one for Eleni. He had even bought her a smaller basketball. He loved the game. She frowned sharply just thinking of her ex.

Minnie saw her looking and said, "Don't you worry. I'm keeping a mindful eye on them."

"Funny," Annice said, "boys that age usually can't stand the company of little girls, or too many big ones for that matter. I notice Corby has a caring manner. His parents have done a good job on him. It's too sad about Maria; she'd be proud of him."

"Yes, she would," Ashley said softly.

"Things happen," Minnie said, "and they don't always happen for the better, it seems to me, but I don't question the Lord's will."

Silence came again and a patina of sadness lay on the group.

"Tell you birds what," Whit finally spoke up. "It's way too hot for Ping-Pong. What do you say we take a long, long dip in the pool?"

"That's a wonderful idea, dear," Caroline said. "We've only been in a few times this summer."

"Yeah," Frank agreed. "King and I worked with the pool cleaners while you were gone yesterday, hon. It's as ready as it'll ever be."

Caroline laughed, her dark brown face sparkling. She looked at her husband of forty years with loving eyes. "We don't call you jack-of-all-trades for nothing." Caroline Steele was a lovely woman with big bones and a queenly carriage. She wore her coarse salt-and-pepper hair in a becoming short cut.

Ashley looked bemused. "You know something, Dad?

You really are a jack-of-all-trades. Neesie"—she turned to her sister—"can I borrow a swimsuit from you?"

"You know you can. Just don't take one that you'll look better in than I do."

Then suddenly Annice's face lit up. "We've got a lot of time to kill before dinner, even with swimming. I haven't been home in a long time and I've missed your singing— even with my CDs. The Singing Steeles, the four of you, come up in my dreams. I'm the only Steele who's got tin ears for music." Her voice got husky. "Sing for me. Sing to me."

Ashley thought she heard a wistfulness in Annice's voice that was often there when she spoke of their singing.

"You're my family," Annice continued, "and I couldn't love you more, but I get envious when you start singing. It's the only time I feel left out of your universe—but only for a little while."

Caroline went to her adopted daughter and hugged her. "You couldn't be more our child if I had given birth to you."

Frank's face looked strained, Ashley noted. Neither of her parents liked talking about the adoption. Frank went to Annice and hugged her and his wife.

"Neesie," he said gently, "I don't want you to ever feel left out, not even for a second. That's why I've often encouraged you to take piano lessons or learn to play the guitar. That way you could play with us. Look at me. Luckily I was ready to retire. The old voice sure isn't what it was before I got that nodule on my vocal cords."

Annice smiled. "You reigned when you reigned, Dad. William Warfield had no better voice. You were magnificent. But you've never let yourself understand. I am completely without musical talent. I only know I love music, but I'm not even a little bit gifted at it. Not *any* kind of music."

Annice's gaze settled lightly on Ashley. "Never mind. I'm going to be one of the truly outstanding psychologists in this world. That's going to be my contribution."

Ashley and Whit hugged her. "Neesie," Ashley said,

"you've got everything you need to set the world on fire, and it doesn't matter what part you stake out."

They clustered around the Steinway grand piano in the large living room, and with sunlight pouring through the windows, Frank sat at the piano to accompany them. Annice sat in a big chair near the piano, thinking.

There they were, her family—her adopted family—linked together powerfully by their music as she was linked to them by her love for them and theirs for her.

She had always been so proud to be in the Singing Steele family of gospel singers, each one more exquisite than the other, with Ashley and Whitley well on the way to being superstars. She wrapped her envy in deep love and it bloomed there. She was their most ardent admirer.

After a swift crescendo of notes, Frank launched into the lead of "Standing in the Need of Prayer."

It's me, it's me, it's me, oh, Lord,
Standing in the need of prayer.

The four voices were powerfully blended—exhorting, praying, pleading with a loving God who never failed them. Annice felt chills go up and down her spine.

Ashley turned to look at her sister for a few minutes as she sang. Annice looked happy now, and Ashley's heart filled with love for her. Her cheeks warmed and her voice felt like pure honey as the meaning of Annice teasing her about Derrick came to mind and lingered there. No, she would never again let a man dominate her life. She had Eleni and she had her music, and it was going to be enough. She had given up so much for Reese, and what had it gotten her? No, never again.

Six

After eating the scrumptious dinner Minnie had prepared, Whit and Ashley scraped the dishes and put them in the dishwasher; then they all relaxed under a big oak tree near the swimming pool. A hedge canopy shaded the area even more. Those who intended to swim had donned their swimsuits and now waited in the hot afternoon.

"Where's Corby?" Ashley asked Eleni.

"He went home to get something. He said his mother had left a doll she'd had since she was a little girl. He's going to give her to me."

"How sweet," Ashley said. "Did he like your dollhouse? I forgot to ask."

"Oh, yes. He says he's way too old for it, but he thought it was neat. Mom, why don't I have an older brother? I sure want one."

Annice shot Ashley an amused glance. "You could always adopt her an older brother."

"I could. We never know what time will bring. But Eleni's a little bundle to handle all by herself."

Caroline fanned herself with a palmetto fan. "I never found the three of you to be any more trouble than Whit was when he was the only one."

"You all kept each other company," Frank said thoughtfully. "Then there were the great times we had on the road. We made a great team."

"We still do," Whit averred.

"Mom, go with me to my dollhouse. I changed the furniture around. Corby helped me."

"Sure, honey. It's hard to believe Corby sat still for that."

"Well, he did."

Eleni slipped her hand in Ashley's as they walked the short distance to Eleni's dollhouse that Frank had built for her two summers past. Painted a sparkling white, with a red tile roof, the house sat in one corner of the Steeles' huge backyard. There was a miniature white picket fence in the tiny house's yard.

Ashley remembered how Frank had worked on that house, with Reese scoffing that it was a waste of time.

"You spoil her," Reese had said. "You all give my kid too much."

"She's only young once," Frank had shot back. "We discipline her, and we let her know that the rights of others matter, but this way she'll have something to look back on. Something beautiful."

Thank God for my father, Ashley thought.

"You're sighing, Mom. What's wrong?" Eleni asked her.

"Not a thing. I'm here with you. What could be wrong?"

"You sure love me a lot."

"Yes."

"I love you, too."

The dollhouse was big enough to accommodate a couple of adults and a couple of smaller fry. Caroline and Minnie helped Eleni keep the little house immaculate. Ashley had bought furniture for a small living room, and the kitchen was surprisingly large, with a miniature breakfast set beside a window. Eleni never tired of it.

Switching gears, Ashley thought, *So Reese thought we were spoiling Eleni then.* Now *he* was spoiling her, buying her unnecessary, expensive things, trying to lure her loyalties away from Ashley.

"Could I go to Gramma's and get you some tea to drink with me, Mom?"

Ashley smiled and shook her head. "We just finished dinner a short while ago, baby. I couldn't hold another swallow. Tell you what: tomorrow I'll come here with you and we'll get a nice lunch from Gramma's. What d'you say?"

"I say that's neat!"

Eleni looked so happy Ashley had to laugh. She was one lucky little girl.

Ashley looked down at her shapely legs, which were shown off in the short white eyelet robe she wore to cover her coral-and-white swimsuit.

"You look pretty, Mom. That jacket is pretty."

"So do you. Your robe is just like mine."

"But yours is bigger."

"I'm bigger."

"I'll be glad when I get bigger."

"Don't rush it, my love. Enjoy it while you can."

Eleni put her hands behind her head. "I'm going to marry Corby when I grow up."

Ashley laughed explosively, taken off guard.

"But I thought you wanted to marry King."

"No. I like Corby now."

"Fair enough." She thought it was a good time to add, "Eleni, when you play with Corby, with anybody, make sure you're within shouting distance of some of us. Things happen nowadays. The world has changed."

"Sure, Mom. You look so serious."

"My love for you makes me serious. I never want you hurt in any way."

"Lighten up, Mom. I'm never going to be hurt. I don't want you hurt either. You used to cry. Daddy hurt your feelings, didn't he?"

Ashley pulled the girl's thin, sturdy body to her. "Believe this, pumpkin: as long as I have you, those tears of the past are water under the bridge."

"Water under the bridge," Eleni said slowly. "Grown-ups

talk funny sometimes. Mom, next year will I be as big as Corby?"

"Maybe never. Stop rushing it, I tell you."

"Okay, but one day I'm going to be a big married lady. Like you and Daddy were married."

"I'm sure of that."

Ashley held the long-legged Eleni across her lap as they sat in a rocking chair Frank had fashioned for her.

"Ashley!" Caroline's panicky voice sounded nearby, and a minute later she entered the room. "Didn't you tell me Derrick isn't letting Corby ride horses right now?"

"Yes. He's not to ride—"

"Then let's go stop him. I didn't let the others interfere. I don't want to frighten him into falling off. Let's go."

Clutching her robe around her, Ashley set off with Caroline.

"I want to go, Mom!"

"No, you stay here, sweetie. Too many people coming over will frighten him."

Eleni went to be with the others in the yard while Caroline and Ashley walked swiftly, then climbed over the white fence; the gate was too far away and they had to hurry.

By the time they got to the other side, Corby was in full view. When they had first spotted him, he had been in the shadows of the line of big oaks—where Derrick and she had shared their passionate kiss.

He saw them and flinched a little, smoothing Black Steed's mane, thinking how beautiful he was. What had gotten into him that he'd had to ride the horse? He hoped Ms. Ashley and Miss Caroline wouldn't tell his father. There would be hell to pay if they did, but they were grown-ups, and grown-ups always stuck together.

"Corby!" Ashley fought to keep panic out of her voice. "Yoo-hoo! Can we chat a minute? I want to ask you something."

"Sure." Corby stayed on the horse. He couldn't seem to get off. It had been so long. . . .

Corby's back was to him, but Ashley saw Derrick walk swiftly to his side of the fence and vault it. He walked quickly to Corby, then slowed his steps. Ashley knew that he was fighting panic, too. He said nothing.

When Corby neared the two women, with Derrick coming up behind him, Ashley said gently, "Get down, sweetheart. I know you're scared. It'll be all right."

She might have been talking to her young daughter, and she saw Corby tremble.

He stopped the horse and got down, releasing the bridle, giving Black Steed's satiny hide another caress. He faced Ashley, not daring to look up. "I'm sorry, Ms. Ashley," he muttered.

"Son!"

Corby nearly jumped out of his skin.

"Dad! You said you wouldn't be back until near dark."

Derrick's voice was gentle steel. "Why were you on the horse when I told you not to ride? And you owe Miss Steele an apology."

"I'm sorry," Corby said again, tears in his voice. He looked directly into her eyes, and his own were full of misery. Then he turned to face his father. "I don't know why I did it, Dad. He's so beautiful, and I miss riding with Mom. . . ."

The boy and his father faced each other; untold pain and sadness lay between them. Ashley was aware of Delia coming up, but she refused to focus on her. Delia reached them, wringing her hands.

"Oh, Corby, how could you? Your father nearly had a heart attack when he saw you on that horse. It's a good thing we got back early. Did you tell him he could ride, Ashley?"

Indignant, Ashley nevertheless said nothing. Delia went to stand at Derrick's elbow.

"I'll handle this, Delia," Derrick said shortly. "Son, I

won't embarrass you further by fussing at you before others, but you and I have to talk. Let's go back to the house. You and Delia go ahead. I'll catch up with you."

Delia gave a sigh of displeasure. "Very well." She and Corby set off. Ashley noticed that Delia tried to take Corby's arm, but he pulled away.

"I'm sorry," Derrick said.

"It's all right," Ashley said quietly. "I've felt pushed to do things I knew I shouldn't do. Don't be too hard on him, Derrick. He's a passionate boy. Be glad for that. He's going to make you proud one day."

With a lopsided grin, Derrick said thoughtfully, "Thank you. I'm going to ground him for a while. With all that passion, he's going to have to have discipline, and his mother never liked disciplining him. He misses her."

"I understand," Ashley said. "He's in a bad place in his life. We want to help in any way we can."

Caroline nodded her assent.

"Thank you both. I'll go back now and do what's going to be hard as hell to do: discipline my son."

"It isn't as if he's a stranger to us or to Black Steed," Ashley felt she had to add. "The boy knows he's a gentle horse. Whenever you see fit, he's welcome to ride."

A tremor convulsed Derrick's face. His mouth tightened. "I'm sorry, but that won't be anytime soon."

Derrick ran the tip of his tongue over his dry bottom lip. Those fabulous legs of Ashley's were going to be the undoing of him. He groaned inside. Her thighs were rounded, not too slender. Those legs were the best.

Laughter bubbled up in Caroline's throat. She saw the way he looked at her daughter, and she was glad; she liked Derrick, and always had. Ashley was much cooler than she usually was. There was something going on here.

"When you're ready to let him come over again, we'll be waiting," Caroline said. "And you come over for a swim any time."

"Eleni is going to be inconsolable," Ashley said.

"I'm sorry. You know I am." His eyes on Ashley were soft. He turned to Caroline. "Speaking of raising kids, I'd say you've done a great job with all yours, but I'm especially pleased with what you've done with Ashley."

Caroline's laughter bubbled over. "Thank you," she said. She was right about these two, and Caroline loved being right about the ways of love.

Seven

Later that night, after it was dark, sitting in the glider on her wraparound side porch, Ashley looked across at the Quinn house, blazing with light, and wondered how Derrick and Corby were faring.

Eleni had fought sleep as long as she could.

"Is Corby going to be punished?" she had asked plaintively.

"I'm afraid so. He won't be coming over for a few days."

"Awww, Mom."

"Riding Black Steed against his father's instructions is serious business, Eleni."

"Corby didn't mean any harm. He loves Black Steed. He told me he does."

"I know, but he had explicit orders not to ride."

Eleni stuck out her bottom lip, which trembled. "Are you going to make me stop riding Goober?"

"Now, why would I do that?"

Eleni shrugged. "Are you?"

"No. I'm not. Now off to bed with you, munchkin."

The child laughed at the nickname, and in relief that she could still ride Goober.

Eleni insisted on being read *Jason and the Polar Bear,* a children's story about a boy her age who lived in Alaska. It was a story she never tired of, but before Ashley could finish the story, Eleni had fallen asleep.

Ashley kissed her child's silken cheeks, brushed back her soft flyaway black hair, and tiptoed out of the room.

Tomorrow Reese would come for Eleni, and she would spend the weekend with him. Ashley frowned. More and more often Eleni seemed upset and cried more when she came home. Ashley had spoken to Reese about it and he had been vehement. "It's your family that spoils her. Don't tell me how to raise my daughter."

"It's hard on a child when there's a lot of bickering going on," Ashley had pointed out. "She needs solidarity and a united front in order to develop survival skills."

Reese hadn't answered that. Anyway, she thought now, at least he had stopped drinking so much. She no longer had that to worry about.

She went into her den and sat at the baby grand piano, surrounded by the luminaries of the gospel world, past and present. Aretha Franklin, the late James Cleveland, Shirley Caesar and many others, all of whom she adored. There were so many superlative gospel singers now, and her heart lifted to think that she was beginning to be considered among the best. She was glad that spirituals were her specialty, for they soothed the soul and gave meaning to life. They were anthems of love sung to God and mankind. There was a history of suffering and triumph behind each song.

Her breath caught in her throat as she saw Derrick's tall figure coming from his side porch and walking a short way down the hill. Her hand went to her breast as she watched him stand in the yard and look around. The new moon was slightly waning now, but it was still brilliant.

Two nights ago Derrick and she had stood in the shadows of the big oak in her meadow and he had kissed her fiercely. She could still feel that burning kiss on her lips. It was no use denying it had thrilled her.

Mesmerized, she watched him reach the bottom of the hill, go to the gate, unlock it, and come onto her property. Both had keys to the adjoining property. By the time he reached her porch, excitement coursed in her veins like wildfire.

"Evening."

"Hello, Derrick." *There.* Her voice was steady. "Won't you come in?" She got up and unlatched the screen door.

"Won't you have a seat?"

"In a minute." He came in and continued to stand, thinking he had been compelled—or impelled—to come to her. He stood looking down at her in the moonlight. She was so damned beautiful. No, not in the sense of perfect features, or perfect hair and skin, but as a woman who had it all going on. She was going places, and in so many ways she was already there. She was already far beyond him, and he was a successful man.

Derrick shook his head. "I'll sit down in a minute. It's times like this when I miss cigarettes."

"You're better off without them. The world needs people like you to stick around a long time."

"You're sweet."

She smiled, thinking *he* was sweet. "How's Corby?"

"He's taking it pretty well. He knows I love him and want the best for him."

Ashley was silent for a few moments. "Derrick," she finally said, "Annice and I talked after you and Corby left. She feels that a sudden act of defiance like that where it hasn't existed before can mean both depression and anxiety."

Derrick sat down slowly at the other end of the glider and partially faced her. "Yeah. He saw a therapist for a few weeks after Maria died. Then he seemed to pull through nicely. He's a resilient kid, but he was really close to Maria. It's plain to me he's still hurting. Do you think I'm doing the right thing by forbidding him to ride just now?"

"How long do you think it will be before he *can* ride?"

Derrick was thoughtful. "You know, the more I talk with you about this, the more I see that this is about me more than Corby. You think I'm wrong, don't you?"

Ashley shook her head sharply. "Not necessarily. I surely do believe you're doing what you think is best for him." She hesitated a long while. "We have no way of knowing for certain what to do with our children, but Derrick, I do want you to think about this: His mother is gone. Don't let him lose you too."

Her words sank into his heart and lingered there. He knew then that he had been in danger of crippling his son to assuage his own grief and his own fears. Corby was damned good with horses; his mother had seen to that. Black Steed was gentle. The boy was in less danger on a horse than most adults were.

Derrick reached over and picked up Ashley's hand nearest him. He brought it to his lips, and his breath felt hot to her. Hot and wonderful. She waited for him to slide over, but he didn't. Instead he placed her hand back in her lap.

"There's so much to you that's really deep," he said. He sat thinking that she was like Maria had grown to be: fiercely independent, but vulnerable. He didn't like clinging vines, but he wanted a woman who was more his than the world's. Yet, looking at Ashley, he silently moaned deep in his throat. Looking down at her legs covered by a long white cotton crepe caftan, a vision of her long, bare curvaceous legs filled his eyes. This afternoon when they had stood in the meadow with Corby and Caroline, he'd felt weak with the desire to make love to her.

He shook himself lightly as Ashley laughed softly.

"Sorry. I'm staring at you," he said.

"It's all right. Your mind is probably a thousand miles away."

His laugh was harsh. "No. It's right here. Ashley, what further do you want to do with your life?"

Startled, she thought a moment. "Keep on with what I'm doing. I like where I am. By the way, I think I told you that what I'm doing may well have been the cause of my divorce. Reese hated my traveling, the crowds, the publicity. . . ."

Derrick wasn't going to lie about it. "With Maria, I came to resent the time she spent away from home with her centered riding. She was going higher. She'd gotten to be really good. She got calls from all over the country."

"And you were jealous."

"Something like that. We had a good business going with the animal farm, and my brain was swarming with ideas for expansion, some of which I put into practice. I thought we had a great life—that is, until the centered riding exploded and she was so taken with it."

She waited before responding. "You ask me what I want to do with my life. I sing, Derrick; singing *is* my life. It's in my blood. I could no more give it up than I could stop breathing. One day I'll retire and teach, but that's a long way away. Right now—"

"You're going to keep going higher and higher, and only a fool would try to hold you back."

Ashley fidgeted, then grew still. Wasn't he going to kiss her again? He'd seemed about to. Had her very honest declaration thrown him off?

He gave a small grin. "Ashley?" he said.

"Yes."

"You've got beautiful legs. I can't resist telling you."

Ashley's face heated. She was glad moonlight wasn't as clear as daylight, when he might have witnessed her turning to mush at his words.

"I'm a leg man. I guess you can tell."

"Well, if that remark means anything."

He tapped the seat beside him. "Actually, I'm a whole-woman man. I want the entire package."

"And you want that package close to you most of the time."

"Yeah. Think I'm selfish—too selfish?"

"No. Each person has in mind a life he or she wants to live. It's the only way to be happy. How long will you be around?"

He drew a deep breath. "Several months, at least. Marty was sick a long time; the place ran down. If I can get Ace to run it for a while—then if Delia wants to sell—it will bring what it's worth."

"And you'll be going down on weekends to your animal farm."

"Yeah, and maybe you'll go with me sometimes. When you're not tied up."

"I told you I'd love to."

"I want to be friends with you. I admire you so much. I love your wonderfully powerful voice. It shakes the hell out of me. It lifts me and spins me around."

"You're a shameless flatterer, but I'd like to be your friend."

"No, this is not flattery; it's real. Friends we are."

They fell silent for a long time before he said, "I've read lately that the measure of comfort we feel with another person is how comfortable we are with silence between us."

"I like that."

"So do I."

But Ashley sat thinking, *I'm comfortable with you, but that doesn't keep my heart from racing when you're near me. I've known you quite a while and I've always liked you, but not like this. Why do I want your arms around me so badly it hurts? Why do I want your mouth on mine, and to cradle your head on my breast?*

Derrick sat smiling a slow, wicked smile. *I've got to go,* he thought, *now.* Minutes more and that kiss of a couple of nights back would repeat itself. Would it go further? Deeper? He could make love to her now and it would be perfect; he was certain of that. It would be perfect because the perfection wouldn't lie in perfect strokes or perfect movements. What they knew would come from the depths of their souls, and it *had* to be good.

Derrick glanced at the luminous dial of his gold Seiko

watch. He had been here over an hour, and it seemed as though he'd just come. He stood up.

"I've got a rough day tomorrow," he said, "so I'd better go and turn in early."

She waited for him to pull her to her feet, anticipating repeated ecstasy, but he bent and kissed her forehead.

"Good night," he said. "I've really enjoyed talking with you again."

"Good night," she answered, disappointment sharp in her breast. He liked her, she was certain of that, but he had his life mapped out, and it didn't include a woman who sang for the world.

Ashley went inside to check on the fast-asleep Eleni. Sometimes she woke up when Ashley came into her room before going to bed to make sure she was okay.

Eleni slept with a smile on her face. Ashley decided she must be dreaming of pleasant things. Kissing the smooth forehead of her child, she slipped out of the room, closing the door softly behind her.

In her own spacious room, which was filled with highly polished cherrywood furniture, she turned back the cream-colored eyelet-trimmed cover of her king-size bed. Reaching into one of the night tables, she took out a short, fat, and round light olive candle set in a brass saucer. Taking a large match, she struck it and lit the candle. In a few minutes, the delightful odor of chamomile, marjoram, ylang ylang, lavender, and bergamot filled the room.

This combination was called a balancing blend. She had many others. But tonight she was torn with disappointment. Slowly she took off her clothes, leaving them in a heap on the chaise longue. Earlier today she had floated with the memory of Derrick's kiss. Ruefully she thought that she could certainly use the balance the herbs were said to bring.

Going to the window she opened the blinds and looked

out at the star-spangled night. The ache of loneliness was sharp in her breast.

Slipping on a peach jersey nightgown, she got into bed and turned off the lamps on each side of her bed. For a few minutes she tossed, thinking of Derrick. She closed her eyes, and Delia's face came up as clearly as if she were in the room with her. Why Delia? Because, she thought fitfully, Derrick was going home to her.

She groaned to herself. She had been thinking that she wasn't ready for an affair, not so soon after Reese and her disappointment in him. She had been foolish to think that Derrick wanted her. One kiss on a moonlit night evidently meant little to him.

She lay with her hands on top of the covers. He had said he wanted to be friends, and she had agreed. She didn't lie to herself: it was going to be hard for her to be his friend. This man she had known so long now moved her, spun her around. Well, she wasn't going to fling herself at him the way Delia did.

Stubbornly she thought that she had her child and she had her music. These gifts were far too great for her to be sad because she didn't have something else she wanted.

She slept soundly then, and did not dream of Derrick or of Delia.

Walking along in the moonlight, Derrick moved slowly. He fought an urge to look back to see if Ashley had gone in. But nothing could stop him from looking down the meadow to the big oak tree where he had held her softness, kissed the yielding lips, and felt her heart pound in unison with his own.

He was glad he was nipping this in the bud. He wanted her for a friend, and she had consented to that. He knew, too, that he wanted to be her mate, her ardent lover. Yes, her husband. But he thought now that he would be a hundred times a damned fool to let himself in for the pain he had known with Maria.

Ace Carter had called. He was coming to see them about the job as Delia's farm manager. If he could be persuaded to take it, then Derrick thought that in a few months Ace could be on his own.

He thought then how he and his brother had grown up in the Tidewater area, both graduating from Hampton University. By then both their parents had died, and he had set up his animal farm in the Tidewater area. But Marty had met and married Delia while in school, where she was also a student. Delia had come from Virginia and she wanted to go back. Marty had refused his young wife nothing. It was enough for him that she had not objected to his wanting to run a breeding and riding stable; she had even found it fun at first. By the time she had changed her mind, Marty had been too sick to care.

The moon was still brilliant, Derrick thought. He hated leaving Ashley. He had been sick with desire to kiss her again and again, to smother her in the passion that was tearing him up. At least, he thought wryly, it let him know how he would feel when she traveled. She was young, gifted, well known, and going higher. Fervently he wished it could have been different, but he was a man who dealt in reality, who prided himself on living in the real world.

He thought then about Ashley's saying that Delia liked him a lot. That was true. Delia was a flirt. He hadn't really approved of the way she had flirted with him even when his wife and her husband were alive.

"Sobersides!" she'd often said. "It would help you if you laughed more. I've gotten Marty to laughing. Now I'm going to work on you."

But he had been resistant, especially when Maria would look at him with love-filled eyes and declare, "I think he's perfect just the way he is."

It sure was a beautiful night, he thought. A beautiful *hot* night. He was going to take a cold shower and fall into bed. But something told him he wouldn't sleep because Ashley Steele was going to fill his dreams with ecstasy, the way she had since the first night he'd kissed her.

Eight

Delia Quinn stood at the doorway of her side porch. She had watched Derrick go down the hill and over to Ashley's house. Anger was a wild thing in her breast. So he had gone again to a woman she hated. Brushing her black hair back with one hand, she turned and looked at herself in the hall mirror. Light filtered into the hall from the dining room. With her gray eyes and slender face, she was beautiful by any standard. Her late husband had worshiped her. She felt she deserved all that she wanted. Her family had mostly seen to it that her every wish was granted.

To look at her, she thought, no one would know how furious she was. Derrick Quinn was to be hers; she had no doubt about that.

"Delia?"

She turned sharply. "I thought you were going to bed early, Corby." She didn't want to be bothered with him just now.

The lanky boy stood in the dining room door that led to the hall. "I wanted to talk to Dad again. Know when he's coming back?"

"No, I don't," Delia said shortly. "After what happened with Ashley's horse, I'd wait a couple of days to talk with your father if I were you."

Corby could have cried. Delia went out of her way to be nice to him when Derrick was around, but when he wasn't . . . well, she wasn't exactly nasty, but she wasn't nice either.

"I think I'll turn in early myself," Delia said, lifting her arms and rolling her neck. "Find another line of work when you grow up, Corby. Horse farms are way too much trouble."

"No. I like farms. I'm going in with my dad when I get out of college."

Delia turned and favored him with a smile. "That's a long way off. Meanwhile, let's concentrate on now, and seeing that you get plenty of rest and stay out of harm's way with your dad."

"Dad would never harm me."

"Figure of speech. He could, in fact, go a little heavier on the discipline with you."

"I'm going to bed," Corby said abruptly. "It's nine o'clock. I wonder if he went to see Miss Ashley."

Delia tensed. "Possibly."

The boy went to his room, and Delia stood at the door a bit longer. In the moonlit night she had watched Derrick's tall figure go to Ashley's house and onto the side porch. Now she folded her arms over her chest. She had a sure thing. Her grandmother had been a voodoo priestess, a *mambo,* and had trained her in some of the intricate ways of that magic. But she had been scornful of it then. It was ignorance personified, she had thought.

With her college degree and good looks, she could do better than voodoo. Still, she had absorbed quite a bit. How long had it been before she'd known that she loved Derrick and not Marty? Long enough. While nursing Marty when he was dying of heart disease, she still hadn't missed a chance to play up to his brother. Maria had been aware of it. Then Maria had died, thrown from her horse. Now she and Derrick were free, and she meant to have him.

A swift thought came to mind: *Be careful, Ashley Steele. Your days may be numbered.*

She reached into the dining room and switched off the light by the door. Going down the hall to her bedroom, she remembered a voodoo spell to bring a lover to his knees, and another to make a man your lover. It had been so long. Had she lost her power? She would talk with Len Starkey tomorrow. The young male hand on the horse farm, he was partial to her. He'd do whatever she wanted him to do. She opened the door of her bedroom and, looking at the bed, she pictured Derrick beside her. A small, narrow smile played about her face. Going to her walk-in closet, she began to select nightwear for a seduction.

On the way back home, Derrick thought that he hadn't stayed long, but even so, he had stayed too long. Why did he keep going to Ashley like a moth to a flame? She wasn't for him. With that voice, she was going higher and higher, with an adoring public. He needed a woman who was his, as he would be hers. Not that he was possessive; he didn't think he was. But he had been so happy when he and Maria had first married, before she had begun to crave a life completely outside him that left her little time for him and their kid.

Ah, Corby, he thought. *Light of my life.* He planned to be gentler in disciplining him. The boy needed him; he had no one else.

In the distance he could see Delia's house and broke into a trot. The exercise felt good. Delia was a woman who loved her home and was content to stay there. She would probably eventually sell the horse farm. Then what would she do? As good-looking as she was, some man would snap her up right away.

He was sober again, thinking of Ashley's contention that Delia liked him a lot. Well, sure, they had had a common bond in Marty. He liked Delia well enough, but he didn't see falling in love with her. His steps slowed when he neared the house. He looked back at the lights in Ashley's house. A vision rose before him of a naked Ashley in his arms, as in the dreams he had of her each night. There were other dreams of her, too: They walked along a path in a deep forest when he turned to her, took her in his arms, and kissed her with a driven passion. Their love was palpable, real. Then he would wake up.

He slowed to a walk, and his voice was husky as he said to himself, "Ashley Steele, do you know how beautiful you are?"

Friends. They would be friends. And that had to be enough.

He wanted to turn around and go back to her. In the house, to his surprise, he found Delia in Marty's old den, the room she had told Derrick to use. She dressed in a dark purple filmy negligee that showed off her black hair and her pale gray eyes, and her mouth was slightly open as she came to him.

"Derrick," she said softly. "I thought I'd stay up a little while to see if there's anything you need to talk with me about regarding the farm."

Just having left the opulence of Ashley and her deep womanliness, for the moment he simply looked at Delia. What was he thinking? she wondered. It had been over a year since Marty and Maria had passed on.

Derrick was thinking ruefully that life threw wicked curves. Here was Delia, interested in him. Why couldn't he be interested in her?

Delia knew enough not to push it. Derrick looked keyed-up, but it wasn't for her. She would play it cool, but she had loved him—or realized she loved him—for two years now, for a year *before* Marty had died. Now she intended to do something about it.

"Could I get you some coffee?" she asked. "Latte?"

"No. I'm going to turn in. Corby's in bed?"

"Yes. He was out here in a short while ago." Maybe concern about the boy seeing them was the reason Derrick wasn't friendlier. She made up her mind then. She wouldn't tip her hand. She'd just be with him as much as possible. Work with him. Delia couldn't remember a time when she hadn't gotten something she wanted.

Derrick sighed. "Does he seem to be in a good mood?"

"Well, you had to do what you did to punish him, so he's a little pouty about that. But I'd say he's okay." In spite of her pledge not to come on to him, her lips opened a bit as she looked at him. Did he know? How could he not know? And how did *he* feel? She was dying to know.

"I guess I'll turn in early," he said. "We've got a long way to go tomorrow with Ace coming down."

"Um, yes. Derrick, are you sure I can't fix you something?"

"I'm fine. You'd better get some rest."

Rest, she thought, wasn't what she needed.

Going to her room, Delia walked about fitfully. The house was so quiet. After an hour or so, she picked up her cell phone and dialed a number.

"Yeah," a man's gruff voice said.

Delia cupped her hand around the receiver. "Len, I'm going to need you to do something for me within the next couple of days."

"Sure. Name it and I'll do it," the gruff voice promised. *Helpful Len.* He had been with her for two years, and he never asked unnecessary questions.

"I need two things: a half-pint jar of a female goat's blood, and about a quart of graveyard dirt."

She paused awhile. They had been over this route before. She had cast a spell on a woman she hadn't liked, and the woman had left Crystal Lake.

"Is that all?" he asked.

"There may be a couple of other items, but those are the crucial ones. Get back to me as soon as you can, and money is no object."

"Sure thing, Miz Quinn; I'll get on it right away."

"Thank you for all the help you give me."

"Don't need to thank me, ma'am. That's what I'm here for."

Hanging up, Len Starkey, a swarthily attractive man, stroked his short black beard. He'd walk a mile on hot iron spikes for Delia Quinn. She was usually pleasant and soft with him, but once in a while her temper flared. What he went for was the way she flirted with him sometimes, as if—if he didn't know better—he could get close to her if he dared.

Len laughed and breathed hard. It would be a fine day in hell before that happened.

Sitting on the edge of her bed, Delia slowly pulled off her negligee and looked at her reflection in her dresser mirror. By the next week, she would have a strong potion made up. There was a shop in New Orleans that would send her supplies by FedEx. When Len brought her the two items she had asked him to get, she would hide the goat's blood in the back of the refrigerator until she was ready to mix the potion.

Power she hadn't felt since her great-grandmother had died flooded her now. She had played along for the past year, certain that Derrick was slowly falling in love with her. Now Ashley Steele had come into the picture. He had known Ashley before. Why now?

Delia's mouth tightened. She didn't know why Derrick was so attracted to Ashley now, but she intended to put a stop to it—and soon.

Nine

The ringing phone had awakened Ashley. She rubbed sleep from her eyes. Eleni was with her father, so had not nudged her awake with her cheerful morning chatter.

"Ashley? Derrick here. Is Corby over at your place?"

"No, I haven't seen him. Let me look outside. He may be in the woods beyond the meadow."

"No. I've looked over your meadow. I've been looking for over two hours and I can't find him. He left me a note that said only, 'Dad, I'm sorry.' My poor, mixed-up son."

"Listen," Ashley said quickly. "I'll get dressed and I'll help you look for him. I'll get my family to help, too."

"Thanks, Ash." His use of the diminutive of her name warmed her, but she had no time for that. Maybe Corby had wandered farther back on her parents' land. He had admired the sycamore grove on the south twenty acres. There were thick blackberry bushes and wild plums growing in back of the grove; it made a good hiding place.

She hadn't seen Derrick in two days. Was he avoiding her? She shrugged. Maybe it was best that way.

She dressed hurriedly and quickly drank a cup of instant coffee and some orange juice. Calling her parents, she alerted them to what had happened. She was waiting on the side porch, having watched Derrick from the time he left his house.

Winded with his haste, he reached her as she stood up.

"We've pretty much gone over our acres," he said. "Ashley, I was too hard on him, wasn't I? It looks like I keep using up all my chances."

She paused, then patted his shoulder. "You're doing the best you can," she said gently. "We can't ask more of ourselves than that."

By ten o'clock that morning Ashley's family, Derrick, and she had gone through the smaller buildings on the farm, calling Corby's name. No Corby.

Ashley and Derrick found themselves a little away from the others. "What did you say to him?" she asked.

"Just that he lost his TV privileges for the week and he wasn't to visit over here for that week. It didn't seem too harsh at the time. Was it?"

Ashley shook her head. "I wouldn't think so."

"There's this," Derrick said. "The horse that threw his mother is a bit like Black Steed. I guess that's why I went off the deep end. I may have raised my voice at him. He isn't used to that."

"I hate to think of it," Ashley said, "but he may have hitched a ride. He's thirteen, adventurous."

"I sure hope not. So much that's really evil is going on these days."

"Hey!" Whit called. "King and I see somebody asleep behind the blackberry bushes. We're going to check it out."

"I'm coming, too," Derrick said. He grabbed Ashley's hand and pulled her along with him.

Derrick's breath was short with anticipation. His only son. He murmured a brief prayer of supplication as they swiftly walked on.

Awakened by the voices, a slender man no bigger than Corby sat up. "Yeah," he said. "You got me. I, uh, came in through the back fence. Don't call the police on me. I'll leave quietly. I just can't stand being shut up at night."

They introduced themselves. He was Pete Fletcher.

By that time Caroline had come up with Frank. "How long has it been since you've eaten?"

The ginger-colored man looked surprised. "Oh, ma'am, I had a real good meal day before yesterday. Yesterday I drank a bit and forgot to eat."

Looking at the man, Ashley felt—as did her mother—that he looked honest enough.

Derrick stood, sick with disappointment.

"Walk back to the house with me," Annice told the man, "and we'll get some breakfast and coffee into you. You're not sick?"

The man grinned ruefully. "No, ma'am. I always look like hell when I've had too much."

Annice and the man set off to let Minnie fix him some breakfast. Ashley turned to Derrick, who looked so woebegone that her heart hurt for him.

"We'll find him," she said fiercely.

"We have to." Hot tears stood at the edges of his eyelids.

By noon they had covered her meadow, then gone over the Steeles' much larger lands.

"I'm going to report him missing," Derrick said. "We can't scour all these acres and the woodland. Besides, as I said, maybe he hitched a ride."

"You have to wait twenty-four hours before they'll accept a missing-persons report," Ashley said. "Besides, something just tells me he's around here somewhere."

Annice had come back, and now spoke up. "I think it's a plea for your attention," she said. "And I'm not lessening the importance of that. I think he loves you too much and you love him too much for him to just run away."

"Thanks," Derrick said gratefully. "I needed that."

They had sat down to rest a few minutes around one o'clock when the man they had found behind the blackberry bushes came loping back, loaded down with two big bags.

"Miss Minnie, she sent me along with some breakfast and lunch for you good Christian people."

He handed the big bag of sandwiches and a big thermos jug to Frank, then patted the smaller bag.

"The lady at the house fixed me a bag, too. You say you lookin' for somebody. I'd be real glad to help."

Derrick smiled grimly. "Sure. We're looking for a thirteen-year-old boy. He's usually in jeans and a white T-shirt. Long. Lanky. He's my son, and thank you for helping us."

The homeless man looked sympathetic. Caroline opened the bag of ham-and-cheese sandwiches, and each of them helped himself to the food and the hot coffee, thick with cream.

Finished eating, they set out again. Derrick felt he couldn't stand the wait for the twenty-four-hour period to be up so they could report Corby missing. Ashley's cell phone buzzed.

"Mom! I've been calling our house phone. Where are you?"

"Eleni, love, I'm out in the meadow near the Sycamore grove. Listen! We can't find Corby. Do you know where he might be?"

There was a very long moment of silence before Ashley prompted, "Eleni?"

"Yes, Mom. I don't know where he is."

"Eleni." Her voice was gentle, but commanding: "Tell me what you know."

"Aw, Mom, Corby's my friend. I can't rat him out."

Ashley's heart leaped with hope. Lord, the language the child had picked up in a few days from her older playmate. *Rat him out.* Eleni was precocious enough, but not that much. Had Corby talked with the little girl about running away?

"What did he tell you, Eleni?"

"You won't tell him I told?"

"No, sweetheart, I won't. We're scouring all three properties. You'll be helping him, if you know where he is. If he's in the woods, he could get lost and hurt himself. Please tell me what you know."

It seemed a long while before Eleni said in a small voice, "I think he's in my playhouse, hiding under the bed. He told me he was going to hide there. Mom?"

"Yes, sweetie?"

"Are you mad at me for not telling you before?"

"No, I'm not. In fact, I'm going to give you an extra squeeze when I see you."

Eleni giggled. "Daddy's bringing me home early. He's got a few things to catch up on. 'Bye, Mom."

Derrick had followed the conversation. Now he jumped to his feet excitedly.

"She told you someplace Corby might be, didn't she?"

"Yes. Her playhouse."

Trouping back to the Steeles' backyard, the party looking for Corby was edgily hopeful. They all but ran to the playhouse; Derrick and Ashley went in. Kneeling and lifting the rose dust ruffle around the twin bed, they heard a cough and a sob. Derrick got on his knees, but didn't look under the bed at that moment. His eyes locked with Ashley's in a dance of triumph.

"Son," Derrick said softly.

In a voice muffled by tears, Corby answered, "Yeah, Dad?"

"Are you okay?"

"Yes."

"Can you come out now?"

Scuffed blue sneakers peeped out first, then the ragged blue jeans-clad legs, and finally Corby was out from under the bed. With all his strength, Derrick held the boy to him.

"I hurt you," the boy said. "I couldn't stand hurting you.

You keep thinking the same thing that happened to Mom is going to happen to me. Dad, I'm sorry."

"No, I'm sorry, son. Sorrier than you'll ever know."

Enveloped in his father's loving arms, Corby said quietly, "I won't ride again if you don't want me to."

"We'll set up a dialogue on this," Derrick said. "There's just one thing I want you to know, Corby: you mean everything to me."

"You're not going to punish me for running away?"

"No. I'm too glad to have you back."

Derrick, Corby, and Ashley were in the playhouse. The others stood in the yard when Delia came running up, breathless.

"Where is Derrick?" she demanded.

"Inside," Caroline said shortly.

Delia went in. She laid into the boy. "Oh, good Lord, Corby, you've given us a terrible scare. How could you be so thoughtless?" She took a step toward the boy, who still knelt with his father. She swept a withering glance at Ashley, who ignored it.

"Not now, Delia," Derrick said. "Don't fuss at him now. I'm too glad to have him back."

After a while Corby looked up at Ashley and Delia. "Gee," he said, "I don't want to be mean or anything, but I want to talk with Dad alone." Then he looked sheepish. "That is, if you'll talk with me, Dad."

"Sure," Derrick said quickly. "Want to go home and talk there?"

The boy shook his head. "I want to go to that bench around the oak tree at Miss Ashley's place."

"Okay. Let's go."

Ashley smiled her approval, but Delia looked crestfallen. "I'm going home," she announced as she turned on her heel and left.

"I'll see you later," Derrick told Ashley, "and thank you more than I can say for your help."

"Yes," Corby said, "I'm sorry for all the trouble I caused you. I had no right to get on Black Steed; he's your horse, and you didn't tell me I could. Besides the fact that Dad's told me not to get on any horse for a while. I don't know what got into me."

Ashley saw the boy wring his hands and she patted his shoulder. "We don't always know what drives us," she said softly. "But if your dad ever agrees to let you ride again, you have my permission to ride him."

"Gee, thanks. Can we go now, Dad?"

Sitting with Corby under the big oak, Derrick couldn't help but think of the night he had kissed Ashley under the full moon. He turned to his son.

"I'm sorry if you see me as being harsh," he said huskily. "I want to make your life more joyful if I can, but I think you know why I don't want you to ride just now."

"Yeah, because of what happened to Mom, but she always told me not to be afraid of everything; just to be careful. You used to tell me that too, Dad."

"Corby," Derrick said suddenly, "do you know how much I love you? Can you even guess?"

The boy paused a moment.

"I think I do. I love you, too. Can I *ever* ride again?"

Derrick drew a deep breath. "I think so, Corby. One day in the not-too-distant future we'll find you a gentle stud."

"Mom's horse was gentle."

"Right. You'll know when you have a son of your own, or a daughter, how frantic you are to protect him or her. In the meantime, trust me; bear with me."

Corby threw his arms around his father and hugged him tightly. Visions of a time when he would ride again danced in Corby's head.

Letting go of Derrick, he said, "You like Miss Ashley a lot, don't you?"

"Yeah. Don't you?"

"For real. I like them all. And little Eleni's a neat kid."

"You always wanted a little sister."

"Yeah, I know."

"Let's go home now. Melissa and Len have been worried about you." Both had looked all over Delia's spread for the boy until Derrick had called them.

"I'm sorry," Corby said again, his thoughts still dancing.

"All's well that ends well," Ashley told Whit and Annice as they stood near the swimming pool.

"The more I see of Derrick, the more I like him," Annice said.

"Plus he's a widower, and you're on the prowl," Whit teased her.

Annice shot him a quick glance. "Why, brother, you malign me." A somber look spread across her face. "In case you forgot, I'm just beginning to get over the heartbreak of loving a man who broke our engagement."

Whit nodded sympathetically. "I shouldn't have said that, but Derrick Quinn *is* a good catch."

Annice could not help flashing a sly grin at Ashley. "I think maybe you ought to focus more on Ashley where Derrick is concerned. You know I've been the lighthearted type: love 'em and leave 'em."

"Don't you mean light-*headed?*" Ashley teased.

Annice shrugged. "Methinks thou dost protest too much where the gentleman is concerned, my sister."

"Change of subject, please," Ashley demanded. "Walk up to the house with me, you two. Reese is bringing Eleni back, and I'd appreciate the company."

Annice glanced at her Seiko watch. "He's early."

"Yes. He has somewhere else to go. Maybe a rendezvous."

"Be grateful you're no longer saddled with him," Annice murmured.

They'd been there only a short while, and they were in the kitchen when Eleni and her father came in through the unlocked side door. Eleni quickly ran to Ashley and hugged her.

"Hey, I could use one of those hugs," Whit told the child.

"Giggling, Eleni hugged her uncle tightly until Annice said, "I hate being left out when there's hugging going on."

Reese spoke up: "You're all an overly affectionate bunch. Hi, Whit and Annice."

"Hello yourself," Annice said brightly. "You won't find us complaining."

"Could I have a cup of coffee?" Reese asked. "It's late in the day and I'm still sleepy."

"Certainly." Ashley moved to get the coffee. Reese had been drinking again. How dared he with Eleni there? She looked at his rumpled brown, curly hair and his square, red-brown face. He was right: his body literally slumped with sleepiness. A man of medium height with a smirky smile, Reese sat at the table.

"Cream and sugar?" Ashley pursed her lips a bit.

Reese grinned. "Don't you remember?" He had a day-old stubble of brown beard. What the hell was going on here? Ashley wondered.

"Things change," Ashley said, then added to Eleni, "What did you two do since you left?"

Eleni moved from one foot to the other. "We went to the circus in Springfield, and Daddy got me a *big* banana split, double size, at the drugstore." Then she put her hand to her mouth as she looked at her father.

"Reese," Ashley said slowly, annoyed, "you know I don't want Eleni to have too much sugar. Didn't you remember that?"

Reese shrugged and said complacently, "Once in awhile isn't going to hurt her."

Annice and Whit looked from Ashley to Reese. Without speaking, Reese had picked up a jelly doughnut from a bowl on the table and bitten into it.

Reese ate and swallowed the last of his doughnut before he said, "You know how much I like sweets. I thrive on them, always have. Sweets make you smart. Right, pumpkin?" He brushed his hand across Eleni's hair. The child loved her father, who let her have whatever she wanted when she was with him, but she felt mixed up when he wanted her to leave Ashley and live with him full-time.

"Well, I've gotta go," Reese said, standing up. "Hate to leave good company, but I've got places to go and people to see. I've got to go home and don my courting clothes, put on my makeup, make myself handsome."

Reese talked in nonsense jive talk much of the time. Annice always said it covered depression. As Ashley moved to put a few dishes in the dishwasher, he came up behind her and kissed her cheek.

"I've asked you not to do that."

"Okay. Okay. So affection is okay for everybody else but your ex."

"It's over, Reese. You know it and I know it. Let's let the dead past bury its dead."

"Hmm, going poetic on me, huh?" He blew a quick stream of air. "Now I really do have to go. I've scheduled an early-morning session with my band students. So I'll get where I'm going and get back."

He sounded reasonable and adult then. Reese was a music professor at Crystal Lake College; he was the bandmaster and he loved what he did. It was hard to tell he was thirty-one; he enjoyed playing the role of spoiled brat to the hilt.

He left then. Ashley sat at the table with Eleni, Whit, and Annice, making small talk.

"I was headed for church today," Ashley said, "but I'm so glad we found Corby and he's all right."

"He's a great kid," Whit said. He rubbed his face. "You

know, we're really lucky to have the parents we've had all our lives."

Both Ashley and Annice nodded in agreement.

Then Annice said glumly, "You'd think with parents like Frank and Caroline the three of us would be happily married, with happy kids." She raised her eyebrows at Ashley. "Well, you almost made it. You got the happy kid, and for a while you had a good marriage."

Ashley looked thoughtful. "I wonder if the marriage was ever really good. Reese started cheating pretty early. I wanted something to last and I couldn't face losing him."

"I know the feeling," Whit said. "When I realized that Janice wanted my success more than she did me and that there was at least one other man still in her life and maybe others, I took it hard. She didn't care what I found out. My divorce still bleeds the hell out of me."

Ashley reached over and pressed his hand. "You'll find someone else one day," she said. "Someone you can trust."

Annice looked up quickly. "Think I'll find somebody, Sis? I haven't since Luke."

Ashley got up and stood by her sister's chair, then leaned over and hugged her. "Neesie, you have to get over Luke first. You're a psychologist. You know all about hopeless love that lasts forever."

Annice smiled. "You know, the more I talk to you, the more I know I'm going into training analysis. Damn you, Luke Jones. I won't let you ruin my life."

Ten

Backstage in her dressing room at Constitution Hall in Washington, D.C., Ashley sat at her dressing table and leaned forward. Her eyes were sparkling and she looked like a young queen, but butterflies had taken over her stomach.

Pulling her blue silk robe around her, she checked her makeup; it was fine. She got up and walked over to a big table laden with colorful flowers.

She'd have to check the card later, she thought, but one tall crystal vase of long-stemmed bloodred roses caught her eye. Her breath came faster with surprise as she took time to read the attached card:

> Now and always,
> may you triumph!
> Derrick and Corby

"How precious," she murmured to herself. Would Derrick be here? No, he would have told her if he was coming. Still, it would be nice. . . . She shrugged and smelled the lovely flowers.

The sound of the orchestra rehearsing drifted over to her as she smiled widely. *You're sounding good, group,* she thought. Whenever she sang to a crowd she was always afraid, but exhilarated. God had given her a magnificent voice, and she could do no less than use it for His glory.

Max Holloway, her agent, came in, walked over to her, and bent to kiss her cheek.

"I never need to wish you luck," he murmured. "Luck sits on your shoulder like the bluebird of happiness."

"Thank you. I feel happy."

The young woman who dressed Ashley came in pushing a rack of costumes. Ashley stood up as the dresser selected her gown. Of silk and wool vanilla-hued fabric, the exquisite gown had a boat neckline that flattered her silken brown face. Unbelted, with panels that were pieced together flawlessly, the gown was beautifully fashioned, its long, heavy skirt falling into perfect folds.

This was a new costume, and Ashley marveled at the fine workmanship that had gone into it. Max went out and the dresser moved deftly, smoothing the heavy folds of the gown. Once the gown was fitted onto Ashley, the dresser smiled widely.

"I never fail to marvel," she said, "at what you do for a gown. When I get my own shop, I will beg you to be my customer."

Ashley smiled, butterflies still circling madly in her stomach. "You flatter me," she said.

"No. Nothing I say could do justice to the way you look in that gown."

Max Holloway came back in. "You look splendid," he said as he stood there, his glance moving lazily over her. "We will need to talk soon, perhaps this evening?"

Max was always such a gentleman, she thought, but he could be controlling, dominating. His average build put him on a level with Ashley as he lifted her hand and kissed it. She blushed. He had long ago signaled a personal interest in her, but she had let it go no farther. With his crisp black hair and lively brown eyes, he was polished and debonair, but he didn't move her.

"I'll need to talk with you about our European tour in the spring," he said. "Ward Kaye wants an answer soon. I'm

going to take you as high as Mahalia Jackson, Ashley. You'll
be another Aretha Franklin, one of the great ones, if I have
my way. And I will."

Ashley laughed. "Oh, Lord, just let me get through this
concert. My knees are threatening to check out on me."

"That's another mark of the great ones. They're all afraid,
because where there's fear there's a world of hope. I think
you know your value and you're afraid something will happen to your blessings."

"You could be right."

The butterflies eased a bit as Ashley said a silent prayer
for strength and gave thanks for so many blessings. She
stood with closed eyes, and Derrick's face rose in her mind
as she finished her short prayer. He seemed so real she
jumped, startled.

"What is it?" Max asked anxiously.

She shook her head. "Nothing. I'll be all right." She
touched his hand. "Thanks for everything you do for me."

"I'd like to do a lot more," he said huskily, "and I'm sure
you know it." He took a tentative step toward her, but she
had moved away.

"Ladies and gentlemen, I am pleased to present that glorious
and accomplished woman of gospel soul, Ashley Steele."

The audience rose to its feet as one and a roar of approbation went up. She drew sellout crowds all over America,
Canada, and Europe. The Davis Gospel Singers, who backed
her on many selections, waited in the wings. This time she
would also be backed by a small orchestra on some numbers.

She had rested her voice all day, singing for only half an
hour or so near the time of the concert to prepare her voice.
She was rested, vividly enthused, ready.

She began speaking. Ashley always announced her songs.

"Ladies and gentlemen, welcome! Welcome to my concert tonight. You all know how much I love spirituals, and

you constantly tell me you do, too. My music is firmly based on them. Spirituals mean so much to our race. They are at least in part the reason we have gotten along as well as we have. They have nourished us spiritually, given us hope, driven despair from our souls. Spirituals are a great tradition, and we honor them with all our hearts.

"I'm going to begin with one of your favorites: 'Steal Away to Jesus.' "

There was a spontaneous burst of applause, and Ashley paused before she continued. "There will be many more. We will also sing lining hymns and spirituals. And, of course, no concert of mine would be complete without your and my beloved ring-shouts."

The audience clapped wildly and Ashley paused again.

This time when she continued, it was to introduce the group of four men and two women, the Davis Gospel Singers. They were superb singers, and the audience cheered them.

The orchestra members sat in a section where seats had been moved to accommodate them; the orchestra pit found on most stages was not a part of Constitution Hall.

It was like a miracle, Ashley always thought. Once she had joined psyches with the audience and begun to sing, there were no more butterflies, just the power and strength she prayed for, and a longing to give glory to God.

> Steal away, steal away,
> Steal away to Jesus.
> I ain't got long to stay here.

She sang another part, just as soulful and as entrancing before beginning a verse.

> My Lord, he calls me.
> He calls me by the thunder.
> The trumpet sounds within-a my soul.
> I ain't got long to stay here.

She rested while the Davis Singers exulted, yet mourned, "I ain't got long to stay here."

Backstage Max Holloway bowed his head. She could be nothing other than magnificent, he thought. And tonight would be the night he intended to draw her closer to him.

Ashley's black velvet mezzo-soprano caressed each note, sending it forth bound for glory. She had a four-octave vocal range, and reviewers were forever saying that she was quintessential excellence.

In the fourth from the front row, Derrick sat enthralled. He had paid a scalper dearly when he'd known he *had* to come. *My God.* She could be forgiven if she had turned arrogant with all her blessings, but she was warm, kind, helpful. With the life she had mapped out for herself, they could never belong to each other, but he was so glad they were friends. He leaned forward. He was a devotee of spirituals and other gospel music, but Ashley was a quantum leap over some others he often listened to.

Sitting beside him, Delia licked her lips, thinking that Derrick sat as if in a trance. She had made up her mind: if her plans for Ashley were to work, she had to move closer, become friends if possible. *Do yourself a favor, Ashley,* she thought; *it will be in your best interest if you decide to go ahead with your wonderful career and not get involved with Derrick. I've wanted him too long and I've waited too long.*

Ashley finished on a hushed note, "I ain't got long to stay here."

Delia slid down a bit in her seat, her eyes narrowed, thinking, *And if you decide you want Derrick, Ashley Steele, the words of that song could be your reality.* She smiled mirthlessly.

Ashley sang on, unmindful of any dissonance. Ancestral spirits of Africa filled her. Her soul had caught fire. As much as any devout minister, she carried the Word, a holy message.

Derrick eased down a bit in his seat, letting the soothing

music wash over him. He couldn't remember when he'd enjoyed anything more. Had she had time to know he'd sent roses? He had asked a noted florist to sent out a dozen spectacular dark red roses with maidenhair fern. Ashley had a big stone urn of maidenhair growing on her side porch. For the first time in his life there was a woman he wanted who wasn't for him. That hurt.

Ashley finished the song, and the hall was very quiet as the orchestra continued to play softly "Steal Away to Jesus."

"Our next selection is a lining song," she announced. "How do you feel about doing 'Amazing Grace' with me?"

The audience burst into applause. Derrick clapped loudly; Delia's response was without enthusiasm.

The old hymn that had assuaged so much grief for so many came effortlessly to Ashley's lips as she led her fans: "Amazing Grace, how sweet the sound."

And the audience responded with fervor, repeating the line after her.

She added: "That saved a wretch like me."

Again they repeated the line she had fed them. Derrick felt his heart almost burst with pride in her, his friend.

"I once was lost, but now I'm found."

The audience echoed her.

Derrick prayed. *Help me, dear Lord, to find myself.*

Ashley finished the verse: "Was blind, but now I see."

The audience responded lovingly. With Ashley leading, the audience continued the lining through the entire hymn. The orchestra played on a minute or so after Ashley and the audience had finished the song. Then everyone burst into thunderous applause. She had found that they enjoyed "Amazing Grace" more than anything other than "Lift Every Voice and Sing," James Weldon Johnson's splendid creation.

Intermission came too quickly. Back in the wings, Max Holloway caught Ashley to him and hugged her. "Brava!

Brava!" he said. "You make me shine. I wish I had words to tell you how I feel about you."

"You're a good friend, Max," she told him, and silently added, *But I don't think you can ever be more to me.* She rushed to her dressing room. Derrick's roses were there. Was he in the audience? The thought of him made her tremble. She had sung superbly and she knew it. She knew, too, that she had sung to and for him more than anyone, even though she didn't know if he was there.

Sitting down, breathing deeply, she was glad that Max hadn't followed her into the room. Derrick shouldn't come back until after the concert, if he chose to come at all, or if he was even here, but Derrick seemed to write his own rules where she was concerned. Leaning back in her plush recliner, she smiled as her assistant fanned her with palm fronds that the maid swore relaxed her.

"I saw you from the wings, mam'selle," the wardrobe mistress, an expatriate Frenchwoman, told her. "You were *magnifique.*"

"Thank you. You do a wonderful job of helping me relax."

"Thank you. In a minute I will go and let you have ten minutes alone, as you wisely choose to."

Ashley nodded. The makeup man came in. "Little wear and tear on your face," he said. "There is little to be done to you."

He set his kit on the small table beside the recliner and set to work, deftly finishing in minutes. The dresser would be the last one to come in.

"I will lock the door so that you are alone," the makeup man said. "I will knock in ten minutes."

She patted his hand. "What would I do without all of you?"

"We are so delighted to be with you, Miss Steele."

Alone, Ashley sipped from a glass of cool red-clover tea with lemon slices. She had spread a cloth around herself to protect the expensive dress. She knew she was disappointed that Derrick hadn't decided to come back already. In that moment of candor, she acknowledged she was feeling a lot for this man—far more than she wanted to feel.

She prayed then to her God of love, salvation, and redemption, and to His son, both of whom, she felt, were always with her. It was a short prayer, more of thanks than anything. She kept her eyes closed and let peace settle on and in her. She was ready for the second half of her show.

In the lobby, Derrick made small talk with Delia, preparing to go back into the auditorium. She had been mostly silent.

"You look bothered," he told her. "Have you enjoyed the concert?"

Delia shrugged. "Well," she murmured, "I always say, If you've heard one gospel concert, you've heard them all. Gospel isn't my favorite music, and I don't believe it's yours."

Derrick looked at her with some surprise. He didn't feel like discussing his favorite music with her.

Delia tipped her head back and looked up at him. She was resplendent in a low-cut, dull black satin cocktail dress with emerald jewelry. She was annoyed that he had said only that she looked nice. "I suppose you'll be going backstage after the show."

"Yeah. Join me? They're your neighbors. I'm sure Ashley would appreciate it."

Delia shook her head. "I really don't feel up to it. My head has begun to hurt a bit. I'll wait out here for you."

"Okay."

Delia brought herself up short. What was she thinking? Of course she'd go backstage. It was first step in her game plan.

"On second thought, you're right. I'll go."

"Good."

He glanced at her again, approval written on his features. His reaction made her happy as they moved with the crowd to the cavernous concert hall.

Back in the spotlight Ashley faced her audience, becoming one with them again. Her concert was shorter than some artists, so she frequently had only one costume—always beautifully simple, always elegant. This allowed her the time to relax and recharge. Max felt she should make more costume changes; perhaps she should. Max was so often right.

"Now," Ashley said as the piano softly struck up background music, "I'm going to take you on a journey you've all told me you love. We will ring-shout 'Scandalize My Name'!"

The crowd went wild. They loved the spectacular ringshout versions of spirituals. Ashley knew that the European concept of music was melody; the African concept was rhythm. She knew, too, that you had to feel spirituals to sing them, and she felt that rhythm in the marrow of her bones.

Now the stage was inhabited by Ashley, a pianist and two guitarists, and the Davis Gospel Singers, who were dressed in tuxedos and derbies. They formed a wide ring around Ashley and began to sing, then quieted as her wondrous mezzo-soprano took over.

> I met my brother the other day,
> Gave him my right hand.
> But just as soon as ever my back was turned,
> He took and scandalize' my name!

Calling to her group, she asked: "You call that a brother?"

And they shook their heads vehemently, responding "No, No!"

This was one of the richest of the traditional African-American spirituals, and one of Ashley's favorites. It was so explosively lively, so evocative of the negative side of human interchange.

With the beginning of the ring-shout, the audience was on the edge of their seats, keyed up with joy. The singers sang of sisters, preachers, and others, who, they plaintively complained, had scandalized their name.

Ring-shouting was done with the feet more than the voice. Ashley and the singers knew well that to let the voice explode with emotion was often to strip it of its softer nuances. No such limitation applied to feet. Ashley stepped out of the ring, standing aside while the Davis Gospel Singers let their feet stomp out the rhythm of whoever would scandalize their name.

The Davis Gospel Singers were at their best this night, and for the length of time they took over, she sang on the sidelines and clapped. The song ended with harsh guitar twangs and loud, rippling chords from the piano. With a final loud stomp, the singers abruptly stopped.

This time there was near pandemonium. Ashley and the Davis Gospel Singers had infused this number with such verve, such energy, such deep feeling and spirit, that each person felt touched, moved, blessed to be rid of such an onerous burden of anger. The song had been their release.

Ashley stopped after partial calm had descended and talked to the audience about the blessedness of spirituals, how valuable they were not only to the African-American heart, but to all hearts. They were a never-ending gift from both Africa and America, for they merged the two into a stunning and soothing whole. They made bearable a life that otherwise would have been far less so.

"I'm so glad you liked tonight's ring-shouting," she said. "Now I will sing a song that always pleases you. It closes my show. We have always loved this song, and we always will."

The stage was clear then. She went back center stage, shifted her microphone slightly, and slid effortlessly into "Lift Every Voice and Sing." Standing, the audience joined her. She sang the song in its entirety, with fervent assistance. When she had finished, a hush fell over the hall. It was as quiet and introspective as it had been joyfully noisy a few minutes before. Ashley had always thought that this song was one of the most beautiful she knew.

Eleven

Back in her dressing room after four curtain calls and an audience that didn't want to let her go, an exhilarated Ashley went behind a wide oak screen. Her smiling dresser helped her take off the expensive gown and put on a simpler, long aquamarine gown.

"Très magnifique!" the dresser said, and Ashley thanked her.

Stepping from behind the screen she was immediately hugged by Caroline and Frank Steele, Whit, and Annice. Caroline and Annice wore dark red and navy, respectively, and both were joyful at her success.

Frank hugged her tightly. "I've always known," he said, "that you would be what you are today. You can go as high as any of them."

Ashley grinned. "You're prejudiced, Dad."

"Then we all are," Caroline added.

Minnie and King came forward, congratulating her. Both hugged her.

Looking at Minnie in her strawberry wool dress, Ashley saw that she looked happy. "You look lovely," Ashley told her.

Minnie looked down bashfully. "It don't compare with you," she said.

King spoke up. "You compare with anybody," he declared. "You compare with any queen, no disrespect meant to Ashley."

Ashley looked from one to the other, smiling, thinking they were quite a pair.

Fretfulness moved into Ashley's heart then. She was keenly disappointed that Derrick hadn't come to hear her sing. Well, she hadn't specifically asked him to come. *Don't make excuses,* she scoffed. He liked her voice; he often said so. In fact, he usually used superlatives to describe her singing. *Oh, well . . .*

A short, brown, well-rounded woman came up and introduced herself.

"Brava!" she bubbled. She identified herself as Rena Best, a producer for a Crystal Lake TV show that specialized in the arts. "We would be so thrilled if you would agree to be interviewed for our show. I know you're busy, but it would mean so much. We're all your ardent admirers." The woman's bright eyes pleaded with her to say yes.

Without hesitation, Ashley told her, "I'll *make* time for you. Call me tomorrow, or as soon as you can."

The woman caught her hand. "How can I thank you?"

Ashley grinned. "You already have by being a fan."

Max came to stand at her elbow. She had shaken so many people's hands, been complimented and praised. At that moment she would have given at least half of it up for Derrick's presence. The thought alarmed her. What was happening to her? She wasn't ready for another love; she knew that. But he added spice to her life, a zest that had long been missing, if, indeed, it had ever been there before.

"They're full of heroine worship tonight," Max said. She nodded. A man came up to talk with Max, congratulating her, and as the two men chatted, Ashley's mind went back to Derrick. Wistfully she thought he would have loved tonight's show.

In the nearly four months since Derrick had come, they had not seen each other very often. She and Derrick remained friends and both were very careful not to get too deeply involved. There had been no more earth-spinning kisses like the first one; just light, pleasant times when his lips touched her cheeks, her lips, or when he lifted her hands and kissed them. They were so controlled. But her dreams . . . that was another story.

With a glad cry she saw him as he entered the room. She moved toward him, not entirely of her own volition.

"I'm so glad you could come! I've missed you."

"Congratulations on a truly magnificent performance," he said, smiling broadly. "I wouldn't have missed it for anything."

Did she imagine that they were closer tonight, that something was back and sparkling between them that they hadn't known since that first kiss?

"No," a familiar woman's dulcet voice chimed in, "I wouldn't have missed it for anything. I'm not that fond of gospel, but I have to give it to you, Ashley; you're good. I insisted that Derrick and I come backstage."

Derrick looked at Delia with surprise as she caught his arm. Glancing at Max as he came to her side, Ashley saw that Max's face reflected amusement.

"I want to stay awhile for support," Derrick said smoothly, giving Max the once-over, proud at that moment that he stood half a head taller and was far more fit. "Of course you have a way to get home, but I'd be happy to take you."

Max cocked his head to one side; his eyes went sleepy, narrow. "Ashley has limousines at her constant service," he said.

"Sometimes we don't want limousines," Derrick said smoothly. "They're so cold, formal."

"And elegant," Max cut in.

"I really appreciate your offer," Ashley said to Derrick. "But a group of us have to discuss scheduling. Otherwise I'd take you up on that."

"Thank goodness for that," Delia chimed in. "We need to

get back. We've got a hard day ahead. No one introduced us, Mr. . . . ?"

"Holloway. Please call me Max."

"I am Mrs. Quinn and this is Mr. Quinn. Derrick and Delia." Delia felt a positive joy at the way the two names sounded together.

"I'm glad to meet you, Mr. and Mrs. Quinn."

Delia wasn't going to get away with this bit of nerve, Ashley thought.

"No," Ashley said sweetly. "Delia is the wife of Derrick's late brother."

Max grinned widely. He thought he understood what was going on. "You make an attractive couple," he said blandly.

A naturally even-tempered man, Derrick felt himself getting nettled at Delia and at this Max person. What was he to Ashley? Yeah, her agent. She'd mentioned him, but he'd never met the guy.

"Your roses were beautiful, and the message on the card was very kind," Ashley told Derrick, as if the other two were not there.

"Neither does you justice."

Ashley blushed. Yes, there was something different between Derrick and her tonight. Was it just a culmination of all the short, close times they'd been together? Again and again their eyes met and locked. Was it just that she was happy about another success? She always felt triumphant after concerts, but she didn't think that explained it.

The group moved to the giant punch bowl that held non-alcoholic punch. A woman poured for them. The cold liquid felt good going down, Ashley thought, and it gave her something to do with her hands. The punch soothed her dry lips, which hadn't been dry before Derrick came in. *My thirst,* she thought wryly, *is not for punch.* With a start of surprise, she seemed to feel his lips on hers—a powerful illusion.

Ashley glanced at Derrick and found him looking at her.

"We'd better be making plans to leave," Max reminded

her. "As you told these lovely people, we've got scheduling to talk over. We've got a kingdom to run, and the queen is on the throne."

"Oh, Max, really," Ashley protested.

Max lifted her hand and kissed it. "I tell you no lie."

Ashley quickly looked at Derrick, whose face betrayed no emotion. Delia beamed. "Well, your majesties," she chirped, "we'll leave your kingdom to you. Shall we go, Derrick?"

"Not yet," Derrick came back. To Ashley's surprise, he asked her, "Walk a little way with me?"

"Certainly. The space behind the screen is clear."

Behind the screen his big hands caught the sides of her shoulders and gripped her tightly.

"It's none of my business, I know, but is there something between you and Holloway? You've talked about him, but I never got the idea he was anybody special to you."

Ashley thought a moment. He was jealous! Without knowing she would do so, she asked him bluntly, "Do you care?"

His breath came heavily; his voice was husky as he told her, "You know damned well I do. Ashley, we've got to talk. Soon. I'll call you tomorrow—or tonight."

She nodded, not trusting herself to speak. With a heavy sigh, he let her go and went back into the crowded room. So she was right, she thought: something was changing, *had* changed, and she didn't know whether to laugh or cry.

That same night, Derrick tossed as he tried to sleep. He knew that no sooner would he drift off than he would begin dreaming of Ashley. The power and passion of his dreams astonished him, but he resented the dreams, too, because they took him so far away from his goals for himself. He would raise his son, and yes, he would probably marry again, but his life would be with a homebody whose life centered around her family.

He did not want to be romantically involved again anytime soon. He did not want to be involved at all with a
woman who belonged to the world. And tonight had let him
know in no uncertain terms that Ashley's world went far
beyond him.

Okay, he thought, *I'm not going to toss all night.* He
closed his eyes and drifted off. This time Ashley was in a
clinging sheer black nightgown. They were in her meadow
near the woods, and Black Steed raced on the hilltop. He
took her in his arms and her body seemed to melt into his.
Her buttery-soft, smooth brown flesh and the rich curves of
her body complemented the rock hardness of his own body.
He drew her close, crushed her mouth under his, and would
not let her go.

Slowly he pressed her down onto heavy bedding that had
appeared with the magic of dreams. Impatiently pushing the
gown to her waist, he prepared to enter her and she vanished,
murmuring, "This is a dream, Derrick, only a dream."

He swore as he came awake and sat up. The dream had
been downright explosive. She had been so beautiful tonight
at her concert. He drew a very deep breath. It was at times
like this that he longed for a cigarette; but his deepest longing was for Ashley.

Once home, Ashley looked in on Eleni, who slept peacefully. Max had thoughtfully taken the baby-sitter home. She
shook her head. Max was making more demands on her, and
she wasn't sure how she wanted to handle it. Max was controlling; but, she thought, she had managed to keep their
relationship on a friendly, even keel. What really bothered
her was Derrick. Even his name felt like warm honey on her
tongue.

She was sure it would be several years before she wanted
another relationship with a man, maybe longer. She enjoyed
being friends with Derrick, but his presence shook her. It

was, she scoffed, just that she was used to having a man around, even an unsatisfactory man like Reese, her ex-husband. Then, too, *he* hadn't wanted a professional woman or an artist. So she and Derrick would remain friends.

In the dark, sitting on her bed in her slip, she decided that a bath with powdered oatmeal and soda was what she needed to soothe her. Glancing at a wall that was nearly all windows, she slipped on a robe, walked over, and opened the drapes. The hill at the bottom of her meadow rose sharply in the moonlight. They called it Black Steed's hill. In her mind's eye she saw her horse racing back and forth on the hilltop; it was such a vivid vision. Bringing her attention back to the room, she glanced at several tall cream-colored wooden screens with exquisite Japanese sumi-e drawings on them. She folded one that was set up and sighed. She frequently slept with the windows open, with the latticed screens in front of them.

It didn't take long to set her bath up. She lolled in the tub with French lavender caressing her senses as she stroked herself with a loofah sponge. What was Derrick doing? He had sent her those beautiful roses that now graced her dresser top. Slowly, by degrees, she dared to think of the way they had looked at each other after her concert. Both their bodies had cried out, *I want you!* and it could not be denied. What were they going to do about it? She felt Derrick's pain over the dead Maria, and his decision never again to get involved with a woman whose life belonged to others.

For the first time since she had begun to sing, she tasted regret. Her voice was a gift from God, and it made her happy to use it. Sighing again, she thought Derrick was a gift from that same God. Even being *friends* with him made her life far richer. They had talked about it often; it would be a mistake to become lovers. He would be gone in another several months or so—gone back to his beautiful animal farm in the Tidewater region. Life would be easier then. Max was planning another German concert, with her glorious voice as the drawing card, and later there would be tours in other countries. Max's plans for her knew no bounds. This was what she wanted. Later—perhaps much later, she thought now—she would retire and give master classes, as well-regarded operatic divas did.

The water was warmly soothing, and the smell of French lavender filled her senses. The room was dark and she moved about in the square, oversize, deep rose–colored tub, smiling a bit to herself. She and Derrick were friends, but could they stay friends? There seemed to her something so powerful between them that demanded more. But right now . . . Getting out of the tub, she shivered, dried off, hugged herself, and put on her nightgown.

In bed she thought of her days at Juilliard. Her voice coach had said she would make a superlative operatic soprano, but it was gospel music that she loved. Gospel music, interpreting spirituals. Her eyes grew moist just thinking about the meaning and the soul of the spirituals she sang so divinely.

Drifting to sleep, she dreamed of Derrick, who kissed her the way he had kissed her under the big oak in the meadow. He murmured endearments that she returned. They were in this room, his roses were on her dresser, and he pressed her back on the bed, where he gently disrobed her. Then she disrobed him and they silently made splendid love. After long moments of pure ecstasy, the sound of rain awakened her and she moaned with disappointment. Her bed was empty save for her, and she felt lonelier than she could remember ever having been.

Twelve

In the late afternoon, two days after her Constitution Hall concert, Ashley continued to feel exhilerated. Well rested, she had let her voice lie idle for a day or so. Now she was sitting in the living room sipping a cup of yellow chrysanthemum tea when the phone rang. She was enjoying her high spirits and didn't really want to be bothered.

"Settled down yet?" She loved the sound of Derrick's rich, baritone voice.

"I'm getting there," she answered.

"Could I come over in a half hour or so? We agreed we need to talk."

She tensed a bit. "Sure. I'll be waiting for you."

After she hung up, she went to her closet and selected an outfit, telling herself that she wanted to look nice for a friend, that she mostly tried to look her best all the time. But when she had dressed in her dusty rose silk harem pajamas and thin ropes of Austrian crystal with a matching wide crystal bracelet, she knew she had something else in mind. Brushing her hair back, she fitted a matching dusty rose band back from her brow and stood back, critically appraising herself in her triple full-length mirrors.

"I will definitely do," she murmured to herself. An unbidden picture of Delia Quinn settled in her mind. How could a woman be so physically attractive and so emotionally stunted? She didn't let her thoughts linger on Delia.

Tapping on a bit of Monoi oil she always bought from a

shop in D.C. that specialized in Tahitian imports, she breathed deeply as the gardenialike fragrance drifted around her. The phone rang. It was Annice.

When she told her that Derrick was coming over, Annice whooped. "I'll say good-by in a hot minute, because I've got a hunch you'll be pulling out all the stops. Where's Eleni?"

"Reese picked her up from school."

"Great. Tell me quickly how your day went. Haiku style: few words, lots of territory."

Ashley laughed. "If you weren't my sister, I'd invent you for me. I've just let it all hang out all day, honey and lemon juice for a well-used voice. Neesie, the concert really did go well, didn't it?"

Annice laughed. "I've told you again and again, but you keep asking because you're not certain what hit you at that one. I saw the looks that passed between you and Mr. Quinn, and they were way beyond hot. No, I take that back; it's too common a word. What I saw between you two was deep, Ash, real deep. Don't let him get away."

"I keep telling you he wants a homebody, and I want time—a lot of time—to get over my bad marriage."

"You won't do it passing up guys made to order for you. Okay, go ahead. Give him to Delia."

Ashley's heart constricted a bit with jealousy. "If she doesn't get him," she muttered, "it won't be for lack of trying."

"Smart girl. You go to it!"

"No, I— That's my chimes. He's here, or at least I hope that's him."

" 'Bye, and I hope you're clad in the sexiest outfit you own. Knock him dead, tiger." Laughing again, she hung up.

"Hello, Derrick, how are you?"

"Ready to talk if you are. God knows we need to. I brought you a bottle of Veuve Clicquot champagne. You said you liked champagne. The best for the best." He handed her the bottle wrapped in white tissue paper.

She took the bottle and held it. "I'll bet I've never gotten around to telling you I like *cool* champagne."

"Really? You're so different in so many ways; that doesn't surprise me."

"But I'll pour some for myself, then chill yours."

"Keep it if you wish. You don't have to open it now."

"I want to open it now."

"Yeah, I do, too, on second thought. To toast you. Now or later?"

"I think now. I know you just got here, and as we've said, we need to talk. But after the champagne perhaps we won't be so clearheaded."

"Champagne doesn't affect me all that much. I'll be fully operative."

"Okay. Come with me to the kitchen and we'll set the wheels in motion."

Derrick looked at her, his eyes narrowed, then fully open. What did she mean by that? Ashley blushed then stammered, "I mean, set the wheels in motion for our talk."

Smiling wickedly, Derrick murmured, "Ash, I never thought you meant anything else."

He took the champagne bottle from her and stripped off the tissue, which she took from him. Popping the cork while she got two Steuben champagne flutes from the dining room, Derrick thought, *Cool champagne. This is going to be different.*

He poured the champagne and both lifted and touched glasses for a toast from him. "It's an old Spanish toast: Money, health, wisdom, and time to enjoy them all."

"I love that toast."

The champagne bubbles tickled her nose, and the fruity taste was like ambrosia. They stood close to each other. Finally he told her, "I didn't say it when I first came in because you knocked the air out of me. Ash, you're beautiful all the way through."

His voice had gone husky.

"Thank you. I've got my own compliments to pay. You're a hunk, Derrick Quinn, and I think you're quite a man. You're genuine; I'm beginning to be certain of that."

Derrick set his glass on the table and cupped her chin in his hand. "That color is for you. I've never seen you look this beautiful."

"We don't see a whole lot of each other—" She broke off, then told him, "Thank you for the roses. They're gorgeous."

"You thanked me before."

"A number of times wouldn't be out of order. They're special."

"You're special."

Ashley touched a small, deep scar beside his right eye. "I've wondered how this happened."

"I was kicked by a colt as a child." He smiled with some bitterness. "It seems I've had my trouble with horses, but I keep pitching as best I can."

"It's what we have to do." Her eyes on him were wide; then she shuttered them, afraid of displaying too much . . . what? Love? There surely hadn't been time enough for that. Desire? *Oh, Lord, yes.* And since when, she thought, did love need a certain span of time to happen?

He took the glass from her. "Another round?"

"In a little while. I want to show you how I rearranged your roses."

She led him to her bedroom, where he stood beside her, bemused.

"They were beautiful as they were," she said, "but I have a special Steuben vase for special flowers. I added more broadleaf fern, and voilà! They're lasting, too."

"Yes, that shop promises long-lasting blooms."

They sat on the plush blue couch. The house was quiet

with only the low hum of appliances running. "Do we start talking now?" she asked.

"What do *you* want to do?"

His question threw her. Was he feeling what she felt? It had come so fast, this haze of desire; then she corrected herself. No, it had been there from the first day she had seen him recently, and had never stopped. They had avoided getting too close; they had settled for friendship.

Desire was like a clear, crystal stream warmed by a hot summer sun, rippling through her being. Tipping her head back, he planted a line of kisses down her swanlike brown throat and into the valley of her breasts.

"Lord, how I want you!" he said huskily. He kissed the freckles that bridged her nose and upper cheeks. She closed her eyes and he kissed them, loving the freckles sprinkled across her nose, the long, thick black lashes against her cheeks.

"Derrick, I—"

"Don't talk. Just be still and let me kiss you."

She did as he demanded. Her open mouth received him, and he ravaged the shallows of it with his tongue, asking himself how anything could be so sweet. Then her tongue tentatively explored the shallows of his mouth. Fire leaped between them, dancing in their loins.

He crushed her to him so tightly she thought she might faint; then his lips were hard on hers, hungry and seeking. She was swimming in ecstasy, yet still he held back. Was it time for this to happen? Would she be hurt again?

"Please wait," she murmured, pulling a little away. He loosened his grip and she stepped aside. She went to the windows and looked out at the red-gold streamers of the sun setting over Crystal Lake. It was gorgeous. Then she turned excitedly to Derrick.

"Look!"

He came quickly to her side and she pointed to the skyline and the hilltop, with Black Steed racing back and forth for all he was worth, his beautiful, sleek black body gleaming, his tail and mane streaming in the wind. He was running free. Derrick put his arms around her with her back to him. He stroked her soft breasts and trailed kisses up and down the side of her neck.

In a little while it would be twilight, she thought. Darkness brought so many splendors.

"Help me move the screens in front of the windows," she said.

"I'll move them."

"No, I'll help you." She bit her lips. She felt so eager. Every cell of her body and every part of her spirit surged toward him. In a few minutes, the four screens were placed in front of the window wall. The screens blocked the setting sun, but she and Derrick knew splendor of their own.

He led her to the king-size bed. It was torture for him, but he slowed himself, removing each garment from her body until she was naked. Then she removed his clothes with more haste than he had shown in removing hers. It was early twilight as he sat on the bed.

"Stand there," he told her. "I want to look at you. Model your beautiful body for me."

"I'm not beautiful. Attractive, perhaps."

"Hush! You see it your way; I see it mine. To me, you're beautiful."

He stood up then and drew her to him, his tumescence pressing against her, his rugged body pressing hers. She felt faint with desire, and he felt a triumph he had seldom felt before. It seemed so strange, he thought, that he had dreamed the night before about Black Steed racing on the hilltop, had dreamed of Ashley beneath him; then she had fled him.

He locked her in his arms.

"I won't let you go this time," he said. "Don't beg. Don't plead. You're mine." And in the dream she hadn't pleaded, had merely slipped away.

She wondered through a haze of desire what he meant by *this time*.

"You think I'm talking out of my head," he told her. "I'll explain later. *Much* later."

He pushed her to the bed and onto the warmth of rose-colored sheets, smiling crookedly. "Everything's coming up roses," he murmured.

For moments he propped himself on his elbow, smiling as he looked down at her lying flat on her back. Then he bent and tongued the corners of her mouth. She responded by doing the same to him. He began to trail hot kisses down the length of her body, and she bucked feverishly.

"Derrick, please!" she whispered.

"Tell me what you want. There's nothing I wouldn't do for you. Just tell me what you want."

She hadn't expected to say it. "I want *you*."

It was a long moment before he answered in a strained voice. "You've got me, Ash. You've had me since I came this summer. God help me, I love you. I don't want to, but I do."

His words thrilled her, shook her to her very foundation. She lay there, steeped in tenderness, yearning for him.

"That's good," she told him, tears in her voice, "because I love you. Is making love making both of us a little crazy?"

He laughed shakily. "If it is, then I'll take being crazy any day."

Lying on his side, he buried his face in her soft hair. Almost desperately, he tried to slow the torrent of emotions and physical passion that nearly engulfed him. She lay still, drawing him like a magnet. Raising himself, he bent to kiss and fondle the physical core of her, and she gasped with sheer rapture.

He stormed her then, his big hands caressing her feverishly, his lips patterning wet kisses over her body. When he finally stopped, taking a foil package from where he had placed it on the bed, he barely breathed with raw anticipation. Her soft hands helped him, stroked him. He caught her hand.

"No," he said, laughing shakily. "Don't stroke me. I can't last if you do. You're so damned sweet."

He raised her hips and gently and smoothly entered the waiting sheath of her body, its wetness like the syrup of midsummer fruits, ripe and wonderful.

They moved slowly in perfect rhythm until he slipped into a deeper place, and she cried out and clutched him to her. Her cries spurred him on as she fastened her legs over his. Tumultuous spasms shook her then, and she cried out again.

He was attentive to her every movement, heard every cry, and there was nothing he wouldn't do for her. As she moved her legs against him, explosive ecstasy shook him into a trance from which he had no wish to escape.

They lay quietly then, side by side, spent for those precious moments. The room was in darkness save for a full moon and a heaven full of twinkling stars that sparkled no more than Ashley and Derrick had. That fiery setting sun that had so roguishly led them on had blazed no hotter than they had.

Fulfilled, she lay beside him. "Do you believe in magic?" she asked him lazily.

He smiled. "Look at the world around us. How can we not believe in at least some kind of magic?"

She turned onto her side to face him. He spread a big hand across the top part of her waist, and she thrilled so deeply for a moment she couldn't believe it. He let his hand stay on her waist for a few moments, then withdrew it. She could not remember ever knowing a touch like that or feeling what she now felt.

"Was I too rushed for you?" he asked. "I'm famished. But you were right with me."

"I was, all the way. No, you weren't too rushed. I love the way we make love, Derrick. So natural. So deep. I feel like

I'm living in a paradise on Earth when I'm with you." Her voice held wonder, awe.

"I've been living in my paradise with you almost from the beginning, but it makes me sad."

"Why?" She propped herself on one elbow. He sat up and propped himself against the thick bed pillows.

"What I did to you isn't fair to either of us. I love you, my darling. I'll always love you, but I know what I feel, and it torments me to think of going through with another woman what I went through with Maria. Can you forgive me?"

"Forgive you? For making love with me?"

"Yes."

She was silent for a long moment. "I don't think either of us could help it, Derrick. When you said you loved me, I would have swum through raging rivers to get to you. We're both adults, both been married, been hurt. . . ."

"Would you have let me make love to you if I'd said at the outset that I can't go through again what I've been through?"

She answered without hesitation: "Yes, because I wanted you from the bottom of my very soul. I wanted you inside me so badly I was sick with it. Not everybody gets married. I have my own problems. I haven't healed from my first marriage."

"Listen," he said urgently. "We both know this brings up new problems. We've become lovers now. . . ."

"Aren't we still friends?"

"Sure we are, but we're so much more."

She sat up, feeling the stirrings of desire again. Derrick marveled that no sooner had he hit the zenith of desire and spiraled down than he was ready to begin again.

"I'm thirsty." She sat up, getting her robe from the floor and slipping it on. "Let's kill the rest of that champagne."

"You put it in the refrigerator—you like cool champagne."

"That doesn't mean I don't like chilled champagne. Besides, you did it my way. Now I'm going to do it yours."

He smiled at the double meaning. Ashley was an earthy, natural woman, and he loved that about her.

Derrick got into his brown slacks and they both padded barefoot back to the carpeted kitchen, where they made grilled-cheese sandwiches.

The champagne was cool as they sipped from fresh glasses. "Well, I tried to serve you properly chilled champagne," she said, shrugging, "but neither of us could wait."

"It was worth it."

"More than worth it."

He leaned across the kitchen table and took her hand in his. He kept seeing her as the most desirable woman in the world—his world. How could he share her with millions of others?

Back in the bedroom a little while later, they drew the blinds, turned on soft rose lights, and removed their clothes. The room swam with a rosy glow. Ashley tapped a little Monoi oil onto the bedsheets and put on a Teddy Pendergrass album.

They sat on the bed, naked, while she fed him Godiva chocolates from her nightstand. Whit had given them to her after her concert.

He stroked her thigh. "Brown marble," he said.

She stroked his thigh. "Polished pillars like Samson, like Denzel Washington, and yet belonging only to you. Made in heaven by an expert."

He laughed. "You say the damnedest, most wonderful things."

"I'm glad you like my performances."

"I love you, everything you are. Listen, Ash, is anybody likely to come by?"

"No. You know Eleni is with her father. My parents never come by without calling; they respect my privacy. Annice and Whitley give me space. No, you're trapped here with me."

"You won't see me trying to get away."

Ashley thought that she wasn't going to borrow trouble. Life wasn't perfect. This man had carried her to heights she'd only dreamed of knowing. He was taking her higher than she'd ever been before. With the champagne bubbling in her blood, she put everything else aside. Tonight she was going to live, the way she never had before.

"I want to stay the night," he said.

"Yes. Stay the night."

In lazy luxury they lay on the bed again, relaxed where they had been supertense. Each had spoken his true mind. But what mattered was that they loved each other. With one moment of sadness, Ashley reflected that he was bitterly hurt, and might never get over it. But she was going to gamble, to bet everything. If she lost . . . well, it would have been worth it.

"How beautiful you are," she said as he leaned above her.

"You keep saying that. You're the one who's beautiful. Do you feel this is special, not quite like anything you've known before? I don't mean to pry."

"You aren't prying. It *is* special. I want it to go on and on."

He put his face in the valley of her softly firm breasts. "Then let's get started again."

This time there were all-over wet kisses, loving strokes, and sighs. She sat astride him, her face alight with love. With his powerful hands, he pulled her down on his hardness, and held her there, gasping with pleasure.

Both were too full to speak; fond looks had to serve. Her long hair partially covered her face as he reached up and brushed it back. She leaned down onto him, her lush breasts touching his chest and flat breasts. Then teasingly she flicked her tongue on his breasts and he jumped at the sensation.

"Go ahead," he said lazily. "You got to me fast the first time. This time, prepare yourself for the long haul."

"Promises," she said flippantly as he brought her mouth down onto his, flicking his tongue into her mouth, no longer gentle. It was now as if he would storm her every portal. His hands cupped and kneaded her flesh as he turned her over and continued to lovingly work her with savage tenderness.

Lowering his head to her breasts again, he feasted hungrily on each ripe, brown mound as her nipples hardened in response.

This was a glory he had always sought, and he savored it deeply. The only thing was, having known her, how could he ever let her go? He moaned in the back of his throat as she found a responsive place above his nipple to softly bite, cushioning her teeth with her lips. He laughed aloud.

"You little devil," he said.

"Turn you on?"

"What do *you* think? I nearly jumped out of my skin with joy."

"Whatever you want."

"Ash. Ashley," he said. "I love my son, but if I had to die tomorrow, I'd want to spend my last hours with you. Corby would understand later."

She grasped him then and they hugged as if they would melt into each other. Each was separate, mature. Each saw the other as individual, alone. But these moments were different, enveloping.

Had she really lain here the night before, lonelier than she could remember being? Surely that was light-years away. As her body moved in smooth rhythm with his and joy filled her soul, she wished it would never end. Dear Lord, why couldn't it last forever?

Thirteen

Delia Quinn sat on her screened back porch in the cold darkness, bundled against the chill. She had come out here shortly after Derrick left the house and watched him descend the hill and head toward Ashley's house. Her teeth were clenched with anger; she had come out to clear her head.

Before Derrick left, he had said, "I'll be late. Tell Corby not to wait up for me, and please see that he's in bed by nine."

"Yes, of course," she had murmured. "Will you be driving?" she asked, hoping he was going somewhere other than Ashley's.

"No." He had given no further answer. Testily she had silently mimicked him: *No.* He didn't need a car to go to Ashley's.

Delia still smarted from the memory of Derrick and Ashley at Ashley's triumphant concert, and at what had lain between him and Ashley. She got up and looked at her watch in the kitchen light. Eight forty-five. She got her dark green melton cloth coat from the kitchen closet. She needed to talk with her hired farmhand, Len Starkey.

Walking along the path with a flashlight in her hand, Delia tried to relax and couldn't. Just how late would Derrick be coming back? Len was teaching Corby to play cards. The man and the boy had grown fond of each other. Reaching the cozy small bunkhouse, she knocked lightly. In a few moments the door opened wide and Len stood there.

"Boss lady," he said jovially, "what brings you out here?"

The lights behind him delineated his coarsely attractive features, his kind, dark brown eyes in his swarthy face, and his short, thickset body. An early siege of smallpox had left him with facial pockmarks.

"I came for Corby, and I need to talk with you. May I come in?"

"Sure you can." He swung the door back and she stepped in, looking around at the neat, clean room that was like the man—no frills.

"Uh-uh," Corby said, "I'll bet you came for me. Why didn't you call? It's really cold outside."

"I need to talk to Len. Why don't you run along and get to bed? I'll be on a little later."

"Yeah, sure. I don't guess you'll let us finish this hand?"

She frowned; she didn't feel like humoring him. "Really, it's past your bedtime, and as swiftly as you can move, it's going to take you a little while to get into bed. You know how you dawdle."

"I guess. Where's Dad? And you didn't say why you didn't call."

Exasperated, she answered him. "I'm not sure where your father is. I didn't ask because it isn't my or your business. As to why I didn't call, I told you I wanted to talk to Len. Anything else?"

"Nope. You feeling okay?" Her face looked pinched to him.

"I'm fine. You run along. Len will put the cards away."

The boy got up reluctantly, got his coat from the back of his chair, and put it on on the way out. Grinning, he told Len, "One day I'm gonna beat the socks off you at poker. You wait."

Len laughed. "And one day a horse is going to jump over the moon. Good night, kid. See you tomorrow."

Delia sat at the table where the man and the boy had been playing cards. Leaning with her elbow on the table, she waited as Len sat across from her. He gathered the cards into a deck and boxed them. She gazed at him fondly.

"You've been with me since Marty died, and you were with him a long time. You're like a family member to me."

"Thank you, ma'am. Feels like that to me, too." Deep inside, the heavy man thought that it wasn't being family he wanted from her. He worshiped her, thought her a queen and himself her willing slave. He licked his dry lips. He'd die for her if it came to that.

"Len."

"Yes, ma'am?"

"What were you thinking? You seemed lost in thought. And I've told you that you don't have to say 'yes, ma'am.' I want us to be friends. There are things I want you to help me with that only a friend can do."

"Anything Miz—"

"Delia. I insist you call me Delia."

He tried, but the name wouldn't come out right. "Won't people talk? We've got some right gossipy folks around here. I've always called you Miz Quinn, said 'ma'am.' "

Her voice was sharp when she asked him, "Can't you change? As for the gossip, I don't live my life for other people. You're afraid of the neighbors. *We're* the neighbors, too, you know. There's plenty of space out here, Len. Room to breathe, to live your own life."

"Yes." He swallowed hard and the word came out hoarsely: "Delia."

"That's great. Now say it again."

"Delia." It was more natural that time, but still stilted.

Delia leaned back, her pale gray eyes almost colorless. "There are things I'm going to want you to do for me that you won't always understand. Are you willing to stick your neck out for me a little?"

Len nodded. "I told you when the mistah died I'd do anything in the world you needed me to. I nevah said it again because I felt you understood that I would. You tell me what you want me to do."

"Anything?"

A smile played about her mouth. Her voice held a teasing note that made him uncomfortable. He knew he wasn't in her class. It didn't matter. He was perfectly content to worship and make no demands. He hesitated before he finally said it.

"Well, yes, I reckon I wouldn't want to kill nobody. Anything short o' that."

The smile was gone now and her eyes were level, straightforward. "If someone were going to kill me, would you kill them to save me?"

"You tryin' t'tell me somebody's afta you? You tell me who and I'll see they don' hurt you no more."

"Well said. It may come to that." She looked down, then back. "I'm raising your salary by a hundred dollars a month, retroactive to the first of this month."

Len flushed hotly. "Now, ma'am—sorry—Delia. You don' have t'do that. You pay me right well, and you got Mr. Carter to pay. Things've gone a bit down since the mistah passed on."

"You're right, but Carter's good, and you're doing a damned fine job. Derrick's making changes that seem to be working. We'll be back on top again in no time."

"Thought you might be thinkin' o' sellin'."

"Don't you worry. If I ever did sell, I'd go somewhere else, and I'd find a spot for you."

"Why, that's one o' the best things anybody ever said to me, and I cain' tell you how I appreciate it."

She placed her small hand over his callus-thickened one. It was now or never, she thought. "Do you believe in magic? Voodoo? Hoodoo?" She laughed nervously.

"I reckon." He looked uncomfortable. What was she getting at?

"Ever heard the term *mambo?*"

"Cain' say I have."

"My grandmother was a certified *mambo,* a high priestess of voodoo, which in spite of what you've heard is a religion. She came to this country at a time of great upheaval in Haiti and never went back. She could work any spell you wanted. My mother despised voodoo, so I was torn up about it when I was young. I adored my grandmother; we were very close, and she taught me many of the spells."

She paused to see how he was taking this information. His eyes were half-closed and he was smiling. *Good.*

"I knew there was somethin' different about you," he finally said. "You know magic."

"Some. Are you surprised?"

"A little. You're so smart I don' guess nothin' surprises me much about you. This have anything to do wit' the goat's blood and the graveyard dust I been gettin' for you?"

It was now or never. "Yes. I'll need other things. As soon as you can get it, I need a pint of blood from a pregnant goat. I need a chicken killed at midnight—no other time. Bring the blood, the feathers, and the heart to me. I need the berries from a holly bush. And I need more graveyard dirt. Do this in such a way that they're all fresh. Do you follow me?"

"All the way."

"Try to get all this by the night after tomorrow. I'm expecting Derrick to be visiting over near Baltimore then. Corby will be asleep. I want you to go deep into our woods, and we'll be there by midnight. You'll see me do things that will make you wonder. Be with me. I'll always be with you."

As she spoke, her eyes flashed fire, and Len felt himself tremble and his flesh cool. *What the hell?* he thought. She was so beautiful, so powerful he couldn't believe what he was seeing. Again she placed her hand over his and he could hardly breathe. The thought sprang full-blown in his head of how it would feel to have her body under his, but he mashed it flat. She was out of his class.

Funny how she looked at him as if there were no distance between them, as if she weren't high and he wasn't low.

"I'll always be wit' you all the way," he said hoarsely. He couldn't seem to get his voice out of the trench of surprise that nearly engulfed him.

She looked at the clock on his table. Nine-ten. It seemed to her she had been here much longer; she had gotten so much resolved. With her eyes sparkling, relaxed now at last, she smiled flirtatiously at him. He wasn't going to take it any farther. She felt altogether safe with him.

Getting up, she smiled widely. "Are you comfortable with what I've told you?"

He nodded, not yet trusting himself to speak; then he found his voice. "I nevah knew nobody like you," he said, noting that he still avoided saying her name. "I don' guess I evah will again."

Delia started to kiss his cheek, then thought better of it. She was going to have to tread as carefully with Len as she had begun to tread with Ashley. And how beautifully she had begun to do both. It was only Derrick she couldn't control her feelings for. Being around him and not having him was like starving and dying of thirst in the midst of food and drink. Anything she needed to do to draw him to her side was justified.

"Good night, my friend," she said, getting up.

She probably thought him a clod, but he knew enough to help her with her coat. He just couldn't let himself touch her. He opened the door for her. "Think I oughta walk you up to the house?"

"No," she said quickly, "I'll be fine. "We're going to be great partners, Len. I need a friend."

"You got a friend—Delia."

Fourteen

Going inside her house, Delia found Corby rummaging about in the refrigerator. She drew a sharp breath, remembering the mason jar of goat's blood that Len had brought her.

"Why aren't you in bed?" she demanded.

"Hey, I wanted the Gatorade I hid from myself so I wouldn't drink my last bottle; then I'm going to bed."

"Can't it wait until tomorrow? You're in a new school, Corby. You need your sleep so you can measure up."

"Measure up? I'm ahead. You know how Dad tutors me, too."

He was right, of course. She came to the refrigerator. "I think I'm going to have to insist that you go to bed now."

"Okay," he said glumly; then he found and brought out the jar of goat's blood, holding it up. "Hey!" he said again. "What's this?"

Damn it, she thought. There were reasons she'd never cared for kids.

"Put it back," she ordered. If the fool kid dropped it, it would take a little while to find and get more blood than she had already had Len get, and she needed it soon.

"What is it?" he asked again. "It looks like blood. Hey, it *is* blood, isn't it?"

"Couldn't it be tomato paste?"

"We worked with blood in my biology class last year." Corby had skipped a grade. Swiftly she thought of a good explanation.

"I'm going to make some blood pudding," she said, "if you don't drop the jar."

"I won't. I never heard of blood pudding. How do you make it?"

"Corby, put the blood back!"

At the sharpness of her voice, he quickly complied and pulled out his orange Gatorade.

"Sorry," he said meekly. "I wasn't meddling. Blood pudding sounds cool. Will Dad and me get some, too?"

"Dad and I," she corrected. "It's cooked and made with plenty of rice. It isn't something everybody likes."

"I bet I would. I like oddball things. Dad used to get frog legs from a pond on our farm. You remember when you and Uncle Marty used to come down?"

"I remember. Did you do your homework?"

Corby opened the bottle of Gatorade and wiped the mouth of the bottle with his palm, then drank deeply. "Sure did," he answered.

Finally she said, "You're waiting around for Derrick, and he said to make certain you were in bed by nine."

"Awww. I'm not really sleepy."

She remembered then when Corby had been at another age—the terrible twos. She had absolutely hated the way Derrick and Maria had handled him. She thought they should have been much harsher; Marty hadn't agreed. "It's the beginning of his feeling his individuality," Marty had said. To Delia, it had simply been the beginning of raising a rotten kid.

Now Marty was gone; she had gotten used to his not being here. As long as Derrick was around she felt okay. Bleakly she thought that, now Derrick was off courting, she was certain he would come in late. Anger smoldered in her chest.

"Corby!"

"Going! Going! Gone!" he said, laughing as he left the room.

After the boy left her, Delia climbed onto a stepladder and got a brass key from the edge of a tall, narrow kitchen cabinet. Sighing as she climbed off the ladder, she walked to a room between the kitchen and the back porch, unlocked the door, and went in, closing the door behind her.

Switching on the light, she looked around her. She called this her spirit room, for the African spirits of her ancestors lived here, as well as in the forests and the rivers.

It was too bad, she thought, that she had not really believed in voodoo in her early life. In fact, she hadn't believed until Marty had become interested in her, leaving his fiancée and coming to her bosom. She had wanted him so badly, and although she was considered one of the prettiest girls on Hampton's campus, he had liked plainer girls.

But *Grand-mère's* voodoo magic had gotten him for her. She felt surrounded by powerful spirits in this room. "Damballah," she entreated, "I love Derrick more than I ever loved Marty. I would die for him. *Kill* for him. Help me."

She felt a surge of power throughout her body as she thought of the chief voodoo god, Damballah.

"And Freda Erzulie, goddess of love and desire, I have always worshiped you. Help me now."

She studied the dark plum-colored walls and the white *vévés*—pronounced *vay-vays*—spirit drawings used to worship voodoo gods. She thought for a moment that she needed the blessings of no other than these two; then she reminded herself that it seemed that Baron Samedi, god of the cemetery, was going to have to be called on, too. Baron Samedi, god of death.

The room had permanently covered windows and little furniture. The *vévés* were drawn on the lower walls to honor the great snake god, Damballah. She kept the room locked at all times. She had told Derrick it was because she kept things of Marty's that she couldn't share with anyone. She had set up this room after Marty's death, seeking to draw Derrick to her as soon as possible.

Was it ever going to work? She asked the spirits—also known collectively as *loa*—for so little: Marty. Now Derrick.

"Loup Garou," she said quietly to herself, wondering why she thought of this now. A *Loup Garou* was a childless woman who could fly, who snatched babies from their mothers' breasts and abducted other children. Magic women, they were hated and feared in Haiti, and some were killed. She shuddered. She cared little for children, and she would hurt Eleni to get back at Ashley.

Ashley's name was like gall on her tongue. If all else failed and Derrick did not come to her, destroying Ashley would become absolutely necessary. She had alternate plans—to claim Derrick for herself, through spells and potions, and, failing that, to get rid of Ashley.

Voodoo was a religion of the spirits, drawn from Africa and Haiti, but it went beyond magic. In her studies of magic, Delia had taken it much farther. European magic, with its dolls made in the likeness of a hated figure, was splendid for revenge, *Grand-mère* had said. Delia believed, too, in European magic, especially Welsh magic.

She sat on a rug on the floor and studied the *vévés*. There was a large picture of a mapou tree, so prominent in Haiti, the dwelling place of Damballah and other gods.

She went into a brief trance. She wanted it to be longer, but she meant to be clear when Derrick came home. The spirits were like liquid gold flowing through her veins. They told her everything, except what she needed most to know: What was going on between Derrick and Ashley? When would Delia claim him for her own?

Stiff, her spirits crumpled, Delia came abruptly awake. She had fallen asleep sitting on the floor. Glancing at her watch, she saw that it was two o'clock. Had Derrick come in and closed the front door softly so as not to awaken her and

Corby? She got up, turned off the light, and stood in the darkness on aching legs for a few minutes.

She wanted to know if he'd come in, and she couldn't do that without opening his door. He zealously guarded his privacy. She was learning to be circumspect, to hide her feelings as best she could, but it was hard.

She went out, locking the door behind her, then walked up the hallway to Derrick's room, which was next to Corby's. Bending down at his door, she listened for sounds of soft snoring and heard nothing. Her heart thudding, she felt impelled to know if he were there.

Opening the door gently, she peeked in. She had a ready excuse if he was there: she would say she thought she heard him cry out in a nightmare. Light from the moon shone in. His bed was empty. Jagged streaks of anger struck her; then she quieted herself. It was only two in the morning. People sat around talking, lost track of time. Was that all that was going on?

"Come home, Derrick," she murmured. "Come home to me, where you belong."

Fifteen

Two evenings later, when she was expecting Derrick, Ashley was sitting in her living room when her cell phone buzzed. She picked it up immediately.

"I can't talk," Derrick said quickly. "One of Delia's horses broke out, and she's in labor near the woods on your side. I'm calling on my cell phone. Trask O'Quinn, the veterinarian, is coming to help. It's a difficult foaling and it may take a while. I'll come if it isn't too late."

"I'm sorry," she said. "Come if it isn't too bad and you feel like it. Is there any way I can help?"

"No. We'll be covered when Trask gets here. This is one of our best brood mares and we don't want to lose her. . . ."

"Come when you can. Good luck, and I love you."

"I love you, too."

"Derrick, be careful out there. You've already got a cold, and it can get worse in a hurry."

"Don't worry about me. I'm tough. 'Bye now."

Pressing the off switch, Ashley sighed. She hoped he'd come by later. He sounded so worried, and she worried about him. She'd picked up some echinacea and other herbs at the herb shop for his cold and had intended to give them to him tonight. *Oh, well.*

Eleni came in and sat beside her, then put her head in Ashley's lap.

"Are Gramma and Grampa still coming over?"

"I hope so."

"Who was it calling?"

"Sweetie, that's impolite. I don't mind your knowing, but you shouldn't ask. It was Derrick."

"I'm sorry. Mom?"

"Yes, love."

"Can I call Mr. Quinn *Uncle?*"

Ashley laughed, surprised. "What brings this on?"

"Can I?"

" '*May* I.' I suppose so, but why do you want to?"

Eleni sat up and rocked a bit before she said, "Well, I love Uncle Whit and I call him Uncle. I really like Mr. Quinn, and I can't call him Dad. You're not married to him. Mom, it'd be neat."

"I see no harm in it, if he doesn't mind. You'd better ask him."

"Oh, goody. He won't mind. Is he coming over tonight? He comes a lot more than he used to."

Ashley groaned a bit, thinking little pitchers certainly had big mouths.

"So you like Derrick?"

"A whole lot." Suddenly the child shuddered. "Mom, you won't let Dad take me away from you, will you?"

Ashley hugged her tightly. "No. Never. What makes you think of that?"

"Daddy asks me all the time if I want to stay with just him."

"I'll talk with him about it. I think he'll stop." Damned right she'd talk with him, she thought angrily. He said he had slowed down on his drinking, but had he? Reese could be mean.

The door chimes sounded, and Eleni and Ashley went to the door to greet Caroline and Frank with big hugs, as if they hadn't just seen them that morning.

Frank picked Eleni up and held her high. "You're growing, kid," he said. "Getting fat."

Eleni giggled. "I'm not fat. You're fat."

"That makes three of us," Caroline said. "Of course your grandfather is teasing you, Eleni, but I, at any rate, am packing it on. I've got to watch it."

"Oh, Mama," Ashley said, sighing, "please don't talk about extra weight. I'm fast approaching the twenty-extra-pounds mark. I'm going to take it off before my next tour."

"Nonsense," Frank said staunchly, "you need your weight to carry the singing you do. Fat gives your voice that silken edge. I'm proud my daughter is so healthy."

"Gee, Dad. Health and weight aren't surefire partners. I'd rather be a bit thinner."

"You were born into the wrong family for that." Caroline brushed her hand over her close-cut hair.

Lovingly Ashley looked from one to the other of her parents. "I'm blessed," she said. "I was born into exactly the right family."

"How's Derrick?" Frank asked.

Ashley told him what had happened. He thought about it a moment. "We talked about that mare this morning when I went over. Look, they're going to need all the help they can get. I'm going home to get my windbreaker, then I'll head over that way."

"Might be a good idea," Caroline commented.

"Did he say where the horse is located?" Frank asked.

"Yes," Ashley told him, "at the edge of the woods on this side of their spread. After we talked, I looked back that way and I could see their lantern lights."

Frank got up to leave. As he got his coat, Caroline told him, "Now take care, Frank. You always get some kind of sniffles in bitter weather like this."

"You bet I'll take care. I've got too much to live for not to. Here, baby, come and give Grampa a great big hug."

Eleni jumped into Frank's arms and hugged him fiercely. "I love you," she said. "I love all of you."

After Frank left, the door chimes sounded again, and Ashley wondered who it could be. She looked at the security panel by the door and drew a quick breath before she opened the door to Max.

He came into the room, took off his hat, and unbuttoned his overcoat, unwrapping the scarf from around his neck.

"Sorry, I just didn't seem to have time to call," he said. "Hello, Mrs. Steele, Eleni." Then to Ashley, "I knew I needed to talk with you, and I took the chance even though I knew you might have company."

He was the soul of graciousness—a complete gentleman. Ashley took his garments and put them in the hall closet. She brushed the light snow from his hat and coat. He was coming from D.C., and if it was snowing there, they were likely to get it shortly. She thought of the men outside on Delia's farm, tending the horse in labor.

Caroline had always liked Max, but she liked Derrick better. She very much appreciated what Max had done for her daughter's career. She sat near Max.

"Listen," Caroline said, getting up. "This is a great time for me to visit alone with my granddaughter. I can help Eleni finish her homework and read to her out of her latest Harry Potter book. . . ."

"Yes," Eleni added enthusiastically, "and the new book you got me that the Hansons wrote, with all the great pictures." The Hansons were a young African-American couple who were enjoying fabulous success with their children's books about African-American children.

Alone with Max, Ashley switched on one of Aretha Franklin's albums.

"Why not one of yours?" Max asked. "You're my favorite singer."

"Thank you. What can I get you to eat or drink?"

"I sure could use a whiskey sour, if you could find it in your heart to make me one."

"Of course I will. A snack?"

"Light one. I'd love some sharp cheese, Swiss cheese, and a few Ritz crackers."

"Coming up." She rose from the couch and started toward the kitchen. He followed her.

"Do you mind?" he asked.

She shook her head. It wasn't a good time to talk with him. Her mind was taken up with Derrick. Eleni's tinkling laughter sounded from her room. The child was a happy romantic who adored fairy tales and children's stories.

Max sat at the table as Ashley arranged cheese and crackers on a platter, then added pickles and black olives.

"You're everything a man could want in a woman," Max said smoothly. "Ashley, I have so much to say to you, but tonight I'm going to focus on what I've been outlining in my mind for your career. One day soon, though, we've got to talk about us."

Ashley licked her dry bottom lip. She and Derrick had to talk, too. Tonight was to have been their night. She blushed, thinking of what they had known in her bedroom a couple of days back. Annice knew what lay between Ashley and Derrick. Did Max guess, too?

She fixed a tray of blended whiskey and whiskey-sour mix, set a shaker on it, and gave it to Max to carry.

The fire cracked merrily in the fireplace as Max munched on the food and shook his whiskey sour.

"Ashley." With his drink in hand, he turned to her as she sat on one end of the couch with him on the other. "You're classically trained. Juilliard."

"Uh-huh."

"On your tour to Germany in March—"

"Whoa! You didn't definitely tell me I was going to Germany this March."

"I'm telling you now. I don't boss you around because you wouldn't stand for it, but some things I feel in my gut. A lot of Germans like gospel music, but all Europe adores opera.

"You'll go to Germany in February or March—I haven't quite decided—and a segment of your show will be devoted to operatic arias: *La Traviata, La Bohème, Madame Butterfly.* You'll knock them off their feet. What better place to start than Germany, where you already have a good following?"

"Could it work? I've never really thought of it. I adore classical music as well as my spirituals." She threw back her head, laughing. "Is there any music I don't like? The sound of deep African drums thrills me."

Max slid over, putting his tray on the cocktail table. "You're an artist and a musician to the core of you. Perhaps that's why I feel about you the way I do." He stopped and put his head to one side, studying her before he said, "You look happy, Ashley. Very happy. Is it because you know I'm seeing to it that your career skyrockets, beginning with this trip to Germany?"

No, that wasn't the reason, Ashley thought, but he didn't have to know that.

She said only, "I am happy. I just am."

"Good. I like it when you're especially happy. You will keep your same agent in Germany, Hans Schneider. He is mad about your music. It is he who suggested that you sing the operatic arias."

Max ate several cracker-and-cheese combinations, leaned back, and put his hands behind his head, looking at her with benevolent eyes.

"Now, don't fall in love with some fool," he said with an edge to his voice. "I'm going to make it all come together for you. By this time next year you'll be well on your way to glory. If I have my way—and I will, with your help—two years from now you'll need bodyguards. Hear me, Ashley? Bodyguards!"

A rush of anxiety filled Ashley. She liked her life the way it was, liked the warmth and the love she shared with her audiences. She wasn't sure she wanted to be big-time enough to be covered by bodyguards. Yet nothing ever stayed the same. It made her sad.

"I'm not sure I'd like that," she said.

"It's part of the game. You've got plenty of room here for one bodyguard. We could have a female guard, if you wish, but no, I think a man would be more effective. There are kooks and idiots out there, lurking in wait for wonders like yourself. . . ."

"Max," she said thoughtfully, "I don't want to go too fast. Music is my life, but it isn't my only life. I have family, friends. . . ."

His laughter was short, harsh. "And I don't deny you that life, but right now let me take you to the top. As I said, don't fall in love with some jerk who doesn't appreciate your true worth. You're a gospel princess, Ashley. I can—I will—make you a gospel queen. You'll be on a level with Aretha Franklin by the time I get through."

Sixteen

It was ten-thirty that same night when Derrick came. When Ashley opened her front door, she could see his pickup truck in her driveway. She saw in a second that he looked worn. Closing the door, he caught her close and held her for a long time.

"You've got to be dog tired," she said. "How did everything go?"

He thought a moment. "Fine in the end. But if it hadn't been for Trask, I think we'd have lost mama and baby. That guy is wonderful. He comes down to Tidewater from time to time to double-check on my stock."

"Is the foal a boy or a girl?"

"It's a boy. Since Black Steed is the sire, you can bet he looks like him. Same star on his forehead."

"Oh, wonderful," she said. "Delia and Marty have used Black Steed, but they used others, too. I'll have to give him an extra apple and extra sugar cubes."

Derrick laughed. "You're paying him to have fun." She helped him shuck his outer garments and put them in the closet.

"Sit down before you fall down from weariness." She rubbed her hands together. "Did you take time to eat?"

"Early on. I'm not hungry." He gave a mock leer. "Not for food, anyway."

"I know the feeling. Could you stand a cup of chocolate laced with brandy?"

"I would be delighted."

She prepared the hot chocolate with whipped cream and chocolate curls and was back in a brief while.

Derrick looked thoughtful in his gray V-necked wool sweater and his heavy gray corduroy pants. They sipped their chocolate quietly. The house was silent save for the whir of appliances.

"Would you like to hear some music?"

He shook his head. "I like sitting peacefully with you." He grinned then. "Tell you what, though. I feel like I could beat the socks off you on a Scrabble board."

Ashley laughed merrily. "You're not as tired as I thought, buster. More chocolate? Did I put enough brandy in it?"

"She asks me when it's all gone. That more than hits the spot, and you put in plenty of brandy. Delicious."

"I could give you an extra shot of brandy. You've been out in the cold for a few hours."

"You worry about me too much. I told you I'm made of steel. Bring on the Scrabble board."

Smiling, she took the cups and saucers back to the kitchen, then went to the dining area and got the Scrabble board from a drawer.

They sat at the dining-room table. He snapped his fingers when she had set up the game. "Luck, come to Papa," he said. "What are your stakes?"

Looking at each other, their eyes caught fire. "If I win," she said, "two deep kisses. If you win, your choice of any number of kisses."

"You're forcing me to fight like hell to win. Two measly kisses, no matter how deep, just aren't enough." He tapped the Scrabble board. "Show me love," he told it.

"You're hopeless. I don't know why I love you."

"But I know why I love *you;* everything about you is why I love you."

She played carelessly, feeling sleepy. He played sharply,

building impossibly long and numerous words from the leads she set out.

He sneezed mightily three times as she got a box of Kleenex. Taking the box from her, he blew his nose on two of the tissues. Frowning, she put the back of her hand to his forehead. "You seem hot to me."

"I've got a hot lead here, lady. Don't try to take it away from me."

"I'll bet you took a bath before coming over here."

"Yep."

"Coming back out in the cold when you already *have* a cold and you're damp could be dangerous."

"I drove, so I was out of the elements. You saw the truck. Don't try to take the game by default."

"Derrick, I'm serious. I want to give you aspirin but Dr. Smith has cautioned me not to be too quick to try to break a fever before seeing a doctor."

"You're sending me home? You're a poor loser."

She stood beside him rubbing his back. "You idiot."

"I'll only accept that if I'm a sweet idiot."

"Jam, jelly, honey, all of it. You're the sweetest."

"Thank you." He held her hand, forgetting the Scrabble game. Looking out a small window, where the blinds were open, he told her, "Look, it's snowing. It held off until I got here. Isn't nature wonderful?"

"Nature's not all that's wonderful sometimes. I hope it's a light snow. I'm not in the mood for snow just now."

"I am. I want to snuggle somewhere with you through a snowstorm." He exploded in one giant sneeze this time.

Ashley put her hand on his forehead again.

"Why don't you lie down for a few minutes? You're worn out from helping the horse foal."

"I guess I should have gone right to bed, but I couldn't wait to see you."

"And I'm so glad you came, but don't be difficult, love. Lie down at least half an hour or so."

"Okay. You've sold me. Maybe I'd be better off, though, driving home while I can."

"I say you can't. Wait a little while. Give the brandy time to take effect."

"You're bossy." He grinned. I usually don't like that in a woman, but I like it in you."

Ashley put her hands on her hips. "Come on, mister. Come with me." She teased him, "I'm going to light your fire."

"You're too late. I'm already ablaze."

Ashley drew a deep breath; she was worried. Red had crept under his dark skin, and he looked feverish.

He lay on her bed and she slipped off his boots. When he was propped on her bed pillows with a woolen blanket over him, she got the thermometer and took his temperature. A hundred and three! She knew enough to know that for an adult, that was beginning to be in the danger range.

"Lie still," she said, but he wanted to talk.

"I'm not Corby. I don't need coddling."

Her voice had grown a bit hoarse with anxiety. "Believe me, I'm not coddling you."

"Let me tell you something: I've decided I'm wrong. I'm going to let Corby ride Black Steed."

Her eyes lit up. "That's wonderful. Does he know?"

"Not yet, but soon."

He was silent a long while, and she thought she saw a shadow pass over his face.

"What do you hear from Max?" he finally asked. "When do you go away again?"

"I'll tell you later. Right now I want to think."

"Stop worrying. Tell me now. I've had fevers before."

"Not around me. Max came by early this evening. I won't be going away until February or March."

"A tour?"

"Germany. I don't want you to talk so much."

"He's in love with you."

"Max is in love with Max. He's a brilliant young agent, but he's selfish. He's got a lot of women crying for him. I'm no sucker to be hurt."

"I'll try never to hurt you. That's what I'm trying to avoid doing when I lay it out for you that I need a woman who doesn't belong to the world. Does my saying that hurt you?"

"No. You're being honest, and I like that." But she reflected dully that it *did* hurt. She was beginning to care deeply for this man, and she was beginning to feel that there wasn't enough of her to go around.

She sat on the bed beside him, stroking his hands, examining his roughened palms and the broad, deep fingernails that were in such good shape. He took excellent care of himself—he cared about himself and others. The way she felt these days, it wouldn't take much to send her hurtling over the edge of love's ravine, falling endlessly.

She shook her head as she stroked his face; he was going to sleep. Love wasn't a ravine. It was a safe haven, she thought, but only when two lovers wanted the same thing for each other. He had what she wanted, but what Derrick wanted, she couldn't give.

At midnight he began to toss and she roused him, put the thermometer in his mouth, and waited. His temperature was 103.4, and she was frightened.

"Turn over," she said. I want to get your clothes off. I have a pair of Whit's pajamas here. You can't go anywhere tonight."

"I think I have to. I don't want Eleni to get up in the morning and find me here. Explain that."

"I could move you to another room. I've got five bedrooms."

She told him what his temperature was and he whistled, but he stopped kidding around.

"Okay," she said, standing up, "follow me."

She looked at him as he tried to rise and didn't budge

beyond the few movements he'd made on the bed. A look of fear passed over his face.

"What the hell?" he rasped.

"What is it?"

She saw the superhuman effort he put himself through before he said with a gasp, *"I can't move!* Hell, I was moving a few minutes ago." He struggled mightily, and she saw the fear on his face, in his eyes.

"Don't try to move. Something's wrong."

"Am I having a stroke? No, I don't think I'd be talking this well if I were."

"Don't try to move. I'm going to call Dr. Smith."

Going to the phone, she dialed with unsteady fingers and then heard Al Smith's pleasant voice. When she told him Derrick's symptoms, he listened carefully, then asked about Derrick's past two days, where he had been, what kind of weather he'd been exposed to.

When she had finished he said quietly, "I suppose it could be a ministroke, but I hate making diagnoses over the phone. Listen, I'm not that far away from you. I owe you for all the gospel concerts you've gotten me tickets to—yours and others. I'll see you in a very little while. Keep him warm and tell him to be still."

"I'm afraid he has no choice," she said ruefully.

Dr. Smith sat by Derrick, just questioning him, and drank a cup of café latte Ashley brought him before he examined Derrick. Then he stripped off Derrick's pajama top as Ashley turned up the heat. Derrick put on a brave front, but his fear was plain.

"It's going to hurt like hell, but I want you to sit up as far as you can."

Derrick looked at the doctor, nodding. "Is it a stroke?"

"Let me check something first. If it is, it's certainly not a severe one. Are you doing the things we try to get people to do to prevent strokes?"

"I read the literature. I think I am. I'm not a salt lover. I'm not crazy about fried foods or other heavy-duty fats."

"That's a good start."

Dr. Smith probed and patted, then took out a small, strangely shaped machine and held it to Derrick's side. Then he sat back and slipped the instrument into his bag.

"You've got pleurisy, a simple, hellish case of pleurisy. I had it in med school, so I know what you're going through. Your lung sacs are full of fluid."

Derrick's smile was beatific. "Thank God," he said.

The next morning dawned bright and clear. Sunlight sparkled on the shallow snowfall of the night before. Delia stood at the window of her living room. Derrick hadn't come home again, and she was beside herself with anger.

"Ma'am?"

She didn't turn as the young woman who helped her came into the room and stood tentatively behind her. Mrs. Quinn had a temper, the woman thought, and you never knew when you'd get on her bad side.

"Yes, Melissa?"

"Well, sorry I'm late. Somebody ran into the back of my car. I just wondered if you want me to fix you breakfast, and if I ought to clean out the refrigerator."

"No breakfast. I don't want any. Of course, fix your own and Len's breakfast. And no, don't bother with the refrigerator. I have everything arranged just as I want it."

"Yes, ma'am." The woman turned and left.

It was typical of Delia not to comment on Melissa's accident or ask how she felt.

Delia felt the start of a monster headache, and she put her fingertips to her left temple; that was always where the headaches started.

She looked over to Ashley's house. The fury in her chest was like hot rocks of newly blown lava, but she knew she had to play it cool.

Since she had known she loved Derrick, she had woven many spells to bring his love—three lately. She would weave one more spell to get Derrick's love before she would mix in the headier spells to move Ashley away—or destroy her.

She let the phone ring three times before she answered it to hear a soft voice. "Delia?" the voice asked.

"Yes, Ashley." She could hardly keep the venom from her voice, but she had formulated a better plan now: to be friends with Ashley, get close to her enemy. The magic she knew was powerful, gained from *Grand-mére,* who knew both voodoo and Welsh magic. She thought again that it had gotten her Marty, her dead husband. She had to believe it would bring Derrick to her side.

Ashley was talking, and Delia hadn't heard what she said.

"I'm sorry," Delia said sweetly. "I'm a bit ragged this morning. I seem to be missing a brother-in-law."

"He's here and he has pleurisy."

"Oh, good Lord, I'd better come and get him. I'll bring Len to help him."

"The doctor was here last night. He doesn't want him moved for a few days."

"Oh."

"Yes. He's pretty sick. I suppose it comes from being out in that damp weather and already having a cold."

It nettled Delia that Ashley knew so much about Derrick. She wanted to be his only confidante.

"I don't agree with the doctor. Who did you call?"

"Dr. Smith."

"Whom I stopped going to. I don't think he's very knowledgeable."

"I find him excellent, but then, not everybody gets the same results from a doctor. He was kind enough to make a house call."

"I'm surprised, but I guess when you're famous a lot of things change."

Ashley chuckled. "I'm not famous yet. One day, perhaps. Perhaps not. I can live with it either way."

Delia's mind wandered again. Bad things happened to famous people. They got stalked, attacked. Sometimes not even bodyguards could help. Suddenly a thought struck her.

"What a coincidence this is," Delia said. "I've started some fresh chicken soup I want Derrick to have. And I'm making cream-soaked bread pudding with raisins and lemon sauce. I remember your mother saying it was one of your favorite desserts."

"I have plenty of stuff on hand. The doctor wants him to eat lightly."

At her window, Ashley saw that the sun had gone back under and dark gray clouds hovered, threatening more snow.

"I insist," Delia said. "Please let me do that much for him."

Ashley was a bit taken aback. "Of course," she said. "Come right over. I'll just squeeze orange juice and toast an English muffin for him."

The corners of Delia's mouth turned down. "Thank you, Ashley. You're very kind." Ashley hung up.

"Hey, Aunt Delia. I'm going out early to play in the snow before the school bus comes. Dad in the barn looking at the new colt?"

"Your father's ill," Delia said shortly. "He's over at Ashley's."

"He got sick there?"

"Apparently." Delia didn't feel like talking to the boy.

"I need to see him," Corby said.

"No, you go on to school and go by after school if you wish. But come home first."

"Awww, Delia."

"*Aunt* Delia," Delia said shortly. "And don't argue with me. I'm not your father."

Corby turned on his heel and started out of the room. Delia began to ask if he'd gotten his breakfast, but she was irritated with him. If he went hungry, maybe it would teach him to behave.

Delia had seen the snow clouds too, and they bothered her. She didn't relish being in the deep woods in heavy snow, but she had no choice. Len wouldn't mind; he was hardy. She had thought she might put off casting her spell for just a little while. The blood would keep. With this new development of Derrick's being sick and getting still closer to Ashley Steele, she had to move—*now.*

In the kitchen she found Melissa sitting at the table with Len. Each had a plate of sausage, eggs, grits and ready-to-serve biscuits before them.

"Morning, Len," Delia drawled. "You take your time, but Melissa, I'm going to have to rush you a bit. I want you to make me a fine batch of chicken soup. Start it out in the microwave. I'll do some bread pudding."

"Ma'am, I can do them both in just a little while. You always so admire my bread pudding."

"And I still admire it, but I feel like keeping busy."

She told them about Derrick's illness.

"I figured he was comin' down with something, the way he kept sneezing. I'm sorry to hear that," Len said.

"I'll want you to run me over to Ashley's. He took the pickup. Maybe he'll be in a mood to come home." Under her breath, she muttered, "No matter what Ashley Steele wants."

She got two-day-old white bread and tore it apart, putting it into a big glass bowl. She assembled heavy cream, raisins, butter, cinnamon, sugar—everything she'd need. Delia hated cooking, hated housework, but loved being mistress of some manor or other.

"You seem in good spirits, ma'am," Len said. "I'm sure you and Mr. Quinn will be glad to know the little foal is stumbling all over his stall."

"Good." She wasn't really interested in animals, not even

the ones she owned. She had wanted Marty, and she wouldn't have wanted him if she had known what he intended to do with his life. He had had an M.A. and she wanted him to go into business—*big* business. Then Derrick had bought his farm, utilizing his agricultural master's degree from the University of Maryland. And Marty had fallen in love with horses. When had she fallen in love with Derrick? She wasn't certain, but it had taken a few years, because she hadn't realized it at first.

Bread pudding. She would make this with a beautiful golden crust, tend it carefully, because a plan lay in her mind with the simple bread pudding. She narrowed her eyes and a faintly evil smile lifted the corners of her mouth. There would be other servings of bread pudding for Ashley from Delia's hands. Bread pudding that would not be as innocent as this.

"Miss Delia?" Delia was coasting into space again.

She brought herself up short. "Yes, Melissa."

"Any help you need on that pudding, I'll give you."

"Thank you. Len, remember I'm going to need you to take me over to Ashley Steele's house when we're through here."

"Sure thing, ma'am."

Delia surveyed the two. Melissa was so obviously taken with Len, who didn't know she was alive. She enjoyed knowing that Len was in love with her, would do anything for her. Anything? She was going to get a chance to find out.

"Oh, Derrick, I'm so sorry you're ill." It was ten-thirty when Delia went to the bed and touched Derrick's face. She didn't think this was Ashley's room—it was too small. But then again, it might be.

"I'm feeling a whole lot better. This pleurisy gave me quite a scare."

"That'll teach you to go running off when you don't feel

too well." Delia pouted prettily. "You know you can go home with us. Len can help you."

Derrick smiled crookedly. "I think I'd better follow the doc's orders and stay put for a few days."

"But you'll be all right in a day or so."

"Have you ever had pleurisy?"

"No. Why do you ask?"

Derrick laughed. "Because I feel right now as if I may not get well in a *month* or two."

Delia's jaw fell as Corby bounced into the room.

"You're supposed to be in school," Delia scolded.

Corby looked at his father nervously. "I had to see Dad." His jaw was tight, defiant.

"Okay," Delia said, "you've seen him. Len and I will take you when we leave."

"No, Delia," Derrick shifted on the bed. "I told him he could spend the day. Ashley thinks it's okay." Corby sat on the bed and hugged his father.

"Aren't you something?" Derrick said to him. "You've been hoeing your own row lately, well on the road to becoming a young man. I get sick and you get needy. Okay, just for today."

Delia stared at them coolly. "Corby, would you get me a cup of coffee? I'm sure Ashley has some."

"You've been here often enough," Ashley said to the boy. "You know where the cream and sugar are, and the coffee machine."

Delia drew a sharp breath. She had been depending on getting Ashley out of the room, too. She turned to Derrick. "I think you're wrong in not making him go to school."

"It's all right," Derrick said evenly. "He'll be fine."

"You spoil him," Delia said hotly. "He's going to make you cry later."

"He misses his mother," Derrick told her gently. "He's hurting."

"It's been over a year since she died."

"You know how close they were. Let it go, Delia. Let it go."

Ashley followed Corby into the kitchen after all, and spooned up bowls of the steaming chicken soup from the big-mouthed red thermos Delia had brought. The bread pudding looked scrumptious in a large Pyrex dish. Len stood at attention.

"Sit down, Len," Ashley bade him. "Or go into the living room and watch TV, or turn the one on in here—whatever you choose."

Len smiled bashfully. "It's nice in here. Think I'll stay here."

A lively Minnie came in the back door and greeted them. She held a small snowball in her hand.

"Your mama thought you could use my help, with sick folks here and all. Eleni off to school?"

"Yes. Her bus picked her up."

"See this snowball?"

"What are you going to do with it?"

"I'll put it in your freezer and take it back with me. It'll be extra hard, and I'm going to pay King Johnson back for hitting me with one this morning."

Ashley laughed merrily. Minnie and King kept something going most of the time. Len looked at the small woman; he liked her. Delia Quinn paid him and Melissa well, so they stayed, even when she got a tad mean. The Steeles' help called the family by name; Delia insisted on a title, although she wouldn't have dreamed of giving her servants a title. A wistful smile lingered on his face. Delia was a good-looking woman, and she sometimes flirted with him. He wondered why she did it, because he was certain she didn't want the likes of him. But he often thought wistfully that working for the Steeles would be heaven.

Minnie took the soup ladle from Ashley. "You let me handle this and you go back to Derrick. He'll be needing you."

"Delia's with him."

Minnie raised her eyebrows. "Like I said, he'll be needing you."

On Derrick's third night with Ashley he felt livelier, in less pain. Delia had bombarded him with her presence when he felt she needed to be overseeing the stables, but she left it all to Ace Carter, who was beginning to manage the place.

He ate the ambrosia Ashley had prepared and forewent the wine soufflé Delia had prepared especially for him.

At his bedside, Ashley patted his face and said wistfully, "I'll hate to see you go. Dr. Smith said you're healing so rapidly."

"Aren't you tired of me?"

Coming in the door, Eleni yelled, "Never! Stay with us!"

"I'd like that." Derrick grinned.

"Mom, can he stay?"

"How I wish," Ashley said quietly.

Corby had gone home. He had been at Ashley's much of the time when he wasn't in school. Now, with a couple of rounds of Scrabble behind them, Ashley tucked Derrick in, loving him so much she hurt with it. She smoothed the dark-blue blanket and placed a hot-water bottle wrapped in wool against the more affected side of his chest.

Bending over to kiss him, she was shocked at the hunger he showed for her. "I dream about you all the time," he said huskily.

"And I dream about you. Dare I ask what you dream?"

"That we're together, and often enough that I'm inside you. God, I never knew life could be like this. Still . . ." His voice drifted off, and Ashley took up his thought.

"Still, you want a woman who's not so caught up in a career that she can't be with you as much as you want her to be."

"Something like that. I'm sorry, Ash. You know how much I love you. That will never change."

Ashley felt her heart constrict. "I'm sorry, too. I didn't know life could be like this. What are we going to do?"

"We're two adults. We can work it out somehow."

It was a painful topic, and she didn't want to upset him, so she kissed him lightly and he let her go. She closed her eyes as she looked at him, and he watched the long black lashes on her cheeks; his heart hurt with wanting her.

She didn't expect to sleep that night, but she fell asleep quickly and she dreamed. She sat on Black Steed in the meadow near the big oak. Bright sunlight glowed, drenching the earth. Derrick helped her down, and the horse sped away. Then Derrick kissed her with all the passion he possessed, and she melted.

"Soon," he told her, "we will be together for all time."

They moved into the deep forest, where it suddenly grew dark as storm clouds gathered. Derrick frowned.

"What does this mean?" Ashley asked him. "It was so sunny."

Derrick shook his head. "I don't know."

Then a voice came through the trees like a spirit broadcasting. The voice was low, benevolent. "Be careful!" the voice said. "There will be pain and destruction. Be careful! There will be *death!*"

Ashley sat up quickly. Her skin was clammy in spite of the warm blankets and the warm room. Her heart raced. What did the dream mean? Every dream she had had before of Derrick had been of love and romance. Slipping out of bed, she went to check on him and found him awake.

"Can't you sleep?" she asked him, turning on a lamp.

"I had a bad dream," he said. "A very bad dream."

She held her breath a moment before she asked, "About a storm?"

"How did you know?"

She licked her dry lips. *"I* dreamed about a coming storm. What else did you dream about it?"

"Nothing else, just that we were deep in the woods and there was a storm raging. Then I woke up. You look shaken."

"I just dreamed about a storm and the woods," she said again.

"This is uncanny. What was your dream?"

Quietly she told him, but did not mention the warning voice. He was ill and she didn't want to upset him. She sat there, incredulous, holding his hand.

"Do you know what I call my dreams of you and me?" he asked.

"No. What?"

His eyes crinkled shut with laughter. "Dreams of ecstasy."

She squeezed his hand. "That's wonderful. They're dreams of ecstasy for me, too."

"We'll forget about the storms and stick to the ecstatic dreams."

"Yes," she said, but she sat thinking that streaming sunshine and fair skies had their place in this world, but storms were an undeniable part of creation, too.

Gently she touched his forehead with her lips and went to check on Eleni. For the rest of the night she slept fitfully, pondering the dream.

Seventeen

Delia stood in her bedroom thinking that tonight would be the night she would begin the spells against Ashley. Her earlier spells had been invoked to bring Derrick to her side. So far the spirits had failed. The spells against Ashley would not fail, because Delia would not depend on mere spells. A small thrill of pleasure took her as she let herself into her secret room.

She went to Derrick's room and opened the door. His pleasant scent permeated the air. She went in and sat on the bed. She felt so close to him here.

Corby would be spending the night at Ashley's, and she was glad not to have him underfoot. He would be back at her house tomorrow after school.

She still smarted with the memory of Ashley hovering over Derrick. She had hurt a lot lately, and she swore Ashley would pay for it.

The old grandfather chimed one o'clock. Delia lit a tall black candle in the shuttered secret room and sat down, admiring the *vévés* she had drawn. "I am good at *vévés*. That is a good start," she murmured to herself. "It may be that I have more power than I know."

She missed Derrick and decided she would visit him daily. She would cook and carry him dishes she knew he liked. As she'd looked at him on his sickbed at Ashley's, her heart had begun a simmering fire of envy of Ashley that she knew would burn for a very long time.

Voodoo—*voudou*—worked slowly. She thought of how long it had taken black Haitian peasants to break free of their white masters. But they had persevered and had freed themselves, the only black country ever to do this. And no one thought that it was other than the *loa*—the African spirits—who had given them this formidable strength.

She got up and began to gather two baskets of things she would need for casting her spell tonight. She and Len would leave the house at eleven. She snuffed out the candle with her palm and shuddered at the mild burn.

Ten more hours. This was the beginning of a vast network of spells and magic she intended to weave around Ashley Steele. She meant to separate Derrick and Ashley.

"I hope for your sake, Ashley," she muttered, "that the spells work. It would be a shame to have to completely destroy you."

Eleven-thirty found Delia and Len and their loaded baskets deep in the forest behind Delia's house.

Len had dug a shallow trench about four feet long, two feet across, and one foot deep. Delia talked with him now as if he were an equal.

"I think I know the reason the spells are not stronger," she told him. "I have only used the *vévés* and a few other symbolic things. I need to sacrifice goat's blood more often. *Grand-mère* seldom sacrificed, but then she was a *mambo*. Do I make you understand what I'm talking about, Len?"

"I think so, ma'am."

Delia put down a candle in a holder and squeezed Len's shoulder, which thrilled him. "My valued friend," she murmured. "What would I do without you?"

He began to answer, but his throat was closed with intense joy and excitement. She was taking him into another world much more powerful than any he had known. Would she teach him magic? It was heady just to think about.

Lighted black candles, a foot or more apart, lined one side and the ends of the trench. She placed them well back from the edge. She took black sheets of construction paper on which she had drawn *vévés* and placed them in the trench behind the candles. She called on the spirits then to bless her, to lead her to triumph. If an island of slaves could free themselves with the help of these mighty spirits, they could help her attain her deepest desire.

"Open the jar of blood for me," she instructed Len.

"Yes, ma'am." He sounded like a slave.

She stopped for a moment to talk to him. "Len, my friend," she said, "here, for tonight, and other times we may need to come here, we're on equal footing. You don't have to call me *ma'am.*"

He blushed furiously. "I just couldn't, Miz Quinn. I'm so used to it. Then I'd forget and do it before other people."

That was true, she thought. Oh, well, as long as she had made him know how valuable he was to her.

"I hope you won't be mad at me," he begged. "Do you understand?"

"I do. I just want you to know how much your help means to me."

Hell, he thought, this was nothing. He'd die for her.

She glanced at her watch's dial. It had been five minutes since she'd placed the *vévés* in the trench. "Give me the jar of blood," she said. He handed her the heavy pint jar. Bending, she dribbled the blood just behind the candles from one end of the trench to the other as the black candles flickered. It was ghostly still.

Wrapped in layered woolen garments with her heaviest coat and rubber boots, she hardly felt the cold.

"Are you warm enough?" she asked him. Len never seemed to her to dress warmly enough.

"I'm fine," Len assured her.

Reaching into the baskets, she undid other parcels and opened other jars—special foods in special colors for special gods. When she was finished, she knelt. It was four minutes to midnight. Then three, two, one.

Midnight! "Kneel and be absolutely silent," she said, and he obeyed.

She invoked the spirits then. The *loa*. They were a mixture of deepest Africa and the various foreign countries that had held Africa's people captive. And they were far stronger than any country.

She felt a mighty surge of power in her breast and cried out, "Damballah! Freda Erzulie! Come to me. Grant me this magic. *Grand-mère*! Be with me now!"

She conveniently did not remember that *Grand-mère* had cautioned her, "Do not use your magic for evil, my love, or it will destroy *you* in the end. Use it to gain love and power. Man cannot create in and of himself, so he must not destroy."

But *Grand-mère* had been old and infirm. Delia didn't think the old woman had wanted anything in her life the way Delia burned with lust and love for Derrick.

Delia knew a lot about Welsh magic, too. She fashioned dolls in the likeness of her enemies and tormented the dolls. She would use those, too.

It was a short ceremony, and when she had finished she nodded at Len, who looked at her with awe.

"Cover the trench," she said, and Len took his shovel and began throwing dirt in. She snuffed the candles one by one and covered them. A large jar-shaped flashlight sat by them, and Delia turned it on, sending beams through the trees.

"All right. Let's stamp it down," she said.

Silently she and Len trampled on the dirt, driving it down into the trench, leaving only an inch or so above the surrounding earth. She was very well aware that somebody might become curious and try to unearth what was beneath.

No matter. The strength of the spell took effect when it was given; no one could undo it.

Putting empty jars, bags, and utensils back into the baskets, Delia felt suddenly tired.

In the flashlight's steady glow she looked up into Len's adoring eyes.

"Will you help me again if I need it?"

"Anytime," he croaked.

"I might have to ask you to come along, do certain things. And you will have to perform just as I ask you to. Will you do this?"

He ached to tell her there was nothing he wouldn't do for her. She was so beautiful standing so close to him. For the first time in his life he wanted to be a different man, one who could claim a woman like this.

In her house, Delia pondered her spell for a long time. Next time she would do the doll magic, a spell that *Grandmère* had shown her how to do.

In her bedroom she was restless, and her face in her mirror looked drawn, haggard. She bit her lip. The house seemed so empty. She had started to keep Len around her just to have someone to talk to.

Grabbing her robe, she went to Derrick's room and looked in his mirror. What was wrong with her? She tried to summon a vision of him and couldn't. "Derrick," she said softly. "Come to me." There was nothing.

Going to his bed, she turned the covers back. Crawling in bed, drawing his covers to her cheek, she smiled bitterly. Tonight she would be within the circle of his arms in magic, if not in actuality.

Eighteen

Standing in her backyard, wrapped against the bitter cold, Ashley began to jog around the big yard the way she did most mornings. Dressed in black tights and a pullover, covered by a thick beige cashmere hooded cardigan, she felt ebullient. She had a long day of practice and recording ahead, and tonight Derrick had asked her to double-date with Annice and Ace Carter, the new man who was taking over management of Delia's stables.

Throwing her head back, with her arms reaching for the sky, she laughed joyfully. So little time had passed since Derrick had gotten over the pleurisy attack. He should rest, but he wanted to take her dancing at Wilson's. *Ah, men,* she thought. They couldn't bear being ill. Frank and Whit were the same way.

A thought took the smile from her face, leaving it somber. While Derrick had been there, each day Delia had brought special dishes she had prepared for Derrick. The bread pudding she had made the first day really had been delicious. Whatever else, the woman was a good cook, and she had competent help in Melissa.

After the first night, Derrick had insisted Corby sleep at Delia's, although Ashley had been willing to let him stay, and Eleni had pleaded. In the end, Corby had taken it very well. He had spent the afternoons after school with his father, Ashley, and Eleni.

She could not remember a time when she'd felt so well.

Nursing a man you loved did wonders for you. Looking out over the meadow on her side, she smiled at Black Steed and Goober frolicking. She rode little in the winter unless it was warm, but she missed Black Steed's burnished hide and his smooth gait.

Inside her home studio, Ashley had spread out her music, turned the twin compact disc players on, and begun her trills when the chimes sounded.

She warmly greeted the Davis Gospel Singers who backed her, and her piano accompanist, Clem Patton. There were hugs all around.

Curt, the lead singer, brought two women forward who were strangers to her. He introduced them as the new members of the group, who would travel with her on her trip to Germany. The women had the same effusiveness that Curt had.

"Oh, I'm really looking forward to working with you," the older woman told her. "This is going to be the culmination of a dream for me and my niece." She indicated the younger woman, who smiled and said, "Nothing I could tell you would let you know how thrilled I am."

Going to the home recording center, Curt adjusted the equipment carefully. By then everyone's outer garments were in the hall closet, and after hot drinks, doughnuts, and Danish pastries, they settled in. The pianist ran a few scales on the baby grand piano.

"I've made up my list for Germany," Ashley told them. She named a few of her signature songs and added, "I haven't done 'Swing Low, Sweet Chariot' as much as I want to. There're others. We have new gospel music I like very much. . . ."

Curt Davis turned to her. "Back when I thought I'd be the next James Cleveland, I wrote a few songs. I'm going to present them to you soon."

"Wait a minute," Ashley said. "You're good, Curt. Your group's good. You're not forty yet. Don't give up on your dream of making it big."

Curt nodded. "I know we're good." He expelled a harsh sigh. "But I'm getting to be content just working with you. We think you're headed straight to the top, Ashley. Straight to the top! And I'm hitching my wagon to *your* star."

Ashley talked quietly with him about continuing to pursue his own dream as well, and the others listened, nodding their assent.

"They single you out for praise in every country we tour," she reminded him. "Your ring-shouts are shows in themselves."

Curt chuckled. "Yeah, I guess we've got that down pat. We're going to bring the ring-shout back in style."

Resting between numbers, they relaxed and harmonized. In the large room the men practiced their ring-shouts, as Ashley made suggestions. "I've got a few moons on you," Curt Davis told her, "but you've got a certain knowledge for what puts gospel music ahead."

That afternoon, they all piled into their big van and headed out to Mick Chancellor's recording studio. The bluff, hearty redheaded man met them at the door. Laughing, he bowed low.

"Goddess!" he purred, "and others from Olympia."

His wife, Sileia, a native of Lyric Island in the Pacific, greeted them effusively, smiling so broadly her eyes seemed to close.

"I was absolutely entranced listening to your latest recordings you made here," Sileia told Ashley. "I have decided the sky is the limit for you and your group."

Mick nodded. "Your spirit and the way you deliver reminds me of Gina Campbell, the pop singer."

"She's one of my favorites," Ashley said.

After they had eaten the Tahitian lunch Sileia had prepared for them, they settled down to pineapple and poi and delicious rum-coconut-pineapple cake from a recipe Sileia said Gina Campbell had given her.

Mick insisted that they rest after they had eaten, so they made small talk.

Ashley turned to Mick. "Whenever Gina and I are in the same town, we get together for lunch. I'm leaning on her to stay with me when she comes to D.C. She's one happy woman these days."

Mick looked at Ashley thoughtfully. "Talk about happy; you're flying. I'm really looking forward to what you'll record today, and mind you, our last recording was excellent. You're in love."

It was a flat statement, and Ashley blushed and didn't answer him.

"I'm glad," Mick said. "For me, anyway, love has made the world go round." He blew a kiss to his wife, who returned it.

"Look, I want to see your ring-shouts again. I think I've got an innovation that will go over big," Mick added.

"Why, thank you." Ashley deeply appreciated the comments Mick frequently made. "You know we welcome any suggestions from you."

Rested, relaxed, with Ashley on her performance toes, and the group ready to back her, Ashley closed her eyes and let a thrill of anticipation go through her.

Mick's studio was very high-ceilinged and entirely battery-powered, set to pick up every nuance of voice and instrument. As they began practice vocals, the guitars of the Davis Gospel Singers moaned.

Mick Chancellor was an institution now. Superstars wanted him to record them, but he accepted few. He liked Ashley Steele, had deeply admired her stunning voice with its four-octave range. Today he heard something different in that voice. There was a depth, different nuances. She was dancing to a different drummer today. He hoped to heaven she was in love, as he felt certain she was. Because if what his mind told him was true, she was headed straight to the top of the tallest mountain.

She was excellent now, much admired, but she was going to leave superstar status behind, Mick thought. If she kept this voice, this stance, she was going to be a megastar down to her every pore.

By the time the group reached "Steal Away to Jesus," Ashley knew that things would be different with her. Until she had met Mick through Gina Campbell, she had never been really satisfied with her recordings. Mick's recordings were so clear, even the cheapest boom box reflected that clarity.

"Cut," Mick said at the end of the spiritual. He turned to Ashley. "On the list you gave me, you've added a few new great ones to your repertoire. I like 'Somebody's Knocking at Your Door.' "

It was one of the group's favorites lately, and they quickly agreed.

> Somebody's knocking at your door.
> Somebody's knocking at your door.
> Oh, oh, sinner, why don't you answer?
> Somebody's knocking at your door.

As Ashley's haunting voice swept over him, Mick felt his eyes moisten. The song could have been written just for him.

The group recorded the song twice. Mick was determined that this one be beyond perfect. It was an anthem to love.

After resting, they swung into "Were You There when They Crucified My Lord?"

With the chorus, Ashley swept in with her incredibly clear, magical voice, intoning:

Oh, oh, oh, oh, sometimes it causes
   me to tremble, tremble, tremble.
Were you there when they crucified my Lord?

Singing, interpreting the melodious spirituals, had been
all she wanted out of life, once she'd known she and Reese
wouldn't make it. Eleni and her singing filled her life. Her
voice seemed to her to come from some deep, wonderful
well now. Everything held a new radiance. She didn't want
to love Derrick, didn't want the threat of being hurt again.
But it didn't matter what she wanted; love was having its
way with her, and every fiber of her being reflected this.

That night Ashley, Derrick, Annice, and Ace Carter sat at
a table in the newly opened nightclub section of Wilson
Cartwright's restaurant. Wilson came over, kissed Ashley
and Annice, and shook hands with the men.

"You've outdone yourself," Ashley complemented him.

"I say we deserve the best—the whole of Crystal Lake
deserves the best—and you're the man to give it to us."
Annice was sparkling, already having a good time.

"I'm always glad when people like my place," Wilson
said, "especially the women. How're you pulling along,
Ace?"

Ace Carter glanced at Annice, his attractive, medium-
brown face alight. "I haven't been back in awhile, but I'm
doing okay now, if luck just shows me a little love."

Wilson laughed long and heartily. Many a man he knew
had stumbled on the way to liking and loving Annice Steele.
It had seemed for a while that Luke Jones had ruined her life
for all time, but she looked happy now.

But Annice was not as happy as she looked. At times like
this, she couldn't help but wonder about her biological parents. And she felt guilty because the Steeles were so wonder-

ful to her. Still, she longed to know who she came from, what bloodlines. Who had given birth to her.

The small, excellent band Love'n Us was playing. As their lively, smooth music filled the room, which was growing crowded, the two men asked the two women to dance. On the dance floor, Derrick guided Ashley to the bandstand.

"Knowing you," he said, "you'll want to speak to the musicians."

"Uh-huh. They're among the best. Going places, sure, but they don't want to get too big. They like Virginia."

The eight-piece group was exuberant tonight, at the top of their form. Ellen and Rich, the bandleaders, came off the bandstand to hug Ashley and Derrick, and Mr. Sampson gave Ashley a bear hug. "You are some kind of pretty tonight," he told her. Then to Derrick, "You lucky dog."

Rafe Sampson's elderly face was wreathed in smiles. He held Ashley away from him as Ellen and Rich laughed. "I'm giving her back to you, mister—reluctantly—but my next song is dedicated to her. Guess I'll have to include you in that."

"I'll be waiting," Ashley told him. "Thanks for including Derrick."

Rafe put his head to one side. "He's special to you? You don't have to answer, because I see it when you look at him."

"He's a special man." Ashley stole a glance at Derrick to find him caressing her with his eyes.

As they danced away, Annice and Ace danced by. The two couples were happy, pleased. Ace was courting Annice already, Ashley thought. *Be careful, Ace. Annice has been a heartbreaker so long she doesn't know how to stop.*

Derrick hummed the tune "Old Black Magic" as they danced along. "It's an old song for a young group like that."

"Yes, it is. Of course they've got Rafe who's pretty elderly. That's one of Mama and Dad's favorites. I think that's why they're so popular; they cover the waterfront."

"You dance beautifully." Derrick pulled her close, smelling her jasmine perfume and the delightful fragrance of her hair.

"We haven't danced together much, just around my house and here."

"That's why I wanted to bring you here tonight. I knew you would dance beautifully."

"How did you know?"

He held her closer and said in a low, throaty voice, "A woman who makes love the way you do has to be an excellent dancer. It's a matter of rhythm, movement. . . ." He nuzzled her face.

Ashley and Derrick had started back to their table when the band struck up their newest song, "I'll Want You Forever." Mr. Sampson introduced this number and dedicated it to Ashley.

"He's skating on thin ice," Derrick growled teasingly. "I'd hate beating up a man his age."

"All over *me?*" Ashley teased along with him, pretending to pout.

"All over you." He lightly kissed the corner of her mouth and they danced to the slow tune until it ended.

Back at the table, Annice wanted to go to the ladies' room; Ashley went with her.

In the dusky rose, beautifully appointed room with one smiling attendant, Annice told Ashley, "Nothing like a good nightclub to make me happy."

"Do you like Ace?" Ashley asked.

Annice thought a moment. "He's nice. I've met him before. He came out to see Marty a few times. I met him over at their house. He's a nice man, but he could never be more than a friend."

Looking at her beloved sister, Ashley sprang the loaded question: "When will you get over Luke Jones?"

"What makes you think I haven't?"

"Have you?"

Annice shook her head. "Let me be happy. Happiness

comes in many forms. I don't need Luke. He certainly didn't need me."

"I'm sorry I mentioned it. Bad timing."

"You want me to have the best. It's okay."

The women checked their makeup and went back out to find Derrick standing at the table with his overcoat on, Ashley's overcoat on his arm. He held the coat for her to get into.

"Where're we going?" she asked him.

He grinned wickedly. "I'll lead you."

Ashley let him slip her coat on and she buttoned it. "You'd better be leading me to someplace I want to go. Are we bidding Annice and Ace good night?"

"No. We'll be back."

"Derrick, what on earth . . . ?"

He pressed his index finger to her lips, effectively shushing her.

Out on the big marble balcony, Derrick led her to a well-lighted section. "I won't keep you waiting long. Give me a kiss and I've got something for you."

"Oh?"

"Remember Christmas?" he asked. She murmured that she remembered. Derrick had had to go to Norfolk because of a cholera outbreak on his animal farm. His farm manager, Julian Harkett, had had more than he could handle, so Derrick had spent the holidays there. Before leaving, he had given her a jeweler's box with a slip inside engraved in gold. The slip had read: *I owe you something beautiful.*

"Close your eyes," he told her now.

Ashley did as he bade her until he said, "Open sesame." She blinked when she looked at twin diamonds that flashed fire. Set on a navy velvet bed were one-carat diamond ear studs.

"Oh, Derrick, they're gorgeous!"

"Do you like them?"

"I love them."

He caught her close to him, the heavy woolen garments shielding their bodies from each other.

"Julian needs me to come back this weekend. Go with me?" Before she could answer, he said, "I don't want to be selfish. I know you've got to prepare for your upcoming trip, but—"

"Of course I'll go," she said. "I'll just double up on my practice. Eleni will be with her father. Are you taking Corby?"

"Yeah. It's a strange thing, but Corby isn't too fond of Delia, although she tries hard to make him like her. It isn't often he shies away from people. He adores you. In fact . . ."

"Yes? In fact . . . ?"

He shrugged, smiling. "Forget it. I'll tell you some other time."

"It sounded important."

"It is, at least to me."

"Let's go in," Ashley said. "I don't want you to have a relapse."

"A mother after my own heart."

"I like that compliment."

"And I like you."

"You already know my response to that. Derrick, you're a love of a man."

Back inside the nightclub, Derrick rechecked their coats. At their table, Ashley and Derrick were seated when the champagne trolley rolled up with champagne in an ice bucket and a single glass of cool champagne on a tray for Ashley. She drank little when she was preparing for a concert.

"You think of the darnedest things," she said to Derrick.

"Just hoping it pays big dividends."

Ashley showed Annice and Ace the ear studs. Ace made a complimentary gesture of the A-OK sign.

"Oh, man," Annice said. "If I had a dude who gave me things like this I'd lock him up and throw away the key."

Ashley looked at her sister and laughed. "You always could do excessive things." But a little voice in her head whispered, *I'm beginning to think that's exactly what I'd like to do.*

Nineteen

A winter thaw had set in, but that had little to do with Delia's high spirits. She had invited Ashley for dinner at five today. Glancing at her watch, she idly stroked her face, a look of pure malice lingering on her countenance. Dinner would be at five so that Corby could join them and have ample time for his homework.

Delia looked at herself in the dining room hutch's mirror. It had been a long time since she'd been so pleased. Dressed in a simple black crepe dress that hugged her slim curves, she swung her head so that her dangling emerald earrings caught the light.

Derrick had come in early and was taking a shower. Now Corby came through the front door. "Where's Dad?"

"I'm here," Delia said evenly. "Don't I matter?"

Corby flushed. "Sure, but I want to tell him something. It's after four. I'm late."

"Why?"

"Well, I told Dad I was joining the band. We practiced late."

"You should have called."

Corby shrugged. "I got caught up."

"Well, shower and put on clean clothes."

"Sure. You think Dad's got a thing for Miss Ashley?"

"Certainly I wouldn't know," Delia said sharply. "You're too young to be thinking about such things."

Corby's thin shoulders hunched. "Not really. A guy in

school is fifteen and he had a baby by a fifteen-year-old girl."

Delia stared at him, amused. She always liked correcting him. He was a smarty-pants, she thought. "The girl had a baby by *him,* not the other way around."

"Well, I'm fourteen in a couple of months. . . ." He was in an argumentative mood. "I think he likes her plenty."

"Scram," Delia said suddenly. "Go wash up." She wasn't going to let him ruin her mood by talking about Derrick and Ashley.

Out in the kitchen, Melissa worked efficiently, putting the finishing touches on the prime rib roast and spooning up wild plum jam in a crystal bowl.

"I want everything to be perfect, Melissa," Delia said.

"Yes, ma'am. As far as I can tell, it will be."

"And show a little more spirit. You mope around so."

"Sorry, ma'am."

"Do you have a man you're attached to?" She'd never asked Melissa this.

"No, ma'am. Not now."

Delia started to ask what had happened, but she really didn't want to know. She was in luck: Ashley had agreed to come to dinner. Eleni was spending an after-school evening with Annice and the other Steeles, so she wouldn't be under-foot. She never considered it her fault that she was less than fond of Eleni and Corby. They were such bright and flippant children—never knew their place. When she and Derrick were married, things would be different.

She thought again that Ashley's agreeing to come to dinner was the second step of her plan.

She put on a pretty appliquéd organdy apron, then went to her room and got a packet of beige powder. Slipping it into the double pocket of her apron, she closed her eyes. The spirits—the *loa*—were slow in working this time, and she didn't have a world of time. Sliding her hands into the apron pocket, she touched the packet, smiling grimly as she remembered purchasing the powder from a woman in New Orleans when she'd known she had to have Derrick. It was a triple-threat powder drawn from the poisonous South American tree frog, a deadly amphibian that lived only deep in the Brazilian rain forest and was noted for its poisonous properties. The poison worked fairly swiftly and was very difficult to detect in the body. Given at intervals, three to six times, it destroyed the immune system. Just thinking about it gave Delia a feeling of power.

She had big plans for herself and Derrick. Together they would own a mighty world of pleasure, with Ashley Steele no longer around.

"This beef is wonderful." Ashley smiled as she sat at the table with Derrick, Delia, and Corby, admiring the handmade lace tablecloth, the heavy silver, and the Waterford crystal. "It's a delicious dinner."

"Thank you. I had a major hand in this one. I had Melissa doing other things." It was a lie. Delia was, in fact, a good cook, but Melissa had prepared this meal—except for the heavy-cream bread pudding that Delia had handled.

Looking at Ashley, who wore midnight blue with diamond studs in her ears, Delia reflected that it wasn't going to be easy hiding her hatred of this woman, but she had to do it. Fortunately, neither Ashley nor Derrick seemed to suspect anything.

"I love your ear studs," Delia complemented.

"And I love yours."

"Did you get them in Crystal Lake?" Delia asked.

"Actually they are a late Christmas present from Derrick."

Delia fought hard to stop the rush of blood to her head, which was driven there by her raging envy. She never knew how she did it, but she smiled at Derrick. "Your brother had good taste. He gave me these earrings one Christmas."

"Pretty," Derrick complemented her absent-mindedly. "Wild rice. How I love it."

"I know," Delia said. "You're also fond of macaroni and cheese."

"My choice is the wild plum jam," Corby broke in. "I could eat a whole plate of biscuits and butter and a pint of the jam."

Derrick laughed and looked fondly at his son. "Trust you to get excessive about it."

"Aw, Dad, you know how it goes."

"I remember well enough."

"Eleni can tuck it away, too," Ashley said. "Children!"

Corby laughed. "I miss the twerp."

"I'll tell her."

Delia excused herself, then got up and went into the living room and put a stack of CDs on the player. As she came back in, Ashley's voice filled the air. "This is your latest album, *Signatures,*" Delia said, noting Ashley's pleased expression. Derrick looked at Delia gratefully, liking her for the moment.

"This is such a wonderful gesture," Ashley told her.

Delia smiled, effectively hiding the acid of her hatred. "I told you a little while back that I didn't like gospel music, but listening to you, it's growing on me. The spirituals are beautiful, and your interpretation of them is magnificent."

"Thank you." Ashley felt humble, feeling a bit guilty that she had evidently been wrong about Delia.

When the main course was finished, Melissa cleared away the dishes.

"Servants are wonderful," Delia said. "They make life bearable. Now, I don't hold with them eating at our table the way you all treat King and Minnie. But I guess I treat them well enough."

Ashley smiled. Now, that was more like the Delia she thought she knew. "They're family really," she said. "We all pitch in and help each other. It works out well."

"King's a great guy," Corby said. "And *big*. I hope I get to be that big."

"Keep eating. You're well on your way," Derrick teased him.

Delia had wondered all afternoon how to get the beige powder now in her pocket into Ashley's bread pudding. She had wisely led off by taking her own portion of the dessert first. All in all, she liked the way her mind worked these days. She felt like a goddess walking on Mount Olympus. Then she had it! Now the perfect solution to her problem hit her, and she rose as the last dishes were cleared away and went into the kitchen.

"I'll tell you what," Delia said to Melissa. "Go out to the storehouse and get more of the wild plum jam and the special apple butter you made."

"Ma'am, there're a few jars left in here."

For a moment, panic rose in Delia. "Well, get some of the blackberry jam. I know we don't have any of that in here."

"Yes, ma'am. Do you want me to serve dessert first?"

"No." Delia tried to keep the sharpness from her voice. "I'll serve dessert. You take your time."

Melissa wondered what Delia was so nervous about as she put on her coat and went out to the storehouse.

Delia mixed the powder into Ashley's portion of the dessert and went through the swinging door to the dining room.

Remembering that Ashley's serving was on the upper right-hand side of the tray, she served her first. When the warm pudding had been put before her and she had taken her first bite, Ashley exclaimed, "You could market this; it's that good."

Delia breathed deeply. "Show me you like my delicious concoction. Eat up, everybody!"

The cream-soaked bread pudding, with its huge raisins and lemon sauce topped with whipped cream, was special, and they all praised the cook.

"Gee, Aunt Delia, you outdid yourself," Corby complemented her. "I'm going to need another round."

"Keep it up," Derrick mused, "and you're going to get to
King's size long before you think you will."

"That'd be great."

Derrick leaned over and ran his hands over the boy's hair.
Ashley's music filled the air as they ate and drank good
port wine. Derrick said that Corby could have a little of the
wine, and the boy crowed with delight.

"I made the bread pudding because you liked it so much
the first time," Delia said. "You must come again. It's such
a delight having you here. We can exchange recipes."

"I'm not the world's best cook, except for my chocolate
chip and oatmeal cookies. With those, I excel."

"I like both." Delia put her elbows on the table. "It's just
beginning to hit me as you go up the gospel music ladder:
the soon-to-be famous Ashley Steele is my neighbor." She
raised her eyebrows. "But then, the Singing Steeles were
well known when Marty and I moved here. I've wasted time
in getting to know you better, Ashley, and I'm sorry. Can we
make it up?"

"I'd like that." Ashley still felt guilty that she was leery of
Delia. The woman's glance had strayed to Derrick again and
again and lingered there. But today she was much kinder,
friendlier. Maybe she just missed her dead husband. Was she
giving up on Derrick? Ashley certainly hoped so.

Ashley and Derrick found Reese's Ford Explorer in her
driveway when Derrick drove her home.

"We should have walked across the way and sneaked in
through the side door," Ashley said, smiling maliciously.

"He'd have seen the lights go on."

"It was a pleasant daydream. Reese is the last person I
feel like dealing with tonight. Derrick, I had a wonderful

time. I'm glad Delia's attitude toward me seems to be changing."

"Yeah. Delia can be a nice woman when she tries. How could anyone not like you?"

"You're prejudiced, like my folks."

Derrick hesitated a long moment. "That's because I love you."

Ashley leaned forward and kissed him full on the mouth. "That's for being like a giant panda—lovable and loved."

"We're going to get Reese's dander up," he said.

"Do you care?"

"Hell, no. I'll take on the world where you're concerned."

"That's good to know. Are you coming in?"

"I'm a bit tired. I had a rough day helping riders. This thing could work if Delia were interested, but I don't think she is."

"Then it's a waste of your valuable time."

"Maybe. She still insists she wants to keep the stables."

Reese got out and slammed his car door hard, then walked back to them. Ashley rolled the car window down.

"I just want to go over a couple of things with you. Do you plan to come in anytime soon?" Reese asked.

For a moment Ashley wanted to rile him further, but she felt too good. Derrick got out, came around to her side, and opened the door as Reese stood at stiff attention.

"Evening, Winters," Derrick drawled.

"More like night," Reese came back. "Evening."

They were hardly inside when Reese demanded, "Where's Eleni?"

"She's spending the night at my parents' house. She and Annice had plans for her dollhouse: a new set of pretty curtains and a new bedspread, new doll, that kind of thing."

"She doesn't see enough of you."

"Well, she would if I kept her weekends instead of you."

Reese stared at her a long moment. "I won't kid around with you, Ashley. Eleni tells me you're going to Germany again in March. I hear you've got a long tour planned for late summer and early fall. I don't want my daughter traveling from pillar to post."

With a show of anger, Ashley shot back, "That's why I leave her with Mama and Dad most times I'm away. They all adore each other. She couldn't be in safer hands, which is more than I can say for her being with you, with your drinking problem."

Reese literally swelled with pride. "You won't be able to hold that against me for long. I'm in a great rehab program, and I'm getting engaged. I'll be able to give Eleni a better home than you, with your globe-trotting gospel singing."

Ashley's eyes flashed fire. "I hope you'll remember this time that marriage is between two people, without taking up the slack with other women."

Reese turned red. "You always were a damned impossible woman," he said. "I'm going to say good night, but consider yourself warned where Eleni is concerned. I'm going to fight you for her when the time comes."

Tears of anger came to Ashley's eyes. "You *did* fight me for her," she said, "a little over a year ago. You know it's not good for her to have us wrangling over her like this. Think about our child, Reese, instead of being selfish."

Reese smiled nastily. He liked getting under Ashley's skin. Her even temper in the face of his wrath usually infuriated him. This was far better.

He had not sat down the short while he had been with her. Now he smiled sardonically. "Like I said, my dear ex, prepare yourself for another fight. You could slow down, not travel so much. Make your choice. Okay, I'm leaving."

She saw him to the door and came back clenching her hands. Reese, she thought, didn't understand the parameters of being a good parent. Yes, she was glad he was in rehab, but he needed parenting training, too—and he'd never get it.

She had found out while living with him that Reese saw the world on his own terms. Bitterly she thought that she was just going to have to go the extra mile to protect Eleni from her own father's immaturity.

Twenty

Derrick got up early the next morning, dressed, and went into Corby's room, where the boy slept on his stomach, buried under a comforter. Derrick shook the covers. "Rise and shine, chocolate kid!"

Corby groaned. He had been riding Black Steed in his dream. He threw the covers back, grinning at his father. "Hey, Dad," he said thoughtfully, "you said one day soon . . ."

"I said what, one day soon?"

"Well, that you'd ask Miss Ashley about letting me ride Black Steed."

Derrick nodded. "I've been really busy, son, and I just haven't gotten around to setting a definite time."

Corby's heart leaped with limited hope.

"Listen." Derrick sat on the edge of the bed. "She's already said you can ride whenever I let you. What do you think about this proclamation: Corby Quinn, son of Derrick Quinn, has his father's permission to ride Black Steed if Miss Ashley Steele will permit it."

Springing from the covers, Corby caught his father in a bear hug. "Gosh, Dad, do you mean it? You're really going to let me ride Black Steed?"

"Have you ever known me to go back on my word?"

"No." He threw his skinny arms around his father's neck again and squeezed. "Today?"

"What do you say we wait until the weekend?"

"Well, I wanted to show off to Eleni, and she'll be with her dad then."

"Okay, we'll ask Ashley if you can ride tomorrow after school, just for a short while. You've got to get used to being in the saddle again."

"Thanks a million, Dad. I'll be real careful. I promise."

Derrick drew him close again. "I'll hold you to that. Now get a move on. What're you having for breakfast?"

"Cold oat cereal and two or three toaster pizzas."

Derrick nodded. "Don't forget about eggs and rye bread and all that good stuff."

"I won't."

Derrick looked at him proudly. The boy's skin was like rich chocolate milk. He took care of himself well, as his father did, and Derrick was proud of him.

Corby got up and started to the bathroom, then turned back to his father. "Thanks again," he said with a lump in his throat.

"Sure. Move it, now!" He slapped Corby's backside.

Derrick sat on the side of the bed with memories of Maria washing over him. Maria had loved riding and horses, and they had loved each other and their son. Centered riding had been her life, and it had taken her away from him, first in being away from home more and more, then in death. He thought about the fact that it had been a while since he'd cried when he thought of Maria. He knew his friendship with Ashley had a lot to do with that. She and Maria had liked each other.

Going back to his room he got a heavy tan wool sweater and slipped it on. He was in good spirits, remembering Ashley last night, and he didn't like Reese Winters one damned bit. He smiled grimly to himself. He was jealous of Ashley.

It never stopped bothering him that Ashley was so much like Maria had been—independent, loving. He often ached with wanting her, but he had to remind himself that he'd been up that mountain before. He wasn't going to ruin Ashley's life the way he'd ruined Maria's.

Out in the kitchen Delia moved about crossly, hiding it because Derrick liked his women spicily sweet. A mean spirit didn't go over well with him at all. She wore a red velvet housecoat that draped invitingly across her pert breasts. Melissa was late; she was going to have to talk to that one. Len's eyes always followed her when she dressed like this, and Ace had looked her way often enough since he'd been here.

The toes of her matching high-heeled red slippers peeked out from the full flared skirt of her robe. A car horn beeped twice. "Miss Mag Moore," she said to herself. "She's early. What juicy tidbits has she got for me today?" Delia loved gossip.

Miss Mag operated a small, country store out of her van. She picked up vegetables, sugarcane, peanuts, fruit, and fruit wines from local farmers and sold her wares along the countryside and in Crystal Lake. She did a thriving business.

The dinner the day before had gone well. Ashley should be a little ill within ten days. The potion worked swiftly; that was what made it so effective. No one could reasonably link it to an illness. There was only one problem: a few people were immune to it. Delia's eyes glittered and she breathed rapidly in anticipation of her destructive plans. Yes, she had many plans. She knew many ways to skin Ashley Steele.

As Derrick came down the hall to the kitchen, he, too heard Miss Mag's horn and smiled. He liked her well enough, but didn't care for her fondness for gossip. It seemed a bit psychotic to him, and she ran it into the ground.

Humming to herself, Delia absent-mindedly bent to pick up what she thought was a small leaf from behind a window screen that had fallen off the day before. As her hand almost touched the object, she screamed. A giant cockroach peered at her. Delia was terrified of cockroaches.

As Derrick came into the room, she flung herself into his arms and hugged him for dear life. Her soft, slim body pressed into his. She was trembling so badly she couldn't talk.

"What is it?" Derrick kept asking.

"Oh, Derrick! Derrick!" She was crying softly then as he held her, and the moment was worth the fright she had suffered. She felt his rock-hard body against hers and thrilled to her bone marrow. Didn't he know they were meant to be together?

She lifted her lips to his, her mouth open. A supportive man who always sought to help, Derrick was stupefied by the passion in Delia's eyes. Lust and longing lay on her face as she looked at him before her kiss, and her body trembled as wildly with passion as with fear. He thought he knew damned well that nothing he had done had brought this on.

"Well, I hope I'm not coming in at a bad time," Miss Mag drawled from the back porch doorway. "I blew my horn and I knocked, but nobody answered. The door was unlocked, so I just came on in." An amused look lay on her face. "I'm real sorry if I walked in on a special minute, but I've been young once. Don't mind me."

Miss Mag giggled then like a young girl. "Maybe you want me to come by on my way back."

Derrick disengaged Delia's arms from around his neck. She was shaking so badly he was afraid she'd fall, but she steadied herself, throwing him a triumphant glance. "Just a minute," Derrick said. "Stay, Miss Mag, and Delia will give you her order, but first I have to find out something." He turned his full attention to Delia.

"What happened to upset you so?"

Miss Mag couldn't stop grinning. She thought, *You happened to her, you blind man. She's got a thing for you, as if you don't know. Heard you spent a few days at Ashley Steele's, you good-looking tomcat.*

Half swooning, Delia was nearly oblivious to Miss Mag until Derrick shook her harshly; then she stammered, "A big cockroach over there behind that screen . . . Oh, my God. I *hate* cockroaches."

Surveying the scene with her eyes half-closed, Miss Mag thought that if a cockroach could make her, Miss Mag, fit into the arms of a god like this, she'd gladly tolerate it.

Derrick got a can of roach spray from the cabinet and went to the screen. The roach, surprisingly, was still there. Pressing the nozzle flat, he sent a steady stream of roach killer onto the cowering insect, which staggered a few steps away and turned over, dead.

Miss Mag had taken in the red robe, the high heels. Folks around here didn't dress like that to cook breakfast. *Fancy. Enough to make a strong man weak.* She liked Delia, mainly because few others did. She always stood up for the underdog. Maybe if she passed this bit of gossip on, it would help Delia's cause. If anybody could handle Derrick, Delia could.

Delia sat down, her face pale. "I'm sorry," she said to Miss Mag. "I get so frightened when I see cockroaches. They scare me to death."

Miss Mag took a seat in a chair near Delia's. "Now you tell me if you want me to come back by."

A big platter of bacon and ham and scrambled eggs and cheese sat on the stove, prepared for breakfast. "I'm going to eat now and get started," Derrick said. "Shall I fix a plate for you?" he asked Delia, then, "Miss Mag, we've got plenty here for you if you want it."

The woman's face lit up. He was nice. Delia had never offered her a bite to eat. Still, she liked her because, like her, Delia had so few friends.

"Why, thank you," Miss Mag said. "it's real kind of you, but I load up on food before I leave the house." She peered from behind gold-rimmed glasses. "Now, what can I go and get you?"

Delia thought a moment, anger coursing through her. If Miss Mag hadn't come in, who knew what might have happened?

Corby appeared, got his cereal, put his pizzas in the toaster oven, and poured himself a big glass of orange juice.

"We need to go to the breakfast nook," Delia said, "and leave the kitchen to Len and Melissa when she comes."

Miss Mag's mouth fell a bit open. Well, this one could play queen when she wanted to. She liked her a little less.

"I'm comfortable here," Derrick said. "Corby looks okay to me, and Ace will be along any minute. We're all in this together."

Delia didn't dare look at him with the outrage she felt. *Some people,* she thought, *have no sense of propriety.* She turned to Miss Mag. "I need both kinds of potatoes," she said. "Winter squash. Roasted peanuts and a peck of raw ones. Too bad," she fretted, "Melissa isn't here. She mentioned wanting something from you and I don't remember what. Maybe you'd better stop back by."

"Sure thing, honey," Miss Mag said, getting up. "Boy, those pizzas look scrumptious. I know I just ate. . . ."

Corby brightened even more as he brought his pizzas to the table. "I've got three here," he said. "Take one, or two. There're plenty more in the freezer."

"Yes, do," Derrick urged her. "They're really good."

Miss Mag beamed. "Well, I don't mind if I do. I'll just take one and put it in this napkin." She reached over and got a paper napkin from a stack on the table. As she began to wrap the pizza, she looked at it and took a big bite. "On the other hand, nothing like eating it when it's hot."

"Coffee?" Derrick asked.

"No, thank you. Doctor says I mustn't drink too much, and I've already had two cups this morning."

She left then, and, going out the door, she couldn't help

looking back over her shoulder, thinking, *That is some fancy red robe Delia's got on.* She knew when a woman was after a man. She thought Ashley ought to know about this. Ashley always asked her if she wanted something to eat.

Around ten that same morning, brilliant sunlight flooded the Virginia countryside. Cold earlier, it was warming rapidly as Ashley rode Black Steed in the meadow. Today the horse was fully saddled, whereas she usually rode bareback. Headed toward the woods, intending to come back again, she saw Corby vault the fence and run to her side. When he reached her, he was out of breath.

"Morning, Miss Ashley."

"Good morning, Corby. No school today?"

"Water main break, so we're out all day. Miss Ashley, Dad said I could ride sometime, if you'll let me."

"Wonderful! I'm happy for you, Corby. You can ride this morning while he's all saddled up."

Corby bit his lip. "Only thing is, I wanted to show off before Eleni, and I guess she's in school."

Ashley laughed. "Guess again. I'm taking little Miss Eleni to the doctor at one. Would you like to bet that she'll see you riding and be out here?"

Ashley decided the forty-five minutes she'd spent riding was enough. She dismounted and began to pass the reins to Corby.

"Uh—could I ride him bareback? I love riding bareback."

"Sure. I won't be riding any more today, so take him to the barn and unsaddle him."

Corby was beside himself with joy. He rubbed the horse's flanks, then went to Black Steed's head and dug into his pockets for sugar cubes. He found two, and the horse nibbled them greedily.

"Steady, boy," Corby said, his eyes half-closed, dreaming of whistling in the wind as he rode Black Steed.

As Corby put the saddle away and rode back to Ashley, she turned to see Eleni racing toward her, calling, "Mom! Corby's riding!"

"Yes, sweetheart, Corby's riding. Isn't that great?"

"Yes. Oh, man!" It seemed her joy exceeded Corby's as he reached them.

"Morning, Eleni," the boy greeted her.

"Corby! You're riding!"

"Yeah. Wanna ride in front of or behind me?"

"Thank you, but I'm going to get on Goober." She looked lovingly at the Shetland pony that grazed a bit away from them. Then she giggled. "You even forgot to call me *twerp*."

Corby shot her a sly smile. "I'll remember next time. I'll bet you expected me to be in school."

"No. Minnie's helping us, and we saw on TV that your school had a water break. . . ."

"Water *main* break," Corby corrected her solicitously.

"Yeah, something like that." A sensitive child, Eleni didn't always want to be corrected. Giving a little wave, she trotted off toward Goober, who finally saw her and came to her.

As the children cantered on their mounts, Ashley looked toward Delia's house and her breath caught. Derrick was coming down the gently sloping hill. His gait seemed measured, unlike his usual long strides. He went to the gate rather than vaulting the fence. It seemed a long time before he finally reached her.

"Derrick, what is it?" Then she saw that he looked grim, upset rather than hurt.

"Let's go sit on the bench under the tree."

"Okay."

He said nothing on the walk to the bench, and it was a short while after they sat down before he told her what had happened.

"I'm pretty sure Delia knows what's going on between you and me. Do you think I'm wrong about that?"

"She could be refusing to see. Delia's strange."

"Yeah, I've always thought so. Ashley, I promised Marty on his deathbed that I'd look after Delia. I can't go back on my word, even though I want to. She's helpless in many ways. Naive."

Ashley felt she had no choice but to speak up. "Helpless, yes, in many ways, but not naive, Derrick. Delia's wily, cunning, manipulative."

"I think maybe you're right. I told myself I was making a mountain out of a molehill, that she was overexcited and frightened by a roach. Miss Mag was there. She saw the whole thing."

"Oh, Lord." Ashley groaned, rolling her eyes heavenward. "By tomorrow, to hear Miss Mag tell it, you and Delia will have had a steamy love affair going for ages."

"Yes." He licked his lips. "I've noticed little things for a long time that Delia's done. I told myself she was pretending I was Marty, and maybe she is. . . ."

"Don't bet on it. What do you want to do about it?"

"A simple thing. I'm going to take an apartment out this way in Crystal Lake. I can get back and forth with ease. Delia stayed by herself before I came. Len's in the bunkhouse. Melissa has stayed with her before."

"She's going to take it hard, but that's her way of controlling you the way she controlled Marty."

He didn't comment on that statement. Instead he asked, "Are you with me on this?"

"All the way." She sighed. "I thought she was changing. She's been very nice to me lately."

"I think that's because she knows in her heart that there's no hope for her and me, and she's savvy enough not to take it out on you. I do think she imagines I'm my dead brother."

"Very possibly. As I said, I've always found Delia a strange one, but she seems to have put her hostility toward me aside for now."

Derrick rubbed his hands together. "I don't want Corby

hurt by slander and gossip. I can hear Miss Mag at it now. By nightfall I'll be the greatest two-timing scoundrel Crystal Lake and this Virginia countryside ever saw."

Ashley laughed. That was exactly what she had been thinking. Derrick patted her knee. "What are your plans for today?"

She told him about taking Eleni to the doctor. He asked if the child was ill.

"No. She's getting more sniffles than I like her to have. She's seven and Reese lets her have a little coffee in her cup with her milk. And I suspect he lets her have a few sips of wine and tells her not to tell me."

"Why do you think that?"

"I didn't think about it before, but she said something just the other day about knowing what wine tastes like. When I asked how she knew, she said the word 'Daddy,' then put her hand over her mouth and would say no more. Damn Reese if he's doing that."

"I thought he was in a rehab program."

"That's what I thought. Enough about that, Derrick. You might have a real problem on your hands. I'm free much of the day tomorrow and much of next week. I'll help you find a place. In fact a new building—beautiful—opened up this week. There's an open house this weekend." She caught one of his big hands in both of hers.

"Cheer up, lover. We'll work it out. One thing Delia isn't is a fool."

Her saying it brought to his mind the vision of Delia's face this morning, blind with passion, her mouth and body clinging to his. He moved closer to Ashley. He raised her hands to his lips, saying, "No wonder I love you so."

Back from the doctor visit with Eleni, Ashley restlessly paced in her kitchen. When she heard Miss Mag's distinctive

horn, she had been half-expecting it. The woman knocked
and at Ashley's invitation came in.

"Just wanted to bring you a couple of long, fat, purple
sugarcane stalks. I know you like sugarcane so much."

"Why, thank you," Ashley said, taking the sugarcane and
laying them across the table. "That's so kind of you."

"Got a cup of coffee for an old lady? My doctor tells me
I drink too much of the stuff, but I tell him to let me be. It
ain't liquor I'm drinking." She smiled slyly, "Of course, a
nip or so never hurt anybody, as you well know. A little wine,
brandy . . ."

Miss Mag seemed keyed up, bursting with her usual energy.

From many times of serving her, Ashley knew that the
woman liked lots of cream and sugar in her coffee, and
sometimes asked for a spot of brandy. Today she seemed to
have what she needed.

Miss Mag drank her coffee in silence as Ashley sat across
from her; then she cleared her throat. "God knows I ain't a
gossip, but when I see somethin's likely to hurt somebody,
I'm the first to speak out. Some people appreciate it; some
hate me for it. You know how much I think of you; that's why
I feel it's my duty to stop by on my way home and tell you
what you ought to know."

Ashley could barely suppress a smile. "Go ahead. Tell
me. It's about Derrick, isn't it?"

Miss Mag's eyes flew open. "Well, I swear. You knew all
along something was going on between that movie star—
handsome devil and his sister-in-law." She slapped her knee
and chortled. "Marry him and she wouldn't even have to
change her name."

"What do you want to tell me? I don't know anything bad
about Derrick Quinn. . . ."

"You like him a whole lot, don't you?"

"Yes." She wasn't going to quibble.

Miss Mag told her story then in embroidered detail, with

Ashley thinking the woman would make either a good writer or a good actress. She was hilarious in her depiction of Delia in Derrick's arms.

"Lord, I thought she was never going to let him go." She paused, shaking her head slowly. "Neither one of them knew I was alive." Glory gone for the moment, Miss Mag turned anxious. "I did the right thing in telling you this, didn't I? Men can be dogs. I ought to know. I been married to three. I just don't want to see you hurt, honey."

Ashley looked at her, studying the wrinkled face of Miss Mag, which looked ten years older than her years.

"Was I right to tell you?" She sounded acutely anxious now.

"It's all right," Ashley assured her. "You did what you thought was best. I can take care of it."

Miss Mag's heart skipped a beat. What did Ashley mean, she could take care of it? She pictured Ashley and Delia fighting over this man, a rootin'-tootin' hair-pulling and scratching match, and she sucked in her breath. *Nothing like a good old-fashioned catfight.* She could see Delia in that scene in a minute, but Ashley wasn't really the type. But you never knew. Folks said still water ran deep. So she would take care of it, would she? Miss Mag vowed she would stop by Delia's tomorrow on some pretext, looking for scratches and bruises. Mind you, she thought, she liked Delia. So few people did. But she liked Ashley better, and she was betting on her.

Twenty-one

Derrick waited until the outside and inside chores were done and Melissa and Ace had left before he found Delia sitting in the living room watching a TV sitcom. She looked up as he stood in the doorway.

"Oh, Derrick, come on in. This show is pretty funny, but you've missed most of it."

"Finish watching," he said; "then I need to talk with you."

Delia glanced at him obliquely, her mind no longer on the sitcom. He'd seldom *needed* to talk with her before.

Delia switched the remote off. "This is on every week, and I don't get a chance to talk with you nearly often enough."

He sat down awkwardly, uncomfortable with the adoring look she was bestowing on him. She looked contrite.

"Derrick, before you begin, I want to apologize to you for what happened this morning. I was half-hysterical. I'm scared to death of insects and rodents. . . ."

Derrick looked at her levelly. "I know you are, and I'm glad I was there for you, but . . ." He cleared his throat. "Delia, I'm moving out."

Shock stiffened Delia's features. Her voice was tiny as she whispered, "Moving out? Why?"

Derrick smiled narrowly. "I don't want idle gossip swarming around my son's head, and I don't want the reputation of being a hopeless womanizer."

"Who'd gossip about us? Derrick, please, I need you here." She glanced in the direction of the secret room and the spirits. This was a body blow.

"Remember we had one of our major gossip columnists as witness to what happened this morning."

Delia's eyes flashed sudden fire. "Mag Moore. That *crone,*" she raged. "That *hag!*"

"Delia, don't. The woman is aging; she's lonely. No doubt it's just another way to fill her empty hours. What she saw was easy for anyone to misinterpret."

"If you stay, I promise it will never happen again." She looked at him wildly, thinking she had to get a grip on herself. She could lose everything.

"It probably *won't* happen again, but the damage is done. It's not your fault. You're lonely, as you said. You miss Marty. You two were very much in love."

"Yes." She corroborated the false assumption easily.

For a few minutes Delia was absolutely still, her heart plummeting.

"Where will you go? To Ashley's?"

He shook his head. "That would be gossip heaven, too. We have two kids to raise between us." He told her about the apartment in Crystal Lake, adding, "It'll be easy for me to get back and forth from here."

"What about Corby when he gets home from school?"

"He'll meet me here, help us with the chores, and go home with me." His glance at her was gentle. "You know, Delia, at any rate, I'll be leaving in a few months. I've already been here longer than I intended to be. Ace is a good man. You won't have a chance to miss me."

"Derrick, I'm so sorry. I blame myself. Do you know if Miss Mag told Ashley about this morning? I know she often goes there from here."

"She told her."

"And Ashley was furious. I've been trying to be friends with her."

"I explained what happened."

"And she believes you?"

"I think so."

Delia breathed a sigh of relief. At least that still left her a chance to give Ashley what was coming to her.

Corby spoke from the kitchen doorway: "Dad, is it okay if I go and clobber Len in a checkers game?"

Derrick glanced at his watch—seven o'clock. "Call and ask if he's willing," he said, "and be back by eight. Homework done?"

"Gee, Dad, we were out today, and I did a lot of homework last night. I'm free." He flapped his wings like a bird.

"Then go and let Len beat the stuffing out of you."

"I beat him twice last time."

"Don't brag. What goes around comes around."

"Sure."

Delia stared at the floor until the boy had gone. "I like the relationship between you and Corby."

"Oh, I thought you always said Maria and I let him have his way too much."

"That was before you came and stayed here."

"You've said it here."

"Then I'm sorry. I think you're an ideal father." But Delia thought bitterly that she didn't want him to have a son, and she certainly didn't want him to have another woman. Maria had stood in her way too long. She did not intend to let Ashley Steele stand in her way. Thank God for the spirits, and the poison potion that was going to deliver him to her.

Part of her was sick with the thought of Derrick's not being here with her, but he would be with her each day for a while longer. The nights were going to be the hardest. It had been so sweet to lie in her bed dreaming of him as he lay a few yards away.

"I'm sorry," she said again. "I know I brought all this on. I hope you can forgive me." She sounded humble now.

Derrick shifted uneasily. Why was he seldom really comfortable with his sister-in-law? He leaned forward and patted her hand. To her, a small flash of electricity passed between them; he noticed nothing. Then her mind flew again to the secret room and the *vévé* figures on the walls that would lead the spirits to do her bidding and bring him to her bosom. That would make him hers and hers alone.

Derrick and Ashley found Saturday a good day to hunt for an apartment for Derrick and Corby. They visited sites from one end of Crystal Lake to another and finally settled on a roomy two-bedroom near the city line. There were two baths and a big kitchen.

They had an early lobster dinner at a seafood restaurant and held hands.

"You look just a little bothered," Derrick told her.

She nodded. "I feel a bit off, and I'm not sure why. This morning as I practiced my scales and trills, I got lightly breathless a time or two. Heart? Lungs? Emotions? What's the reason? I almost didn't hit a high note I reached for."

She paused, frowning. Derrick squeezed her hand, looking sympathetic. "You'd better check it out."

"Believe me, I'll be there at my doctor's first thing Monday morning. He'll know how to route me from there."

"I'll take you."

"No, Delia's going to need your help more than ever. She's a needy woman, Derrick. In many ways I feel sorry for her."

"I told her I was moving out."

"Already?"

"Yes."

"How did she take it?"

"Surprisingly well, I thought. Oh, she was upset, all right, and she apologized for her hysteria yesterday morning. . . . I told her I didn't care to be the butt of vicious gossip, for Corby's sake and for yours."

"I can't imagine that going over too well."

"It had to be done. I promise you, Ash, you'll always know what side of the fence I'm on."

Derrick dropped Ashley at her parents' house, but stayed only long enough to carry on a brief conversation. After he left, Caroline, Frank, and Ashley discussed Derrick and Delia.

"My guess is we're the only ones Miss Mag hasn't told," Caroline said. "Not too many people pay her much attention, but I think Derrick is doing the right thing in moving out."

Frank nodded. "The more I see of that fellow, the more I like him."

Ashley flushed. A compliment to Derrick was a compliment to her.

Annice came in with a huge bunch of pussy willows and put them in a very large vase. "So, my beloved sister," she asked, "did you two find something suitable for Derrick to escape the Wicked Witch of Crystal Lake?"

Ashley smiled at the name. "We did."

"And when does he escape said witch's clutches?"

"In ten days to two weeks. Actually, he's only going to be here a few months longer."

Coming in, Whit said, "I heard the conversation in the hall so I feel free to butt in. My hat's off to Derrick Quinn. He's doing exactly the right thing. Miss Mag's gossip may be a blessing in disguise."

He turned to Ashley as they all sat sprawled on the couches and chairs. "Grab him, sis. He's irreplaceable."

"Oh, you," Ashley protested.

Annice laughed. "If for some reason you don't appreciate what that man has to offer, just pass him along to me. I'll worship at his shrine any old time."

"Flibbertigibbet," Ashley told her. "You talk a good game, but I happen to know Marion Johnson couldn't run faster."

Annice clutched her heart in mock dismay. "You hit me where it hurts."

After an hour of so of banter, Ashley felt a headache coming on. She never had headaches. "What is it, honey?" Caroline asked.

"I'm not sure. I spent a lot of time singing today before Derrick picked me up. And I guess this thing with Derrick and Delia has me upset, although I'm very satisfied with how he's handling it.

"I'm a bit cross with Reese, too. He's letting Eleni have a little wine and a little coffee. I've got to speak to him."

"I'm sure he knows better," Whit cut in. "He's such a rascal."

Ashley nodded. "Where is Minnie?"

Caroline smiled. "Would you believe she and King have gone into town to an early movie?"

"There's hope for all of us," Ashley commented.

Annice raised her eyebrows. "Especially for lucky you."

Ashley stood up to go in spite of their protests. "We're singing here tonight. A few neighbors might pop in," Frank told her.

"Thanks, Dad, but what I want right now is some fresh air and a brief nap. I have new songs to master."

Whit said evenly, "You're about as good as they get. It only remains for a guy like Max Holloway and some impresario to put you on display so the world knows it."

"You're up there, too, Whit," Ashley complimented him.

Whit looked somber. "What I want for myself is more what Mom and Dad have. More of a hometown thing. I do nicely, though, don't I?"

They all chorused that he did.

By the time Ashley had walked the half mile from her parents' house to her house, she felt a bit winded. She took off her coat and other outer garments, and, sitting on the edge of her bed, she reflected that the winter air had felt good. She was disappointed, though, that her head hadn't cleared and her heart still pounded and fluttered off and on.

She decided against taking an aspirin. Her doctor believed in letting the body heal itself, in keeping the immune system well bolstered. She placed her hand on her heart and listened. She was so anxious it was hard to tell what she heard and what she didn't.

Kicking off her shoes, she lay across the bed. The room was too cool and she needed to turn up the thermostat, but she couldn't get up. She was too dizzy and the bed felt too comfortable.

In no time at all she was asleep, and a dream came instantly. The room rocked around her. Wet green summer leaves swept through, and a few plastered onto her body. The wall collapsed. She could not get her balance as she tried to stand, and she cried out. She was wet, cold, and shaking from the storm that was sweeping through the room, and she was helpless, about to be swept away with the green leaves.

She came awake, shaking, batting her eyelashes rapidly. The room was still, warmer than in the dream. The window wall stood solid. She struggled up and went to the window, looking out on an absolutely peaceful winter scene. There seemed to be no wind at all.

She wanted to go to the kitchen to fix a cup of peppermint tea, but she was too tired. She could not recall ever having felt like this before, and she wished for Monday morning, when she could begin to get to the bottom of this malady.

Twenty-two

By ten the next Monday morning, Ashley had an appointment with Dr. Smith as soon as she could make it in. She hesitated, then decided to call Derrick.

"I was thinking about you," he said. "I'm a bit worried."

"That's why I'm calling you. I've been plagued with small illnesses all my life, but there's never been anything major. I take good care of myself."

"What time's your appointment?"

"Whenever I can get there."

He cleared his throat as he stood in front of Delia's barn, his cell phone in hand. Three horseback riders were already on the trail. he looked across the way at Black Steed racing, at Goober grazing. "Okay, then. I'm going to drive you in."

"Oh, love, it isn't necessary."

"I say it is. I'll pick you up; then we'll drive by my place and I'll change."

His voice was warmly firm, and she found herself glad that he would do this. "All right, and thank you."

"What I want to thank you for is giving me splendid dreams."

"You had another one last night?"

"Yes, and before now I rarely remembered my dreams."

"I had one, too. We were running in the meadow. I stumbled and you caught me. We kissed—and I'll leave the rest to your imagination."

Derrick laughed heartily. "Dreams of ecstasy," he said somberly. "Ash, you've brought me everything."

"I'm glad, because you've done even more for me."

In Dr. Smith's ivory-and-blue hospital office, he sat across his big mahogany desk from Ashley, who was still in her hospital gown.

"You had a thorough physical a couple of months ago," he said. "This looks like or mimics low iron or low potassium, but your blood tests don't show that. Still . . ." He tapped the edge of his desk with a pen.

"Have you been suffering lately from PMS?"

She shook her head. "I never have."

"I'd say lose weight, but you're not obese, just a little heavier than I'd like, and I won't quibble about that. You may need it for your singing. I don't find much wrong."

He paused for a very long moment before he said, "There's a line of little lumps just inside one of your cheeks, and it puzzles me. When I went out a moment ago, I looked up this symptom and I talked with Dr. Nathan Domingo. He's an ear, nose, and throat man. He's worked largely in South America, but he's a wunderkind, just knows about everything. He's coming in to talk with us."

"That sounds useful."

A knock sounded, and a wiry, short, gray-haired man with tender eyes came in. Dr. Smith introduced her.

With caring hands, Dr. Domingo examined her, then sat down beside her. "The symptoms you describe here," he said, "are like those I've often seen with South American jungle dwellers. It comes from a poisonous tree frog, and the only antidote is a rare lily that grows in the swamps. But there are other symptoms that the poison carries, and you have none of those.

"You are not terribly sick," Dr. Domingo went on, "and that's good, because the poison kills in ten days to a couple of months with a terrible wasting illness. Another thing is that in rare instances certain individuals build up a quick tolerance for the tree frog venom.

"But what am I talking about? We're light-years away. Have you been on tour in South America?" Dr. Domingo asked. "I know you're a singer."

"No, not recently. I'm scheduled to go next fall."

Dr. Smith nodded. "I'll continue to check this and talk with Dr. Domingo. I'm going to give you a tonic that should make you feel better. I can pretty much assure you that it's not poison, but have you been in the woods lately?"

"No," Ashley answered. "Not since summer." She thought about the search they had all made for Corby that past summer.

"I think it's likely something much simpler." Dr. Domingo got up and paced with his hands behind his back. "I looked over the results of your blood tests quickly. I'm pretty sure this is a fluke of sorts. Perhaps nerves, do you think?"

"That's certainly possible. I get tense a month or so before I am to give a major performance."

Dr. Domingo smiled. "I have heard you sing, and you are indeed magnificent."

Ashley blushed. "Thank you."

"I have many family members in Rio de Janeiro. They will like you, as you will like them. If you will permit me, I will introduce you via phone and Internet."

"How thoughtful of you."

"The honor will be theirs."

Ashley got dressed then and returned to find the two doctors waiting for her. They made another appointment for her to come in the following Thursday. She drank a yellow liquid from a paper cup—a tonic, Dr. Smith explained. Already she felt better.

In the waiting room, Derrick fretted and tried not to show it. When she came in view, he couldn't stop himself from saying, "Well?"

"I don't think there's much going on. Nerves. I've been there before."

Derrick put his head to one side. "But what does the doctor think?"

She told him about the entire conversation and the poisonous South American tree frog whose venom sometimes caused an inner mouth rash.

"We looked for Corby in the woods, but that was too long ago, and this isn't South America."

"Yeah. I'll bring you back Thursday."

"Delia's going to fire you for missing so much time."

"Think I could really make that happen?"

As they left the hospital hand in hand, Ashley felt suddenly happy, well, glowing. She patted her handbag, which held a prescription for a tonic. She laughed now at Derrick's answer regarding Delia. "You know, Derrick, I think you remind her of Marty, and, like Miss Mag, Delia's lonely."

"I guess. Corby and I are enjoying not living with Delia any longer. Things are shaping up beautifully. Since our talk, she's kept her distance, but she's been cordial."

"Derrick, she's changed in this short period. She's kinder, more even-tempered with me when I've run into her. She's living proof that people can change. I still think she's got a crush on you. . . ."

"And I've got a hell of a case for you."

He stopped and kissed her cheek. "Talk about gossip," she said, laughing.

Derrick laughed with her. "I'll shout it to the world. I asked the angels to show me love, and they brought me to this woman."

But with all his happiness, Derrick felt a wide swath of misgiving. They were coming to love each other, and that was a miracle, but he had been this route before. In his gut he still felt guilt about Maria. She had needed him and he had failed her. He could not let himself do that to Ashley.

He stopped at his car in the parking lot and helped her in. Silently they drove to her favorite drugstore and went in.

She gave her prescription to the pharmacist and she and Derrick walked around the newly renovated store, admiring the new fittings. They came up behind two women who seemed unaware of their presence.

"He makes a great addition to the neighborhood," one of the women said. "If I were ten years younger, I'd pitch my tent in his bedroom."

The other woman laughed shrilly. "Well, I've got a couple of years on you, and age sure wouldn't stop me."

"I think he's already got two women on a string, according to Miss Mag and a few others."

"But he's moved near you and me. He moved into an apartment building near our house, or so Miss Mag says. I'm going to set up a watch. Talk about tall, dark, and scrumptious. . . ." She made a kissing sound.

"You're a fast woman, Maisie." The woman's friend laughed heartily.

Maisie knocked on a wooden shelf. "Well, with so much outrageous competition these days, all of it fast, I've got to do something to get myself noticed."

What Ashley wanted was on a shelf directly in front of these women, one of whom she recognized.

"Rita," Ashley said. "How are you?"

The pale, attractive Rita blushed to a bright red. "Why, Ashley Steele. I haven't seen you in a month of Sundays. I hear you're still singing like an angel. I didn't make your last concert in these parts."

"Thanks for the compliment. I'm well."

Rita introduced her friend and Ashley introduced them to Derrick. The other woman shook hands gingerly, but Rita held on to Derrick's hand a long while, soulfully gazing into his eyes.

"My, my," Rita's friend murmured. "Some people have all the luck."

* * *

By the time Derrick dropped Ashley off and headed back to Delia's, she felt good. Her prescribed medicine was like the liquid in the paper cup at the hospital. It was as if she had not known a spell of sickness at all.

Her cell phone rang and she picked it up.

"Where in the hell have you been, woman?"

Ashley was taken aback. "What's wrong with you, Reese?"

"I asked where you've been."

"That's really not your business. What can I do for you?"

There was an angry silence; then Reese barked, "Eleni's with me."

Alarm bells went off inside Ashley. *"Why* is she with you?"

"She's coming down with a cold and she vomited a bit. The school nurse thought we could ward off the cold by putting her to bed now."

"Wrap her up well and bring her home, or I'll come and get her."

"The poor kid needs someone who's always there for her."

"I was at the doctor's, Reese. I wasn't gone very long."

"Okay. Okay. I'd keep her, but I'm giving an exam this afternoon. So I'll bring her over."

"Let me talk with her."

"She's asleep in the other bedroom."

Ashley doubted that, but Reese could be more difficult in small ways than anybody she'd ever come across.

Ashley was in her studio going over a playlist for songs she and her group would record Thursday and Friday, if Eleni was well enough. She hummed a few bars of "Steal Away," and it set up a deep sense of sadness and pining for a world she had yet to know. She stopped for a moment. Since she had known Derrick this time, there seemed little darkness in her life, except that she knew he was torn. That he loved her was evident, but he was blunt in saying they could hurt each other.

When the door chimes sounded, she rushed to the door to find Reese carrying a heavily bundled and drowsy Eleni. She reached for the child, but he shook his head. "Let me carry her to her room."

Ashley bent to kiss the child's soft cheek. "How do you feel, angel?" she asked.

"Kinda sick, Mom, but I'll be okay," Eleni murmured sleepily.

"You bet you will," Ashley assured her.

In her room with the cutouts on the ceiling depicting the solar system, Reese pulled back the covers before Ashley could do it. Ashley got Eleni's animal-print pajamas from her closet and brought them to the bed.

"Let me undress her," she said.

Reese shrugged. "Once she's in bed, we need to talk briefly."

"I thought you had something else to do."

"That can wait until I can get something off my chest."

Exasperated, Ashley said sharply, "Heaven forbid that you could have something on your chest and not discharge it immediately."

"That's right," he shot back acidly. "What happens to me and what I want doesn't matter; the only thing that does is what goes on in *your* glorious world."

She unbundled Eleni and got her into her pajamas, then tucked her in, hesitating a moment.

"Give me a kiss, Mom."

Smiling, Ashley kissed the child's cheek several times. "Now go to sleep and you'll feel better.

"What about her medicine?" Ashley asked Reese.

Reese reached into his overcoat pocket and handed a bottle of red liquid to her. He sounded petulant when he told her, "I see you've got nothing to say about my statement that yours is the only world that matters." Had she really once loved this man?

"Your world *does* matter to me, Reese," she said slowly. "You're my child's father. That has to matter. *You* have to matter. I listen to your complaints, but you insist on being unfair. Let's go out to the kitchen or somewhere else. Eleni needs to sleep."

But in spite of the negative conversation going on around her, Eleni had fallen fast asleep.

Ashley chose her studio to accommodate her talk with Reese. She felt comfortable there, uplifted. He took off his overcoat and threw it onto a chair. Reese looked around him. "Ashley Steele, the great," he said mockingly.

"Not yet," she said calmly, "but I may well be one day if I keep putting my heart and soul into it."

"Meanwhile, the rest of us, including me and Eleni, can go to hell."

"That's not true and you know it."

He let out a harsh breath. "I don't have much to mention to you, but there is one thing. You and Quinn are getting serious, aren't you?"

"You might say that."

"Are you going to marry him? We've only been divorced a little over a year."

"That's not something I want to discuss with you right now," Ashley said easily.

Reese's voice rose. "If it's going to happen, I need to know. I'll have plans of my own to make."

"Meaning?"

"It takes two to tango, sweetheart, whatever that means to you. Ash, let's cut the crap. I notice Eleni's calling Quinn Uncle . . . Why? They're not related."

"They're fond of each other. She asked me if it was okay. I certainly think so."

"She's my kid, too. Why didn't you ask me?"

Ashley looked up, her mouth slightly open. "This is such a small thing, Reese. I saw no need to ask you. After all, if Derrick and I were to get married, she'd be calling him Dad."

Reese struggled with his anger. "Well, make up your mind. Are you marrying that bastard or not?"

A milder strain of anger flashed in Ashley as she told him, "That's none of your business, Reese, and you know it. There's nothing between you and me now except Eleni, and that's a big 'except.' "

"You're being hateful."

"And you're not?"

"Let me warn you. Don't marry this jerk in haste and repent at leisure."

Ashley smiled narrowly. "Thanks for running my life, Reese. It didn't work when we were married and it won't work now."

Reese's pale brown face reddened with frustration. Ashley had never known a woman's place, he thought. "I can tell you this, if you haven't already heard it: Quinn is messing around with Delia. It looks like he's pulling both yours and Delia's strings."

"I can take care of myself."

Reese stood up abruptly. "I'd advise you to watch your step. You constantly yapped about me and other women. At least I wasn't *living* with one of them."

With satisfaction, Ashley told him, "If you listened to *all* the gossip, you'd know Derrick has moved away from Delia."

Reese looked surprised. He started to say something when the door chimes sounded. Ashley went to the door to find Delia standing there. She greeted her none too warmly, noticing the thermos she carried.

"Ashley, I didn't call because I didn't want you to tell me no. May I come in? I'll only be a little while. Promise."

"Of course. What's in the bag?"

"That's why I'm here." By then they had reached the studio and Reese, who spoke warmly to Delia.

"As always, you're looking gorgeous," he complimented her heartily. Blushing, Delia thanked him.

"If you'd like to see a movie or just to go riding, please feel free to give me a call." Reese flirted mightily, glancing out of the corner of his eye at Ashley.

"I thought you were leaving," Ashley told him.

"Not on my account," Delia urged him. "What I want to ask will take only a little while."

Reese grinned. "I really do have to go, but I'd like to be a fly on this wall while you two ladies talk about matinee-idol Derrick."

"Oh, really." It was Delia's turn to blush again.

"Good-bye, Reese," Ashley said levelly. "You've done enough damage for this visit. Don't forget to call and see how Eleni's doing."

"Do I ever?"

Once Reese was gone, Ashley went back to Delia, who had uncapped the thermos. She held it up.

"I know I said I didn't like root beer, but I find Len and Melissa, my helpers, are crazy about it, even in the winter-time. I've been trying to make it for a while now, and I'm not doing something right."

Delia poured the cap half-full of the root beer. "Would you be good enough to taste it for me, tell me what I'm not doing right?"

"Sure. I'll be glad to. It's not hard to make."

Taking the thermos cup, Ashley tasted the brew, ran some over her tongue, and took another swallow. In a few minutes she held the liquid in her mouth and thought she had the answer. She swallowed and exhaled. "You need much more sugar," she said. "Otherwise everything else seems top-notch. You've got about the amount of root beer flavor I like in it."

Delia looked at Ashley, a warm, pleased smile on her face. "I have to keep my help happy. They're all I have now. I'm sure you know Derrick's moved out, and, considering everything, I think it's for the best. I wish country and small-town people weren't such avid gossipers. God knows there's enough to do without meddling in other people's business."

Ashley shrugged. "I'm sure it was like this even back in biblical times."

Delia seemed humble when she spoke. "Ashley, thank you for being kind. I want you to know I've thought about it carefully and I wish you and Derrick the best of luck. I searched my heart and found I'm so fond of him because he reminds me of Marty. My husband and I were so much in love, and I can't seem to get over him. I hope you'll both forgive me. I wish Miss Mag hadn't been such a vicious gossip."

"Ah, well," Ashley said evenly, "like all of us she has her problems. Of course I forgive you, Delia."

"I wonder if Derrick ever will."

"He doesn't seem to me to hold it against you. He has his noon meal with you. He wouldn't do that if he were angry."

"Yes, but he only takes a big sandwich and a salad. He cooks at night for himself and Corby. Corby wants a snack after school, which I give him. I'm afraid I've made a bit of a mess of things."

Looking at her, Ashley smiled. "Give it time. I'm sure it will all work out."

To Ashley, Delia seemed so different from the arrogant woman she had recently been.

Three horn taps sounded outside. Ashley went to the window to find Miss Mag's van parked in her driveway. In a moment the chimes sounded and she let Miss Mag in, leading her back to the kitchen. The woman's mouth fell open when she saw Delia. Miss Mag shifted awkwardly as she handed a big bag to Ashley.

"Well," Miss Mag said, "I don't see you out and around much. This is a surprise."

"There's nothing like starting fresh," Delia said pleasantly.

Miss Mag nodded and said to Ashley, "I'm on my way home. I forgot to bring you that gallon of cane syrup you wanted, and here it is." She set the bag on the table, looking from one woman to the other. What was going on here? She'd give her eyeteeth to know. As long as she lived, she'd never forget the sight of a lush and passionate Delia clinging to Derrick Quinn.

Delia stood up as Ashley asked Miss Mag to sit down. The older woman shook her head.

"I've got places to go and things to do," she said. "Folks think you get old and life's over. Well, mine is beginning. Who knows but what I'll find me another man one day."

"It could happen," Ashley assured her.

Delia touched Ashley's shoulder. "Thank you so much. When I think it's just right, I'll ask you to sample it again. I'm determined to get this just so."

Turning to Miss Mag, Delia asked, "Could I get a ride home with you?"

"You bet you can." Miss Mag loved company.

Twenty-three

From her kitchen window, Ashley watched Miss Mag's van until it stopped at Delia's house. Pulling on a heavy sweater, she stepped outside to get a flowerpot to transplant a geranium. She bent to examine the pot and shake dirt from it.

"Your *can* can freeze in weather like this. You need a coat!"

Holding the pot, Ashley stood up. "Neesie! I'm so glad you all came by." King Johnson carried a big bag, and Minnie a smaller one.

Annice hugged her sister fondly. "Did Miss Mag stop by here?"

"She did. Why do you ask?"

"Let's go inside. You don't want a cold along with your daughter."

Outer garments removed, the three sat around the kitchen table, drinking hot chocolate Ashley had made.

"Now, why did you ask if Miss Mag stopped by?"

Annice shrugged, smiling wryly. "Did she tell you any gossip about your ex?"

"No. Reese came by to bring Eleni. Then Delia popped in."

"Delia? What was her reason?"

Ashley looked amused. "She's a neighbor. Does she need a reason?"

Annice looked at her sister. "My darling, there's always a method to Delia's madness."

204   *Francine Craft*

"She wanted me to critique her root beer. She makes it for Len and Melissa."

"That was her *apparent* reason. I wouldn't trust that witch behind a split broomstick."

Ashley laughed. "And psychologists are supposed to be benign, forgiving."

"That's the old-style ones. What did she have to say to Reese?"

"More like what he had to say to her. He flirted outrageously."

Annice drank the last of her chocolate and put the cup down. "That's like saying the sky is above us. Doesn't he always flirt? You know, sis, the luckiest women in the world are the ones Reese Winters didn't marry."

Ashley laughed heartily. "What about Miss Mag's gossip about Reese?"

"Oh, yes. He seems to be stepping out with a very young music instructor at Crystal Lake College. Miss Mag said she wouldn't be surprised if they jumped the broom. According to her, he's nuts about her, and she feels the same."

A twinge of anxiety pinched Ashley. Touching the unopened bag, she asked King what was in it.

"A good helping of freshly roasted peanuts," he said. "Your folks and I know how you and Eleni like them."

"Thanks for thinking about us."

"And I brought persimmon wine," Minnie chimed in. "This came out top of the line." Minnie took the sparkling bottle of pale-yellow liquid out of the bag and set it on the table.

"Beautiful color," Ashley complimented her. "Could I open it and pour a bit for anyone?"

King patted his foot. "Not right now. I'll be getting a whole bottle for myself, if Miss Minnie shows me love."

"Don't count on it," Minnie teased him. Both women said they'd pass on the wine for now.

Reaching into the bag, Ashley got a handful of peanuts and shelled them one by one, eating the nuts as she did.

"Delicious," she told King.

King looked pleased. "Thank you, ma'am. Now, I could've sent them by Annice and Minnow, but I wanted to be close to Minnow as long as I could." He looked boldly and lovingly at Minnie.

Minnie flushed and looked down. "One of these days, King Johnson."

King laughed. "You promising? Or threatening?"

Annice smiled at the two, then asked, "How's Eleni?"

"Still sleeping when I looked in on her a little while ago. She seems to me to be breathing a lot easier. I haven't had to use the nose drops. I think the nurse was bothered by the fever. Eleni gets those. It's never been serious."

"Then I won't wake her," Annice said. "I'll just hang out with you."

King put his arms behind his head. "I'll be shoving off. I want to groom Black Steed. Didn't have time this morning."

To their surprise, Minnie chimed in, "I could help you, if you have a mind to let me. You've had a rough day chopping wood and digging up those old tree stumps."

King looked up with surprise. "You'd do that?"

"I said I would," Minnie shot back sharply. "Don't make me change my mind."

King slapped his thigh, laughing. "Man, I got to be doing something right to get an offer like that."

When King and Minnie left, the two sisters looked at each other, giggling. Annice got another cup of chocolate and sat sipping it.

"I've been thinking," Annice said slowly. "You're going to Germany in March. I've got some time owed me. I'd love to keep Eleni. I could stay here, or she could stay with Mama and Dad and me."

Smiles wreathed Ashley's face. "Neesie, she'd love that,

but Mama always takes care of her when I'm on tour. Are you sure? You always have so many things to do."

"I'm certain, and I won't take no for an answer, so let's change the subject. How's Crystal Lake's own Denzel Washington?"

"Derrick?"

"Who else, girl? Crystal Lake ladies will be crying in their soup when he goes back home. Including me."

"We were slated to go down to his farm this weekend, but I guess we'll have to set another time because of Eleni. Derrick's very caring that way."

"Yeah. I could keep Eleni, but you'd never leave her when she's sick."

"Don't be surprised if she's okay by then. She recovers from her small illnesses miraculously."

"That's the stuff the Steeles are made of. I'm a fine one to talk, but you and Derrick need each other."

"I know, but Derrick really wants a stay-at-home wife, and that's his prerogative."

"And you?"

Ashley thought a moment. "After Reese, I'm still wary. People change, and not always for the better. . . ."

"Derrick moved out from Delia's to spare you and his son the gossip. Reese would never have done that. Don't make the mistake of thinking he even *might* be like Reese."

"I don't want to be hurt again. He doesn't want to be hurt again."

Annice studied her sister a long time before she spoke. "Being alone can hurt worse than what anybody can do to you. Learn to gamble, Ash. It's the only way to live."

"Spoken by a woman who takes few chances anymore."

When she got out of Miss Mag's van at her house, Delia hurried inside, relieved that Derrick didn't need her help with the riders this afternoon. She had other things to do.

Pausing in front of the door to the secret room, she closed her eyes and put her hand over her heart. Derrick had said he and Corby would be leaving early. It galled her that she needed him so; with Marty she had held the upper hand. Soon she would need more goat's blood; bless Len, who always did as she asked him.

She had to be careful, she thought. Ashley was no fool. When would she put it together that she sickened when she had eaten food Delia had prepared? She was fortunate that by nature Ashley wasn't a suspicious person.

"Delia!" Derrick's voice sounded at the back door, coming into the kitchen.

"I'm in the hall, Derrick; coming right away." She sounded cheerful.

She stopped a few feet from him, her eyes grave. "Derrick, how can I ask you to forgive me?"

He shook his head. "There's nothing to forgive, Delia. People misinterpret what they see. That wasn't the first time, and it won't be the last. I just hate vicious, mindless gossip."

"I do, too. I loved having you and Corby here. I get lonely."

It wasn't the first time she'd said it, and he felt sorry for her, but his own life came first.

"I know," he said, "and I'm sorry, but I'll be going home in a few months anyway. The man who came out yesterday made you a good offer, in case you want to sell. Ace Carter's a really good man if you want to keep the place, which I don't think you do."

She shrugged. "I just haven't made up my mind. Ace is okay, I guess."

"He's tops with horses. His divorce cost him his own horse farm; otherwise he'd be rolling." Derrick grinned. "He'd be good marital pickings for you."

Delia recoiled as if he'd struck her. "Not my type," she said tightly. "Not after Marty."

Derrick looked at his sister-in-law keenly. Lately she had

made a demigod of his brother. They had quarreled plenty when Marty was alive. Surely she hadn't forgotten so soon.

"You're quiet," Derrick said, "but you like people around you. You might consider at least getting to know Ace better. Marty liked him."

"I know. Marty liked everybody."

"My brother was a winner."

Delia nodded. It was on the tip of her tongue to say that he, Derrick, was the winner. Her heart clamored in her chest. She had to have him for herself.

Melissa puttered around the kitchen, still doing the dinner dishes; she didn't like dishwashers.

"Art hasn't got a lot of education," Delia said slowly.

"He nearly got rich and didn't need a fancy education. He's smart. Next time he'll get better financial advisers."

She was going to risk it. "I like smart men, Derrick, men like Marty . . ." She hesitated. "And you."

"You'll find someone, but you've got to let yourself love again."

He was playing the Dutch uncle role and she hated it.

"Right now I'm only concerned about your forgiveness."

"Don't be. I can live with what happened. I saw you get out of Miss Mag's van."

"Yes, I ran into her over at Ashley's."

Derrick's eyebrows shot up, questioning.

"I've come to like Ashley," she said slowly. "I'd like us to be friends. She's a nice woman, aside from a fast-becoming-famous one." She grinned unexpectedly. "I'd like to be able to say I've got friends in high places."

"Now you're talking." He reached out and patted her shoulder. "You're okay in my book, Delia. We're a lonely pair, you and me. The only thing is I hit it lucky. Your turn will come—if you let it."

She could never understand how she did it, maintaining this calm exterior when she was screaming with need and desire for Derrick inside. Then suddenly she knew: in spite of the pain, hope filled her to bursting. Somehow, some way, Derrick Quinn was going to be hers. She would never stop trying.

"I'm listening." Delia shifted her stance, relaxing. "Right now I only need to know that you forgive me for clinging to you so hard, for almost kissing you, that you understand."

"I do understand, and I forgive you—and believe me, I can live with it. You lost your emotional balance. Lord, Delia, I wish I could help you more."

Delia's face lit up. "You'll never know how much I thank you," she said throatily, basking in his nearness. He patted her shoulder again.

"I got lucky finding Ash. You'll get lucky, too."

"Thank you."

Derrick turned sympathetic eyes to her. "I want to help you, Delia. Marty would want me to. You deserve it." He drew a deep breath. "Call me if you have an emergency at any time, but right now I'm picking up Corby from basketball practice at school." He glanced at his watch.

"Derrick," she said suddenly, looking and feeling like a waif, "would it bother you if I kissed your cheek?"

Derrick looked startled. He wasn't sure what his answer to that ought to be, but he said, "Sure, go ahead. You're my sister-in-law."

Desire mingled with gall in her veins as she thought, *What I want to be is your lover.*

Derrick was still at Delia's when Ace Carter came in, talked to Melissa for a few minutes, then came to Delia and Derrick.

"Thought you'd be gone by now," Ace said to Derrick.

"Shooting the breeze," Derrick answered. "Corby would like me to be a couple of hours late picking him up from school. That boy is a hoop fanatic."

"He's a great kid." Ace looked at Delia. He wondered if

she knew she was in love with Derrick. Probably so, but
Derrick was gone on Ashley Steele.

Melissa speeded up her cleaning. If she got through before Ace left, she would offer Len some of the peach cobbler
they'd had for dinner to take home. Not that he'd ever look
her way romantically. It was plain he had his head set for
Miss Delia, and she had all the chance of a snowball in hell.

For once late that evening Delia wasn't lonely. When the
house was empty, she unlocked the door and went into the
secret room. Closing the door behind her and locking it, she
lit three fat black candles that stood in holders on the floor,
then knelt down to them. The flickering light was eerie.
There was something special she intended to do that night.

Grand-mère, the voodoo priestess, the *mambo,* had
known and taught her a lot about Welsh magic as well as
voodoo. Death dolls were one facet of that magic. *Grand-
mère* swore by them, said they were even stronger than the
spirits. Now Delia took materials from a large cloth bag,
along with a partially finished doll, and began to work on it.

She could have been an artist, she thought to herself. So
far she had fashioned a very good likeness of Ashley: expensive natural hair like Ashley's hair, long black lashes, and an
oval face. She had chosen to dye the fabric of the doll's
modeling-clay body with black walnut hulls. It had given the
doll a nearly exact replica of Ashley's skin color.

The doll had a tall, graceful body. She had bought a fancy
white silk dress in a doll boutique, a dress that looked a lot
like the ones Ashley wore onstage. She would finish the
death doll tonight. Working swiftly she began inserting pins
of death in the doll's body at strategic points: sharp pins in
the scalp, in the mostly fabric body. There was something
special she wanted to do when she had inserted all the pins.

The intricate *vévé* designs on the floor and on the lower
parts of the walls seemed to her to beckon her. They called

the spirits, helped them work their magic. A statue of a
completely black-clad black man stood in the middle of the
room, propped on a stand: Baron Samedi, god of death. Only
a white shirt broke that cloak of blackness. He wore a black
derby. Delia felt a delicious shudder course through her.
Grand-mère had been a *mambo*. Perhaps she, Delia, would
go back to New Orleans and find another *mambo* who would
teach her. But there wasn't time now. Unexpected things
were happening too fast.

In a very short while she had all the pins in place, cursing
with each pin. "Die, Ashley, die!" she said harshly. "Derrick
is mine; he will never be yours."

The death potion nearly always worked, along with the
voodoo *loa,* the spirits that blessed and when necessary
damned. More and more she felt a surging confidence.
Grand-mère had told her that confidence mattered more than
anything. The trouble was, she had too little time. In the
beginning she had wrongly thought it necessary only to cast
a spell to make Derrick love her. That was all it had taken
for Marty. Now an obstacle had to be removed. Black magic
frightened her a little, but she couldn't turn back. She knew
what she had to have.

Delia pushed the bag against the wall and got up, stamp-
ing her feet a little to stop the cramping in her legs. Snuffing
the candles, she went to the hall closet, got a heavy green
loden cloth cape, and slipped it on.

Twenty-four

Walking along the short path to Len's place, the tack house, Delia felt cold, yet curiously comfortable. As she walked along she saw Len come out his front door. He stood for a moment, looking up at the clear sky.

"Why, Miss Delia," he said cordially.

"Were you going somewhere?" she asked.

"I was thinkin' about takin' a run into town."

She reached him. "Let's go in for a moment," she said. "I need to talk to you."

"Sure." Len licked his dry lips. Did she know how beautiful she was? he wondered.

In the warm, clean room with one light left on, Len shucked his heavy overcoat. She saw then that he was nicely dressed in sporty clothes and his hair was brushed back.

She had to be careful how she put this. She wanted his cooperation; he was all she had now. "I have no right to ask you this," she said softly, "but I have to. I'm alone for the present, and I need you. Please tell me when you're going out at night. Now that Derrick is gone . . ."

"Sure, ma'am. I'd be glad to." He hesitated a long time before he continued. "After your hus— ah, Mr. Quinn passed on, Melissa stayed with you, before Mr. Derrick and Corby came."

Delia nodded. "So she did, and I may ask her again, but right now I don't especially need someone in the house with me. Just knowing you're out here is fine."

"Sure. I'll be here." He started to ask her to have a seat, but she was the boss; it was up to her to set the pace. She took off her coat.

"Is it all right with you if I visit a spell?" Her smile was charming, and his head spun with her direct, seductive gaze.

"You know it is."

Delia sat on the couch and he began to sit in a nearby chair. He had rough but perfectly decent furniture. She patted the sofa. "Sit by me. You're a handsome man, Len."

He nearly choked on that one. Did she really think so?

Her voice was warmly soothing. "Don't you know you're handsome? Don't you catch women looking at you in a certain way?"

Delia wondered what in the hell she was up to, but she gave herself permission to go ahead. She could handle Len if he got out of line, but she had to be careful. She needed him, and he was no pushover. He sat down gingerly on the couch a little distance from her.

"Do you believe in magic?" Delia smiled, holding her head to one side, studying his swarthy face, his close-cropped black hair. She rarely thought about him except when she needed him.

"Well, ah, well, my mama plumb hated what she called hoodoo. . . ."

"But you, Len, what do *you* think about it?"

He shrugged. "What little I know, it sounds like a lot of fun."

She patted his knee, and his leg caught fire from her touch. "You're right," she said, laughing. "It *is* fun. I don't think I've ever quite thought about it that way." She leaned forward. "But it's something else, Len. It's *power,* pure and simple. It's power the way most people never feel it."

"I expect it is."

"Have you ever had a spell put on you?"

Len caught his breath. He'd never thought about it. "Well, no, I don't think so."

"How would you like to know how to get whoever you want for yourself, get rid of your enemies, drive people away you don't want to be bothered with?"

Len shook his head. "I dunno. My mama always said . . ."

Delia felt his discomfort and reveled in it. She could read more easily him this way.

"You're a man now, Len. Away from your mama."

"She died a while back," he said sadly.

"Then you have to go on with your own life. Would you like me to teach you magic?"

Len looked at her with alarm. "Well, ma'am, now, I dunno. I mean—"

"Would you? Okay, don't answer right now. Think about it. You could have so much. . . ."

"I never figured I needed too much. I'm a simple man."

"You're a wonderful man. I'll keep mentioning it to you, and if you want to know magic, I'll teach you."

"Thank you, ma'am. It's really kind of you."

"No, you're the one who's kind, doing things for me. You like horses, don't you, Len?"

"Oh, Lord, yes, ma'am. Mama always said my daddy marked me buying a new horse just before I was born."

"Charming! That kind of thing is magic, too. Nature is full of magic."

"I guess."

She caught her breath as she turned to him. "I may need more pregnant goat's blood in a few days to work a spell."

"I'll get it for you."

"Do you have a hard time finding this blood?" She had never asked him before. What if he was lying to her? But she trusted him. He wouldn't dare.

"I know a man farther down in the Tidewater area. He raises goats. We grew up together, and he'd do me any favor."

"Does he question you about what you need the blood for?"

"No, ma'am, but I expect he knows. He believes in hoo— I mean magic."

"Does he ask you who you get the blood for?"

"No." It was a quick lie, because his friend asked a lot of questions. Len's face got hot when he thought about how he had told his friend he had a girlfriend who wanted the blood. His friend had laughed loudly and clapped him on the back. "Make sure she don't work no spells on *you*." He got the blood for Delia. *Girlfriend? Fat chance that will ever happen.*

He explained further, lied further: "My frien' is a man who don't pay too much attention to other folks' business. We been friends a long time."

Delia was never sure why she said the things she said to Len. She liked playing his heartstrings. "You should never get married," she said now. "Have you ever wanted to get married?"

"Once or twice. Why d'you say don't get married?"

"Because you're what they call a hunk. Pass yourself around to a lot of lucky women. Believe me, you could make them happy. Don't confine yourself to one woman. You'll hurt the rest too badly."

When he was silent she asked him, "Have you ever been hurt?"

"I been hurt."

"Were you in love with her?"

"I reckon. Ma'am, I don't want to hurt your feelings, but I feel some devil blood coming up in me when I think about that woman."

"It helps to talk about it."

"No. I jus' cain't. I could take me a gun and shoot up the world when I think about that woman. Don' try to make me talk about it, because I jus' cain't."

Startled, Delia looked at Len's countenance, which had gone unbelievably stormy. *Well,* she thought, *you never know.* A little warning bell went off inside her head. She told herself to tread carefully. Len Starkey was not a man she'd want to cross.

Looking at him with kind eyes, she told him, "I'm sorry you were hurt. All the more reason not to let it happen again. Play the field, Len. Have fun. And yes, as you said, magic is fun."

When she started to rise, Len got up, too.

"It's cold and you got on no gloves," he said. "You'll catch your death of cold."

"No. I'm tough." Stepping nearer to him, she touched his face. "You're such a good friend, and you've helped me so much. I'm going to give you the foal that was born recently."

Pleasure warmed him like the noonday sun. "Oh, ma'am, you don't need to do that."

"Yes, I do, because I'm going to need your help. Be there for me, Len, and you'll never regret it."

"You name it, you got it," he said huskily. "Only reason I'd fail you is if they put me six feet under."

"You're precious," she said, and kissed the corner of his mouth. "Please don't think I'm coming on to you. It's just that you're such a dear friend."

That kiss unnerved him, set his world on fire. He wanted to say something, tell her anything she wanted to hear, but he couldn't speak. A woman had hurt him badly, he thought, and this one could shatter him anytime she chose to work her magic.

Len walked her back to her house and saw her in.

Walking back to the tack house, Len felt alive with shivers of delight. He didn't want to go into town now, didn't want to see anyone else. He didn't let himself be fooled. He knew the score.

Although a young man in his twenties, he'd led a hard life. He thought Miss Delia was sweet on Derrick. Miss Mag had covered the countryside with her gossip. But by God, if Miss Delia wanted to use him, he was willing. He'd been used before.

And yeah, he thought, it wouldn't hurt if she taught him magic. Maybe he could get good enough at it to make her turn his way.

Once inside, Delia paused at the door of the secret room and decided against going in. *Let the Ashley doll spell work more deeply.* She thought about the larger pins she had put into the doll's head.

"Work, magic," she whispered. "Work for me!"

As she undressed in her bedroom she felt a faint chill, although the room was warm. Stroking her body, she thought of Derrick. She pulled on a red jersey nightgown and, going to the mirror, smiled at the billowing black hair about her sultry face. She was making Len love her, because that was the certain way she could get him to do things for her.

Going to her dresser, she opened a middle drawer and pulled a male doll fashioned of modeling clay from it. She looked at it a long time. It was a wonderful likeness of Derrick, even better than the Ashley doll. She held the doll against her heart and closed her eyes.

"Get used to being without her," she told the doll. "When she is gone you'll turn to me as you were turning to me after Maria died."

How fortunate, she thought, that Maria had had the accident. She had just begun to cast the spells back then. Had the spells possibly caused the accident? She shrugged.

She sat on the edge of the bed, looking down at her long, narrow feet. Ashley had swallowed the poison twice now, and Delia had a perfect excuse to lure her into ingesting more when she asked her to taste the root beer a second time. *Grand-mère* had told her that the poison nearly always killed on the third to sixth time. She was going to have to be sharp to keep Ashley from suspecting anything. *Two down.*

Crawling into bed with the doll fashioned after Derrick,

she held it close to her breasts. "Derrick," she whispered. "I love you. And you were beginning to love me, too. I could feel it. You were tender, concerned about me. You were beginning to care. Even now you're drawn to me. I can feel that, too."

Derrick belonged to her, and she would have him—no matter the cost to anyone else. She kept the light on once she was in bed with the Derrick doll beside her. "Love me," she whispered three times. No sharp pins were needed here, only caresses and murmurs of devotion. Once he was hers, he would be happier than Ashley could ever make him. "Freda Erzulie, Earth mother, goddess of love. Take me into your heart and bless me. Make him mine." She had unlimited faith in what she was doing. She was the granddaughter of a *mambo* and could not fail.

She would leave the light on so she could look at the Derrick doll. Kissing the face of the doll, she said aloud, "You will be mine, no matter what it takes."

Twenty-five

"Mom! I'm feeling great!"

In her bear-print flannel pajamas, Eleni jumped up and down on her bed as Ashley stood in the doorway.

"I'm glad, baby, but be careful you don't land on the—" Ashley's hand went to her head as excruciating pain shot through her skull. She steadied herself against the doorjamb.

Concern flooded Eleni's face as she scrambled off the bed and went to Ashley.

"Mom, what's wrong? Does something hurt?"

When Ashley couldn't answer, the child asked again, "Do you hurt?" She buried her face against Ashley's body and patted her. "It'll be all right, Mom," Eleni comforted her. "I'll take care of you."

Ashley patted Eleni's back. The pain left as quickly as it had come. "I'm okay, love," she assured the child. "Just a short pain in my head. Now what is this about your feeling so great?"

"Yay! I can go to school tomorrow."

"I don't know. It might be best for you to still stay in. I'll keep my trip with Derrick for a later weekend."

"Mom, no! We're doing research on the computer on swans tomorrow, and Dad's taking me to the zoo Saturday. Mom, I've got it all planned out. Please?"

Ashley bent and hugged her daughter tightly, feeling the steady heartbeat in the thin body.

"Okay. Okay. You've won your case. Let the defense rest."

"What does that mean? Why're you talking all funny?"

"Because I'm so glad you're feeling great, it makes me silly."

"I love you when you're silly."

"And I love you any way you happen to be. I want you to stay in today and entertain yourself. I'm mapping out my German tour and I'm going to be a bit busy."

"You went to Germany last year. Can I go next year?"

" 'May I,' and perhaps you can. How is it you don't ask to go this year?"

Eleni shrugged. "Dad's going to take me on a trip to New York while you're gone. We're going to the zoo, to museums, to see some dancers somewhere. . . ."

"The Rockettes at Rockefeller Center?"

"I think that sounds about right. I don't altogether remember. Daddy said they were high-kickers. Gee, I wish you were coming."

"What about school?" Ashley asked a bit testily. Trust Reese to take the child on a vacation right in the middle of the school year. She had to find some way around this.

"Daddy says we get education in lots of places besides school."

"I'm sure he'd know about that," Ashley muttered.

"What, Mom?"

"Nothing, sweetheart."

As the child looked at her, Ashley saw her own bright brown eyes reflected. "Daddy asked me if I hated your going to Germany."

"And?"

"I told him I was a little sad," Eleni said slowly. "Then he started telling me all the places he would take me and what we would do. Daddy's got a girlfriend—Alice. She's nice. I think she's coming with us."

Ashley felt happy for her ex. As selfish, as thoughtless as he was, he needed someone.

Dr. Smith called shortly after Ashley had fixed breakfast for herself and Eleni. They had eaten, dawdling for a long time, in spite of Ashley's having work to do.

"I'm calling a bit early," Dr. Smith said. "How are you feeling?"

Ashley collected her thoughts swiftly. "I was feeling much better. That tonic you gave me really hit the spot." She told him then about the pain in her head that morning.

"Explain it as exactly as you can."

"As though I'd been shot and you or someone had immediately anesthetized the pain."

"Have you ever had this kind of pain before?"

"I think once or twice in the past two years. Do you think it's stress?"

"It could very well be. Although your blood sugar isn't high, other symptoms make me think you could have hidden diabetes. Cut out sweets entirely. Your tests are all just fine, but I'll want to test you again in three months if all goes well.

"As for the pain in your head, I'd hazard a guess that this is an early arthritic dagger stabbing you."

"Arthritis?"

"Uh-huh. You're thinking you're too young. Not so. Stress often brings it on. Now, Ashley, if I need to ask you to cut back on your scheduling, could you do it?"

Without hesitation, she answered, "Of course I would. I've got to be here for Eleni, and I can't do it if I'm ill. I'm already on a reduced schedule because we're putting together a special world-tour package for next year that my agent and I feel will put me on top."

"So I've got your cooperation."

"Completely."

"That's good. Now if you have any more symptoms, please call me immediately. You're one of my healthiest patients and I want to keep you that way. Watch the weight. You're not harmfully over. Pay attention to the little things. Your diet and supplement regime is just fine."

Dr. Smith could picture the woman on the other end of the line. *Superfine!* He chuckled to himself. If he didn't have the wife he had, he'd go after her. Then he chuckled even harder. He had four kids and wouldn't give up a hair of any of them.

As she began to hang up he called her name and she responded. "Thinking this over," he said, "I'd like to see you about two weeks before you leave for Germany instead of the three months I mentioned. Just for safety's sake. You take care now."

With Eleni happily putting puzzles together in the living room, Ashley showered, dressed in black jeans and a heavy gray sweater, and went into her studio. She stood in the middle of the floor, feeling the peace of ages she always felt when she came in here.

The high-ceilinged walls lined with photos of the great and near-great always nourished her spirit. She paused before the specially lighted one of Aretha Franklin and shook her head. How could anyone be that superlative? Mahalia Jackson. Both incomparable. In front of Mahalia she stood with her hand over her heart in a gesture of deep respect. In front of Aretha she placed her hand over her heart with the same deep respect, then murmured, "You go, girl!"

She picked up the phone on the first ring.

"Could the beast who is Max speak to the beauty who is Ashley Steele?"

"Max, how are you?"

"I'd be better if you called me more often."

"My line is always open to you. Eleni's had a mild cold,

and I'm working hard on our plans for my world tour next year."

"That's good. I haven't pushed you this year so far, but get ready for me to keep your feet to the fire for the rest of the year."

"I'm working with you. I've dug back for very old spirituals, ones we don't hear very much now. Beautiful songs. Max, I love these spirituals."

"As I do. But my dear, don't forget that in Germany—and if all goes well in other places—we'll also be doing the operatic arias you do so grandly."

"I won't, but they're not my first priority."

"Ash, you could be among the world's top opera singers. You've got it in spades. Your natural talent and that magnificent training you got at Juilliard isn't being fully used to your advantage."

It was something Max often said. Sometimes it merely irritated her; sometimes it hurt that he didn't feel the same passion she felt for the spirituals. Oh, yes, she enjoyed classical music, but she became *one* with each spiritual she sang.

"Are you there, Ash?"

"I'm here."

"It nettles you that I don't love spirituals the way you do."

"Well, you've got your own taste."

"The spirituals go deep with me, perhaps because you sing them so superbly."

"That's sweet of you to say so."

"Well, that's my good news. The bad news is that Vintage Records has decided to put off your album release and your party celebrating same until later this spring."

"Oh. Why is that bad news? They'll still have it later."

"Most assuredly. They're giving you the best publicity, pulling out all the stops. You know they'll be giving your party on a waterfront yacht in Alexandria."

"Sounds very splashy."

"Their publicity department knows what it's all about. I'd say sometime mid-May will be the date."

"Max, wait. You know Mama and Dad always hold their May songfest in May. I won't let anything interfere with that."

Max laughed easily. "I'll see that it's a couple of weeks apart. Maybe I'll lean on them to change it to April. Disappointed?"

"Thank you. No. I'm not disappointed."

"I care about you, Ash, and I want the best for you. I mean the top of everything. Sometimes it seems to me that you settle for far too little."

"Are you trying to tell me something?" She was certain he was talking about Derrick.

"I don't have to. I think you know what I'm talking about."

Twenty-six

When Ashley came awake, she couldn't place herself for a few moments. She knew only that she was happy. In the darkened room with one window open a bit, she looked at the cold sunlight sweeping in and drew the covers more tightly around her. Then it all came at once.

She had driven down to Derrick's place with him and Corby the night before. Eleni was with her father, feeling super, and here she was. There was no sign of any pain anywhere.

Throwing the covers back, she padded over and pulled the window down, shivering a bit. Derrick had shown her the thermostat; she switched it higher.

In the lovely, big ivory bathroom that adjoined her room, she began to draw her bath, then stepped back into the bedroom to select a few garments from her bag. She could sing with happiness. *Oh, happy day!*

Derrick stood in Corby's bedroom beside the bed, gently shaking the boy awake. "Hey, sleepyhead! Are you getting up anytime today?"

Corby grinned delightedly. "I need plenty of sleep. I'm a growing boy, you know."

"Sure, I see it happening by leaps and bounds. Get dressed, boy. Clara is fixing a big, big breakfast with all your favorites—sausage, grits, eggs, and pancakes. I heard Ashley's tub running, so she'll be ready soon. Scoot!"

In one bound, the boy got up and went into the bathroom.

Derrick went to the window and closed it. Corby liked to sleep with all the windows thrown wide open.

Derrick sat on the edge of his son's bed. Lord, how good it felt to have Ashley under a roof with him. He had lain awake with heated dreams and fire scorching his loins. He had slept only toward morning. Listening to Corby's changing voice in the shower, he thought how proud Maria would be of their son. *Maria.* He had betrayed her trust. Oh, not with another woman; he had betrayed her dream. People survived horseback accidents, bad ones. A few tears stung the corners of his eyes. She might have lived if her heart hadn't been broken, if he hadn't insisted on her being what he wanted her to be instead of what she wanted to be.

One thing he knew: he would never do that to Ashley; he would die first. It was bad enough that he couldn't forgive himself for Maria's death. He refused to have Ashley's giving up her dream on his conscience.

He laughed a harsh little laugh at the last thought. Ashley Steele was a strong woman with a magnificent gift. Could he or any other man interfere with what she was doing with that gift? And, he thought with a trace of bitterness, Max Holloway would do everything he could to push her to the top. The man loved her; he wore his heart on his sleeve where she was concerned. Well, Derrick loved her, too. He put his hands to his head and groaned aloud. They had sworn to always be friends, Ashley and he, but he knew damned well friendship didn't begin to be enough. They were destined to be lovers, but what exactly was their destiny?

Corby came out with a towel wrapped around him. "You know, Dad, Mr. Whit invited me to go fishing with him this weekend. He and four other boys and men were going out on a catfish lake."

"This weekend?"

"Yeah. I didn't want to hurt your feelings about coming here."

Derrick laughed aloud with relief. His heart leaped. His

son was choosing to go somewhere with another man the son admired. He wasn't clinging frantically to him anymore, the way he had since his mother's passing.

"You like Whit a lot, don't you?"

"He's a great guy. After you, though, Dad."

Derrick pulled the boy to him and hugged him. "You get another invitation like that and you take it. It takes more than one tree to grow a forest."

"Yeah. Dad, I like them all. Are you going to marry Miss Ashley?"

Derrick laughed nervously. "I don't know. Would you like me to?"

"I'd love it. She makes a great mother."

"She'd be my wife. Think she'd be a good wife?"

"Yeah, she's super. Dad, I don't dream of Mom so much now, and when I do she's always smiling. She told me she wants you and me to be happy."

Derrick nodded, studying Corby. "I'm going to do everything I can to fulfill your mom's wishes."

Outside after breakfast, Ashley patted her stomach as she and Derrick walked over his farm. Clara, the middle-aged cook with the beaming face and salt-and-pepper hair, had urged food on them until they nearly burst. Ashley passed up the syrup and had fruit on her pancakes. The coffee was out of this world, but she chose skim milk and stevia sweetener for hers.

A stocky, barrel-chested man came to them as they stood near the barn, watching the horses being fed.

"Ashley, may I introduce you to Julian Harkett, my right arm—and for that matter, my left one."

The man laughed easily and took Ashley's gloved hand in his. "She certainly lives up to your press about her. I'm really glad to meet you, ma'am. You do justice to your photographs."

"My photographs? Oh, you mean my publicity shots."

Julian shook his head. "Those and private shots."

"I've taken shots of you," Derrick reminded her.

Ashley laughed. "Yes, but I thought you left them at home."

"Whither I go . . ."

He was looking at her as if they were alone, and she loved it.

"Derrick tells me you've been friends for a very long time," she told Julian.

"Yeah, Derrick, Marty, and I go back to childhood. We lived on adjacent farms." He grinned suddenly. "I'm glad you came along, lady. My friend is swimming in a sea of love. You're damned good for him."

"Hey, buddy, you're telling all my secrets."

"She knows, man. Women always know."

Ashley smiled. "I know no such thing. Derrick and I are the best of friends. We're very fond of each other. Now, let's go deeper for you. Is there a Mrs. Harkett?" Derrick had told her a little about his best friend.

Julian smiled ruefully and drew a deep breath. "There was, but there ain't anymore. Unlike a lot of people, it was amicable—the divorce, I mean. No children, to my sorrow."

"You've got lots of time."

"And he's wined and dined lots of women," Derrick teased.

"They just don't take my case," Julian said sadly.

"I'm racking my brain," Ashley assured him. She and Derrick looked at each other and chortled as one. "Annice!"

"Who's that?" Julian demanded.

Ashley grinned. "Someone I know."

A wide smile spread across Derrick's face. Corby came across the yard and joined them. "Here, sport, I'll need your help," Julian said to him. "We only have a few groups scheduled today. Next Wednesday we're crushed." He glanced at his watch. "Eight forty-five. Our first group is at ten-thirty."

Proudly Derrick took Ashley around, showing off his spread, introducing her to the workers. Animals of every description were everywhere.

"I think you said you have five hundred acres?"

"A little more. Like it?"

"I love it." Across from them, two awkward emus watched them steadily. White-pink, black-spotted, and red, sleek pigs and hogs wallowed in their pond.

"How many different kinds of animals and birds do you have here?"

"Oh, Lord, about fifty different types. I'm thinking about cutting some out. Help's getting harder to hire."

In the near distance the rolling Chesapeake Bay spread out before them, and at the foot of Derrick's land a yacht was anchored.

"I'd certainly be a boat person if I lived here."

"That's my boat down there."

"You own a yacht?"

"A small one."

"No matter. Derrick, you're wealthy, aren't you?"

"Does it matter to you? I can take care of you. Of course, if you're going to be the twenty-first-century Mahalia Jackson, I may be hard-pressed. Do you require more than three minks?"

"I don't require any."

"Tomorrow I'll take you to look the yacht over—or maybe this afternoon. I try to give Julian what help I can. I've practically deserted him to help Delia, who isn't easy to help."

"She's still been perfectly pleasant to me lately."

"To me as well. I guess moving out was best after all. Subject change, please. I'm feeling too good to ruin it with thoughts of Delia. You raved over that sausage this morning."

"It was beyond merely good. Best sausage I've ever eaten."

He took her gloved hand and squeezed it. "I'm putting it on the market next spring. It's getting raves all over this neck of the woods. I picked up a master's a couple of years back and I'm going for more training in marketing."

"You're going to be a very rich man yet."

"I'm not doing badly now, but then I'm playing the alpha male with you and bragging."

"Brag on. You deserve it."

In her bright red turtleneck sweater, with her black suede, fleece-lined coat keeping her warm, Ashley felt a flood of joy course through her.

With a small jerk of his head, Derrick told her, "Follow me. I've got something special to show you."

They walked past sleek horses, ponies, cows, geese and ducks, and a pond with several black swans and a few white ones floating beautifully. Another pond lay farther on. "We grow catfish there," Derrick said. "That's one of many things you'll get for dinner tonight."

The land rolled gently, with a mountain range in the distance. "If only we could think when we're worn and beaten down with pain that better days will come," she said. "Splendid days will come."

Derrick listened to her beautiful voice and loved everything about her.

Finally he paused in front of a small fieldstone house with a fence around it. Taking out a key, he let them in. To her surprise, there was a banked fire in the fireplace. Taking the poker, Derrick stoked it.

"Does someone live here?" she asked. "This is a lovely place."

"I'm glad you like it, because it's becoming another haven for me. It's special to me, so I want it to be special to you."

A huge brown bearskin rug lay in front of the fire. Brown leather couches and chairs were set about. Bookcases lined the walls. She looked at the titles; nearly all had to do with business.

"Where do you find the time to read all these?"

"When I'm here I make time. Ashley"—his voice went husky—"I'll be coming back home at least by June. I'll have to insist that Delia make up her mind. I can't stay away any longer. I'm needed here. She'll probably sell. I'm advising that."

"I think that's best. You're very kind."

He helped her with her coat, then removed his own and threw them both over the back of a chair.

"I think I told you that Marty asked me to look after her. He was on his deathbed; I couldn't refuse him. He loved her so, and she loved him. She still worships him."

Ashley thought that yes, Delia probably had loved her husband, but she didn't feel that the woman had given up on Derrick. But perhaps she had. People changed, saw the light.

In the midst of all his happiness, Derrick felt a surge of sadness sweep through him. His son was growing up and he needed a mother, as he, Derrick needed a wife. How could it happen when Ashley was anchored fast in his bloodstream and he could never be free of her, nor did he want to be?

They sat on the bearskin rug looking at the dancing flames. "I want to bring you back here tonight," he said. "I want us to make love to each other. Oh, God, Ash, if I only had words to tell you. There could be everything between us, and Corby adores you, too."

"I'm all for him. But, sweetheart, we have to tread carefully. We have differences, you and I. I want to sing, Derrick. I've *got* to sing. Every day the feeling grows stronger; there's a world out there, and I've got a message for it. Spirituals are my lifeblood, and I've got to sing them. I love the hustle and bustle, the hoopla, the crowds. I think I could never give it up."

"You once said you wanted to teach, to train."

She closed her eyes. "And that will come many, many years from now."

He drew her to him, crushing her body to him, and smoothed her hair. His mouth on hers was bruising, punishing with love and desire. "You are mine," he whispered. *"Be mine."*

She heard a voice within her, not speaking of her own volition, say "Yes, I am yours."

Twenty-seven

It was after nine when Derrick brought Ashley back to the tack house. Flames leaped in the fieldstone fireplace. A big crystal vase of roses sat on an end table, and their perfume filled the air. A magnum of champagne sat in an ice bucket to one side of the couch.

"Compliments of Julian, the romantic," he told her. "There's a smaller unchilled bottle if this one is too cold. You like cool champagne. I aim to please."

He had asked her to wear a short skirt under her long, heavy coat and she had. Now she asked him why he had requested this as he helped her take off her coat.

He shrugged and didn't answer until he had removed his coat; then he turned to her, his eyes narrowed as he studied her legs.

"Those legs are enough to drive a sane man crazy."

Ashley laughed explosively. Dressed in a wool-lined black leather skirt and an ivory cashmere sweater that set off her allspice-brown skin, she felt alive and well, basking in his compliments.

"They're just legs."

"They make my knees weak. I'm glad you wear pants and long skirts a lot. I need to be functional most of the time."

"I think the man likes me," she teased.

"Multiply that many times over and you're right."

He'd bet she had little idea how she affected him. She knew he liked her, but for him that was just the tip of the iceberg. She nestled in his heart like a brown dove, and he wanted her to stay there forever.

A light, cold rain had begun to fall, beating against the windowpanes as if demanding to be let in.

She curled up on the deep, tan sofa as he poured them champagne. Her breasts in the powder-soft cashmere seemed to beg for his attention. Sitting beside her, he lifted his champagne flute and made a toast.

"I have only one toast, a Spanish proverb," he said. "I've told you before. Health and wealth and wisdom, and time to enjoy them all."

"I like that," she said, "I have to add 'deep love, long love.' "

"Where does that come from? I like it."

"My heart."

"Good toast. Is the champagne too cold?"

"It's perfect, but are you sure you like it this way?"

"I've come to like cool champagne very much."

"I'm glad. It's something else to share."

Suddenly something crossed her mind and she frowned.

"What is it?"

"How is Corby taking it that you're spending so much of your time with me?"

Derrick laughed. "It seems he's adopted your whole family. He's waiting for a chance to go fishing with Whit. He's stopped clinging so hard to me. As for you . . . well, he'd marry you tomorrow."

Ashley laughed delightedly. "I love him, and he knows it."

"You bet he does."

Putting his glass down, he spread his hand over the breast nearest him. "I want to feel them under me, in my mouth, tasting all that sweetness. Ash, the few times we've made love, I've been nearly crazy. I *dream* of ecstasy with you, but with you it simply is real."

"I know. That's the way I feel."

"I've wondered: having your music, I've thought you probably don't need a lot more. Love, yes, but . . ."

"With you, I get much more than love. I get rapture."

"So do I. But where are we going?"

"To the heights again, and soon. Tonight."

"I mean something much longer than that, something more lasting."

"Where do you want us to go?"

"All the way to the top and forever. Babies. At least one between us. Lovemaking that just gets better. You believing in me—and God knows I believe in you."

"That's good. You've helped me get over Reese. What about Maria? You spoke of secret feelings. Guilt."

Pain lanced his heart then. It was time to talk about it. She set her empty flute down; his already sat on the table. Now he took her hand, pulled her up, and guided her to the tall windows. Opening the drapes and blinds, they looked out at the cloud-laden sky. It was so dark, she thought, no stars. To her it seemed they were sealed in with each other.

Derrick caught her to him hungrily. It was time, he thought, to let her know what was in his heart.

"I wanted to stand close to you when I told you this. I do feel guilty. Maybe I should." His face was grave.

"I'm listening. You could never do a bad thing to someone knowingly."

He caught her hands in his, and the two of them were outlined against the windows. Nature, he thought, was mirroring his own cloudy thoughts tonight. His passion for the woman he stood with raged inside him, but the guilt raged inside him, too. Would she understand?

He began then, holding her hands cupped in his as if for needed support. "The night before Maria died, we quarreled bitterly. She told me she was going to travel more, expand her share of this place. I didn't mind her expanding, but I didn't want her to travel so much. Can you understand that?"

"Yes."

"I was furious because she didn't seem to listen to me at all. Corby was spending the night with a friend, so we were alone. 'I need a life of my own,' she yelled at me, and I yelled back, 'If you do, maybe you need it with another man.'

"She asked me if that meant we were finished. I said I wouldn't go on like this. I actually said she had to make a choice. I can't believe I was so cold, but I thought we'd get a chance to talk again about it, and soon."

"But it didn't happen that way," Ashley said gently, longing to draw his head down onto her breasts.

"No. The next morning she was still furious with me. She was training a group several miles down the road. I can imagine the mood she must have been in. The woman who owned the centered riding stable where she was training students came to me around noon. A horse had thrown Maria and she had died on the way to the hospital. I never got the chance to talk with her again."

"My God. I'm so sorry."

"So am I. I've beaten my psychic hide relentlessly. The guilt just doesn't go away."

"Do you believe in God, Derrick?"

"Yes, deeply."

"Don't you know God forgives you? You were wrong, and you know you were wrong. But you both should have listened, tried to work it out. Think about it, Derrick; a year or so ago you were younger, and the young can be blind."

"Twenty-nine isn't so young."

"It can be for some people. You've always been wrapped up in your business. You didn't really take time to think deeply about a relationship. Maria was busy, too. Raising Corby took time." She paused a long time before she said, "I believe in redemption. Do you?"

"I hope I do."

"Then do what God would want you to do and forgive

yourself. You won't do it all at once, but you must—for your son's sake and for your sake."

Her face was like a madonna's turned up to his, and he kissed her hard, then roved over her face with his open mouth. Her skin tasted like the elixir of love. He couldn't stop, nor did she try to stop him.

"Thank you," he whispered huskily. "I'm going to make it."

"You bet you are."

He closed the blinds and drew the drapes then. Going to the fireplace, he put up a screen that covered it completely. Coming to where she stood by the sofa, he helped her undress; then she helped him.

Naked in the warm room, he caught her to him and pressed her voluptuous, yielding body to his rock-hard one. Rising mightily against her, he probed the depths of her open mouth, then held her tightly as his mouth traveled over her face, her throat, her breasts.

She could only murmur, "Derrick, my love. How I want you."

He felt wild with wanting her. Flames danced in his body the way flames danced in the fireplace. Lifting her, he held her in his arms for a long while, then placed her gently on her back on the big bearskin rug. Bending over her, he swept her body with kisses from her scalp to her toes. Kissing her beautifully manicured feet, he held them to his cheeks. The simple gesture set her on fire, and she moaned deep in her throat. "Derrick, please."

He reached out to the table behind them and got a foil packet, opened it and slid on a thin latex shield, then lay back down. He teased her to slow himself. "Show me you want me. Beg me."

She beat his chest with tender fists. "Oh, you nut. Keep doing what you're doing and I'll be no good to you."

He poised above her then and entered the blazing, nectared sheath of her body. Wrapping her legs around his back, she gave him deeper entrance, then cried out in rapture as they climbed the heights together—natural and altogether wonderful.

They lay spent, blissfully touching each other.

"We're really good together," Ashley said huskily.

"We're way better than good. We're phenomenal." He took the tips of her fingers in his mouth and nibbled them. Kissing her palms, he then let his tongue begin patterning kisses up her arms. Then he rolled over and began to get up.

"Running away?"

"Purposeful running." He went to the end table and opened a drawer. Crossing the room, he brought back a two-pound box of Belgian chocolates.

"I'll let you open them," he said.

"Derrick, thank you so much, but I can't eat them. I told you I may be becoming a diabetic. I don't want to take chances."

"They're for diabetics. I wouldn't forget that."

Ashley took a rounded piece from the box and popped it into her mouth. It was dark cherry and delicious.

"Like them?" he asked her.

"Love them. I'd say the makers are chocolatiers to kings."

"And a queen." He leaned forward and ravished her mouth, which now tasted like chocolate and cream. Her heart and soul surged toward him, claiming him for her own.

Getting up again, he went into the kitchen and to the stove. On the back burner, keeping warm, were small sandwiches of sliced chicken, ham, and roast beef, all spiced with brown mustard. Putting a number of sandwiches on a napkin-covered plate, he took it back to Ashley.

"Oh, honey, we ate at six, but . . ." She rolled her eyes comically. "You know I am a bit hungry . . . just a little."

"We burned off a lot of energy in a little while. Best exercise in the world."

"Agreement here." He was looking at her hungrily again, and she blushed. Well, she thought, she was looking at *him* hungrily again. She ate just two of the smaller sandwiches. He ate more, and they each drank another glass of champagne.

"This cool champagne grows on you."

"Are you trying to get me drunk?" she teased him.

"No way. I like the way you operate when you're sober too much."

He got up again. "You're restless tonight," she said.

"Last time, but this trip is necessary."

He went to the crystal vase and selected three roses from the two dozen or so. Getting an envelope from the end table drawer, he stripped the petals from the roses, put them in the envelope, and brought them back. Kneeling, he scattered the petals over her, bruising some onto her body.

Laughing, she asked him, "Oh, good Lord, what are you doing to me?"

"Leading you astray. Tell me you don't like it."

"I won't lie. I love it." The path of fire was circling them again, binding them. This time they were slower, measured. She felt his tumescence and gloried in receiving it within her body. He throbbed like a massive heartbeat, and she felt his heart beat hard against her own.

They were like swimmers traversing lazy, warm waters. He cupped her face in his hands and kissed her, blotting out the world. Silent now, they moved in unison, rhythmic strokes, glory in action. After one long stroke, he rolled her over on top of him and entered the warmth of her body again, shuddering with delight.

"I love you," he whispered. "Love you. Love you."

Placing her hands alongside his face, she drew him to her open lips, where her tongue ran over the outlines of his wickedly sensual mouth. *Glory days!* she thought. "I wish this could last forever," she murmured.

"Next best thing is to get it again and again," he said, laughing.

She arched above him, her hair swinging around her face as his movements shifted her.

"You didn't say you loved me when I said I love you."

Touching her tongue to the corner of his mouth, she told him, "Because I don't just love you. I *adore* you."

"And I adore you. Ash, we've got to find some way to build a life together."

Waves of steam heated ecstasy fused them now. Inside her, he felt exalted, and holding him deep within her she felt she had the best life had to offer.

They were together a long time in the soft rose light. The logs were burning down and the champagne bubbled merrily in their blood. With one smooth, long thrust he felt tidal wave–strength tremors rush through his body. And lying beneath him she felt the rhythmic trembling of her body as they both lay spent, swept onto nature's blessed shores that had no beginning and no end.

Twenty-eight

It was one in the morning when Derrick and Ashley walked back to the main house hand in hand. The night had cleared, and clusters of twinkling stars hung in the still, damp air.

"I love the earth, nature," Ashley said softly.

"So do I. Sometimes you wonder how anything could be so beautiful."

She laughed a little. "When I was a teenager and my parents seemed impossible in not letting me have my way, I used to say I loved nature but didn't always like people."

"Oh? Teenagers have a rough time of it. Still feel that way?" he teased her.

Ashley's laughter pealed on the night air. "No. People are just like nature; I think I've figured that out. Nature is kind, wonderful, with her star- and moonlit heavens, oceans, gorgeous plants and flowers, and oh so many other things. But she can be really cruel with her storms and hurricanes, poisonous insects, vicious animals. . . ."

"We have to take it as it comes."

"Yes. I hate to go in. I'd like to stay out here all night."

"One day soon we'll do just that."

"Mmmm. I'll look forward to it. Derrick, you were wonderful tonight."

He stopped and turned to her, then hugged her body in her greatcoat, and covered her face with small kisses. Then his mouth fastened on her open lips and his tongue slipped inside for a few moments.

Raising his head, he sighed. "Making love with you is what I've dreamed of," he told her. "We're going to have to find a way to stay together, because I cannot do without you."

Ashley thrilled to his words, and her heart raced as she kissed his leathery throat.

Inside the house he took her hand and led her down the corridor, past closed doors and people sleeping.

"I want to show you something," he said.

He opened the door of a medium-sized darkened room, where he stood silent for a little while.

"What is it?" she asked.

He switched on the table lamp and she blinked to get accustomed to the light.

"Look around you."

She did as he requested and gasped with surprise as he held her elbow. The table was covered with her CDs, her albums, with photos of her.

"Don't talk," he said. "Look around."

She walked around slowly. There were books in the bookshelves about gospel music—many books. Photos of other gospel singers were there, deceased ones and those still singing their hearts out.

She stood before a large photo of Mahalia Jackson, another of the Clara Ward and the Ward Singers, and still another of Aretha Franklin.

"I'm just getting started," he said. "Look at the CD and cassette shelves of the entertainment center. I think I've got every record you ever made. I've always been fond of gospel music. I've learned a lot more than I knew since I met you. . . ."

Her hand swept out. "But all this . . . the time it must have taken . . ."

"I did it a bit at a time. Julian helped. He's got a bug for gospel music. His father sang with a gospel quartet."

She picked up a recent book on gospel songs, put it back, and picked up another very old book by James Weldon Johnson. Just holding it made her feel close to her gospel origins. Things were so different then. But her forbears had been resourceful; they had had unlimited hope. They had been close to God and the angels.

"Derrick," she said softly. "Thank you. You're becoming a man with a mission."

He shook his head and took her hands in his. "I've become a man in love," he said.

They slept late, and after brunch Corby had come in from riding. In the big kitchen, they sat at the flower print–covered heavy oak table after eating Clara's waffles, sprinkled with cheese, sausage, and bacon bits. Ashley had poured herself a second small glass of orange juice as Corby came racing in.

"Did you see me ride?" he demanded of Ashley.

"Yes," she told him. "You ride beautifully, but then I've seen you ride before and complimented you."

"That's my special horse, Jupiter," he said. "He's been at the vet's a few days. Julian brought him home this morning." Corby shrugged. "I guess he's not as beautiful as Black Steed, but he's mine."

"Don't compare what you have with what others have," Derrick said easily. "There's plenty of room in the world for everything that is."

"Okay, Dad. I read you."

Buses began pulling into the far side parking lot around eleven-thirty. Julian and two other men went out to greet them. Before he left, Julian told Derrick, "I think we can handle everything. You take care of Ashley." Eyes twinkling, he told her, "You're good for my buddy. It's been a long time."

"How kind of you to say so." His eyes on her were warmly complimentary.

In his study, Derrick and Ashley talked. "You've got a large spread here. I knew you were successful. I just didn't know how successful you are."

"I do well. I could take care of you, even as Ashley Steele, stellar rising gospel singer."

Ashley blushed. "That wouldn't require a great deal."

"It would, you know."

Derrick picked up the phone on the first ring as Ashley tried not to listen.

"Have you called the vet?" he asked after a moment.

Was it Delia calling? Derrick's voice was cool, even.

"Yes, I can believe it's serious, Delia, but I'm not going to be able to get back early. We'll be back by noon tomorrow. Len's wonderful with the horses. You can reach Ace. Lean on him. He'll like that."

He listened a minute or two then and seemed more annoyed. Finally he said, "Tell you what, *I'll* call Trask and talk with him. He may not be able to get there immediately. He's a good guy, and people sometimes take advantage of him. You call him, too, and I'll back you up—and don't forget about Len. I'm going to be out a lot today, so you might not be able to reach me."

In a moment he said good-bye and hung up the phone, turning to Ashley. "She's upset again over a limping horse I think she's going to have to sell. The horse is great with children, but he keeps developing hamstring trouble. Delia goes to pieces when there's nothing to get upset about. The more I know her, the more I feel she should sell out and just choose something else she wants to do."

He expelled a harsh breath. "It takes passion to run a

good business, and she's not passionate about it the way Marty was."

Ashley smiled a bit grimly, thinking that Delia's passions these days were all wrapped up in Derrick, even though she was hiding it. She shrugged. "I don't know how she's going to make it after you're gone."

"She can. She didn't need to call me with Ace available. He's top-drawer. Of course, he's building up a place of his own over in Maryland. But he's offered to handle her spread for a long time. She keeps quibbling."

"I hate to think of your not being next door to me, coming back here to stay, as much as I like this place."

"You could come—" He broke off, grinning. "I won't pressure you." Then he added, "Not now, at any rate."

"You look a bit bothered," Derrick commented after he hung up.

"I'm thinking about Eleni." She had talked with Derrick about her unhappiness over the things Reese insisted on letting her eat. "He's livid over the fact that I'll be traveling more and he keeps hitting me with it."

They sat on a love seat and Derrick reached for her hand, squeezing it. "Anything I can do to help, let me know. You're the best of mothers, Ash. Believe in yourself completely."

Looking at her now, his heart hurt with longing. But he was here on his beloved ranch, scene of the worst failure in his life: his marriage to Maria. He didn't trust himself to love another woman, not to hurt another woman. He was torn up with wanting and needing this woman. It was Maria and their debacle all over again.

"Now *you* look bothered," Ashley said, pressing his hand.

He put a hand on her knee and a small thrill coursed along her spine. "Yes," he said evenly, "I *am* bothered. About us and where we're headed. Work and pray hard, Ash, as I am working and praying hard—for us. We've got to find a way."

* * *

Derrick and Ashley walked along paths that led to deep woods. They passed the section that held the animals, the large man-made lake with its black and white swans, two more large ponds, the usual cows, pigs, horses, and chickens. There was a large aviary filled with brightly colored, twittering birds. Then there were the exotic emus and ostriches. Squealing children watched and came with an adult to touch them. Julian and two other men shepherded the children with their parents in attendance.

There were fences and open spaces. Ashley thought it was one of the most beautiful places she had ever seen. It reminded her of the splendid farms of Switzerland and France.

As they walked toward the crowds watching the birds and animals, Ashley laughed delightedly. "I don't wonder you're in a hurry to get back here." A big ostrich looked at them sideways and seemed to flirt with them. An emu walked haughtily away.

They walked among the crowd, greeting them and chatting. Suddenly a girl of fifteen or so studied Ashley and burst out, "Ma'am, I don't mean to meddle, but you look just like Ashley Steele."

Derrick cocked his head to one side. "Do you like Ashley Steele?"

"Yes!" the girl exclaimed. "She's about my favorite. I love gospel music. Love me some Ashley Steele. I've got all her CDs and tapes."

Ashley touched the girl's silken brown face. "I *am* Ashley Steele," she said, "and who are you?"

"Katie Walker," the girl said, hardly breathing with excitement.

Ashley held out her hand. "I'm so glad to meet you."

The girl seemed delirious and about to faint. Suddenly she turned back to the crowd she was with, who had watched her, and called out, "This lady is Ashley Steele, you all. *Ashley Steele!*"

They thronged about her then, shaking hands, asking for her autograph. Most of them had no paper with them. The girl, Katie, asked her to autograph her tan cap, and others followed suit with jackets and other articles. A smiling man gave her his Sunday paper to write on. They pressed in on her, complimenting her, asking her to sing.

Quite humbly Katie said, "If you could sing for us now, it would be one of the greatest things you ever did. You see that big, tall man in the gray cap? That's my father, and he loves you, too."

Derrick looked at her and smiled. "Feel up to it?"

"I feel up to anything," she answered.

The sun shone brightly now, and the day was warming. Ashley pushed the knitted scarf back from her face and hair.

"How about 'Amazing Grace'?" she called out.

"Sing it, lady!" a man's voice called back, and others took up the cry. She saw Julian then with Corby and the other men who worked for Derrick. Corby looked enthralled, proud.

So she began, "Amazing grace, how sweet the sound . . ."

She closed her eyes as the wonderful music poured from her lovely throat. She sang to Derrick, who stood beside her bathed in her melody, and for her audience whom she loved—not the way she loved Derrick, but loved neverthe-less.

"Beautiful," Derrick murmured in a brief lull. "Amazing *you.*"

The crowd was rapt, listening. When she had finished the last verse, she called to them, "Sing it with me!"

And they did sing it with her. In the crisp winter air, there were no sinners, only the saved.

When she had finished, they surged around her, glowing with goodwill. She talked with them singly and in groups. Then Derrick's hand was on her elbow, and he said they needed to go in. He pulled the long scarf back onto her head. "We have to protect this gorgeous voice," he said to the crowd. "She's got to go in now."

They let her go as easily as they had held on to her and her music.

Walking back to the house, she laughed, excited now. "I was going to sing another song."

"No," he said. "It's still cold and it's a bit damp. I'm protecting your voice." Then he said ruefully, "I'm protecting your voice so you can travel away from me."

"Thank you, as I thank you for so much."

They stopped then, and Derrick turned to her. "Know this, my darling: I will always protect you. Always."

Twenty-nine

Ashley woke up happy the following Tuesday morning. Dressing to go to school, Eleni stood on one foot and looked at her. "Gee, Mom, you look pretty in that robe."

"And you look pretty in your yellow snuggies. Now get a move on. The bus will be here before you know it."

"May I have waffles for breakfast?"

"Yes, if you hurry."

Eleni came to her and hugged her around the waist. "If you and Uncle Derrick got married, he could be my daddy, too."

Ashley laughed. "Would you like that? Not that it's going to happen, at least not anytime soon."

"I'd *love* that. He's a neat man."

Derrick had brought Eleni a dozen gold-painted pinecones from the area, and she had taken a few to school for show-and-tell.

Ashley looked at her daughter fondly. She was sure Reese had something in mind, but what? Sighing, she went out into the kitchen, smoothing the blue trapunto-quilted robe Eleni had admired.

She had an eleven-o'clock appointment with Mick Chancellor to record several spiritual singles and the operatic arias that would be released for summer. She was always happy to see Mick, who knew so much about music and how to bring out the best in an artist.

She didn't particularly feel like seeing Max. He was

pressing her more and more. If she didn't have the voice he always praised as "magnificent," would he want her? What if she were not Ashley Steele and headed up? She felt he wanted not her, but merely the glory she could bring him. Somberly she rethought her feelings. No, he cared about her a lot. But Max was sophisticated, suave. Once he realized that she belonged to somebody else, he would get over her easily. He had been good for her career and she had been even better for his. Derrick was another matter. Sitting across from Eleni, drinking coffee, Ashley had only to think about the weekend Derrick and she had just spent together to thrill to her very soul.

"Mom, you're smiling so great."

"Yes, baby. I'm smiling so great. You said it earlier; your Mom is very happy."

Getting up, she had shepherded Eleni into her room and into her outer winter clothes only a few minutes before the school bus horn blew. She pressed the thin, bundled child to her closely. "Minnie will be here when you come back from school," she told her, "but I'll be back just a little later."

"Sure. Minnie always gives me something special."

She was out the door then, and Ashley reflected with a lump in her throat that the child herself was everything that was special.

Ashley had drawn her bath and laid out the baggy old clothes she would wear to record when the door chimes sounded. With deep irritation she wondered why Max always came so early. Looking out the door viewer, she was surprised to see Delia standing there. Delia knew enough to call before coming over. Why hadn't she? She carried a bag with her.

"Invite me in for only a moment and I'll be out of your hair."

"Well, come in, but I am getting ready for an appointment."

Delia looked at Ashley in the flattering robe and felt a sharp pang of envy. "The life you lead makes the lives of the rest of us seem drab."

Ashley shrugged. "There's always something particular that a person wants to do. Find out what it is and voilà!, at least a certain amount of happiness. Is this something else you want me to taste?"

"How did you guess?"

"Then let's go back to the kitchen. That's my tasting lab."

As she followed her, Delia's eyes narrowed. This would be the third time Ashley had ingested the potion. Would it work, or was she one of the ones who built up a quick tolerance for the poison? Delia felt so tightly wound that she thought she might snap. She handed the bag to Ashley, and Ashley took out the now familiar red thermos and opened it.

"See, I even brought a plastic cup so I wouldn't put you to any unnecessary trouble."

"That was thoughtful." Pouring out a full measure, Ashley sipped the cold liquid, rolling it around on her tongue, then drank the rest. She took a deep breath as Delia exulted. Would the third time be the charm?

"My girl, you've hit the jackpot," Ashley told her. "This is really good."

"I added a lot more sugar, and let it sit longer. Ashley, I can't thank you enough. I'm going to serve it at the May Songfest. My small contribution. Thank you for being such a sweetie."

"No problem. You seem pretty contented these days."

Delia nodded. "I am," she said quietly, but inside she was jumping for joy. She admired the way she was keeping her cool these days. No one could possibly know that the woman she stood before, smiling, friendly, was someone she meant to hurt.

Delia paused. "Bear with me a minute longer. Be honest

with me, Ashley. Has Derrick forgiven me for what he must have felt was my coming on to him?"

Gently Ashley told her, "I can't speak for Derrick, but I know he's a forgiving person."

"I'm sure you know I called him while you two were away. I was worried about one of the horses." She sighed. "Marty always said I worry too much about every little thing. Ace came from over in Maryland on his day off. It wasn't a lethal cut the horse got from getting entangled in fencing wire, but it could have crippled him."

"But you got through it?"

"Yes. Ace took care of it. He decided not to call the vet. I'm sorry I called Derrick. I really am. It's just that I don't always know what to do. I depended on Marty."

Deep inside, Delia wondered if her act was good enough: the widow hurting, longing for her mate. She was a good actress, and had given stellar performances in her college plays.

Finally Ashley said quietly, "You can't go on feeling you're doing everything wrong. I'd say Derrick understands. Give him credit. Now I've got to get started."

"I can't thank you enough." Outside, Delia was all charm and pleasantness. Inside, the storm clouds pressed on her brain and icicles of rage chilled her. How long could this continue? she wondered, then thought: *Derrick's love is worth the time, worth the effort, well worth the trouble.*

Max came shortly after Delia left. Ashley never stopped admiring his smooth grooming, his suave demeanor. Today he wore a steel gray suit by a Savile Row tailor, highly polished tasseled black loafers, and a pale gray shirt. His tie was a work of art—red, gold, dark red, and light gray coin dots of different sizes.

"How spiffy you look," she told him, offering her cheek for his kiss.

"I see I'm too early again."

"You mean I'm not dressed. This is what I'm wearing."

Max looked at her carefully, gauging what he would say. "Ash, you're too beautiful a woman to go about looking like that. You have an audience to please. . . ."

"Well, I don't think I'll be seeing many fans behind the tinted windows of the limousine and at Mick's studio. I like being natural sometimes, Max. You know that."

"Lord, how can I tell you how much I want you to do justice to yourself? The rest of this year is a crucial one for you, and next year is more so. Lady, I've got great things lined up for us."

Ashley laughed, teasing him. "Yes, sir, Mr. Holloway, but could I take your hat and coat?"

Max shook his head. "We've got to get moving."

"Can I get you anything to drink? Coffee with brandy?"

"No, but I do thank you. You say you're ready. I've got to be back at the airport by midafternoon and I want to hear as much of the recording as I can."

Mick Chancellor stood at the door of his gray stone house waiting for them. His ruddy face brightened as they drove up. They had picked up Ashley's piano accompanist and the Davis Gospel Singers. Mick came out to the limousine.

"You're early," he said, "and that makes me happy. I've got a lot of plans for this session."

Inside the studio the temperature was perfect, the way Mick kept it for recording.

The group practiced together for a while before Mick said, "I'm going to record the gospel music first; then those not involved in the operatic arias don't have to stay."

"I think we all want to listen," Max said. "We're a close-knit group. We're not all classically trained the way Ashley is, but we've all got a great ear for music."

"Sure thing," Mick agreed. "I like looking at it that way."

As he always did, Mick demanded absolute quiet then. All electricity was cut off so no electrical hum could disturb the sound. Everything was battery operated, with specially made batteries.

They began with "Deep River," and Ashley swept into the song.

> Deep River, my home is over Jordan.
> Deep River. I want to cross over
> into campground.

As she sang it with guitars moaning, the tambourines and the piano thrumming, Mick felt warm tears come to his eyes. He was a dour man who had known too little joy. *His* home, he thought now, was over Jordan, and *he* wanted to cross over into campground. His wife, Sileia, had brought him untold happiness, but this music touched the pain he had known all his life.

Sitting on the bay window seat, Max folded his arms over his chest and simply listened. He reflected that the recordings Mick made had contributed greatly to Ashley's success. He hoped one day to make her come to her senses in her life as well as in her music. She could be better than most of the others—as good, if not better, than the top few.

The gospel music recording went swiftly. "Are you tired?" Mick asked them. No one was.

"I have a favor to ask," Mick said. "I want to record just the group without Ashley. Could I settle you in another room to rest, even if you aren't tired?" he asked her.

"Certainly," Ashley said.

Max stood up. "May I come with you?"

At the moment Ashley wanted to be alone, but she nodded okay.

They sat in a small sitting room. Sileia brought them hot apple cider with cinnamon sticks. "Your days are blessed," she said to Ashley. "I can tell. Come to see us when you are not recording. I always remember you are a friend of Gina Campbell."

"I will," Ashley answered, liking the tall, slender Tahitian woman.

The warm mug felt good in her hands. Max turned to her as they sat on the sofa.

"I wanted to come with you because I want to ask you to begin thinking hard, Ash, long and hard and often. You've got one of the greatest voices, one of the greatest futures ahead of you I've ever witnessed—and I've witnessed a few. But it requires collaboration from you. You've got to be free to travel, to perform, often when you'd rather be home."

She mulled over his declaration before she said slowly, "I want Eleni to be old enough to withstand my being away."

"She has her father."

"She has me." She had never discussed Reese with Max, but he had gleaned much from the divorce and had always offered to help in any way he could.

"Of course she has. We can work it out. Please choose the fame and fortune that are swiftly beginning to come your way. Ward Kaye has heard you sing and is interested in taking you under his wing. That would mean the blessing of angels. Think what you could give to Eleni then. You have suddenly come into your own. Strike while the iron is hot. Your last album went only a bit below double platinum. This one could go triple."

"Always I thank you, Max, for what you do for me. Eleni already has everything she needs"—she paused—"except a full-time father."

Max stiffened when she said the word *father,* because he thought about Derrick Quinn. Max had little wish to be a father, but he could tolerate the child to have Ashley for his own. *Ah, Quinn,* he thought, the one fault in a wondrous plan he was unfolding.

Thirty

It was a warm day for March, so Ashley chose to ride Black Steed. This time she saddled up. King Johnson saw her and came to the fence.

"Need help?"

"No. I managed. How is everyone this morning?"

"Well, Whit's in New York, and Neesie took a brief trip down to Richmond. Your mama and daddy couldn't be better."

"What about you? Minnie?"

King laughed. "I'm fine, and Miss Minnow is as ornery as ever."

Ashley made a face. "Keep trying, King. Trying is the water that wears the rock down."

"Oh, she's a rock all right. A sweet little old rock. Well, I got to be getting back. You coming over today?"

"I don't think I'll have time. I'm going away, you know, and I've got a lot of things to do."

"Going to Germany?"

"Yes. I wish I could take you all with me."

He sounded wistful. "I've always wanted to travel some more. I was in the merchant marines, you know, and the only reason I'm out is I fell under the weather. Then I met Minnie. She don't have no mind for travel, so I gave it up."

"She's got to marry you one day. We'll work something out."

"And I'll be your slave for life." King laughed then, long and happily, then started back to Frank and Caroline's.

The horse's sides felt good under her legs. The saddle was expensive burnished black leather. Going toward the woods, she paced the horse, liking the feel of his smooth muscles beneath her pants and his black raw-silk mane. She slowed as she saw Delia come down the hill.

"Can you ride to the fence?" Delia called.

Ashley did as she asked, and dismounted at the fence.

Delia blushed. "Oh, I didn't want to put you to the trouble to get down. I just wanted to say hello."

"Anything special going on?" Ashley asked her.

"How are you feeling these days?" Delia countered. "You must be under a lot of stress preparing for your trip and everything."

"Well, I seem to be just fine, stress or no stress." She started to mention the violent headaches and the weakness, but both had stopped, and she really didn't want to talk about it with Delia.

"I'm glad. I worry about you. Now, I know that sounds pushy, but when we're older, we may look back and be glad we became friends."

"Stranger things have surely happened." Ashley felt uncomfortable. It was true Delia was no longer being the emotional despot she had been with her, but she didn't altogether trust her. She thought she'd just keep her at arm's length.

The women leaned on the fence for a few minutes.

"Ashley, thank you so much for being so decent when I've been such a bitch. I hope you've really forgiven me."

"There's nothing to forgive. Each one of us has his or her own personality. You didn't know me before. I was married, singing and busy. You were married and busy with your life. . . ."

"Then Derrick came along and brought us together." Delia paused. She didn't want to go too far. She felt like a sorceress weaving a silken web of necessary deceit.

Delia clasped her hands over her breasts. "I'm making a nuisance of myself, but I feel so bad about seeming to come on to Derrick, and I want him to forgive me so."

Ashley looked at Delia closely. She felt she had said everything necessary to make her feel better about kissing Derrick. What was she looking for? Nevertheless, she felt constrained to say pleasantly, "Stop worrying about it. I'm sure he forgives you. He's always the gentleman."

"Like my husband." Delia closed her eyes. "Like Marty."

Ashley thought she saw a glint of tears in her eyes and felt compassionate.

With a deep sigh, Delia said, "Ashley, thank you *so* much. I'll be going back now. Derrick and Ace drove over to Ace's house, as I'm sure you know. Ace is dickering to buy a farm. And, of course, you know Derrick goes back to his spread late this afternoon. I don't know what I'd do without him."

Ashley knew that Derrick would drive down to his spread, and wished she were going with him again. She closed her eyes as scene after scene washed over her of the past weekend. It was as if Delia were not standing there.

Delia shuddered a bit with biting envy at the rapt expression on Ashley's face. She could be thinking about only one person: Derrick.

"I've got to go," Delia said. "Take care of yourself. Damp cold is hell on the respiratory system, and we don't want anything to happen to your gorgeous voice. Ashley, I'm running it into the ground, I know, but thank you, thank you, thank you."

She turned then and walked to the hill and began her climb to her house. Ashley got back on Black Steed, slapped his rump, and let him gallop. Goober grazed peacefully, looking up from time to time.

Dr. Smith sat in his office in his shirtsleeves, his hands clasped behind his head. He was thinking about Ashley

Steele. He was deeply concerned about all his patients, as an internist who went the extra mile. What did she have? A razor-sharp headache. Temporary weakness. What did it tie into? There were so many chemicals in the air these days. The water wasn't always safe, and E. coli bacteria lurked everywhere.

He had talked again with his Brazilian doctor friend at the same hospital he was affiliated with. The doctor had said the symptoms were nearly always present in the poison of the Brazilian tree frog. The Brazilian doctor had laughed. "We are many miles from the rain forests of my country. This country has its own poisons. Test."

But the tests for poison he had run had proved negative. Now Ashley felt fine. She'd be okay; she took good care of herself. Dr. Smith smiled a bit. She was a good-looking woman and she deserved the best life had to offer. Twenty years older than Ashley, he thought he would have loved having her for a daughter. Then he grinned widely. He'd prefer having her as his wife.

With Derrick and Corby gone, Delia was left to her own lonely devices, and she knew just what she wanted to do with that time.

Freshly bathed, with gardenia fragrance surrounding her, she made her plan. She dressed in black silk crepe with a plunging neckline, as she would dress for a lover. Smoothing lotion on her hands, she went down the hallway, unlocked her secret room, and went inside.

What she had to do had to be done twice, with ample time in between for the spells to take effect. Strange, she thought, how she had begun to deeply believe in the spells she wove. She had never felt so powerful.

True, the poison hadn't worked so far, but there was still much time. She had let herself doubt, and *Grand-mère* had said the weaver of spells must never doubt. Just when you least expected it . . .

In the darkened room she pulled the door shut, locked it, and stood in the darkness, invoking the spirits who never failed. There was no one in the house but her, so she could call to Damballah and Freda Erzulie as loudly as she wished. Excitement coursed through her blood as she stood there, her eyes closed. She felt the spirits enter her bloodstream and set her body trembling at a very early stage.

Groping on the table by the door, she found a flashlight and turned it on. Reaching into a table drawer, she took out Marty's old lighter and lit three slender black candles and placed them on the floor. Having spied the old pack of cigarettes that she saw each time she opened this drawer, she began to crave one.

Opening the package carefully, she tapped out a cigarette, lit it, and inhaled deeply. Once she had been a heavy smoker, but Derrick had turned her against smoking. Marty had smoked. She needed the tangy bite of the tobacco in her lungs. She would get a carton when she went into town.

The Ashley doll lay in the drawer, too. Inhaling deeply, Delia bent and blew a stream of smoke in the doll's face without picking it up. Ashley had been so damned beatific in the meadow this morning, she thought. "Enjoy it while it lasts, Ashley Steele," she said aloud, "because it isn't going to last much longer."

She turned on a record player that sat on the table and turned it low. The sound of jungle drums rolled into the air, and the flickering candles seemed to dance with the rhythm—heartbeat drums, more powerful than any other music.

"You've got your music, Ashley," she said snidely. "I've got mine."

Picking up the Ashley doll, Delia murmured. "I will dance, and Derrick's love for you will die."

Holding the doll in the air, she laughed once, bitterly, then

flung the doll to a corner of the floor, dashing it to pieces.
She had made one more Ashley doll lately. There would be
time for that one later.

Winded, she drank a medium-size glass of neat rum that
sent her senses reeling, then sat on the floor in front of the
flickering candles. Her slender arms were weaving in the air
as she sang:

> Damballah, I am possessed by you.
> You are the god of gods, my love.
> Bless me with your power,
> Enter me and fill my heart completely.
>
> Erzulie, you are one spirit with me.
> Bless me as you enter my woman's heart
> and with Damballah possess it completely.
> Give me that which I want.
> Give me that which I cannot live without,
> and I am your subject forever.

The spirits couldn't fail. She had only to believe. Already
she felt the powerful quakes of her body as she began to
writhe. The floor was carpeted in thick, shaggy dark green,
and Delia imagined it was jungle grass as she slid her body
into its crisp wooliness. The silk of her black dress and the
wool of the carpet excited her even more. The silk was her
skin and the wool was the goats she sacrificed.

In a little while her body trembled violently and she didn't
talk anymore. She saw the spirits as plainly as she had seen
her own face an hour or so before. With the drums still
beating, swelling, and eddying around her, the rum took full
effect and she grew sleepier. Just before she passed out, she
knew now she would win. Her life depended on it. Somewhere it seemed a telephone rang, but it didn't matter. Nothing mattered now except the spells and the spirits that
empowered her to weave those spells.

* * *

Len thought about going to bed early, then decided he'd stay up, watch the fire in the fireplace, and read a men's magazine. He had a new copy of one. Leafing through it, he licked his lips at the photos. Good-looking naked women, but he'd bet they had nothing on Miss Delia.

Picking up the phone, he thought he'd call her, check to see if everything was all right. The phone rang six times and a recording came on. He held the phone away from him. It was nine-thirty. Where was she? She never went to bed until midnight. Maybe she had gone into town to see a movie. He worried about her. She wasn't as tough as she thought she was. He'd call back at eleven or so. He had repairs to make on the barn tomorrow, and he'd be off Monday. He picked up the magazine and looked long and hard at the lush centerfold, then at other photos of skantily clad women, and sighed. Miss Delia would beat every one of them, he thought, in spades.

Len came back alive at one particularly provocative photograph. Whistling long and low, he wriggled his heavy shoulders. Lord, but he could use a drink. He started to get up to make himself a whiskey sour, then sat back down. He was craving liquor too often these days. The son of an alcoholic who had died early, he watched his step, not drinking at all for months just to prove he could do it.

The knock was soft and he wasn't sure he heard it; then it came louder. Len had few friends, and he seldom visited or was visited. Miss Delia usually called before she came.

"Yeah, coming," he yelled. He opened the door and Delia stood before him, her head thrown back, laughing.

"Are you going to invite me in, Len?"

"Why, sure." He stumbled over the words. "Why, sure, Miss Del—"

Coming close to him as he closed the door, she put a finger to his lips. "I thought we had that all worked out.

Okay, so you're bashful, but I want you to call me Delia—
when we're alone, at least. That's an order."

"Maybe I'll forget and call you that when other folks are
around. That wouldn't be too good."

"Damn other people." She moved closer and he moved a
foot or so back. He could smell the liquor on her breath.

"Help me with my coat." She unbuttoned the heavy coat
and he slipped it off her shoulders, then walked over and laid
it on a table.

"Put it in the closet," she told him. "I may be staying a
while."

His hackles rose. What was she doing? The low-cut black
silk dress hugged her every curve, and he thought she sure
didn't have much on beneath it. He stood awkwardly as she
came to him and wrapped her arms around his neck. Goaded
by the magazine photos and faced with Delia's curves, he
felt desire like a red-hot poker down his spine. Her lips
touched his. *Lord, forgive me,* he cried inside.

She put his arms around her. "I want you, Len. Don't you
wan't me?"

Hardly able to talk, he blurted out that he did; then what
he added hurt him, but it was the truth. "You don't want me,
Delia. You want my help, and I tell you, you don't have to
do nothing to get my help. I'll do anything you need done,
but you been drinking and you ain't used to liquor."

Delia laughed shrilly. "That shows how much you know.
I've been drinking since college. I hold it well."

He felt uncomfortable. How the hell was he going to get
out of this? "You don't owe me nothing," he said in a growl.
"Nothing. I always've done what you asked me to, ain't I?"

"You know you have, but I want to be held. I want you to
hold me."

"Just hold?"

Delia's fingers played upon his face. "Well, it could go on
to something else—we're both adults. Although you're act-
ing like a silly schoolboy."

"Yeah," he said; but he felt like Samson. His arms had fallen to his sides, and she put them back around her. The silk of her dress felt wonderful beneath his fingers. Only half knowing what he did, he drew her to him and kissed her long and hard. She came to him like filings to a magnet, and he groaned. The kiss lasted until hot tears of anger came to his eyes.

Len was a man who saw the world clearly. He'd been a loner all his life. He knew with everything in him that this woman would use him, and he was willing to be used by her. But he knew, too, that she wanted Derrick Quinn. Right now Quinn loved Ashley, but who knew when or if he would one day turn to Delia?

If he, Len, let himself be drawn into Delia's magic web, he would someday be dumped like so much trash. He closed his eyes then, because it had happened once before. He had been dumped, laughed at, and he had had to run to keep from killing the woman who had dumped him.

Delia's smile was tantalizing as she leaned back in his arms. "I'm your boss. You're supposed to obey orders."

A woman he had loved more than life itself had teased him, led him on, and had nearly sealed her death warrant. The flashback cleared his mind, cooled his ardor.

"No, Miss Delia," he said firmly. "I'll always help you in your magic. I hope you'll teach me how to work it. But I won't let you use me and throw me away."

"Oh, Len," she said softly. "You big baby."

"I'm a man. You wouldn't be wanting a baby."

His words cooled her, driving some of the liquor from her brain. She saw his resolve and bowed her head. She was angry that he didn't take her. Who was he to turn her down? But she didn't want to appear the fool.

"Very well," she said evenly. "I'm sorry I bothered you." She tried to make her voice sound hurt and succeeded. He was fooled.

"Holding you back's the hardest thing I've ever done," he

ll but whimpered, "but you think about it and you'll know
'm right."

"I'll go now," she said dully, feeling the fool in spite of
herself.

She didn't go. Instead she stood there, still close to him.

Suddenly she said, "I've been smoking a lot lately, drinking a lot. Did you know?"

"I seen you smoke a time or two, smelled liquor. Hell, I
drink, too."

"Know something else, Len? I go out on the highway that
bypasses Crystal Lake. I go out early in the morning, two or
three o'clock, and I race the old red truck. Marty had a great
motor put in it. Have you ever driven very, very fast, just for
the hell of it?"

"No. I can't say I have."

"Would you like to go with me some morning?"

He shook his head. "I dunno. I don't think so. Maybe you
hadn't oughta be going either."

"Scared?"

"Yeah."

She took his hand and put it to her face. "Don't be afraid
of life, Len. Take it on your own terms and nobody else's.
Demand what you want. *Take* what you want. The strong
rule, Len, and the world belongs to the strong."

He nodded. At least they agreed on who the world belonged to. The only thing was, he wasn't one of them.

"What you do. It sounds dangerous."

Her eyes lit up, sparking fire. "It is. And you're scared?"

"Yes," he said slowly. "I'll walk you back." He helped her
with her coat.

"No. I can make it on my own."

"Are you mad at me?" he asked her. Maybe she'd fire
him, he thought. She was a woman who usually got her way.
But being out of a job was better than being without freedom, in prison.

"Yes," she answered honestly. "I'm angry. I offered you the gift of myself and you refused me."

"That ain't the way it is. You know it."

She touched his face. "Maybe I do. Good night, Len. Remember your offer to help me with anything."

"I won't forget, ma'am."

He was impossible, she thought as she went up the walk alone. It was an overcast night and she needed someone. The pain of wanting Derrick was like shards of glass in her heart. She didn't realize that Len stood in his doorway in the cold watching until she let herself into her house.

Later, when she couldn't sleep again, she got up and went out to the truck that was parked near the end of the driveway nearest the road. She had dressed warmly, and in a short while she was on the stretch of the road she rode most often at night.

There was little traffic and she could speed along, exhilarated. Marty used to drive too fast. Derrick never did. Why did she love him so?

Slowly a plan began to form in her mind, a plan that pleased her greatly. It had to do with Ashley Steele, and it was fresh, appealing. Not paying attention to her driving, she came too close to a tractor trailer, and he blew his horn shrilly. She passed him and he cursed, yelling a lusty string of oaths.

It didn't matter. She had in mind what she was looking for. She had been out for such a short while, but at the first turning point, she turned the truck around and started home. She drove at a moderate speed, as Derrick would have. *Derrick.* She thought she had it all together now.

Thirty-one

Onstage at Germany's Deutsche Opera Berlin, Ashley raised her arms in greeting to the audience, who cheered her loudly and long. Clad in an intricately draped periwinkle-blue silk jersey gown, she wore a knotted rope of marble-sized cultured pearls. She felt wonderful. She looked wonderful. She was also haunted with missing Derrick.

This was a special concert by invitation from one of Germany's premier choral groups. Behind her the tambourines rattled softly. The guitars twanged their heartfelt music, and the Davis Gospel Singers hummed. Her German agent had introduced her and the song she would sing. Now she slid into an old, old spiritual, in a rare arrangement by James Weldon Johnson, "Nobody Knows the Trouble I've Seen."

> Brothers, will you pray for me?
> Brothers, will you pray for me?
> And help me drive old Satan away.
>
> Nobody knows the trouble I've seen.
> Nobody knows like Jesus.
> Glory hallelujah!

The crowd listened raptly, with her all the way. It had come to be another signature song.

Then, breathing deeply, she launched into "Every Time I Feel the Spirit." The song was lively, challenging, and the

Davis Gospel Singers and Clem, the pianist, backed her with
their best. She asked the audience to clap with her as she
sang, and they did.

Hans Schneider, her German agent, had explained that
this opera house was best for gospel music. He had
shrugged. "My countrymen are not noted for their love of
variety, or for that which is different. Here you will gain
accolades." And she had.

Now she sang a verse she loved.

> Upon the mountain,
> my Lord spoke.
> Out of his mouth came
> fire and smoke.
>
> I looked all around me,
> it looked so fine.
> I asked the Lord
> if all were mine.

Audiences everywhere seemed to like the third verse of
the spiritual.

> Jordan River,
> chilly and cold.
> Chill the body,
> but not the soul.

She had the audience in the palm of her hand. It was a
near miracle, Hans Schneider had said when she had sung
here for the third time in as many years. "We Germans—so
many of us, anyway—are music lovers. We will listen to
good music, and we will listen with all our hearts."

After the third song, she took a bow to deafening applause
and went backstage to change gowns.

After the makeup artist and the dresser had done their

services, she had a few minutes to spare. Hans came and sat beside her in a chair by her chaise longue. Max came and kissed her cheek.

"I always swear," he said, "that you cannot be more magnificent, yet each time you prove me a liar. Keep your wits about you and we will be at the pinnacle of heaven—soon."

She smiled at him, missing Derrick with a physical ache, and missing Eleni. She and Max and the others had spent two days in Paris before coming here. She was puzzled that she hadn't heard from Derrick.

"You looked stunning in both your gowns," Hans told her, admiring the very dark-red crushed velvet that bared her shoulders. She wore an obsidian choker and dangling matching earrings.

"Thank you both," she told them.

"You know," Hans said, "my grandfather was very fond of spirituals. He spoke often of the Fisk Jubilee Singers and the Utica Jubilee Singers, from Tennessee and Mississippi, respectively. It was in the twenties and the thirties that they took Europe by storm. They sang before the crowned heads of Europe. . . ."

He closed his eyes in remembrance. "I have dreams of arousing this same fervor in some of our European breasts. Music is cyclic, like anything else." He paused. "Time to go back out, my beauty."

Max's eyes glowed with planning a splendid life for Ashley. And he kept in mind his plans for her—with him. Ashley loved her music, and he was the one to bring her to glory.

Back onstage, she felt more relaxed now, the music thrumming in her blood. This time, with only Clem accompanying her, she sang, "My Lord, What a Morning."

By the time she reached the words that told what would happen on that morning, "when the stars begin to fall," it was as still as in the womb. The first verse began, "You will hear the trumpet sound," then "You will hear the sinner moan," and last, "You will hear the Christians shout."

This was one of two ring-shouted songs, and the rhythm of supple bodies was beautiful to watch. The Davis Gospel Singers had the spirit with them tonight: fire from within, lavish support from without. It was their only ring-shout for the night, and they poured their all into it. Their feet told the story as their voices sang.

They finished abruptly, on cue, and the audience called out its approval, as they had with Ashley.

"Applaus! Applaus!" they roared, enchanted.

It was a favorite, and applause burst forth before she could finish.

The Davis Gospel Singers sang another two spirituals; then the next part of her show, the operatic arias, loomed before her.

Again she met with wild applause as she finished a spiritual and the concert broke for intermission.

This time she had a chance to relax more, drink a glass of grape juice, and eat a small dish of oatmeal and juicy raisins. Hans went to talk to people in the lobby, and she was left alone with Max. "You and the oatmeal," he teased her.

"It soothes my throat."

"It signifies the child in you."

"I had a happy childhood."

"I've told you a million times, your adult years with me could be more splendid than anything you've known, if you'd let them be."

A voice inside Ashley whispered, *I have known the pinnacle with Derrick.*

"I have one failure behind me," she said wryly. "Don't wish me another one."

"We wouldn't fail, Ashley, if you'd give me a chance."

Ashley's eyes glazed over. She was really fond of Max, but she didn't think she believed he wanted her as much as he thought he did. It would be a marriage of convenience, and she didn't want a marriage of convenience.

She went behind the broad screen, and when she emerged, Max whistled. "My God, what a woman!"

Ashley blushed. "You're very kind."

"You're very beautiful."

This time she wore ivory silk crepe, with beaded teardrop pearls and a trumpet bottom, showing off her hourglass figure. This time she made her own announcement to the audience that she would sing operatic arias from *La Traviata, Tosca, Madame Butterfly, La Bohème,* and *Tristan und Isolde.*

This time she was backed by a full orchestra, and she looked nervously toward the orchestra pit. Classical music was something the Germans *did* worship. They had known Wagner. The revered composer might be lacking in human tolerance, but he composed great music. And there was the gifted, tragic Schumann.

From the beginning her big, powerful mezzo-soprano voice dominated the room, sweeping and undulating. Notes of glory. Words of love. For what was music, she always thought, but love put in motion?

Her voice lilted on "Sempre Libre," the aria from *La Traviata,* and the applause fed her, sustained her. It was one of her favorite arias. At Juilliard, a coach had once told her wistfully, "I'd like to see you do more of the classics. God knows, there would be nothing between you and the top if you chose this way."

And she loved classical music, but even when she'd been a child, the spirituals had begged her to sing them, and they still begged her. She was on a journey to paradise with all her music.

The Liebestod from *Tristan und Isolde* was her last selection. In her hands, in her rendition, the ill-fated lovers were forever memorialized. When she had finished, the room was hushed for moments, then the crowd went wild, standing, shouting, *"Applaus! Applaus!"*

She took three curtain calls, and still the audience did not want her to leave the stage. Max and Hans beamed in the wings. "Thank you from my heart," Ashley told the audience. "I will do a good-night number for you from my childhood. And she sang them Brahms's *Lullaby.*

Unwilling, they let her go then, and backstage she laughed with joy at the approbation, the palpable love in the air. Then she saw him standing by the door and flew into his arms.

"Derrick!" She gave a small scream.

"I wasn't sure I was doing the right thing, bursting in on you like this."

Her lips met his and she closed her eyes. "Seeing you is always the right thing. Did you hear the concert?"

"I saw some of it on TV in the lobby and the hallway. You were, as usual, magnificent. I've run out of accolades for you, love."

Max's face was cool, but he hadn't gotten where he was by tipping his hand.

"Oh, let me look at you." Then she laughed. "We haven't been apart but a week."

"And that's a week too long. My plane was late. I intended to be here much earlier, do some sight-seeing tomorrow with you. I had business in London buying special show horses for my spread." He paused. "That's partly true. I'll tell you the rest later."

"And where is Corby?"

Derrick chuckled. "Would you believe he *wanted* to stay and go fishing with Whit and some of Whit's friends?"

"In this cold?"

"They know a river in Florida. Besides, fishermen don't get cold."

Hans had followed the couple with his eyes since Derrick

had come in. Pacing up and down, he held his hands clasped behind his back. Finally he came to stand before them.

"Please introduce the gentleman, Ashley."

Ashley did as he asked, and a huge smile lifted Hans's face.

"This is the man who brings you to your zenith," he said slowly. "We were to go to Mäcki Messer, the famous restaurant, tonight and, of course, Ashley is already ensconced in one of the finest hotels in all Germany, but I have an invitation."

He put his forefinger to his cheek. "I am a romantic, you see. If my wife were not in Paris, she would be here with me tonight."

Max strolled up and spoke to Derrick. Then Max asked coolly, "What point are you making, Hans?"

"Just this, and I will be brief. Lately my wife and I have had the large tower of the small castle we live in outside Berlin renovated. It is a suite and it is beautiful. My dear, I want to invite you both to stay with me."

"But, man," Max exploded, "we have plans for the entire group to share a meal at Mäcki Messer. We all have suites at Reimer's Hofgarten. The whole group is expected to follow through. People who play together must be together often."

Hans shook his head. "It is clear you are *not* a romantic, my friend." He turned to Ashley. "I saw the love on your face when you looked at this man and when he looked at you. My castle is enchanted. You will not be disappointed.

"As for dinner, the owner of Mäcki Messer is a friend. He will send you a splendid meal. Will you do this for me?"

A sense of reckless wonder swept over Ashley. She looked at Derrick. "Are you game?"

Derrick grinned. "Am I game? How often do I get to sleep in the tower of a castle?"

* * *

Hans Schneider's castle was as romantic as he had promised. It was very late before they were settled. Photographers and journalists had covered her well, and the audience had demanded autographs she was eager to give. "You must come again," a small, wizened lady with clown-white skin and bright blue eyes had told her. "My dear, in my long lifetime I have rarely heard such superb singing."

Now Ashley and Derrick stood in their round castle suite, surrounded by beautiful windows all around. They walked through the room with Hans, arm in arm. "Did I lie to you?" Hans asked.

"It is gorgeous," Ashley told him as Derrick nodded. Done in multiple shades of blue, with pale walnut furniture, the living room, bedroom, powder room, and den were all one could ask.

Hans bowed, smiling. "I will go now. Your dinner will be served shortly. I promise you the best."

Hans took Ashley's hand, kissed it, then shook hands with Derrick.

Once they were alone, Derrick and Ashley fell into each other's arms. Derrick felt half-crazy with longing for her, and Ashley's body was limpid with wanting him.

In a very short while a knock sounded, and at Derrick's invitation a man came in with a large food cart and bowed low.

"I am Pierre, and Herr Schneider instructed me to serve you. He commanded that I do it well."

Derrick looked at the cart and back at Ashley. "I'll tell you what," he said. "I thank you very much, but *I* wish to serve the lady. We will put the cart back in the hall when we are finished. Please don't take exception."

The man's eyes almost closed with mirthful understanding. He bowed low. "I understand," he said evenly. "I, too, have a lady I serve. I wish you well."

He left them as Ashley and Derrick dissolved into laughter until the tears came.

"I can wait no longer," he said. "Our food will stay warm."

"But it's such special food," she told him. "After Hans has gone to all this trouble."

He wasn't listening to her. He unzipped her from her last costume change, the beautiful ivory silk crepe that flattered her so. She unfastened her jewelry and took it off. When she was naked before him in the warm room, he groaned with aching desire. For a moment he seemed to struggle with his tie, until with steady hands she undid it for him, then undressed him slowly, tantalizingly.

"If you were my valet, I'd fire you," he teased her. "Why so slow?"

"Because," she teased him back, "you can sometimes be a hothead when you want to make love. The longer we wait, the better it gets."

"I disagree. We have only one kind of lovemaking—stupendous. Come on, Ash. Move it."

Lovingly she touched his protrusion, which had long come to stand at attention for her. He kicked off his shoes and sat on the bed to remove his socks, turning for a moment to pull back the bedcovers of the heavy walnut bed that sat on a platform.

She stood beside the bed, looking down at him. "Now I want to study your beloved body," she said.

He reached for her arm and pulled her down on top of him. "Like hell you will," he said in a growl. "I promise I'm going to study you from the inside, and I dare you to deny me."

She started to laugh, but then the laughter faded. Wild thrills were racing through her body. An ache began in her belly, seeming to reach for his body with greedy fingers. There was no time now for kisses. Their caresses were frantic, unguarded. Reaching up to put his mouth to the hollow of her throat, he pressed smoothly and slowly into the depths of her body. Her grip was like a tightly fitting glove, and the nectar she gave him was sublimely satisfying.

It was over too soon. "You have only yourself to blame," he said. "Playing with me like that. But you were with me all the way. I felt you bringing me along."

Ashley smiled. "What a lover you are."

"Lovers extraordinaire," he whispered, his narrowed eyes on her. He reached for her again.

"I'm starved," she said. "I think I burn thousands of calories in a concert. You told the man you'd serve me. I hold you to that."

Hans had had someone pick up their suitcases from the hotel. Now Derrick dressed in a robe and pajama bottoms, and Ashley put on a watermelon pink robe with a full skirt. He uncovered the delicious food. "I'm going to take pity on you and help you," she told him. "What do we have here?"

The food on silver trays under silver domes was still piping hot. A menu lay on one of the trays. Ashley read it as she helped Derrick put out the food.

The meat dish was done to a turn. "Roast beef," she read, "coated with red rice. Fish soup. Several vegetables. Two bottles of red and two bottles of white wine."

Dessert was flan with blackberries and cream. Pierre had thought of everything. There was a bottle of Grand Marnier to furnish the flames when the liqueur was poured lightly onto the flan and lit.

"I don't think I'm going to risk setting this flan on fire," Derrick said. "We'll save that until next time. It seems to me there's already a lot of fire in this room."

Pursing her lips, her eyes dancing as they sat down, she said, "You speak for yourself."

"I speak for both of us. I know what I know."

The dinner was superb and they lingered over it. Ashley had cleared the table of the main course and Derrick had set out the flan when the phone rang. It was Caroline.

"Mama. How are you?" Ashley asked.

"Well, I'm fine. Now don't get rattled when I tell you this," Caroline said. "I waited until your concert was over. Eleni fell from the low bough of your big oak late this afternoon. She has a hairline fracture of her arm. She's asleep or I'd put her on."

Ashley's heart raced.

"How badly is she hurt?"

"Dr. Smith saw her. We took her in. She had X rays. He thinks it's a clean fracture and she'll be over it in a jiffy. She was to go to New York with Reese but he delayed the trip a couple of days. He put her in a light cast because she's so active. I don't know what got into her, climbing that tree without asking me."

"She's climbed it before many times. I let her. I never thought there was any danger. I'll be home day after tomorrow."

"She's in great spirits, so you don't have to rush."

"Mama. Derrick's here with me."

"Derrick? My, that's nice."

She talked with Frank, Whit, and Annice, all of whom urged her to stay as long as she wished. Eleni was in the bosom of her family, safe and loved. She and Derrick could talk with Eleni and Corby tomorrow. Ashley glanced at her watch. It was tomorrow now.

It seemed she had hung up only a few minutes, after telling Derrick what happened, when the phone rang again.

"You sure are a damned hard woman to catch up with," Reese barked.

"What is it, Reese?" she asked sourly, knowing what it was.

"Eleni had a bad fall. She's been in low spirits since you left. I've gone to see her almost every day."

"That wasn't necessary. She has the best of care."

"Does she? She hasn't fallen out of any trees when she was with me."

"Accidents happen to everybody, Reese."

"You're sure calm, lady. I'm going to tell you something to rattle your cage a little. I'm going to file to get sole custody of Eleni. You've got a world of travel to do beginning this fall. I don't like the way things are going for our little girl."

Ashley was stunned. What in hell did he think he was doing? She hung up and pressed her hands to her head, repeating to Derrick the conversation with Reese.

When she finished, Derrick was silent. What was he thinking? she wondered. Still silent, he got up, went to the closet, got something out of his suit jacket, and jammed it into his robe pocket.

As he came back to her, his face was somber. "Sit on the couch," he ordered.

"Derrick? What . . . ?"

He took her arm and guided her to the couch, where she sat. Then, smiling slightly, he went on one knee, took a navy blue velvet box from his robe pocket, and snapped it open.

"If you marry me," he said, "you'll have the best situation for Eleni. I love her as if she were my own, as I think you love Corby. You'll have Reese hands down, and I'll have you."

He took the ring and slid it onto her left ring finger. Her eyes filled with tears. The five-carat oval diamond glittered in the light.

"Oh, Derrick," she said softly. "I love you and I want to marry you, but you're not comfortable with my traveling so much. You don't want to hurt someone, or *be* hurt, again."

His finger on her lips silenced her. "I'm under your spell," he said. "All I know is that I love you, I want you. I mean to have you for myself."

As elated as he felt, deep down inside Derrick knew a rush of panic. He could not bear to hurt another woman as he had hurt Maria.

After undressing again, they made slow love, hot to very

warm to hot again. After a time they got up, stacked the dishes on the cart, and pushed it into the hall.

"The man is going to wonder what took us so long to put the cart out."

Derrick grinned. "Remember he told us he has a woman of his own. He'll understand."

They went to bed, but neither could sleep. Ashley could not stop looking at the beautiful ring. Their kisses now were the stuff of passion. He covered every inch of her with hot, moist kisses and stroked her gently and deeply.

He found a book of Arabian love poems in the night table and read them to her. Then she read to him. They lay and looked at the starlit heavens. By dawn they were sated with each other, and they watched a rosy winter dawn rise in the eastern sky. Then they slept in each other's arms.

A pleased, laughing Hans picked them up the next afternoon. "Your flight is tonight," he said, "and you *must* visit our best flea market at Seventeenth and June. You missed it last time. It is like nothing else you will see. I trust all went well with you." He had immediately seen the diamond she wore and said simply, "Congratulations to you both!"

They went through heavy traffic in Hans's black Volvo. The building was large, sparkling clean, and loaded with beautiful things, reminding her of certain parts of a museum.

"You see," Hans said gravely. "We Germans take our flea markets seriously. The goods here are often heirlooms, antiques, often the best a family has to offer."

Hans was quiet, thoughtful. As they browsed, admiring the beautiful articles, Hans now said, "Pierre told me, Herr Quinn, that *you* wished to serve the lady. She seems happy enough."

Derrick laughed. "We can never thank you enough."

Hans bowed, saying to Ashley, "In a couple of years,

when you have reached the zenith of your talent, I can look at you and think that I helped to make this happen."

Ashley chose a beautiful heavy ivory lace tablecloth for Caroline, a Russian carved male wooden doll for Frank, a female carved wooden doll for Annice, and a carved wooden sea bass for Whit. Eleni would have her heart's desire with a Bavarian porcelain doll, and Corby would get an old-fashioned fishing lure. The gifts would be mailed.

Ashley had not thought of Delia. Now she felt a rush of sympathy as she spied a large and beautiful frosted Steuben vase.

"I'd like to get this for Delia," she told Derrick. "She may be hurt when she knows about us."

Derrick said glumly, "You may be right. I think it will send clearer signals if it comes from you rather than both of us."

"Yes, I think that's true."

A shudder took her then. Goose bumps peppered her arms in the warm room. "Goose going over my grave," she murmured.

On the plane that night she slept and dreamed of a wild storm around her in her bedroom. Winds nearly swept her off the bed. Wet green leaves slapped at her, stinging her face. She came awake with Derrick shaking her gently.

"You're having a nightmare," he said, letting the armrest down so he could hold her. She looked outside at a moonlit, starlit sky, a sea of calm outside. What was going on inside of her?

Thirty-two

Sunday was filled with brilliant spring sunlight. A week after Ashley and Derrick returned from Germany, the Steeles threw them an engagement brunch, down-home style. The house was filled with white narcissus and gladioli.

"Mama, you shouldn't have gone to so much trouble," Ashley complained.

Frank answered for his wife. "We're hoping this is the second, counting me and your ma, in a long line of successes in love. This ought to show you that bad luck doesn't last forever."

Coming up to them, Whit laughed. "What if he changes in midstream and beats her? I don't promise to hold back this time."

Annice, who stood nearby, drawled, "You mean hold back from punching whatever brute does this?"

"You bet I mean that, Neesie."

Annice shook her head. "Derrick's true to his nature. He's a mature soul, and I'm so glad you came to your senses and snagged him, sis." She came closer and hugged Ashley.

Caroline, glowing as much from her husband's loving eyes on her as from her daughter's engagement, pursed her lips. "I get the feeling," she said, "that although this is an almost impromptu party, word is going to get around. I think we're going to be swamped."

One of the first to come was Miss Mag, who lugged a big bag. "I brought you a dozen jars of muscadine preserves,

made like only your mama and I can make them," she told
Ashley.

"You remembered I love muscadine preserves," Ashley
told her.

Miss Mag grinned. "I don't forget much."

There were very few people milling about. Derrick hadn't
come yet, and Ashley kept her eye peeled for him.

"I've got news about *me* this time that I want you all to
hear," Miss Mag said. She shushed them with a raised hand.
They listened.

"I got me a new friend. Now, I didn't bring him because
I won't be here long and he's bashful. We ain't engaged, but
anything can happen." She blushed, and her pale, weathered
face reflected happiness.

"Congratulations!" Ashley told her, and others present
took it up.

"Thank you. I reckon I might as well put it out myself.
You know how people gossip. He's living with me." She
turned to Caroline. "He's the man you found on your land
back when the boy ran away. He helped you try to find him.
He's a real nice man."

"Oh, yes," Ashley said. "I run into him from time to
time."

"Yes, and you always give him money. One thing I'll say:
the Steeles ain't no slackers. You all are the best there are.
I'm going t'bring him by when I get him past being so
bashful."

"You do that," Frank said. "We'll be glad to entertain you
both."

Miss Mag lifted her head. "Don't I smell catfish cooking?"

Caroline smiled. "You do. Catfish, whiting, perch, all
kinds of good things. Some of the catfish is ready, but not
the other things, I'm afraid. Wait a bit and you can take a
plate home to your friend."

Miss Mag shook her head. "I promised him I'd be back

early. Just give me a coupla pieces o' catfish and I'll go on. I'm planning on cooking him a big dinner. This'll come in handy."

Caroline went back to pack the food for Miss Mag as Ashley arranged the eight gleaming pint jelly jars in a double line on the table.

"It ain't fancy or nothing, but it comes from my heart," Miss Mag declared. She went back into the kitchen then to hurry Caroline along.

Derrick came shortly after Miss Mag was packed and ready to leave. She looked him over. "I always thought you had the right stuff in you," she said. "I never listened to none o' that gossip that was goin' around." She touched his shoulder and Ashley's arm. "You two be happy. I mean that."

She left then as Ashley and Derrick went to a window and watched her start up the old van and drive away.

Derrick grinned. "In a way it was dodging her and her gossip that brought us closer. We owe her."

Smiling, he looked at her, then whistled low. "You look wonderful, love. Brown leather skirt split to show off those incredible legs, pale-blue cashmere sweater. The diamond studs I gave you." His eyes went to her feet in banded brown leather sling-back shoes and he whistled again. "If I won the Nobel Prize I couldn't like it more."

Ashley chuckled. "Hey, you're coming on strong. I'm just little old me."

His eyes nearly closed, then blazed as he studied her. "You're my *woman*, Ash. And I'm your man."

"Like Porgy and Bess?"

"Like every set of impassioned lovers in the world."

Fairen Carrington, a journalist, came up to them, offering congratulations. "I can't stay long," she said. "My husband was going into Germany as you two were leaving. I had to come. You both are so lucky to find one another."

Eleni and Corby came up together, then spoke to Fairen, who hugged them both.

"I guess you're too big a boy to be hugged," she told Corby, who grinned.

"No, I'm not."

"Especially by a good-looking woman," Derrick drawled.

Without planning it, Derrick and Ashley were both dressed in brown and complementary colors. Looking at him in his tan tweed jacket and brown wool gabardine pants, with his deep cream shirt, tieless, Ashley found him drop-dead handsome, and blushed when his eyes met hers.

"I'm coming by next week to finish interviewing you for our article on you. So many people call and ask us to do an article about you. Is Wednesday okay?"

"I'll make it okay."

Fairen greatly admired the exhibited gifts Ashley had brought back to her family. She had once given her own daughter a set of Russian nesting dolls.

"Mom, we're going outside over by the oak," Eleni said.

"Fine. Just don't climb any trees."

"She won't," Corby answered. "That's why I'm going with her." As the children left, Fairen said, "Your families seem to be blending well."

"I guess we're just lucky," Ashley said. "Eleni worships Corby."

"And he's crazy about her," Derrick added.

There were quite a few people in the big, high-ceilinged rooms by then. The handmade ecru lace tablecloth Ashley had brought Caroline from Germany graced one of the tables. The other tables were covered with cream damask. Crystal and silver graced the tables.

Around one-thirty, Caroline, Minnie, and Annice began to set out the food. King and Frank gave them a hand.

"What gorgeous food," Fairen exclaimed, looking at the beautiful golden brown of the catfish, whiting, and perch. There was also macaroni and cheese, fried sweet-potato planks, potato and cheese casserole, German-fried potatoes and onion, french fries, hush puppies, and king-size biscuits.

Vegetables made the scene colorful, and salads were put out in abundance.

"Take your choice," Ashley told Fairen. "What do you want to drink? Beer is in the fridge. Wine. Lemonade. You name it."

Fairen asked, "You wouldn't happen to have hot cider."

"We *would*. I'll get you some."

Fairen blushed. "I've been craving cider for a week. I think I'm getting my third little blessing."

Ashley hugged her spontaneously. "Oh, Fairen, let's hope you are."

Annice had been near them. Now she went to get the hot cider.

"Well," a voice said behind Ashley. "Great party, or at least it seems that way."

Ashley turned to see Delia standing there. She swayed a little and she had liquor on her breath. Derrick, Ashley, and Fairen spoke, and Delia smiled bitterly.

Annice came back and handed the cider to Fairen. "Don't mind me," Delia said. "I love wine with my lunch, and I had a glass too many. I'm so happy for you two." She tried to look happy and almost succeeded. Derrick gave her an A for effort.

"I'm happy, too," Annice put in. "The only thing I'd rather have Derrick for than a brother-in-law is a husband."

Delia's face went paler. Derrick laughed explosively with pleased embarrassment. "A sister-in-law after my own heart," he declared.

Ashley laughed. "Stop teasing him so."

Annice shrugged. "Who's teasing?"

"Beautiful food," Delia said to Caroline as she walked up.

"Hello, Delia. My, you're looking well. You're one of a few women who are gorgeous in black."

And Delia did look good in a black crocheted dress that hugged her figure and was a little fancy for this gathering.

Long diamond earrings glittered in her ears as she twisted the big diamond ring she seldom wore.

"Thank you," Delia returned. "You're always so kind."

"It's easy to be kind," Caroline said, "when you're faced with beauty."

Delia looked at Ashley's engagement ring and pain stabbed her heart, but she wasn't giving up yet. Marty had been engaged when she had begun to want him.

Delia glowed a bit at Caroline's compliment, and she glowed more when Reese came in and walked over to them. Before he had reached them, Annice grumped, "He has his nerve. Talk about a skunk at a picnic."

Reese was feeling no pain, and he and Delia quickly found each other. He gave Delia a fairly loud wolf whistle and people looked around.

"Talk about a living doll," he said before he looked coolly at Ashley.

"I don't know how you won this one, Ash," he said. "This is one bee-yoo-ti-full babe."

Delia's chin lifted an inch or so. She held her generous breasts higher.

"You're the doll," she told Reese.

"How's your beer supply holding up?" Reese asked Annice. She was never a favorite of his, but he liked to goad her.

"I'd say coffee would serve you better," Annice said evenly.

"Ah, Neesie, get off it. You've been known to tie one on."

"But I know when to stop," Annice flashed back.

Reese shook his head. "I didn't come to argue," he said. "I'm being one of the good guys. Eleni is with you because of her arm. That was carelessness on somebody's part."

"That's a lie!" Annice told him. "A child has some freedom. I'm sure she's climbed that tree when you were with her."

Reese shrugged. "Where is she?"

"Out playing," Ashley said.

"Get her," he ordered Ashley. "I've been by to see her every day since she fell."

"Not in this shape, I hope," Ashley said bitterly.

Reese shot Derrick a wry look. "Like I've told you, man, with Ash, what you see isn't always what you get."

Derrick met Reese's childish banter with grown-up even-handedness. He didn't take it further.

"Why don't you walk out to the oak tree? She's playing out there with Corby."

"That's another thing," Reese said. "Eleni's used to being the only child. . . ."

"That was never *my* plan," Ashley said heatedly.

"Nothing like a second chance," Reese muttered.

"Come on, Reese, walk out to the oak tree with me," Delia coaxed him. "I just wanted to give my congratulations. I'd love your company."

Gratefully Reese turned to her. "You've got a date."

It was late when Max came to the party, bringing Ward Kaye the noted impresario. A very tall man with dark brown skin, snow-white hair and a thick mustache, he lifted Ashley's hand upon introduction and kissed it.

"I'm charmed to see you again," he told her. "I keenly follow all your concerts. Max sends me tapes, and you are more than ready to take advantage of what I have to offer."

As he paused, Ashley thanked him, pleasure rippling through her at his words.

Ward Kaye laughed ruefully. "Here I am, business as usual, and I have not yet congratulated you on your engagement. Your ring is stunning. I see love on both your faces. Be happy."

Ashley and Derrick thanked him, and he continued: "Another two years or so and you will be on top of your world. With me, and with Max guiding you, you will storm every major city here and abroad. You will travel as a queen, with your subjects worshiping you. Oh, how I hope you are prepared to travel!"

With shallowed breath, Ashley glanced at Derrick, who smiled, but she clearly saw misery in his eyes. They loved each other, but he was marrying her to give her the clearer rights to her child that being married could bring. What was he letting himself into? And could she let him do it?"

"We will talk later," Max murmured.

Ashley moistened her dry lips. "I may not be able to travel as much as you'd like."

"Nonsense! Of course you will travel. Rio de Janeiro. Europe. You will be in every major American city at every turn. Get ready for Ashley Steele, our next undisputed queen. I have gotten feedback from Germany for both your gospel and operatic music. You were stunning, my dear. There is nothing you cannot have if you work with me."

When Ashley introduced her family to him, Ward was the soul of charm. He kissed Caroline's hand. "The Singing Steeles. How long I've admired you, and I only met the mama and papa and Whit once or twice." He blinked a smile at Annice, bowed, and brought her hand to his lips. "I have not had the pleasure of meeting this charming, lovely woman." As Annice beamed, Ward Kaye turned his attention back to Caroline and Frank. "You chose to cling to your home base. Please help me persuade Ashley that she cannot do the same. A voice like hers belongs to her audiences."

Frank nodded. "What you say is true, but it is up to her."

"Yes," Caroline backed him. "It is up to her." Then she added, "You must enjoy our food. We have plenty that is kept hot. There is catfish, perch, chicken, roast beef. . . ."

Bowing, Ward kissed her hand again. "You are gracious, Mrs. Steele. I have eaten splendid food the world over, but the food I see on your table moves me. There is nothing I love more than catfish, nothing I love more than soul food."

Thirty-three

Silvery moonlight late that night found Eleni in bed, with Ashley and Derrick walking in the meadow. Everything seemed so serene. Bundled in heavy coats, they walked toward the big oak.

"I seem to be remembering a kiss under this tree," Ashley said.

"I don't remember any kiss," Derrick teased her.

"Oh, you! Don't get unromantic on me now."

Derrick laughed. "What I remember is a too-brief time of passion so deep it scared me."

"Still scared?"

"Aren't you?"

"No," Ashley told him. "I think I can truthfully say you've laid my fears to rest, but I haven't been able to do the same for you, have I?"

Derrick pondered her question a moment. The moonlight was stunning, and he didn't want to focus on anything but that and the woman beside him. He brought himself up short and answered truthfully.

"Ash, I'd be lying if I said I'm no longer afraid. What are we letting ourselves in for? Where are we going? We love each other too much to hurt that love."

Ashley stroked her finger with his ring on it. "We won't rush this," she said. "I believe in long engagements sometimes. We can wait a year, try talking it through, try a marriage counselor if it's necessary. If nothing works . . ."

He reached out and pulled her bundled body to his. "It's got to work," he said fiercely. "It's just got to work."

They were silent a long while before he said, "Something seems to be bothering you."

"Yes. How well you know my moods." She sighed deeply. "I keep thinking about Reese's filing for full custody because I'll be on the road so much. Judge Lewis is known to be partial to fathers. God only knows what will happen."

"We're getting married, remember? That should make it less likely that Reese will get Eleni."

She squeezed his hand. "It's bound to make a difference, but Judge Lewis is very partial to the rights of fathers." She thought now that she didn't want Derrick to sacrifice his life for her.

"I think I can come through as a worthy father."

"I know you can. I'm a worrier. You know that."

"Worry about my loving you so much it hurts."

"I don't ever want to hurt you."

He squeezed her hand tightly. "You bring me more joy in a second than any pain I'll know. I love you, Ash. I'm sure that's always going to be true."

Delia watched the same moonlit night as she stood on her back porch. She had also watched as Ashley and Derrick had walked across the meadow to the oak.

Reese had stayed a long time, and they had drunk a lot together. He had grinned. "You'd never know I'm in alcohol and drug rehab, would you?"

"That's for weak-knees."

"I agree. I'm no alcoholic. I can take it or leave it, and I stop completely from time to time just to prove to myself that I can. I'm celebrating today. My lawyer tells me he's sure I can get Judge Lewis to rehear my custody case. To-morrow I'll be stone-cold sober and stay that way until the hearing."

"You get your kid on weekends. Isn't that enough? From what I hear, you're a busy man."

Reese stiffened. "I love Eleni," he said tightly. "How in hell can Ashley take the best care of her now when she's on the road plenty? I talked with her agent. Ward Kaye was there today. He'll take her to the mountaintop."

"I've always been satisfied to be a wife," she had said.

"Bully for you. We ought to see more of each other."

His words left her cold. She liked being admired by him, but she didn't want him. There was only one man she really wanted.

"Well," he urged her, "think that's possible?"

"Anything's possible." She had been slurring her words by then.

"Give me an answer. I think you could be the answer to my prayers." He moved to kiss her and she let him, but felt nothing. She had felt more for Len because she could control him.

Delia shifted her stance. Her coat wasn't heavy enough for this weather. She hadn't meant to stay out so long. In the end, she had rushed Reese, because she had something to do.

In the secret room, she sat on the floor, yoga-fashion, with just one fat red candle burning. Where were the spirits tonight? She was having difficulty summoning them. But on the third deep try, she felt them filling her body and her mind. The spirits never failed if you believed in them. They hadn't failed her with Marty. They wouldn't fail her now.

She spoke her incantation: "Spirit of Freda Erzulie be with me now. Derrick, be with me now. Under deepest cover of night I steal your heart and keep it mine forever!"

She repeated it twice more, slowly. The room was absolutely still. She let her words sweep through her, then wing their way to him. She needed no drums tonight, only the incantation repeated three times.

Staggering up, she nearly fell. She had always refused, like Reese, to accept that she didn't handle her liquor well. At the door she bumped into the doorjamb and swore, feeling she might pass out.

But in her bedroom she opened her blinds and made it into bed, shuddering. She felt so cold. "Spirits, warm me," she muttered, then more harshly, *"Warm me!"* She frowned in the darkness. Something odd was happening.

For the first time since Marty had died, she felt alone in the worst sense of the word. Without aid. Without support. Would the spirits fail her after all? She fell into a deep, dreamless sleep in which there was only blackness and icy emptiness and despair.

Thirty-four

"I'm glad we waited for me to interview you. This way I can do a spread of the Steeles' annual May picnic in a very little while and do consecutive runs on this. I like to get started early, the way we're doing today."

Fairen Carrington grinned happily. "I guess I'm one of your fiercest fans."

"I'm glad, too," Ashley told her. "I'm really looking forward to this."

Set up for sound with two microphones about her body, Ashley felt keyed up, happy, but she was edgy, too. The sound man and the photographer hovered as Fairen suggested angles. Strobe lights flashed. The sound engineer frowned. "I'm not getting my best voice reading," he said. "Relax and try that again."

Ashley did as he asked and he gave her the A-OK sign. "Beautiful! Remember to stay as relaxed as you can."

Photographs were being taken for a TV spot as well as a newspaper article. Time sped by as they shot photographs and she talked. The sound engineer was ecstatic. "I can guarantee that this is going to be hot," he assured them.

The two men left, and Ashley and the journalist were alone. "I've been doing the interviewing for a TV journalist who's also a great admirer of yours. She was sick that she couldn't make it. She's going to interview you later for a longer spot on her same TV station."

"I'll look forward to that. Let me get you coffee, or café latte, if you like it."

Fairen groaned. "Don't my hips tell you I never met a café latte I didn't like?"

Ashley laughed. "I'm sorry the two guys didn't have time to wait the short time it takes me to make it."

"They were rushing to Howard University to do a photo shoot on a theater group. I'll go in the kitchen with you, if you can tolerate that. I get inspired seeing you move about your day."

"Come right ahead."

As Ashley set the machine up and got supplies from the refrigerator, Fairen kept up a steady stream of chatter.

"After this," she said, "I'll want to ask for copy on Eleni. And, oh, yes"—she wiggled her eyebrows—"I need a photo of Mr. Handsome Quinn."

Blushing, Ashley nearly dropped the cup she was holding.

"The article is about you, of course, so I'll give him enough space so everyone knows what a catch he is. I understand he doesn't live with Delia anymore. How would you suggest I handle this? Readers like to see people in action. Delia's stables?"

Ashley shook her head. "It's after hours for you, but I'd suggest his apartment. I think he'd be more comfortable there."

"Fine. My beloved editor keeps me on call half the time when I'm off. I'll go by one Sunday or one night. I'll call and set up an appointment. I'll also call later and set up a time to interview and shoot you with Eleni."

"Fine. I'm sure Derrick and Eleni will enjoy that. He liked you when you met at our engagement brunch."

"And I liked him immensely."

The two women took their café lattes back into the living room and settled down, Ashley still feeling keyed up, Fairen with her pen and pad and her tape recorder. Questions and answers. Probing questions. Honest answers.

"When do you plan to marry?"

"We haven't set a date yet. It may be a long engagement."

Ashley sounded a bit sad, and Fairen wondered about that.

"You're going up fast, lady, steadily climbing the charts, becoming an icon. Double platinum. That's kind of heady stuff. You really love singing, don't you?"

"Yes. I love singing. It's always been an enormous part of my life."

"Where do you see yourself a year from now? You've got a world tour planned for next year. Where do you see yourself five years from now?"

"Whoa! I'm going to go as evenly as I can. I've got a beloved daughter to raise, and she takes a lot of time. She'll travel with me with a tutor sometimes."

"Any regrets about that?"

"Some. She's very happy with my parents. Her father keeps her most weekends. . . ."

Plainly something was troubling Ashley, and Fairen paused.

"Say anything you wish—and you have free rein to cut anything you don't like. I know you'll be fair."

Ashley nodded. "I was thinking that Reese threatened to give me trouble if I take Eleni on the road with me too often."

Fairen pursed her lips. "I know the gentleman, and he can be unpleasant when he wants to."

"As much as I love singing, Eleni is my life before anything else. I wasn't in favor of Reese's getting to keep her almost every weekend. But you know Judge Lewis's reputation. He's very much on the side of fathers."

"So I hear."

Ashley sighed. "I haven't wanted to burden you with my problems, but I've been a bit out of it. Reese and I have an appointment to talk with Judge Lewis this afternoon."

Fairen looked compassionate. She leaned over and

touched Ashley's hand. "I'm sorry. I could have come another time."

"No, I *wanted* something to make the day go faster. You've done a great job. Wrap the picnic up in a couple of weeks and send me copies of the articles, which I know will be top-of-the-line."

Fairen laughed. "That's praise, coming from a highly valued source. Ashley, I'm going to say it again: I *love* your house, your meadow, that gorgeous horse and the nifty pony. I promise you the best I have to offer."

Ashley was a bundle of nerves that afternoon. She went to her side-porch window and saw Derrick vault the fence and come across the meadow. She went out on the porch and waved to him.

When he was inside he kissed her long and thoroughly, and she clung to him.

"I came," he said, "because I wanted to give you support."

"Thank you, but I know you're always busy. Just calling would have been enough."

"Did you know you're trembling?"

"Yes."

"I want to hold you, kiss you, make it all come out right. Why must Reese be such a bastard?"

"He does love Eleni. I guess being a bastard is just in his genes. I promise you he hid it very well before we were married."

"Should I go with you?"

"No," she said sadly. "Thank you so much, Derrick, but it would just make it worse. You help more than you could ever know. Judge Lewis has a rep for being long-winded. It could be late when we leave. Minnie is going to pick up Eleni from school."

"I'd be glad to do it."

"No. Leave it this way. Sweetheart, I've got to get ready to meet Judge Ogre."

"Are you okay? This is hurting you, and I don't like it one damned bit."

"It's all right." Hot tears spilled down her face then. As he dabbed her eyes with his handkerchief, her heart seemed to squeeze dry. Would the judge really grant Reese full custody and leave her with only visitation rights?

"No, you're *not* all right," he said fiercely. "Ash, how I wish I could spare you this pain."

She breathed more easily then. "Being with you helps me so much. I'm praying for myself, Derrick. Say a prayer for me and Eleni. Then maybe we both should pray for Reese, that his heart be changed."

Derrick held her away from him. "I love you, Ash. In all the world, there is nothing and no one who loves you more than I do. My son and you are on an even keel for me, everything that matters."

At her urging, he left then, saying, "Call me from the courthouse. I'll be waiting."

She watched him cross the meadow and couldn't know that he spoke prayers of supplication that she would win in her battle with Reese over Eleni.

Judge Madison Lewis was an imposing man. Five-foot-eight, with a well-kept body, he was bald and walnut-skinned, with piercing black eyes. He was known to occasionally drink too much, but he was politically active and he never paid a price for his overindulgence.

The judge, Ashley, and Reese sat around a table in the judge's opulent chambers. Reese looked stone-cold sober, impressive in his business suit and carefully matched shirt and tie.

"Ah," the judge said, grinning slightly, "the battling Winterses."

"The name Winters for me was some time ago," Ashley told him. "I took back my maiden name."

The judge looked at her coolly. "Maybe I'm just recalling the way things used to be. If you had been more reasonable, *Miss* Steele, we wouldn't be sitting here today."

Ashley didn't know how to answer that. Did his cool demeanor mean he intended to turn her world upside down?"

"I understand your little girl fell out of a tree and got a hairline fracture to her arm."

"That's right, sir," Reese spoke up. "Ashley was in Germany when it happened."

The judge nodded. "I see your career is expanding greatly," he said. "Do you really have time to properly look after your child? Wouldn't Mr. Winters be likely to be the one who has the necessary time during the week to best look after Eleni?"

"No," Ashley said breathlessly. "I take her with me on trips from time to time." She told him then how Eleni adored her parents.

"Who spoil her relentlessly," Reese cut in.

"That isn't true," Ashley said. "Reese is the one who spoils her. All the sweets she can swallow. Letting her taste wine . . ."

Judge Lewis pulled a silver canister toward him and uncovered it, displaying hundreds of multicolored jelly beans. "I'm a candy addict," he said pleasantly. "Have some?"

Ashley said no, but Reese took a handful, and he and the judge munched on them silently.

"As for wine," the judge said, "the French practically let their babies drink it. Most civilized people in the world."

By then Ashley's heart had sunk to the bottom of her shoes, and Reese was beaming.

Finally Judge Lewis spoke up, his manner subtly changed. "I must say that you're one of my favorite singers, Miss Steele. You have a truly magnificent voice."

"Thank you."

"I have a wife who might have been a successful concert pianist, but she chose to be with our children. She tells me she's never been sorry. Now I have grandchildren."

Where was he leading? He looked from one to the other, his face seeming to soften.

He looked keenly at Reese. "You filed a petition to turn my custody arrangements upside down."

"Yes, sir, because I think it's in my daughter's best interests."

"You love your daughter, Mr. Winters. I'm sure of that." He paused, then went on. "But I'm sure, too, that Miss Steele loves her at least as well. How is your drinking problem, Mr. Winters?"

What did the judge care? Ashley thought bitterly. He had something of a problem of his own.

"I'm in rehab, sir, in a private place where I go for outpatient treatment. I promise you that in six months or less, I won't be drinking at all."

Liar! Ashley screamed inside. *You were drinking at my engagement brunch. Is the truth nowhere in you, Reese?*

"Good. I'm happy to hear that. Congratulations on your engagement, Miss Steele. I wish you all the best."

Ashley thanked him, and he turned to Reese. "Have you similar plans, sir? A family with two parents is superior to just one."

Reese stuttered a moment. "I'm seriously dating a young woman. We'll probably be married within the year."

The judge nodded at Ashley. "You're engaged."

"Yes." Ashley felt a lift of hope.

The judge leaned back, rocked in his chair. After a very long while, he said, "It's no secret that I tend to favor the father in my cases." He sighed. "I can't say I believe in all the psychological palaver, but I can see that some things are true.

"I've bent over backward to be fair to fathers, because in my first marriage, when I was a young lawyer, a judge was fair only to my wife. She took our child to the islands and I've seen my daughter only one or twice in the past twenty-five years. I love this child dearly, but she was and is lost to me."

His voice had grown softer, and there seemed a glint of tears in his eyes. He lifted and spread his hands.

"I want to suggest that we handle this informally. Let the arrangement stay as it is." Delicious warmth spread through Ashley. "If you insist, Mr. Winters, I'll rule against you. Can you see my point? Eleni reminds me of my own daughter, whom I lost. I no longer wish to hurt a woman in order to help a man. I have daughters of my own and they now have children. You both are reasonable people. Be reasonable about this."

Ashley felt as if the weight of the world had been lifted off her shoulders. She looked at Reese, who looked stunned.

"Thank you, Judge Lewis." Ashley swallowed past the lump in her throat.

"And you, Mr. Winters? I know you're disappointed. If you're determined, this doesn't have to be the end of the road for you, but I'd advise against pursuing it. If I had been a more fair-minded man, you would have gotten only bi-weekly visitation rights, or less.

"At her present stage, Eleni needs her mother. I want to compliment you both on doing a superb job. When I talked with Eleni when you were away, she seemed to me a very happy child."

"You talked with Eleni?" Ashley looked up in surprise.

"Didn't Mr. Winters tell you?"

"No. And I guess Eleni forgot. Reese, you didn't tell my parents either."

But there wasn't room for bitterness now. The judge looked at Reese. "You should have told her or her parents," he said.

Reese sounded strangled. "I'm sorry, sir. I guess it just slipped my mind."

"Really," the judge said, half closing his eyes. "My grandchildren are mellowing me. Perhaps in time, Mr. Winters, some bit of fate will mellow you."

Thirty-five

May brought perfect weather, and the day of the May Songfest couldn't have been lovelier: blue, cloudless skies, warm breezes, and a sun that beamed its warmth on them all.

By eleven o'clock, the south twenty acres of the Steele place were partially filled with people milling about.

"Looks like we can look forward to another success." Frank Steele stood on a platform at the end of the meadow and tested his guitar.

"It's always a success, even when the weather doesn't cooperate," Caroline answered. "I hope everything goes well."

"Why wouldn't it?"

Caroline shook her head. "Since I got older I get a feeling in my bones sometimes, like something's not right. Turns out sometimes I know what I'm feeling."

"Aw, Callie. Tell your bones to be quiet. This is going to be a glorious day." He called her Callie only when he wanted to reassure her.

Frank put his arms around his wife and kissed her cheek. "Callie, let it ride," he said. "Be my happy wife. This is *our* day."

Caroline smiled a bit, but she couldn't stop the feeling.

The platform was loaded with guitars for the Davis Gospel Singers, and guitars for Whit, Caroline, and Frank. Now Frank plunked out a comical tune, and the lead man for the

Davis Gospel Singers laughed. "Man, you got a style I never get tired of hearing. You two need to be back onstage."

Frank grabbed Caroline's hand. "What about it, Callie? You want to go back onstage?"

"Never." Caroline laughed. "I had enough while we were there. I'm satisfied with what we've got now."

Wilson Cartwright, who owned Wilson's restaurant and nightclub out on the highway, came up. A bluff and hearty dark brown man, he clapped Frank on the back and kissed Caroline's cheek.

"We've about got it all set up in the food line," he said. "Barbecue's on, ready by one-thirty. We started before daylight this morning. When's the singing begin?"

"Around twelve." Frank looked thoughtful. "I suspect it's good for us to sing awhile, eat awhile, then sing again."

"Folks do have a good time at these songfests."

"We have a great time giving them," Caroline told him.

Caroline saw Derrick and went over to him. "Do me a favor, son," she said.

"I'll be glad to."

She dimpled a bit. "Well, two favors. First, please feel free to call me Mama. I've told you before, but I guess you forgot."

Derrick laughed. "Sure, Mama."

"Second, I've fallen down on my end of the job. I was to pick up aspirin, antacids, and two first-aid kits. Then I was to drive out and pick up Reba—you know, the nurse—just in case somebody gets sick. And she loves to be here anyway. I must be getting old. I got to going back and forth and forgot them all."

"I'll be glad to do it. I know where Miss Reba lives."

"Bless you. Ashley's not here yet. Whit and Annice are coming in a bit late. You're my godsend." She patted his back.

Derrick left. On his way to his car, Delia came to him.

"Hello, Delia. I wasn't sure you were coming." Looking

at her keenly, he decided something was wrong. Then he clapped his fist to his forehead. Today was the anniversary of Marty's death, and he had forgotten.

He made a mental note to call Delia that night and see if she felt up to having Ashley and him over or letting them take her to dinner.

"Oh, yes." Delia gave him her brightest smile. "I wouldn't miss it for the world. Where're you off to?"

"Into town for a few items for the Steeles."

"Ashley's late."

"She's supposed to be. She'll be here shortly."

He turned away to go to his car, which was parked in the very large area set aside for the guests. Delia went back toward the crowd, but watched Derrick as he got in and drove away.

She breathed a sigh of relief when she stood on the same spot and watched Ashley cross the meadow. Saturday. Eleni would be with her father. She needed to talk to Ashley.

The singing began early. It was an entertainment-by-participation event. Frank took the microphone to say, "Folks, we weren't going to start singing until later, but I'm in the mood. What do you say we start now?"

Cheers and cries went up. Guitars twanged and tambourines rattled lustily. Clem, Ashley's piano accompanist, strummed a mean guitar now.

"Tell me what you want to lead off on."

A great number of voices chose "He's Got the Whole World in His Hands." And Frank led off with the first verse. As soon as he arrived, Whit stepped onstage as the crowd cheered him. Caroline went to see if she saw Ashley. She soon caught sight of her walking toward the crowd; then she saw Delia speak to her and talk a moment. She shrugged. She'd catch her later, but Ashley called, "Mama," leaving Delia to come to Caroline. When she reached Caroline, Ashley asked if Derrick had come.

Caroline nodded. "I asked him to go into town to pick up some things for me."

"Oh, fine. Delia wants me to drive over to her house to get a great bouquet of flowers she left."

"She doesn't have to do that. We've got everything we need, except what I forgot."

"Don't go worrying about your memory now. Delia doesn't look well, Mama. I think she may be taking Derrick's engagement hard."

Caroline scoffed. "Somebody's got to lose when somebody else wins."

"Poor consolation when you're hurting."

"Probably she's still grieving Marty."

Ashley said nothing, but thought, *Maybe, but I don't think so.* She got onstage, sang a song with the group and the audience, then found Delia again.

Looking bleakly at Ashley, Delia felt a hard stab of envy. Dressed in blended shades of pale to medium yellow, she looked freshly ready for a photo shoot.

"Mama thinks you shouldn't put yourself to all this trouble," Ashley told her.

"Nonsense. I want to do my part. Please let me."

"Of course. It's very thoughtful of you."

Delia took a loose cigarette from her shirt pocket and lit it, drawing heavily. Ashley saw then that she wore very high heeled black boots.

Delia saw her looking and laughed, lifting a small foot. "I'm being glamorous today."

"They're pretty."

"Thank you. I bought a huge bunch of gladioli and dahlias. I promise you'll like them. A good-sized pot of red tulips. Beautiful. They'll do the table proud."

As the people eased into their third song, Ashley and Delia quickly found Delia's old red pickup truck and got in. On the seat was the Steuben vase Ashley had given her.

"Am I losing it, or what?" Delia asked. "With the vase to

remind me, how could I forget? Thing is I had it fastened down on the truck bed. I put it up here when I realized I had left the flowers—after I drove onto your folks' property."

"We can't remember everything all the time."

"You're sweet. Thank you so much for coming with me."

"Why didn't you send Len?"

"Because I think I left them in my bedroom and Len would hate going into my bedroom, looking for something for me. No, it's better I get the flowers."

"Well, let's get started," Delia said, fastening her seat belt.

Fiddling with her seat belt, Ashley frowned. "I'm having trouble with this."

Delia snapped her fingers. "It's got a glitch. I thought I'd take it in to the nearest gas station or garage. Don't worry, I'm a careful driver, and we're only going a short distance."

"Okay," Ashley said reluctantly.

Driving out the gate, Delia turned right, explaining that she had one errand to run in town and wanted to get the seat belt fixed. The crystal vase sat in splendor between them. Ashley touched it. "That was a beautiful thank you note you sent me."

"Not half as beautiful as the vase. It was so thoughtful."

Ashley frowned as Delia swiftly smoked another cigarette and half tamped it out. Ashley saw that the ashtray was loaded with half-smoked butts, some still lit, and she wished she had passed this trip up.

Ashley glanced at Delia's blanched knuckles on the wheel. She braked sharply at the back of another truck and swore. Her face had gotten tense, angry. The vase had begun to slide and Ashley stopped it, then kept her hand lightly on the lip of the vase to steady it.

"Hey! You missed the turn to go into town."

"I thought about something else I've got to do," Delia said pleasantly, her tone belying her expression.

Exasperated, Ashley cautioned, "Well, I can't stay out

long. I'm going to lead another one of the songs and I want to be back in plenty of time to tune up."

"Don't worry about it. I'll go in, pick up the flowers, and have you back in no time, after I do my errands."

"I knew you'd understand. Just where are we heading now?"

"I won't say until we get there." Delia's voice had a surprisingly hard edge, and Ashley looked at her more closely.

"Delia, is something wrong?" she finally asked.

"Wrong? What could be wrong?" Delia asked flippantly. "Celebrations are in order. Songfests. Engagement brunches. And don't *weddings* come after engagements?" Delia's voice had cracked with anger. *My God,* Ashley thought. What was going on here?

Zipping along the highway, Delia slowed a moment, picked up the vase, and held it up. "Beautiful, isn't it?" She threw the vase out the window with all her might into a concrete barrier, and looking back with shock, Ashley saw it shatter.

"Are you mad?" she demanded, trying to keep her balance.

"I don't need your damned vases. Do you like going fast? I find it exciting. I've got a seat belt and you haven't. I have a chance, but you're going to *die,* Ashley. Scares you, doesn't it?"

"Yes. Delia, you're upset. If it's about Derrick, there are so many men you could—"

"Shut up! Men can be weak. Derrick was beginning to love me before you began to slither up to him, come on to him." Her voice spewed acid. "You whore!"

Ashley hardly heard her, she was so intent on moving suddenly. Then she had her foot on the brake of the old pickup truck. But she was outmaneuvered by Delia, who viciously smashed her high heel into Ashley's bare instep. The pickup jerked and dragged with the conflicting commands, as Ashley yelped with pain. Then Delia pressed the

accelerator to the floor and cut the wheel sharply to the righ
The truck crashed through the guardrails and began to son
ersault down the steep hill, rolling over and over until
came to rest at the bottom of the hill. Then all was quiet.

Driving back through the gate at the Songfest, Derric
stopped as a disturbed-looking Len hailed him. The man
face was rigid. He could barely talk.

"It's Miss Delia," he said. "I'm worried about her. Sh
and Miss Ashley drove off in her truck."

"How long ago? And why are you so bothered?"

"Because she's not herself. She's been drinking, and thi
morning she had a lot of coffee, so when she got here sh
seemed all right, but I don't think she is. She didn't turn le
to go to her house. She turned *right.*"

Derrick listened intently, but he needed answers. "Thin
she might have gone into town?"

In a wild rush then, Len told him about Delia's early
morning drives on the highway. "We've got to find them,"
Len said. "I got a bad feeling about this."

"Get in!"

Time moved at a snail's pace to Derrick as he drove to th
stretch of highway Len guided him to. He willed his jumble
mind to empty, then filled it solely with finding his beloved

They both looked for signs of the red truck or a wreck
along the road, and it seemed forever before Len yelled
"There! At the bottom of the hill!" The red truck lay man
gled there.

Derrick parked on the wide shoulder, took out his cel
phone, and called for an ambulance. He had to stay calm.

Len had raced ahead, but both men reached the wreckage
almost at once. Ashley had been flung twenty or more fee
from the twisted truck, but Delia was still inside. The smell
of leaking gas was strong in their nostrils.

With trembling hands he willed to be steady, Derrick

ound that Ashley was still breathing, groaning, and Derrick's time was taken up with her. He checked her faint pulse, her faint heartbeat, then called 911 again and squatted beside her, waiting.

With hellish pain tearing through him, Len thought he knew from the minute he touched Delia that she was dead. He checked for vital signs and found none. He managed to get the door on the passenger side open and undo her seat belt. He pulled her out of the truck's cab.

"Let's take them a good distance away!" Derrick called. "There could be an explosion."

Len lifted Delia. He knew she'd been smoking, too, for a couple of days. She did it off and on. If she was smoking as she drove, there might be still-lit butts in the cigarette tray, but he didn't have time to check for that.

"Get here, damn it!" Derrick ordered the absent ambulances before he heard sirens whining in the near distance, then, finally, at the top of the hill. They had moved nearly fifty feet away when the ambulance attendants came down the hill and took over.

Derrick's face was hot with tears. At least she was still alive. He didn't have time to think about anybody else.

A heartsick Len looked at Delia's beautiful, twisted face and wept with anguish. She would never have been his, but he wondered how he would fill his life without her.

Flames leaped as fire ignited from the lit cigarette butts. As the ambulances pulled away, they heard the explosion and saw spewed debris littering the valley and the hillside.

Thirty-six

"Delia, don't!"

Derrick's heart leaped with joy. Ashley's voice was litt more than a whisper, and a medical team was leaving th room. The doctor had told him he could stay and he ha Now Ashley's wounds were dressed and her rib cage wa tightly bandaged. She had a broken rib.

"Derrick?"

"I'm right here love." He got up and bent over her as th doctor smiled.

"Don't let her talk too much," the doctor said. "She's on lucky woman. It won't take her long to pull out of this. The were no other internal injuries—no serious ones. A ligh puncture to her liver. We've given her a sedative, so she going out on you. Nothing else. As I said, she was ver lucky."

Derrick wanted to crush her to him, hold her.

"She was going to kill me, kill us both."

"Sssh. Don't talk, love. You've got to be quiet."

"Did they arrest her?" Deep inside she was afraid Deli would come after her again.

"Delia's dead," he said firmly, hardly believing it himsel

"Dead? Delia's dead?"

"Yes. Now you've got to stop talking. I'll tell you a about it when you wake up."

"Yes. Wake up. I'm not dead. I will wake up. But I don want to go to sleep, want to be with you."

The sedative kicked in then and she drifted into a nether-world of fear and passionate murder. And she murmured again, "No, Delia, *please.*"

It was morning when she came to in the brilliantly sunlit hospital room. Derrick had gone home briefly and come back. Corby had wanted to visit, but Derrick wanted to shield him at the moment from Delia's mad act.

He came loaded with a pot of purple African violets and a big fruit basket.

"Derrick!" She greeted him with joy laced with sadness.

"Ash! How do you feel?"

"Better. Much better. Was I out long?"

"Not too long."

A nurse took the flowers, put the fruit basket on the table, and went to find a vase. "How beautiful," she murmured.

"Open the fruit and help yourself to it," Ashley told her.

Derrick sat in the chair pulled close to the bed.

"I've got something really important to tell you," he said.

Her tender gaze questioned him, but she said nothing.

"On the way to the hospital, waiting until I could see you, had a good chance to think, Ash. I knew in a split second that I wanted you, wanted us to belong together no matter what differences we have."

"I'll make changes, sweetheart. I love you so."

He shook his head. "You're an artist, my love. Your voice is God-given, and no one has a right to ask you to curb your singing. I want you to go on. Travel the world. Get to the mountaintop, and I'll be there with you in spirit if I can't always be there in person.

"I know now, Ash, that problems in love are God's way of letting us know the value of what we can know together, if only we will."

"That's beautiful, but are you sure? Have you forgiven yourself yet for Maria's death? You have to, you know."

He squeezed her hand. "With prayer I will, and you'll [be] there to help me."

He got up, bent over, and kissed her forehead, her chee[k], and her lips. Tears pooled in her eyes as she touched his fa[ce].

"I love you, my darling," she said quietly, her heart filli[ng] with his presence.

"We're going to make it, you and me," he said softly. "[I] never knew dreams of ecstasy until I met you."

"I'm glad. I have ecstatic dreams, too, but do you kn[ow] why I love you so?"

"Why?"

There was both joy and sadness in her then as she told hi[m,] "Because you take me higher than I've ever been before."

Epilogue

"Abby Quinn, beloved daughter of Ashley and Derrick Quinn, may you know passion, love, and honor throughout your long life, the blessings from God and the Savior, and the warmth, respect, and cherishing of your fellow humans. And may you *give* these things to yourself and your fellow humans and get them back manifold. In God's name I seek these blessings. Amen."

The pastor beamed as he blessed baby Abby in his arms. His white surplice was snowy, like Abby's christening gown.

Derrick stood proud and tall, his love for his wife and his tiny daughter mirrored on his face as the pastor placed the baby into Ashley's waiting arms.

The church was dressed with red and white roses and tall ferns. Soft organ music played. Family and friends were there to witness this holiness. Now they would move on to a reception at Ashley and Derrick's spread, out from Norfolk.

It had rained off and on all morning, with intermittent brilliant sunlight. It was cloudy when they left the church.

Derrick held a big umbrella over Ashley and the baby, but only a few drops of rain fell.

Eleni moved happily along with them a few steps, then dropped back to be with her grandparents.

Ashley and Derrick's home was only a short distance away, and as the group stepped into their split-level living room, the odor of freshly baked meats and breads filled their nostrils.

Standing in the middle of the room, Caroline stroked her granddaughter's face with one finger, smiling as Frank came to her side, then Whit and Annice.

"We're going to mark her," Frank said. "All this food, all this celebration for one little baby."

"One *precious* little baby," Derrick said drolly, to which they all agreed.

"Let me give you some relief," Caroline said to Ashley. "You circulate. We'll mind the baby."

And Ashley did circulate, but her thoughts were very much with Abby, too. The baby would not have been here if she and Derrick hadn't beautifully worked through their lives. She was more famous than ever. Her tours had put her near the top, but she would not work for a year or so to give her baby, Abby, the at-home sustenance she needed to thrive.

"All the best," Ace Carter said, coming up. He was buying Delia's farm, and he was in love with Annice. He followed her with haunted eyes.

Look elsewhere, Ashley wanted to advise him. *My sister's heart has been shattered and may never be whole again.* But she knew they were friends and took solace from each other.

As Annice walked away, Ashley followed her movements, Ashley's heart leaped with hope for her emotionally injured sister.

"Hello, there! You going to ignore me?"

Ashley looked into the beaming face of Miss Mag. "Hello, yourself. Ignore you? Never! You're looking well. I'm so glad you could come."

"Well, I just told your folks straight up I wanted to see this baby, seeing as how I always admired you and Derrick and came to your wedding." She turned, calling to a man nearby. It was the man, homeless then, who had helped them when they were trying to find Corby.

"Honey," Miss Mag told him, "give Ashley your blessings. Pete," she scolded, "now don't drink too much."

"Promise I won't."

Ashley smiled widely at the two; they grinned in return.

"You might like t'know I don't have time to gossip so much no more," Aunt Mag said. "Besides, I got a bit o' gossip from the folks myself when Pete and me took up, before we got hitched. I guess the shoe was on the other foot for a while. You be happy. Your ex has got a new girlfriend, and I think it's love."

"I'm happy for him," Ashley murmured.

Going to Caroline and Frank, Ashely touched her baby's face. Was that a toothless smile? Or gas? Walking to a window she thought about Reese. He had driven down shortly after she and Derrick had moved. He had been coming back and forth to get Eleni and bring her back. Then one day he had looked more sincere than she had ever seen him.

"Ash, I hope you can forgive me," he'd said. "I think I'm in love again, and I don't intend to screw up this time. We've talked it over, my friend and I, and we've decided I'll see Eleni once a month. Too much going back and forth isn't good for her. I hope you'll forgive me the pain I've put you through."

He had looked then like the Reese she'd married, and she had complimented him and wished him well.

"Mom, I'll keep the baby for a while, if you want me to." Eleni was deliriously happy with the baby, calling her hers more often than not.

"Thanks, sweetie, but let's let Mama and Dad hold her while they can. Tell me, Eleni, do you ever miss seeing your father every weekend?"

Eleni mulled it over. "No, I enjoy seeing him when I see him. He doesn't drink much anymore, and he's nice. But I love Uncle Derrick and I'm happy here, Mom. Honest."

The child moved away then to join her baby sister and her grandparents as Ashley walked over to Whit, who looked out the window pensively.

"Penny for your thoughts," she told him.

He chuckled. "I'm thinking our luck has to change now.

You've got great things going. Great marriage. Smashing
career, now a great baby. Maybe Annice and I *can* get with
it, too."

Ashley touched his face. "You were hurt, Whit, savaged.
So was Annice. You can get over it. So can Annice. It just
takes time. Your career is flying now. You'll find someone."

Ashley's eyes were on Len Starkey, who had come with
her parents. His being here brought it all back, and he
seemed to move toward her reluctantly, apologetically.

"Miss Ashley, I hope you don't mind my coming."

Ashley reached out and touched his shoulder. "I'm glad
you came, Len. You'll never know how glad I am."

"The baby, she's beautiful," he mumbled. Were there tears
in his eyes?

"You saved my life, and you always have a place in it. I've
told you before, your telling Derrick when you did made all
the difference."

Yes, there *were* tears, she saw plainly now. "I wasn't quick
enough to save *her*."

"No, you weren't." Emotionally, Ashley and Len differed
here. She had come to realize that Len loved Delia. Delia
had wanted—no had *tried*—to kill her. A cold shudder went
the length of her body.

"One day you'll get over it, Len," she said gently. "Just
as I'm getting over it. Are you working now? We've got jobs
available. Good jobs."

"And I might take you up on that. Mr. Derrick has offered
me a job before, but me and Ace, we do well together. You
know he's going to buy the farm. I'll stay, I guess. But thank
you. I'm glad I could help save you. She was out of her
mind, Miss Ashley."

His eyes glazed and he touched his heart. "The Delia I
know was too deep into living to kill." Ashley noted that he
had said Delia, not Miss Delia. Her heart hurt for him.

Ashley was standing alone when Derrick came to her,
took her arm, and guided her to a window. The weather was

clearing, and a rainbow stretched across the sky. *Glorious!*
With his arm around her shoulders, he kissed her brow.

"Rainbows yet, Ash. A kind of benediction?"

She looked at him through misty eyes. "Yes."

"We've got it all, Ash," he told her huskily. "At last,
we've really got it all."

ABOUT THE AUTHOR

Francine Craft is the pen name of a writer based in Washington, D.C., who has enjoyed writing for many years. A native Mississippian, she has also lived in New Orleans and found it fascinating.

Francine has been a research assistant for a large nonprofit organization, an elementary school teacher, a business school instructor, and a legal secretary for the federal government. Her books have been highly praised by reviewers. She is a member of Romance Writers of America.

Prodigious reading, photography, and writing song lyrics are Francine's hobbies. She presently lives with a family of friends and many goldfish. She loves your letters and promises to answer every one.

Francine Craft
P.O. Box 44204
Washington, DC 20026

COMING IN APRIL 2002 FROM
ARABESQUE ROMANCES

__**LOVE POTIONS**

by Leslie Esdaile   1-58314-289-4 $6.99US/$9.99C

It begins as a lark—four friends throw a few harmless psychic-reading pa
Then an ex-cop moves in to bust their operation. But not before Nikki g
the sexy private eye a potion that makes him fall head-over-heels in love—
her! But who's going to keep Nikki from falling beneath the spell of
irresistible man?

__**THE PROPOSITION**

by Shirley Harrison   1-58314-220-7 $6.99US/$9.99C

Carolyn Hardy can't believe how passionate football star Michael Henne
feels about re-igniting their simmering attraction. When a scandal dest
Michael's reputation and threatens to ruin his life, Carolyn confronts her
doubts to discover the truth . . . and her own heart.

__**FALLING FOR YOU**

by Kim Louise   1-58314-283-5 $5.99US/$7.99C

Martial arts expert Sabin Strong knows she should ignore her growing fee
for Montgomery Claiborne. After all, she's been hired to protect the hands
businessman from whoever's been trying to kill him. And if Montgomery f
out the truth about her, she's sure he'll do more than blow her cover . . .
break her heart.

__**LOVE'S DESTINY**

by Crystal Wilson-Harris   1-58314-285-1 $5.99US/$7.99C

Savannah Raven Dailey had it all, until the day her husband cleared out
bank accounts and disappeared. Shattered, she has no choice but to pic
the pieces and go on. What she doesn't know is that she will emerge
woman determined to track down her runaway spouse . . . with help fron
irresistibly passionate man.

Call toll free **1-888-345-BOOK** to order by phone or use
coupon to order by mail. ALL BOOKS AVAILABLE APRIL 1, 20

Name _____

Address _____

City_____ State _____ Zip _____

Please send me the books that I have checked above.

I am enclosing $_____

Plus postage and handling* $_____

Sales tax (in NY, TN, and DC) $_____

Total amount enclosed $_____

*Add $2.50 for the first book and $.50 for each additional book
Send check or money order (no cash or CODs) to: **Arabesque Roman
Dept. C.O., 850 Third Avenue, 16th Floor, New York, NY 10022**
Prices and numbers subject to change without notice. Valid only in the U
All orders subject to availability. **NO ADVANCE ORDERS.**
Visit our website at **www.arabesquebooks.com.**